RED
BISHOP

ROBIN T.W. YUAN

Published by
Red Robin Publishing
www.RobinYuanAuthor.com

ISBN (hardcover): 978-1-7377894-0-6
ISBN (paperback): 978-1-7377894-1-3
ISBN (ebook): 978-1-7377894-2-0

Book cover design by Liz Demeter, www.demeterdesign.com
Page design and production: Domini Dragoone, www.DominiDragoone.com
Map design by Nat Case, incasellc.com
Author photo by Robin Nicole Yuan
Images are from the author's personal collection.

DEDICATED
TO FAMILY

CONTENTS

CHINA 1911-1945

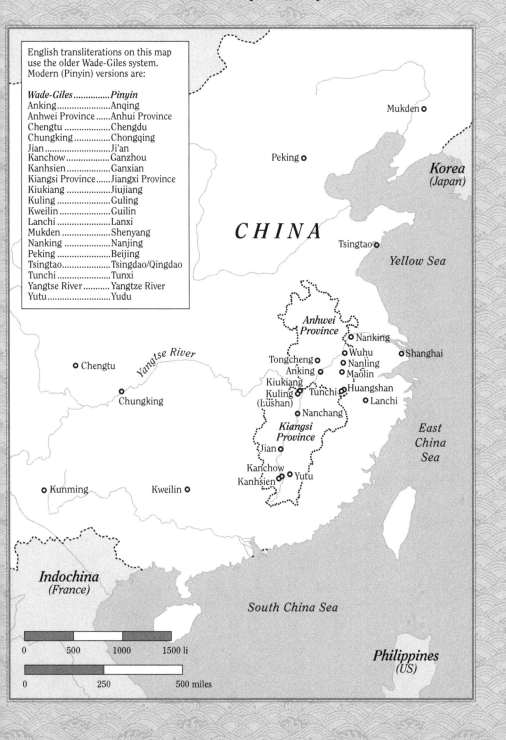

English transliterations on this map use the older Wade-Giles system. Modern (Pinyin) versions are:

Wade-Giles	Pinyin
Anking	Anqing
Anhwei Province	Anhui Province
Chengtu	Chengdu
Chungking	Chongqing
Jian	Ji'an
Kanchow	Ganzhou
Kanhsien	Ganxian
Kiangsi Province	Jiangxi Province
Kiukiang	Jiujiang
Kuling	Guling
Kweilin	Guilin
Lanchi	Lanxi
Mukden	Shenyang
Nanking	Nanjing
Peking	Beijing
Tsingtao	Tsingdao/Qingdao
Tunchi	Tunxi
Yangtse River	Yangtze River
Yutu	Yudu

Mukden

Peking

CHINA

Tsingtao

Korea
(Japan)

Yellow Sea

Chengtu

Yangtse River

Chungking

Anhwei Province

Tongcheng
Anking
Kiukiang
Kuling
(Lüshan)
Tunchi

Nanking
Wuhu
Nanling
Maolin
Huangshan
Lanchi

Shanghai

Nanchang

Kiangsi Province

Jian

Kanchow
Kanhsien
Yutu

East China Sea

Kunming

Kweilin

Indochina
(France)

South China Sea

Philippines
(US)

0	500	1000	1500 li

0	250	500 miles

Chapter 1

THE WORD

Zzzzz ... Zzzzz ... Zzzzz ...
Worn tires whirling on rusted spokes hummed as Helene strained to push the steel pedals, struggling against the heavy weight of her human cargo. She pumped furiously down the main boulevard towards the hospital, fearing her efforts would not be enough.

The bishop, her father-in-law, lay still at the bottom of the wooden cart trailing behind the bicycle, his frail body quiet, his wasting face cradled in Constance's lap. The half-century spent with his wife had come to this apparent dead end on the streets of Shanghai, strewn with the rubble of social upheaval.

Small crowds of students from the shuttered university, armed with frenzied ideas of revolution, wandered noisily from corner to corner. Some pointed fingers at him as the cart passed by. Others just stared blankly.

Big-character posters of black ink on white paper, *ta tzu pao*, were plastered auspiciously on every building, proclaiming the wisdom of Chairman Mao: "Smash the Four Olds—old ideas, old customs, old cultures, old habits." Banners carrying familiar slogans from Mao's Little Red Book hung from every tree and lamp post.

All reactionaries are paper tigers.
Political power grows from the barrel of a gun.
Form a united front to oppose the U.S. imperialistic policies of aggression.

The bishop's eyes, jaundiced and dull, caught a glimpse of a group of much-too-young Red Guards hauling on a tangle of ropes, bringing the steeple of a church, its image burned into his mind, crashing to the ground—fervor and naïveté clashing with the idea of a new China.

A year earlier, he had been paraded by others like them in front of accusers who denounced his Western ties. How ironic—and perhaps just. He *had* wronged others. Betrayed them. Friends and colleagues, all in the name of patriotism. But that was at the very beginning of it all. Was it truly wrong? Had he committed a grave sin? Was it difficult for these revolutionary neophytes, as it had been for him?

The white cross, just a moment before glistening like a flame on the steeple, exploded as it toppled into a mushroom cloud of grey dust, like a bomb going off in his soul. But he had closed his eyelids to veil his hazy, pinpoint pupils; his ears were already deaf to the commotion around him.

Constance gently stroked his face with gnarled fingers, blue veins revealed through skin as translucent as rice paper. This would be their last trip to the hospital. They were done. The end. She wiped the droplets of blood seeping from the corner of his mouth. The red had stained the collar of his grey tunic jacket; the ubiquitous uniform of nearly every citizen of the revolution had long ago replaced his ecclesiastical robe.

The bishop coughed weakly, spraying a mist of crimson. Constance did not flinch, accepting the blood as if it were her own. She let the droplets coalesce upon her cheeks and lips. She felt no shame, no fear—those were words they had conquered in their many decades together.

"Soon—there!" panted Helene as she glanced back at him. Sweat dribbled down her brow, mixing with tears that trickled down her high cheekbones.

The world was quiet now for the bishop. He raised his heavy lids enough to see the wintry sky overhead, dotted with white clouds. It was against just such a fresh, azure background, shimmering in the morning sun, that he saw his father, leaving with him for St. James Mission Middle School many years ago. He remembered kind Sister Louise, his first English teacher, her firm voice and soft smile. He heard the prescient words of his friend, Bishop Lloyd Craighill, years later at their unusual joint consecration. A lifetime ago.

Most of all, he missed Grace. Chen I. Number One Daughter. He shut his eyes tightly, as if trying to coax her forth from deep within his memory.

China's world had been upended. Children scolded and turned on parents. Students lectured and beat teachers. Doctors and scientists, with bodies bent in half, planted rice, and slept in pig sties in the countryside. Christians, especially their leaders, belonged to the counterrevolutionaries, *fan ge ming*, one of Chairman Mao's Five Bad Elements. But he believed the Lord would provide. The Word would survive. And smashing the Four Olds would bring a new China.

The bishop knew he would never see it, but he held faith deep in his heart, which had endured so much. He strained to lift his head, and he pulled Constance closer. His lips nearly touched her ear. He drew a deep breath and whispered one word—without anger, without hate, with complete conviction. It was a most Christian word. A simple word.

He settled back into her arms, let his head sink into her lap, and managed the very faintest of smiles.

Chapter 2

YOU ARE THE
BEGINNING

It seemed the whole Anglican community in Wuhu, which included a sizable number of English and American expatriates, had turned out for the ceremony on a grey, chilly day in November of 1940. Grace, a bit over seventeen, stayed in the corner of the garden just outside St. Lioba's Church, the mission's main building of worship. She and her mother, dressed in a deep purple *chi pao*, watched the three bishops arrive in their formal garments and red sashes: Bishop William Payne Roberts, the American from Peking, Bishop Arnold Scott, the Englishman from Shanghai, and Bishop Lindel Tsen, her father's old teacher and colleague from Honan. Her father arrived in a heavy tunic coat, wearing his familiar top hat and a grey wool scarf encircling his neck to insulate his throat from the cold air.

It was later that Grace, overhearing the elders converse, grasped the gravity of the day. Japanese forces had already occupied her hometown for three years after they swept through Shanghai in a barrage of bombs and street combat. Charging through Shanghai, the Japanese forced Generalissimo Chiang Kai-shek's Nationalist Army to retreat through Wuhu and farther west to Chungking. Grace and her family fled to the mountains, often sheltering in refugee camps or hiding from the Japanese army in limestone caves.

The occupation normalized over the years, allowing her family to return home. But travel was still dangerous throughout the middle of China, where Nationalist, Communist, and Japanese forces connived among, and plotted against, each other. Each side sought advantage over the others through whatever dubious double-crossing scheme they could devise.

The train carrying the bishops and Christian guests from Shanghai also bore Nationalist officials suspected of plotting with the Japanese against the Communists. Rebels rigged the tracks with explosives to eliminate the traitors. It seemed that everyone, especially the wife of Lloyd Craighill, the new bishop, saw the protective hand of God on this momentous day. The explosives detonated fifty minutes after the train passed the spot, sparing the Christians and the colluding Nationalists. But a second train full of innocent Chinese citizens was derailed.

"How horrible! Those poor Chinese!" Mrs. Craighill whispered to Grace's mother.

"Yes, horrible," echoed another American guest.

Her mother nodded with mute solemnity. Grace heard those sentiments echoed by so many foreigners. It was part sympathy, part pity. Nothing seemed to change. Poor Chinese.

"Lloyd admires your husband," Mrs. Craighill commented, sounding heartfelt. "He is a true patriot ... *and* a servant of God."

"He is grateful to serve the church," Grace's mother replied with humility. It was no secret that Grace's father was universally beloved and respected, and that could be worrisome; the head of the chicken is the first part to go.

A servant of God? Of course. But a patriot? It was hard to know exactly what that meant in the current civil conflict, Grace thought.

The two men had served the Anglican church through much turmoil. China and the church had seen no peace for so many years, ever since her father was born. They had all witnessed interminable hostilities that brought them to this very day.

Grace knew the church wanted more native leaders. Her father's consecration would cause him to be absent from the family even more than he already had been. He was to become one of a handful of Chinese bishops—a local shepherd for the diminishing flock, surrounded by foreign foxes and domestic wolves.

Her education was most important to him, and he wished great things for her and for the country. No. He expected, even demanded, it of her. *Everyone needs to help the country,* she heard him say, over and over. There was no mistaking that he meant those words for her as well.

As she watched him walk behind the cross with the other ministers and bishops, his robe flowing and his face smiling, she was fearful, because of things she had already heard and experienced in her young life. The more important you were, the more attention you drew, and the more dangerous it could be.

The ceremony brought the young local Chinese clergymen together with the three bishops of the English, American, and Chinese churches. Grace observed Bishop Scott, the presiding bishop from America, consecrate Reverend Craighill, who in turn assisted Bishops Scott and Tsen in her father's consecration.

"These two did not care for their lives, but only for the name of the Lord Jesus Christ," Bishop Tsen read from the Book of Acts.

After the garden party and the posing of pictures, the new bishops disappeared into the rectory. Grace, her mother, and the guests were left to receive congratulations from the familiar congregation. She held the tiny hands of one of the orphaned toddlers, who was her responsibility this celebratory day. A group of Japanese soldiers, rifles slung over their shoulders, sat on a stone wall outside the church grounds, smoking cigarettes. They seemed to watch the gathering with more interest than she had noticed before, and she instinctively pulled the toddler closer.

LLOYD REMOVED HIS ROBE AND SASH AND POURED HOT TEA into the porcelain cups. Robin sat on the small couch in the rectory's greeting room and received a cup from Lloyd.

"Bishop Chen!" said Lloyd, as he raised his tea in a salute.

"Bishop Craighill!" Robin responded, rising from the couch. He bowed slightly.

"*Gang bei!*" exclaimed Lloyd as they clinked cups.

The other bishops came into the sparsely furnished room, laughing and offering salutations to Lloyd and Robin. The day had given them a small wisp of hope, amidst the turmoil the country and church were facing. They each accepted a teacup from Lloyd and settled into well-worn chairs. Lloyd took a soft white cloth and dipped it into a ceramic basin of water. He wrung it out. As he began to wipe down the silver wafer plate and wine chalice the altar boys had left, he glanced at Bishops Scott and Roberts.

"Alpha and omega. The beginning and the end," he proclaimed, tipping the shiny chalice in their direction.

Lindel shook his head solemnly. He was a thoughtful and serious type.

"That war should end. God willing."

"The Generalissimo will maintain his alliance with Mao against the Japanese. But the end ... the end will take time," Scott opined.

"China *always* has time," Lindel commented.

The room joined him in uncomfortable laughter.

"Not the war, Lindel." Lloyd pointed the cloth at Scott and Roberts. "British. Americans. The devils." He punctuated *devils*, indicating himself, as the bishops acknowledged the partial joke with another laugh.

"We *have* overstayed our welcome," Roberts chimed in.

Lloyd turned to squarely face the Chinese men and stated with emphasis, "Lindel, Robin. *You* are the beginning."

Robin looked at Lloyd intently as the weight of the words sunk in. He nodded agreeably to Lindel, who returned the nod.

"Lloyd, will you stay," Robin asked, "until the end?"

"There is much work to be done. Chinese people have grown on me. I will stay as long as I am welcomed," the new bishop answered.

"That you are," confided Lindel, as the others murmured their consent.

"Chinese are hard-working. Salt of the earth," said Roberts, with admiration.

"Prosperity will eventually come," Lloyd predicted. "Time—"

"Prosperity is an empty vessel," Robin interrupted. "China needs more."

"The Communists ... they are a problem," scoffed Lindel.

"They promise a socialist ideal," noted Robin matter-of-factly.

"... led by atheist beliefs!" Lindel continued without taking a breath. He hadn't touched his tea during the discussion.

"Gentlemen!" Lloyd jumped in as he opened the glass door to the room's lone mahogany cabinet, which stood against the wall. He carefully placed the plate and chalice inside.

"China has existed for thousands of years without us. It can do so for thousands more. Will communism win? The Nationalists? That is not the real question! Your politics is something we can never solve. It is a *Chinese* problem," he continued, positioning the plate and chalice symmetrically on the shelf.

"What can spirituality offer China? What sacrifices are you willing to make? Robin ... Lindel ... *these* are the questions you must answer," he paused. "You *are* the beginning."

He closed the door with a bang and turned the latch with a click. The metallic sound echoed throughout the sparsely furnished room.

There it was again. The heavy and hopeful words Robin would remember.

So, it was—the beginning.

Chapter 3

THE SYMBOL

"*Lai! Lai!*" Come, come!

Mr. Chen called out to Jian Chen as he hurried through the tight hallway of his modest home in Wuhu. He paused at the small family shrine as he did every morning. On the altar table was a bowl of oranges and an iron censer in front of a painting of Kung Fu-tzu, known to Westerners as Confucius. He poured a cup of hot tea for his deceased grandparents and lit an incense stick for each, while whispering the names carved into small wooden tablets. Black and white photos of his parents stood beside the tablets. Once the sticks released their wispy smoke, he bowed to the images.

There was a smaller picture behind his parents. A toddler—a girl. His firstborn. She would have been Jian Chen's older sister. Death came easily in China.

Mr. Chen straightened his tailored suit, centered his tie, and placed his black felt top hat over his hair, which was pulled back in the queue style of the day. He opened the front door and motioned to the awaiting rickshaw driver.

Jian Chen, handsome and healthy, short of fifteen years, bounded down the staircase into the hallway; his queue whiplashed like a horse's tail swatting flies from its rump. Mr. Chen shot his son a stern glance, causing him to stop at the shrine. He dutifully lit an incense stick and bowed reverently, if perfunctorily. His father waved at him, and he ran out the door. They settled into the rickshaw together, sitting side by side. The driver expertly turned the cart and trotted energetically out of the courtyard.

JIAN CHEN FELT EXCITED ABOUT THE PROSPECTS OF STUDYING at St. James Mission Middle School. His father had a secure position working as an accountant for the local police department and was able to afford a rickshaw driver and his own house. But it had taken him a bit of moving around from Anking, working various jobs as a crewman at the river port and on the railroad. His father had never passed the imperial entrance examinations, which caused great embarrassment since his father's own father was a government official—in fact, an instructor in the Temple of Confucius and administrator for its student examinations. His father's failure prompted high expectations for his number one son.

Jian Chen eschewed mindless recreation for reading, especially classical novels like *Romance of the Three Kingdoms* and *Dream of the Red Chamber*. His parents were acutely aware of the vices—mainly cigarette smoking and petty gambling—that tempted teenagers and were determined to deter him. The mission school was the best in the region, particularly for learning English. As a son is a reflection of his family and, foremost, of his father, they hoped he would eventually make something of himself.

The rickshaw passed through the bustling streets of the river port, where coolies with long queues trailing from the top of their heads to below the nape of their necks clamored for clients. Street vendors singing in shrill voices vied with each other, like river cranes calling out for their mates. They hawked fruits, steamed buns, and roasted chestnuts from their carts. Western-dressed bankers and their customers entered masonry buildings that displayed English words, in stark contrast to more familiar Chinese signs.

His father had noted the influx of English-speaking foreigners in his daily encounters. Most did not speak Chinese and used company translators. Missionaries, who often studied Chinese prior to their assignment, were the most fluent. His father impressed upon him that competency in this Western language could be the difference between an elite position in the government and a hard life toiling as a commercial journeyman.

Jian Chen studied diligently and, after primary school, passed the government middle school entrance examinations. The choice was now easy; his father would do anything to get him into the mission school.

As the rickshaw jockeyed for position on the unpaved streets, Jian Chen noticed beggars in the street, some crippled and blind. Most were ignored. But odd-looking women in white hoods and loose, light blue robes stopped and offered money or food. He had no idea why they did that.

A pair of ragged boys about his age taunted an old man leaning on his cane. The boys danced around, poking at the man's long white beard. The man waved his cane at the boys. While one of the boys drew the man's attention, the other quickly stripped the man of his pocket watch. The boys scampered away, leaving the old man hobbling helplessly after them. Jian Chen had seen it happen many times before.

The rickshaw turned towards the turgid Yangtse River, the lower portion of Chang Chiang, or Long River. The murky waterway was crowded with barges laden with coal, rice, and tea. The boatsmen called out to one another. Smaller "three board" boats, or sampans, drifted closer to shore, along with three-sail junks and houseboats with straw covers. Men and boys dotted the banks with bamboo fishing poles and cast nets, hoping to catch dinner or a few trophies large enough to sell to the local fishmonger. The river was the lifeline of the country, an important means of transportation and the source of necessary irrigation for crops. His home city had profited well, becoming one of the largest and busiest ports on the river, thanks in part to foreign businesses. But at times, it was a raging serpent, over two miles wide in some places, which during an extraordinarily wet season could devour everything in its path. Many shoreline villages and cities had been mercilessly swallowed throughout its turbulent history.

The trio moved towards a cluster of small hills just outside the city. The driver powered the carriage up the gentle incline with ease. He sang Chinese folk songs, which helped him breathe and broke the monotony of running. The driver was often proffered a gift of food that Mrs. Chen made on special occasions, such as the Lunar New Year. Despite the grueling job, the driver was always smiling, simply happy to be able to feed his wife and two growing boys.

As the rickshaw climbed north from the low-lying city toward the mission, the road became narrower and the European-style houses larger and spaced farther apart. Anglican missionaries had purchased land with funds from the United States, steadily piecing together lots to form the existing compound. Surrounding hills were similarly owned by the Jesuits, the Disciples of Christ, the Presbyterians, and Methodists, as well as wealthy foreign businesses. Many missions occupied this prime area, since the hills afforded protection from the floods and an inspiring view of the serpent coursing through the lower landscape.

THE RICKSHAW CAME UP THE DIRT ROAD, AND A LEATHER-skinned worker opened the wooden gates leading into the grounds of the mission. Mr. Franz E. Lund, the tall, Swedish headmaster of St. James Mission Middle School, sporting a short, light brown moustache and a bowler hat, was waiting for the Chens at the office entrance. Mr. Lund had been sent to China by the Swedish Missionary Society, along with a host of other Swedes. After being ordained to the ministry in 1899 with his countryman, Rev. Carl Lindstrom, he was stationed in Wuhu to develop the school system. He was among the more fortunate of these self-sacrificing Swedes, many of whom had become victims of the anti-foreign, anti-Christian Boxer Rebellion of 1900 in Peking, nearly a decade ago.

Mr. Lund shrewdly consolidated parcels of the land, named Lion's Hill, by appeasing landowners with the sale of excess landfill from the mission's acreage. This allowed owners to shore up their low-lying properties in exchange for legal transfer of contiguous lots that benefited the mission.

He greeted Mr. Chen with a warm handshake and deep bow.

"I am Mr. Lund," he said, extending his hand to Jian Chen.

Jian Chen recited his name in reply. He mimicked his father and took the headmaster's hand. Mr. Lund opened the door to the red-brick office building and led the pair inside.

The headmaster noticed that Mr. Chen was dressed in a Western business suit but sported the traditional Chinese queue, bridging the culture of the current Ching rulers and the trappings of foreign influence. The queue was a Manchurian tradition imposed on the Chinese Han subjects during the early years of the dynasty. An imperial edict ordered the shaving of the head and braiding of the hair, under penalty of death. The mandate was a source of embarrassment, even insult, for the predominantly Confucian society, where alteration of body parts was an affront to ancestors and, as important, symbolic of the invaders' dominance over the native Chinese Hans. Thousands of Hans lost their lives battling over these precious strands of hair, and more than a handful of the Manchu officials lost theirs from retaliation by rebellious subjects resisting subjugation. After two hundred and fifty years of Manchu rule, the queue had become more a fashion adaptation than a legal requirement. Still, half a century earlier a Brit's well-publicized use of the term *Chinaman's tail* had served as a rude reminder of its demeaning overtones.

"Why do you want to send your son to St. James?" Mr. Lund asked politely.

"Learn English," Mr. Chen answered deliberately and pointed to his son. "Jian Chen … learn English."

"He will learn English better than boys in America," said Mr. Lund. "Also, math, science, and geology."

"English. Learn English."

Mr. Lund was not sure how much Mr. Chen understood him, but he understood the father.

JIAN CHEN DRIFTED AWAY FROM THE TWO MEN AS THEY talked, drawn to photographs hanging on the corridor walls depicting scenes from the mission's history. The first showed men in clerical garments standing on a bare hill, surveying the surroundings. There was another of Chinese workers erecting the office building. The next showed boys with books, sitting at desks. A foreign woman stood watch over the children.

As he walked down the corridor, he imagined himself in the photos: planting a vegetable garden, playing with a feathered shuttlecock, reading a book under the wide canopy of a large magnolia tree. The next-to-last photo depicted a crowd standing in front of a small building as a large cross structure was raised off the ground by workers. The people were smiling and clapping. Such a happy world!

The final image was a medical clinic with men, women, and children lying on beds—local peasants not unlike the ones he saw begging in the streets. The man who had greeted them, Mr. Lund, was holding a book and stood over a man lying in one of the beds. The man's eyes were closed, hands folded across his waist, a cross lying on his chest. Jian Chen leaned closer. Was he sleeping or dead? Perhaps he was sick. What was that book? Something serious was going on.

His father and the headmaster disappeared into a room off the corridor. Jian Chen ran to catch up. He followed them into the room. It was then that his life changed.

THE WINDOWS WERE SHUTTERED, THE ROOM NEARLY BLACK. Everything was hidden in the darkness, as if he were blind except for the very center of his vision. There, he saw a column of light, catching fine particles of dust floating in the air, coming from a single window high on the front wall. Jian Chen's eyes fixed on the column of light. It drew him in like magic. At the bottom, in the very center of the beam of light, was a solitary cross on a table. The cross appeared metallic as the light, reflecting off its veneered wooden surface, produced a vital sheen, as if emitting energy. *Ch'i.*

As his eyes adjusted, he saw rows of benches in the middle of the room. Large Chinese-style lantern sconces and wooden chandeliers hung from the walls and ceiling. He glimpsed his father and the headmaster standing just inside the door.

"Mr. Chen. We are Anglican. Church of England," explained Mr. Lund. "This is our chapel."

"Confucian," replied Mr. Chen as he pointed to his chest and to his son.

Mr. Lund smiled and said, "Every Christian used to be something else."

"My son ... learn English," repeated Mr. Chen.

Mr. Lund did not belabor the point. Attempts at conversion of natives to Christianity had proved not to be very fruitful. Most Chinese were suspicious of foreigners. Two Opium Wars and the resultant Unequal Treaties in the first half of the last century had ceded unprecedented influence and protection to foreign powers in port cities like Wuhu and, while good for trade, left a bitter taste for many Chinese. Western missionaries flocked freely to these open ports, inevitably linking their evangelism to the growing commercial, cultural, political, and even military dominance of the Western powers, successfully riding these coattails to influence. While missionaries generally opposed the use of opium, it did not help that England and the United States were the primary importers of the illegal and highly addictive drug until the Unequal Treaties forced its legalization upon the populace. Missionaries served as interpreters and couriers for foreign businesses. As such, they were not saviors but alien spies, imperialists, and capitalistic predators worthy of suspicion and spite.

With such heavy historical baggage to carry, the focus was mainly on educating the Chinese and teaching them English. A quiet approach was necessary following all the violence during the Boxer Rebellion, when two hundred missionaries and over thirty thousand Chinese Christians were slaughtered.

Mr. Lund threw a switch, turning on the wall lights. A clean white cloth covered the table, and two chairs stood guard on either side. A deep-purple velvet curtain hung as a backdrop.

The cross itself was simple. The table reminded Jian Chen of the family shrine. He felt something powerful in its simplicity. It must mean something to stand all alone, in the center. He took a seat in the back row and continued to stare at the cross.

Why was this cross on the table? What did it represent? If it was a shrine, who was it honoring?

Jian Chen realized his father and the headmaster had already left the room. He stood up and scampered out of the room into the corridor; his mind was full of questions as he raced after his father.

THE TWO MEN HEADED TOWARD THE CLASSROOMS.

"I can offer a scholarship," Mr. Lund explained. "No need to pay."

"I pay," Mr. Chen said without hesitation, pointing to himself.

Mr. Lund nodded. He liked the boy's father. He was proud and direct. He clearly wanted a good future for his son. Jian Chen had done well on the entrance examination and deserved a chance to walk the path his father desired.

"I'm sure we can work something out," Mr. Lund replied as Mr. Chen waved at his son to join them.

The country needed educated, forward-looking citizens to progress beyond the feudalism of the imperial system. Mr. Lund believed that most of China's future leaders would come from the Christian mission schools. He knew the country would have to engage with the rest of the world and inevitably be pulled forward by the West. Most important, he was convinced that any one of his boys could have an influential hand in shaping that future.

Chapter 4

THE SISTER
AND THE FRIEND

Jian Chen settled easily into mission life. His classmates came from many parts of Anhwei. Most were from families like his, whose fathers were prosperous enough to afford the modern education that mission schools promised. A few were from families that needed a place to send their children so they would have a roof over their heads, plenty of food, and medical care when they needed it. Not many were there to study the Bible or learn about the religion that had brought China so much turmoil.

Jian Chen wondered why these foreigners came from overseas to teach English to Chinese children. His father told him about the influence English-speaking people outside the mission brought to China—different clothes, different customs, different behavior—as if to warn him. They often strutted around like mandarins and treated his neighbors with little respect, but they did bring more trade. That was good for the people.

The power of foreigners was unmistakable. They had exacted a terrible price from China in reparations for the murders of Christians and destruction of church properties during the Boxer Rebellion. The Empress Dowager was forced to pay hundreds of millions of taels of silver to the eight foreign nations that dominated the Chinese main cities. Her Ching government was obliged to open its border to preachers of this Christian god and its ports to foreign ships with their foreign goods. Having his son master English would improve the chance of success with these outsiders, or at least give him an advantage over Chinese who did not. For that reason,

Mr. Chen ignored all the trouble this religion might bring to his family. The country's resentment of foreign powers and, by association, these Christian missionaries, had been soundly quashed. The foreigners, mainly British and Americans but also Swedes and Germans, Russians and French, had won. They were all here to stay.

"Learn English. Be respected," Mr. Chen explained in Mandarin. "Become someone."

That was that. Jian Chen would study English and make his father happy.

THE FIRST TASK WAS TO LEARN THE ALPHABET. JIAN CHEN already knew how to say a few simple words and phrases.

Hello. Good morning. How are you today?

But reading and, especially, writing were more difficult. The good thing was that none of the new students knew how to read or write, and some did not know English at all, so Jian Chen was ahead of most of them. The older boys who applied themselves progressed quite far and could carry on conversations and write simple essays after a few years.

Sister Louise, an American nun wearing that funny hat and blue robe, took an immediate liking to Jian Chen. Mr. Chen had so firmly impressed upon Mr. Lund how important it was that his son excel in English that Mr. Lund appointed the young missionary as Jian Chen's personal tutor. Jian Chen studied diligently. The worst thing would be for him to disappoint his father, who had gone to the expense of lending him to Mr. Lund and the mission teachers. Like other families of means, Mr. Chen bought a chair and a desk for Jian Chen's personal use. It was here that Sister Louise would sit with him every afternoon following the regular classes, to help him with his English.

When Jian Chen was introduced to his tutor, he judged her to be perhaps twenty-five years old, maybe younger. A foreigner's age was hard to guess since he knew very few of them and, unlike the Chinese women he knew, her skin was light and smooth. She had hair the odd color of a chicken's yolk that fell just below her ears, and he had never seen eyes that were as blue as the summer sky. But it was her gentle smile and deep laugh that put him at ease right away. Even though they looked completely different, she could be the older sister he did not have.

"A," started Sister Louise.

"Apple," recited Jian Chen during his first lesson.

Sister Louise chuckled lightly, nodding with encouragement, as he struggled to hold the pencil correctly. He used the traditional ink brush to write Chinese calligraphy. That required a light grip at the ends of his fingertips and movement controlled by the wrist and arm as a unit. The Western grip placed the pencil tip closer to the fingertips and used less wrist and arm movement and firmer finger action, as if strangulating the instrument. The shapes written with the pencil seemed more abrupt and angular, often retracing a path, as opposed to Chinese ideograms. They did not seem to flow easily from one letter or stroke to another. Writing Chinese with an ink brush seemed like water flowing down a gentle hill, while writing English with chalk or pencil felt like etching wood blocks. One was caressing and painting, the other just scraping and scratching.

"B."

"Boy."

Every afternoon he practiced under Sister Louise's mindful and critical eye. He forced his fingers and hand to follow the outline of each letter on the tracing paper, even though it was awkward and unnatural—sometimes moving from right to left, sometimes from left to right. Chinese character strokes went from left to right, top to bottom. There was a structure and convention to the script. English was backwards, read left to right, then top to bottom; Chinese was read top to bottom, then right to left. Sister Louise sat with him patiently, curling her soft fingers firmly around his like a warm mitten to guide his movements.

"C."

"Cat."

"And China!" added Sister Louise.

Jian Chen gave her a puzzled look.

English did not make sense!

Sister Louise seemed to read his mind and laughed.

It was only after completing his tutoring sessions that he was allowed to play with the other students. Mr. Lund showed them the game of American baseball with little success. The boys were more at home with a stick in hand running after an old iron wheel or kicking shuttlecocks to others. Some showed tricks using yo-yos, *kong tzu,* they crafted in the workshop. Jian Chen liked to play Chinese chess, or *hsiang,* with his best friend, Hsiao Wang.

He first noticed Hsiao Wang when they were introduced to the Bible, the book he had seen in the photo. The class took place in the chapel. The room was free of ornamentation except for the cross at the altar and another wooden one hanging on a side wall.

Because of a shortage of Chinese Bibles, each book was shared by two students. His partner was Hsiao Wang, who was unusually quiet and shy. He was noticeably thin and smaller than most other boys in his grade, with a queue hanging nearly to his waist, as if siphoning nutrition like a tapeworm in his belly. While he kept a clean face and hands, his clothes were worn and hung loosely on his body. His shirt exposed his skin at the elbows and the blue dye of his pants faded at the seat and the knees. The open-toed sandals he wore despite the cool fall temperatures were not made of leather or cloth, but straw.

The Bible was written in Romanized Chinese. Mr. Lund or his Chinese assistant, Lindel Tsen, who was like a son to him, read passages, alternately explaining in English and Mandarin the meaning of the stories and ideas that were often difficult to understand. Jian Chen found it hard to believe how a man could live nine hundred years or that the entire world could be created in just six days. Walking on water seemed even more improbable. It sounded more like Chinese myth or legend. Mr. Lund called it *faith.*

"It is not important to understand the unbelievable. Learn to live life," Mr. Lund told the boys.

Jian Chen found that much more agreeable since he could see how what he read was practiced by the people in the mission. His father believed that having the correct behavior was honoring their ancestors. What the Bible said was correct behavior was honoring this thing or person they called God. Was there a difference between honoring his father and honoring this God as long as behavior was good?

"Faith will come later," Mr. Lund said to the boys.

"Do you understand Headmaster Lund?" Hsiao Wang asked Jian Chen when they were alone, playing with their crickets.

"Not all things can be understood," Jian Chen suggested.

"I understand what I see," Hsiao Wang replied, placing his cricket in the palm of his hand.

"Headmaster Lund teaches us about things we cannot see."

"But what I cannot see, I cannot eat," replied Hsiao Wang, putting his pet back in his lacquered box. "What is the use?"

"You feel happiness when you see your cricket." Jian Chen peered at the box as Hsiao Wang placed the cover over the cricket. "But you only see your cricket."

THE TEACHERS SPENT AS MUCH TIME WITH JIAN CHEN AS HE wanted. They saw he was more curious and open to learning new things than the other boys.

"Why fear God?" he asked.

"*Fear* means to respect," one of his teachers answered with a smile.

"Why I and me? Am I not me, the same?"

"I is when you are the subject. Me is when you are the object," explained Sister Louise.

"Why he and she? Man, woman. We call both *ta*. They are same."

The teachers stared at him blankly, then burst into laughter.

"Jian Chen, in America, men and women are definitely not the same!"

The nurses in the clinic were just as gentle and patient. Jian Chen saw they went out of their way to help anyone who showed up. They did not shy away from coughs or open sores or rashes on the face. They never turned anyone away.

Jian Chen and Hsiao Wang visited the nurses on the weekends and watched them apply bandages to small scrapes and scratches. They observed how the nurses talked to and comforted patients. They saw women give birth to babies that later were deposited in the mission's orphanage, their destitute parents unable to care for them.

Hsiao Wang eagerly helped clean wounds, pound on a chest full of congestion, and apply salve to infections. He was good with his hands and did not mind getting his fingers dirty. He did what he was told to do. But he did not say much. He never asked questions. He was like a good soldier.

Most of the boys got along with one another despite their diverse backgrounds. Mr. Lund was very fair-minded, and Western and Chinese teachers were strict on everyone. They all worked long and hard, spending time with students. If students did not learn and never reflected the Christian spirit, then the mission would be a failure. Most of the boys were well-behaved, but there was always one wayward child who strayed and caused a ruckus. One day, Hsiao Wang ran into this rascal.

Hsiao Wang was walking through the courtyard playing with his *kongzhu,* which he expertly twirled on a string tied between two wooden sticks. He had carved the two discs from bamboo, working in the workshop after classes for two weeks. One of the peasant boys tapped him on the arm and asked to play with it. Hsiao Wang twirled the *kongzhu* and tossed it in the air. It landed on the string with a hum. A rocking motion and quick pull with the sticks made it spin more quickly. Balancing the spinning discs on the taut string, he held it out for the other boy to take. The boy reached for it. Suddenly, another hand reached in and grabbed the sticks.

"*Bu shing!*" No, growled an older boy. He was one of the biggest students and a couple of years older than Hsiao Wang. "Give me!"

The *kongzhu* flipped off the string and pirouetted on the ground.

Hsiao Wang stooped to retrieve the *kongzhu,* but the older boy quickly snatched the toy. Hsiao Wang reached for his *kongzhu* and the two were quickly in a tug of war. Before either could blink, Hsiao Wang was on the ground as the older boy held his head and pulled his arm. They rolled over twice, kicking up dust like two squabbling roosters. The older boy ended up sitting on Hsiao Wang's chest, forcing him to gasp for air. The other boys were yelling and cheering. Someone laughed.

Jian Chen pulled the older boy firmly off Hsiao Wang as if removing a sack of rice. He stepped in between the two schoolmates, aware that the older boy stood nearly a head taller than him and he stood more than a head above Hsiao Wang.

"Why do you steal Hsiao Wang's *kongzhu*? Go make your own!"

"What do you care?" argued the older boy.

"Why make trouble? Don't you see? He has nothing," Jian Chen reasoned. He knew neither would really fight, because Mr. Lund would expel a troublemaker. "If you want the *kongzhu,* Hsiao Wang will show you how to make one."

"I know how!" the older boy shot back. With that, he trudged away, his face as ruddy as his pursed lips.

Hsiao Wang picked himself up off the ground and brushed the dirt from his clothes, his fingers catching a new tear near his knee. Jian Chen retrieved the *kongzhu* and handed it to Hsiao Wang. Hsiao Wang immediately offered the *kongzhu* to the peasant boy, who sheepishly took it and put the toy in motion.

Jian Chen saw that Hsiao Wang was unharmed, so he turned and walked away without saying a word. Even in their silence, he knew they would become good friends.

Chapter 5

THE BEATITUDES

Jian Chen and his classmates practiced their new language by reading the Bible. The school had few texts, except for Chinese classics and English books for the upper classes, like *A Tale of Two Cities, Romeo and Juliet,* and *Treasure Island.* There were primers the missionaries wrote themselves or brought from overseas, hardly more useful for everyday conversation than the Bible. If the students were going to learn English, the Bible was as good as any book.

To Jian Chen, the stories were more than tales. Every passage seemed to have a second meaning or lesson. It was not like reading about cats chasing balls of yarn or boys chopping trees in a forest. His favorite was the Beatitudes. After a few weeks, he could recite it from memory.

"Blessed are the poor in spirit …" began Sister Louise in one class.

"… for theirs is the kingdom of Heaven," the students responded.

"Blessed are those who mourn …" Sister Louise continued as she paraded between the rows of desks, observing each student closely as if they were young seedlings in a garden.

"… for they will be comforted."

Jian Chen saw his Chinese people in the Beatitudes every day. They were ones who slept unclothed in the dirt streets or showed up in the clinic asking for medicines. They stole from street merchants and buried their children in shallow graves or surrendered them to the mission orphanage.

His eyes wandered to the crucifix on the wall and then fell onto each of the boys in the room. He had been at the school for two years and felt so comfortable with the missionaries and other students. His life had changed. He had given up cigarettes. He did not gamble on cricket fights. He thought about people beyond his own family. He wondered and worried about his classmates and their lives, not only about his own future. He learned about concepts he could not see, like love, forgiveness, and trust.

"Blessed are the peacemakers ..." read Sister Louise. Her voice seemed far away.

"... for they will be called the sons of God."

His gaze found Hsiao Wang, sitting on the far side of the room. At times, his younger schoolmate seemed so helpless. His family were poor tenants working for a rice farmer on less than ten *mu* of land. The only reason he was at St. James was so his family would not have to feed him. They never came to the mission, and Jian Chen wondered where he would end up in life. Would Hsiao Wang grow rice for the rest of his life? Would English save him?

"Blessed—!"

The ruler slapped hard on his desk, shattering his daydream and making him jump halfway out of his seat. The boys turned and stared at him. Someone in the back row tried to stifle a giggle.

Sister Louise gave him a stern look, continuing, "—are those who are *persecuted* because of righteousness ..."

He quickly put his head down and focused his eyes on the Bible. He joined the rest of the students in response.

"... for theirs is the kingdom of heaven," he recited with vigor, making sure his voice was heard.

Sister Louise nodded with approval. He forced an apologetic smile and thought he detected the slightest smile on her face as she passed him.

"Rejoice and be glad, for great is your reward in heaven ..." she went on.

She was standing right in front of his desk. All the boys had her attention. But it seemed as if she was speaking directly to him.

"... for in the same way, they persecuted the prophets that were before you."

༄ ⊕ ༄

SINCE HE LIVED SO CLOSE TO THE MISSION, JIAN CHEN WAS allowed to go home on weekends to visit his parents. While he still bowed at the shrine in the hallway, it was different than when kneeling in the chapel. He was respectful, but his gesture felt repetitious. When he was in the chapel, because he sat for a longer time, often in the solitary shadows of early dawn or late dusk, he felt that the "worship" of God, *shang di*, went deep into his very existence. Confucian teachings helped him behave in a "good" and "harmonious" manner, but the Christian God seemed to be responsible for his life, his future—like a father to a child. And the promise of everlasting life: Was it just a grand, complicated story like *Dream of the Red Chamber?*

At dinner, he told his parents and younger brother some of the stories from the Bible: feeding five thousand people with two fish and five loaves of bread; bringing the dead to life; the young child teaching elders in the temple. They listened politely, amused, and pleased at his enthusiasm and his improving English. They said little and asked less. They were simply happy he was learning something that kept him out of trouble.

"Why cannot this be in China?" he asked one evening.

"*Shen ma?*" What? his mother asked.

"Feed people. Take care of people who are sick."

"China is a big country. We must take care of ourselves," his mother replied.

"Why did Hsiao Mei die?" he asked.

"Don't talk!" his father said sternly.

His parents glanced at each other. His father went on eating. Everyone knew someone who died. Why? If God was able to prevent death, he might have had an older sister. But if the stories he read were fantasies—tales from these foreign people about their foreign God—then so what? They were no more or less useful to him than the Monkey King.

Could what he learned and saw at the mission really help China?

That night, he opened the lacquered leather chest that held many of his clothes. He found a cotton shirt and a pair of trousers with a drawstring at the waist. At the bottom of the chest, there was a worn, but clean, pair of sandals made of heavy canvas. Good enough. *Not straw,* he thought. His family was not rich, but he did not have to worry about food or clothing.

He carefully folded the shirt, placed it on the trousers, and then positioned the sandals on the shirt. He rolled up the trousers into a tight package, starting at the bottom, and tied the drawstring around the bundle. When it was neat and secure, he placed it next to his books that he had brought home. It was not much, but it was something. He lay down and went to sleep.

⤳ ✦ ⤳

THE FOLLOWING DAY WAS SUNDAY, AT LEAST IN THE MISSION. Jian Chen returned to the school in the rickshaw. The younger boys who stayed at the school over the weekends because their families lived too far away, or because the mission kitchen saved their families money, were tending to the garden next to the dormitory. They broke open the soil with tools donated to the mission. A Chinese worker supervised the boys, who worked well as a team. One group turned over the soil with a pitchfork. Another shoveled the dirt onto a screen to sift out the large rocks. Another collected the rocks and debris in a wheelbarrow to be carted away. A fourth group patted and stomped the soil to a flat surface with their bare feet. Hsiao Wang was in this last group.

Jian Chen kept his distance, observing from under a plum tree as Hsiao Wang methodically smoothed and compacted the earth. His friend was focused and exact. When he was finished, the ground was as level and smooth as a tabletop. Hsiao Wang went to a water spigot and washed his feet. He took out his straw sandals, which were tucked into the waist of his trousers, and slipped them on. Jian Chen could see some of Hsiao Wang's flesh peeking through the many defects in the sandals.

Jian Chen waited until Hsiao Wang was a distance away from the other boys and then approached him. He waved his arms to catch Hsiao Wang's attention.

"Hsiao Wang!"

"Jian Chen," Hsiao Wang answered, surprised to see his friend. "Why are you here?"

Jian Chen held out the package of clothes he had wrapped the previous night. Hsiao Wang took the package cautiously. He seemed unsure of what to do. Jian Chen nodded reassuringly.

"What is this?" asked Hsiao Wang.

Hsiao Wang began to untie the drawstring. He unrolled the trouser legs as though unwrapping *ba bao fan*, the sweet eight-treasure rice pudding bundled into a banana leaf, and revealed the shirt and sandals. He took a few seconds to stare at the sandals. Jian Chen could hardly suppress his grin. He watched Hsiao Wang turn over the shoes as if admiring a trophy caught from the river. Hsiao Wang took off his straw sandals and pulled on the canvas ones.

Jian Chen quietly stole away and was already halfway to his dormitory when he saw Hsiao Wang spin around, searching for him. As he entered the building, he was filled with unspeakable joy. For the first time in his life, he felt an exhilaration, a giddiness; he was on the verge of uncontrollable laughter.

What Jesus said in the Bible was true. It *was* more blessed to give than to receive.

Chapter 6

TWO KINDS OF CHESS

Jian Chen spent part of every school day with Sister Louise, practicing his grammar and reading stories from the Bible. He asked as much as he could about Christianity, and Sister Louise was all too happy to oblige. The more he read the Bible, the more his English improved. They spoke freely with each other, less as teacher and student and more like *Jie Jie* and *Dei Dei*—older sister and younger brother.

Sister Louise was fond of playing chess with the other teachers, but few mastered it to any degree to give her a challenge. On this bright, sunny day, she sat with him at a stone table in the cool shade of a cherry blossom tree. She opened a wooden box, unfolded the chess board, and began to place the pieces in their positions. She needed a new partner.

"These men are called pawns."

"Why are they men?"

"Perhaps they could be women," Sister Louise mused with a chuckle. "They move one space at a time, slow, like foot soldiers, except the first move can be two. When a piece is in front, to the side, the pawn can capture it. Because there are many and they are weak, a pawn is often sacrificed."

"Like Chinese peasants," Jian Chen observed.

He studied each piece as he copied Sister Louise. He confused his queen with his king, and the good sister corrected him.

"The queen's crown is different, you see, and she sits on the king's right. She can move in any direction, as many spaces as she wants, and can capture any piece in her path. She is the most powerful piece."

He laughed, "Like you, Sister."

She answered through her own laugh, "No, I am not the king!"

"China does not have kings," he said matter-of-factly.

"Neither does America."

"England has a king."

"And you have emperors and empresses," she noted.

"Yes, every country is different."

They continued to set up the board.

"Why does the king wear a cross?" he asked.

"In England, the king is also head of the church," she explained.

"Hmm," he pondered. "What is England like?"

"I have only been in China."

"How long have you been here?"

She thought. "Five years."

"Why did you come?" he asked with a serious look.

He had not thought much about the teachers. He just assumed they were there, like trees in the compound. Foreigners had been present in Wuhu for as long as he could remember. It was not until he had been at the school for nearly two years that it dawned on him: they had all made a decision to come from somewhere else. As the school grew and new buildings were erected, it was obvious that people and money were coming from outside Wuhu, from another country. He never thought that there had to be a reason why people like Sister Louise and Mr. Lund left their country to come all the way to China. But there had to be. Someone planted the first trees.

"When I was a teenager like you, I did not know what to do with my life. I was lost, so I became a nun," she laughed. "China was far away. We did not know much about your country. I wanted to learn more. I took my vows, a promise, to devote myself to the church. I could not wait to come here."

"To teach us English?"

"To show God's love."

Jian Chen looked at her thoughtfully.

"Teaching English was my way of serving God," she continued. "I could teach English anywhere. I chose China."

He thought a while as he doubled-checked the placement of his pieces against hers.

"You are brave to leave home."

"Leaving home was easy. And coming to China was exciting. But choosing to serve God, *that* was brave."

"Why?"

"If I failed in China, I could always go home. But if I failed God, I would be lost again."

"I am glad you chose China," he said.

He looked at her intently.

"Sister Louise, what is this God's love?"

She stared at him.

"No one has ever asked me that before."

She paused.

"God's love is giving what is most precious," she said measuredly. "Love so great, you give of your own life."

It was a strange answer to Jian Chen. He had always thought love was to feel good about something he had—to love his mother's cooking, to love his parents, to love his Bible. But love was about giving. Was that why it had felt good to give Hsiao Wang his own clothes?

"How can God give his own life? He cannot die."

"He gives us what he loves the most," answered Sister Louise.

"What is that?" Jian Chen asked, squeezing his brows hard.

"His family. His only son. Jesus Christ."

It was Jian Chen's turn to pause, staring at the chessboard.

His family. His only son ...

"What about *your* family?"

"The church *is* my family," she explained. "Our work is not only about teaching English. It was about forming a family. To build a community where each person is devoted to the community and willing to give his or her own life to the community."

"You gave up your family?" he asked.

He saw that she could not speak, so he looked at the other pieces, one shaped like a horse's head and the other with its top like a tower from *Chang Cheng*, the Great Wall. He knew about the king and queen. But there was a piece that did not look like anything he had seen before.

"What is this?"

"That is a bishop," she answered.

"Bish-op," he slowly enunciated. A funny-sounding word.

"A bishop is a minister, a leader in the church. Often an adviser to the king," she continued. "There are two for each side. One on the right, another on the left.

"What does bishop do?"

"It moves diagonally, as many spaces as it can … all the way across the board. It is a good attacking piece."

"Are bishops real?" he asked.

Sister Louise giggled.

"Yes. We have a bishop. Bishop Huntington. He lives in Anking. One day, you will meet him."

Jian Chen jumped up so quickly Sister Louise did not have time to say anything. He dashed towards his dormitory. Within half a minute he reached his desk and pulled out a wooden container from its drawer. He sprinted back to the stone table as fast as he had left it. He emptied the contents of the box and unfolded a flat, rectangular piece of wood. It had lines on the playing surface, like a grid, and an empty space in the middle dividing the board into two halves.

"This is *hsiang ch'i*."

He held a round, thick disk the size of a quarter, carved out of wood with a Chinese character in black etched into its top surface. He dangled his forearm in front of his face and tossed his head back as he waved his arm. His voice emitted a sound like a horn.

"*Hsiang*," he repeated.

"Elephant?" she guessed.

He nodded, though not understanding the word. He picked up another piece with a different Chinese character on the top in red.

"*Hsiang*," he said with a slightly flatter intonation.

"Elephant."

He shook his head.

"Bishop."

He pronounced the word slowly and put the two different bishops together. He then placed them in position; red on one end of the board and black on the other. He moved the red piece like a bishop, two intersections at a time in the shape of a diamond on one half of the board. He did the same for the black elephant piece on the opposite side of the board.

"Black … el-e-phant. Red … bishop!"

Sister Louise took the red piece and mimicked his moves.

"*Hsiang* cannot cross the river," he said, pointing to the blank section in the middle of the board. "*Hsiang* always stays home."

"I see," Sister Louise remarked.

"*Hsiang* never leaves our country. Always protects his general." He returned the bishop to Sister Louise. "No queen. Only general."

Sister Louise laughed.

"If a pawn reaches the other side, it becomes a queen," she informed.

"Like America!" exclaimed Jian Chen. "The weak can be powerful, the most important."

"You are right. That is America!"

She laughed. Jian Chen smiled and shook his head, placing the red disk in its position.

"In China, it is different," he said.

Chapter 7

A TURNING EVENT

I t had been more than three years since Jian Chen entered St. James, and, with Sister Louise's help, he was nearly fluent. Mr. Lund offered him a full scholarship, and his father and mother were pleased he was happy and away from more idle boys.

But outside the mission, a tumultuous change was taking place. Under claims of corruption and a spreading national disenchantment with the imperial system and foreign rule, the Empress Dowager relinquished Manchu control of the country to a loose coalition of revolutionaries. One of the more Western-influenced of these native leaders was appointed provisional president of the newly formed Republic of China in January of 1912. With that, four millennia of dynastic imperialism abruptly ended.

Over thirty years prior to this historic and relatively bloodless event, a Chinese laborer turned successful businessman, Sun De-zhang, also known as Sun Mei, had recognized the importance of the English language in a China progressively influenced, even dominated, by Brits and Americans. More and more business, diplomacy, and law were conducted in this foreign language. With this wise prescience, he sent his younger brother, Sun De-ming, also known as Sun Wen, to an Anglican school in Hawaii to learn English. It was a practical strategy geared toward employability, not at all a religious one. The Anglicans were known for a high standard of education and an equal dose of moral expectation not nearly as rigid or ritualistic as the Catholics.

While the adoption of Christianity was not mandatory at Iolani School in Honolulu, attendance at daily chapel prayer and Sunday church services was. Christian principles of equality—the first shall be last, and sacrifice for the common welfare—began to ring true to Sun Wen.

Fearful that his brother was coming under the anti-Chinese, anti-Confucian spell of Christianity, the traditionalist Sun Mei recalled Sun Wen to Hong Kong. Undeterred, Sun Wen studied at another Christian school, the Diocesan Boys' School, and then a public secondary school. He was so influenced by these teachings, he eventually converted to Christianity. At age eighteen, he was baptized in Hong Kong despite his brother's objections and given the name Jih-hsin by a Congregationalist minister. Soon after, he met a pastor who gave him the Mandarin name Sun I-hsien. He had other names: Nakayama Sho in Japanese and its Mandarin counterpart, Sun Chung-shan, or Middle Mountain. But after receiving a medical degree in Hong Kong, he was most famously known by his Cantonese name, Dr. Sun Yat-sen.

Confucian respect for the body prohibited the cutting of hair, which was often wound into a tight bun at the top of the head. With the fall of the Ching dynasty, Western style and culture prevailed. Jian Chen and most of his classmates, even the coolies in the city, cut off their queues. Since Dr. Sun spent much of his early revolutionary life outside of China, courting financial support from overseas Chinese, his Westernization, particularly his conversion to Christianity, helped his cause. Americans identified more easily with Dr. Sun than with the Empress Dowager; he often wore Western suits and ties, was fluent in English, and spoke about Western ideas like democracy.

The new government promoted a flood of missionary activity. With the renewed interest in Christianity, attendance at the St. James Mission School was robust. Funds from overseas flowed into its treasury, especially from the widow of Rev. E. Walpole Warren, the former rector of St. James Church in New York. Through her generosity and that of others, new buildings, including a middle school and church, had been built a decade before. Teachers were added and nuns from the Episcopalian order of the Sisters of the Transfiguration in Ohio came to service the diocese.

Jian Chen sensed that belief in the common good could be important to motivate both wealthy and poor to help propel China out of its imperialist and feudal traditions into a modern future. He was eighteen years old and needed to find his place in the new China. The traditional beliefs and order had been upended by the rise of Dr. Sun and his Republic. He would have to look toward the future, to what should be, not what already was. He was not particularly good in math. He had no interest in business or law. Perhaps he could teach, like Sister Louise. But what?

The stories in the Bible inspired him. The idea of the Son of God bridging the divide between man and his creator to bring salvation and a sense of oneness to humans appealed to his hope for a better life for his fellow Chinese. The mission school allowed many of the boys from poor homes to have an education not available from the old government examination system. Likewise, the clinic in the compound treated people who could not afford to visit a doctor or even a local herbalist or acupuncturist.

Suddenly, everything was clear to him. He did not know where it would lead, but he knew the path was the right one. He needed to tell someone— but not his parents.

SISTER LOUISE KNEW JIAN CHEN HAD PUT A LOT OF THOUGHT into his decision, but also his trust in her. She was not sure of his father. The row she had had with her own father when she declared her devotion to the order came back vividly. Facing her father at the immature age of fifteen was frightening. She remembered his wrath and how it prompted her to run away. That was where she might help Jian Chen.

While many Chinese had welcomed the change that swept the Manchu government out of power, not all, but a minority, embraced the new ideas and customs of the West. Abandoning the queue was not the same as adopting Christianity, an import from the oft-despised West. While it promised the fruits of modern education and medical care, it also carried the stigma of foreign betrayal and dominance. The educated, contemporary class had an easier time accepting Western ideas. Many of its youth, like Sun Mei and Jian Chen, were educated in Christian institutions. They knew about Lincoln and Moses, and Congress and the Apostles. The masses, and the older generation, were more apt to cling to their native traditions of Taoism, Confucianism, and Buddhism.

Sister Louise met Mr. Lund at the walkway leading into the garden. Chinese gardeners were fertilizing the soil. A few boys were playing croquet in an adjoining field, while others kicked hacky sacks or crowded around freshly caught crickets—not for fights, but as singing pets to prod and pester in captivity with long twigs poked through their cages.

"Thank you for seeing me about the Chen boy," she said.

"Jian Chen? His English has improved."

"Although he doesn't read the classics."

"The classics are essential to proper English!" Mr. Lund exclaimed with feigned indignation.

She laughed.

"His English is as proper and clever as it comes. To him, the Bible is better than Dickens," added Sister Louise with a smile.

"Better than Dickens?" he replied, twisting the end of his mustache.

She walked a bit further, then blurted, "Mr. Lund, Jian Chen loves the Bible. He wants to become a minister."

She waited for that to sink in. Mr. Lund did not miss a step.

"He'll have to be baptized," he said bluntly.

"Of course."

"You know his family is Confucian," Mr. Lund posed.

"To him, we are protectors of China."

Mr. Lund turned toward Sister Louise, his eyebrows raising quizzically.

"He sees the good work we do," she said, answering his questioning look.

Mr. Lund's eyebrows drew together more tensely.

"It is possible the father will not think it favorable and pull him out of school. That will not be beneficial to the boy."

"Reverend Tsen converted at the same age."

"Lindel had no parents, no family, no one to answer to." Mr. Lund continued pacing through the garden, which was abloom with an array of colorful spring flowers. "Has the boy approached his father?"

"He is afraid."

"What does Lindel think?"

Lindel Tsen was like a son to Mr. Lund. Plucked from a ragtag collection of sorry-looking, wayward waifs when Lund first came to Wuhu in 1898, Lindel, or Ho-P'u as he was then known, was a homeless orphan. Unlike some other schoolboys at the mission who were prone to street vices and could be more correctly characterized as delinquents, Lindel was serious, showing intelligence beyond that of the typical peasant child.

Mr. Lund revitalized the school, which at the time of his arrival had deteriorated into an unproductive receptacle for local lost souls. The boys, often runaways, and the school were languishing under the corrupt misguidance of the presiding instructor, who was known to spend more time inhaling an opium pipe than exhorting his students. Mr. Lund cleaned house and sent the insolent instructor and unmotivated urchins packing. But something about the fifteen-year-old Lindel made him take pity on his sorry state of destitution, and he gave the boy a full scholarship at the new mission school. Lindel turned out to be a diligent student, demonstrating a mature concern for the younger boys. Upon graduating from Divinity School, he became a deacon and was appointed by Lund as headmaster at St. James Mission Middle School, just as Jian Chen arrived.

Three years later, unencumbered by parents, Lindel was consecrated a priest in the Anglican tradition. Because of his singular path from discarded orphan to Christian clergy, his opinion was especially valued in assessing fellow native boys.

Lindel's transformation was not the only time Mr. Lund had rescued a native son. The mission authorized him to use the resources of the church to salvage hopeless souls left behind by the ineffectiveness, corruption, and sheer vastness of Chinese feudalism. In an earlier incident, while stationed at the diocese's mountain outpost in Nanling, south of Wuhu, he had been returning to the mission late one snowy winter night when he heard groaning and whimpering in the frigid dark. Drawn to the agonized cries, he came upon a young boy of ten, seemingly more animal than human and half frozen to death. His hair was matted into a tangled mess. The weeping ulcers and painful red lesions of chilblains on his feet rendered him effectively crippled. He looked and smelled as if he had not seen a clean bath for weeks, if ever.

Mr. Lund learned that the boy's mother had died of starvation during the recent famine. The boy was put out of his house—not out of cruelty, but hopelessness—by his father, who could hardly afford to feed the boy's younger brother. The insensitivity and inertia of society had left this helpless soul to perish alone in the cold, at the mercy of a stranger's pity and generosity.

Mr. Lund gathered up the child and nursed him back to reasonable health. He placed him in the mission's primary school. Local Chinese heard about the boy's salvation and contributed some money here and there. The boy prospered in the school, and soon the school had more children than it could handle clamoring to be educated. Mr. Lund believed Jian Chen, like the young Sun Mei and Lindel Tsen, or any poor, solitary, lost soul could be instrumental to the church and to China.

Sister Louis looked down at the dirt path. "Lindel believes he has an extraordinary gift, a gift of insight … of seeing and seeking truth. He is an honest and innocent soul, bursting with desire to help his people."

Mr. Lund paused and turned. He looked earnestly at Sister Louise.

"And what do you think?"

She looked back at him with the same intensity.

"He is one of the most curious and sincere young men I have ever known. He reminds me of me."

Mr. Lund was silent. A croquet ball rolled into their path, and Sister Louise kicked it back to one of the boys. The boys laughed and ran around as they banged the ball at the wickets plugged into the bare ground. Mr. Lund and Sister Louise smiled proudly at their students, all of whom were progressing nicely as students, but also, more importantly, as good citizens with kind hearts. They were nurturing a promising generation of young Chinese men with opportunities not to be squandered and talents not to be buried. They knew Jian Chen was not only one of the absolute best of these young men, certainly one of the brightest and most diligent, but also perhaps possessed with the primary reason for optimism in the whole group. He was a leader.

Mr. Lund drew in a deep breath as Sister Louise continued strolling, watching their boys play in the field. Students like Jian Chen and Lindel came around rarely. The Swedes had sown the Gospel for years at the school with little to show for it, but perhaps things in the new Republic were changing for the better. He and the other missionaries had wished for this day ever since Jian Chen came to the school, and Sister Louise knew he must seize the moment, even at the risk of losing the boy.

"Permission must come from the parents," he said as he stooped to pluck a red rosebud.

"He trusts us, and he needs our help."

"If he is as you say, Sister Louise, then we must not stand in his way."

Chapter 8

THE REQUEST

Mr. Lund alighted from the rickshaw in front of the Chen home, well-aware that an audience at the elder Chen's house was a sign of respect. He hoped it would soften resistance to the request.

A manservant opened the door and led Mr. Lund through the front hallway. As they passed the family shrine, Mr. Lund noticed a polished orange in the porcelain bowl and a portrait of Dr. Sun Yat-sen positioned next to Confucius. With the recent fall of the Ching dynasty and the establishment of the Republic, pictures of its Christian leader were everywhere.

Mr. Lund entered a sitting room neatly appointed with black lacquered chairs and silk pillows embroidered with entwined twin birds and chrysanthemums. The manservant disappeared.

As he waited, Mr. Lund noticed the bare wooden floor was spotless. Its surface glistened with a smooth varnish finish. The walls held a few scrolls of Chinese calligraphy, and there were a couple of large, cobalt-blue ceramic vases in the far corners of the room. Otherwise, there was nothing to suggest anything but a respectable Chinese household, comfortable but not excessive.

Within a few seconds, the manservant reappeared, and Mr. Chen came into the room, accompanied by his wife. His wife was quite pretty, with her hair in a bun and wearing a stylish yellow *chi pao* fitted exactly to her figure. She sat in one of the chairs as Mr. Chen bowed to Mr. Lund. Mr. Lund returned the gesture, being sure to bow even lower. He extended his hand. They shook briefly before Mr. Chen took a protective position next to his wife, as if a sentry on duty.

"*Chen hsien sheng,*" Mr. Chen, Mr. Lund started in his rudimentary Mandarin. "Thank you for inviting me to your house. Regarding your son, we at school, all are very happy."

Mr. Chen nodded politely and replied in Mandarin, "We, also, are very happy."

"Your son very much enjoys reading the Bible."

"He tells stories. Very nice. My English, also better!"

Mr. Lund chuckled politely. He searched for the Chinese words, pondering how to formulate the next sentence.

"Sorry, my Chinese compared to your English is not as good. May I—" he hesitated, "speak English?"

Mr. Chen smiled and nodded.

"Your son is a good student," explained Mr. Lund, taking care to speak slowly. "He learns quickly. When other students do not study well, he helps. When they fight, he makes peace. When they do not have clothes, he gives his own."

Mr. Chen whispered a translation to his wife. She broke from her stoic demeanor and grunted her approval with a hint of a smile.

"He is good boy," Mr. Chen replied.

"He believes our work, our—" Mr. Lund hesitated. He could not think of a better word. "Mission."

There was no easy way. The request was going to be accepted or not. He wasn't about to sell Christianity to a Confucian.

"Mr. Chen, your son, Jian Chen, would like to become Christian."

Mr. Chen did not react. He bent over and whispered something to his wife, who nodded.

So far so good, Mr. Lund thought. *No outrage.*

Mr. Chen seemed to stare straight through him. Perhaps he didn't understand that his statement was an implied question awaiting a response.

"Mr. Chen. I—" Mr. Lund began to explain.

Mr. Chen suddenly held up his hand. His voice began quietly, as if reading an official statement.

"China, my country. Armies come from Menggu. Manchukuo. One hundred years, British come … sell opium … force treaties," he said, becoming more animated and gesturing with his clenched hands. He punctuated each word. "We fight British ... French ... German! Outsiders, *wai guo ren*, take ports ... take land ... walk free in cities ... get special privilege. Should guest follow custom of host?"

"Of course," mumbled Mr. Lund. Things were suddenly not going well.

"I give my son. Learn English. No God. English!" Mr. Chen said, his voice rising. He slapped the back of a fist into his opened palm.

Mr. Chen moved from behind his wife to the window, looking out at the garden at the rear of the house. He gazed at Jian Chen, who was seated on a stone bench under a flowering cherry blossom tree, reading his Bible. Mr. Chen spent a long time looking at his son while Mr. Lund waited patiently.

As Mr. Chen turned away from the window and walked towards him, Mr. Lund began to fidget, rubbing his thumbs into the sides of his palms.

"I, Confucian!" Mr. Chen suddenly declared, again pounding his right fist into his left hand. "My father, Confucian! Teacher ... in Temple of Confucius! Loyal to family, friends. Seek harmony. *Ho hsieh*. You, teach forgiveness ... love. Every day, I give respect to ancestors. You, pray to God. *Shang di*."

"You know much about Christianity."

"Because my son."

Mr. Chen's voice softened, and he went to Mr. Lund's side and took his arm. "*Lai*."

He led Mr. Lund gently, but purposefully, into the front hallway. His wife never moved. He stopped in front of Dr. Sun's portrait. Dr. Sun's eyes seemed expressionless, betraying no thoughts, as if staring into the unknown future. His hair was dark, straight, and parted on the side, and he sported a wide mustache above his resolute, tight lips. He was dressed in a suit, high-collared white shirt, and tightly knotted dark tie. As he studied the new president's photo, Mr. Lund thought he could easily have been from Stockholm or New York.

"Doctor Sun, free us. He Confucian. Study in mission school. Learn English. Now Christian! Doctor Sun say God, his spirit, help free China. My son, the same. Jian Chen, he loves China. *All* Chinese *love* China."

Mr. Chen left the shrine, went back to the sitting room, and returned to stand at his wife's side. Mr. Lund obediently followed him into the room.

He had nothing to say. The church was not there to take over Chinese lives. They had learned their lesson. China was on its own, in control of its own destiny. Foreigners like him must heed China's own people. If the Chinese wanted Christianity, it was there. But if they did not, they did not. While others thought differently, missionaries like him at St. James were there to help China, not conquer it.

Mrs. Chen lifted her hand as Mr. Chen stood behind her. It was the first time she had moved since she came into the room. Mr. Chen took her hand and faced Mr. Lund. The two men both stood erect, facing each other directly, as if in a standoff.

"Jian Chen. He is eighteen years. A man," said Mr. Chen.

Mr. Lund watched as Mr. Chen opened his hands and gestured towards his son outside as if introducing his son.

"Jian Chen, my son, he *is* Christian."

Mrs. Chen opened her mouth. Her voice—soft, but steady, in perfectly understandable although heavily accented English—was certain and final.

"He is yours."

Mr. Lund left to bring the good news to the boy, whose parents had endowed the church with a treasured gift, a new convert. In the process, they had given their number one son a most precious present. His freedom.

Chapter 9

YUNG CH'I

By the time he entered upper middle school, Jian Chen had mastered the game of chess. He proved himself a worthy opponent for Sister Louise, besting her on more than a few occasions. It was a more exciting game than *hsiang ch'i*. Though both games used sixteen pieces per side, all the pieces in chess were free to move anywhere. There were situations where he found his king on the opposite side of the board, deep in the opponent's territory. That would never happen playing *hsiang ch'i*; the general with his advisors were confined to one side of the board within the palace, an area three by three "spaces." He thought it quite appropriate. Chinese emperors rarely strayed from their homeland, but imperialist kings thought it their duty to expand empires into distant countries.

Since chess was new, Jian Chen preferred it to *hsiang ch'i* and taught the game to some of his classmates. None gave him much competition, but Hsiao Wang enjoyed the game enough to play with him. Hsiao Wang did not have any siblings and rarely went home to see his parents. Ever since he was saved from the rascal four years ago, Hsiao Wang had followed him around like a little brother.

"What will you do when we leave this school?" Jian Chen asked Hsiao Wang as they set up the board one spring afternoon.

"Be a doctor. Help people," he answered in perfect English.

"Good! China needs doctors," Jian Chen agreed.

"*Ni ne?*" You? asked Hsiao Wang.

"I want to become a minister."

"Aiyaaaah!" exclaimed Hsiao Wang as he slapped his forehead. "You want to catch fish?" he joked. "Too hard!"

"Why?"

"You need big, big—" Hsiao Wang thought hard for the right word as he spread his hands far apart, then pounded his chest with his right fist, "—*yung ch'i!*"

"*Yung ch'i?*" Courage? Jian Chen answered with a puzzled glance.

"*Dui!*" Yes.

They each played a few moves.

Jian Chen, hand on his chin, squinted hard at the pieces.

"Why does a minister need courage? If you believe in the Bible, you can teach others, help them become good people."

Hsiao Wang castled his king, tucking it safely behind a row of pawns. He pointed at Jian Chen, shaking his head slowly.

"Teaching is easy."

"Then why need *yung ch'i?*" asked Jian Chen as he moved his queen's bishop forward.

"You will see, Jian Chen," Hsiao Wang answered, wagging his finger intently. "You think it is simple. But it is hard, impossible, to *always* obey God."

Jian Chen playfully slapped his friend's leg and smiled.

"Man is not perfect, but I will try."

Hsiao Wang remained silent and dropped his gaze, avoiding Jian Chen's scrutiny. He shook his head again.

"You will see," he finally whispered to himself.

Chapter 10

BAPTISM

A merican Anglican minister Daniel Huntington was elected bishop of
the diocese of Anking in 1911. Due to the commotion of the revolution that was underway to overthrow the Empress Dowager, he could not
be consecrated in a formal ceremony until 1912. He oversaw a diocese that
geographically encompassed Anhwei Province, one of the poorest provinces,
and parts of Kiangsi Province to the south. Wuhu was the largest city in this
diocese and one of the most important and active centers for Episcopalian
missionary work.

Huntington was instrumental in organizing separately functioning missionary organizations from English-speaking countries into a unified entity.
The perception of Christian churches as foreign institutions run by foreign
ministers and bishops made it difficult to reach and relate to the local people. The idea was to develop a distinctly Chinese church from the Church
of England, the Episcopal Church of the United States, and the Anglican
Church of Canada. The ambitious transformation from a foreign church
to an indigenous Chung Hwa Sheng Kung Hui, CHSKH or Holy Catholic
Church of China, propelled many native Chinese, like Lindel Tsen, Bernard
Tsen, Hunter Yen, and Reuben Nieh into formal priesthood. They were the
first ordained by Huntington, but behind them came a growing number of
well-schooled young men dedicating themselves to the Christian faith.

It was in this environment in 1912 that Mr. Lund welcomed Bishop
Huntington to St. James to preside over Jian Chen's baptismal ceremony.

Huntington was in his early forties, a Yale graduate, with dark hair oddly parted down the middle and plastered flat against his skull. He wore a full beard and a lush, neatly groomed moustache that effectively hid his lips. His eyes were heavy, almost tired-looking, effecting a kind but weighty appearance.

"Bishop Huntington, thank you for coming," said Mr. Lund.

"It is always a pleasure to welcome new members into our fold," Huntington replied dryly as he greeted Jian Chen before the service. "We are but humble fishermen," he added, looking Jian Chen directly in the eye. "Fishers of men."

He finished with a wink to Mr. Lund.

Jian Chen felt at ease with this otherwise imposing figure—his first real bishop—although the man's words, which he interpreted to be messages from heaven, seem to magically emanate from behind his thick facial hair.

As Bishop Huntington and Mr. Lund waited in the alcove outside the church, the room began to fill with Chinese teachers, American missionary workers, and the students' family members, who sat in a section separate from the handful of boys waiting to be baptized. Mr. and Mrs. Chen took their seats behind Jian Chen, who was dressed in a long, dark gown buttoned at the neck and reaching to his sandals.

Jian Chen's parents were not enthusiastic about his conversion, but neither did they oppose him. They understood the change China was undergoing. Mr. Lund explained the attributes the church could impart: the limitless learning, the connection to the important world beyond Wuhu, and the opportunity to lift up people and help China. Jian Chen knew they wanted a good future for him and a superior education to ensure that future. If joining the church provided that, then they accepted his decision. Besides, he had his own mind, and they always wanted him to use it. He had.

"Who presents this child to be baptized?" asked Bishop Huntington when it was Jian Chen's turn to kneel before him.

Mr. and Mrs. Chen stood and nodded politely. Jian Chen looked for any hint of a smile before they sat down.

"You have chosen an English name. Robin," said Bishop Huntington. "And a Chinese name. *Jian*. See. *Chen*. Truth."

Jian Chen had cleverly chosen a homonym for his new name. With a slight change in tone and an entirely different ideogram, he transformed a meaningless familial name into an adopted one with deep significance.

To others, it fittingly matched his ability to cut through the fog and see the landscape as it truly was, much like his skill for analyzing strategic positions of chess pieces or knowing when a classmate needed help with schoolwork. But to him, it was more of a search, a challenge. It was not a talent he possessed but a goal to pursue. His name focused him on everything he did and said. Not "see truth" as he saw it, but "see truth" as he *sought* it—a constant reminder to strive for the truth.

"Robin Jian Chen Chen, do you wish to be baptized?"

"I do," he replied.

He did not take the initiation into the faith lightly. He was acutely aware of the upheaval occurring in China with Dr. Sun's ascendency to power. Core values had been changed almost overnight. Old China lost to new China. The feudalism of Imperial China was replaced by *San Min Chu I,* or the Three People's Principles, developed by Dr. Sun. Instead of dynastic rule supported by an elitist civil service system within an imperial hierarchy, a republic was born and itself baptized with nationalism, democracy, and common welfare.

He was finally able to discuss his conversion to Christianity with his parents, thanks to Sister Louise and Mr. Lund. It was so clear to him that the ideas taught at St. James aligned with the principles behind Dr. Sun's forward-looking republic. The missionaries cared about him and his country and had pledged their lives to help China. Everything seemed so purposeful and the questions easy to answer.

"Do you renounce Satan and all the spiritual forces of wickedness that rebel against God?" asked Bishop Huntington.

"I renounce him," he answered.

"Do you renounce the evil powers of the world that corrupt and destroy the creatures of God?"

"I renounce them."

"Do you believe in God, the Father?" continued Bishop Huntington.

"I believe in God, the Father Almighty, creator of Heaven and Earth."

"Do you believe in Jesus Christ, son of God?"

"I believe in Jesus Christ, His only Son."

Sister Louise and Hsiao Wang had helped him memorize his lines.

"Do you believe in God, the Holy Spirit?"

"I believe in God, the Holy Spirit."

He did not have to even think.

"Will you persevere in resisting evil?"

The words rang more seriously, as if from God, filtered through the bishop's beard.

"I will, with God's help."

There was so much going against China. He had not really thought about what God's help would entail or how that would come about. He could not foresee the future of his Christian path in China. He only held the faith that God's help did exist, and at some point, he would need it. The forces of the world around him were greater than he as a solitary man could manage, let alone understand.

"Will you seek and serve Christ in all persons, loving neighbors as yourself?"

"I will, with God's help."

Christianity had taught him that central theme: *all* persons—all living things, near or far, predator or prey—were creations and children of God. He felt deeply for the poor and destitute people he saw every day. Mr. Lund did not have to lecture him about the suffering and death brought by the famine in 1907, or the devastation of crops and great starvation of people after the floods in his home province of Anhwei in 1911. He had seen them with his own eyes. He bore witness to peasants with nothing but tattered cloth on their wasting bodies; peasants who perished in the cold, crowded streets at the feet of insensitive strangers struggling for their own survival. He sensed the futility of his fellow Chinese, whose basic needs could not be provided for by disloyal, and often uncaring, government officials. But he had also seen the tireless efforts and generous financial gifts offered by a network of overburdened, underfunded, inadequately staffed missionary organizations.

Where there were problems, there were opportunities, and he was eager to be part of this rebuilding effort swept in by the new republic.

"Will you strive for justice and peace among all people and respect the dignity of *every* human being?"

Bishop Huntington's soulful eyes, heavily hooded by the many difficult years of bringing Christianity to Chinese life, bore deeply into Jian Chen's lively, hope-filled eyes. The task seemed impossible and the burden too heavy, yet it was too late for him to avoid.

Coastal and treaty cities teemed with every sort of pleasurable activity. What he knew came by way of loose talk. Foreigners brought money and an appetite for the exotic. He had heard about Shanghai's tens of thousands of prostitutes. Gambling houses abounded with games of cards, *pai gow* (literally, 'eat dog'), *mahjongg*, horse racing, and cock fights. Opium production had resumed as local governments and farmers pursued cash to support their needs. There was a resurgence of smoking dens full of stupefied Chinese, and large ports had every kind of nightlife vice.

"I will, with God's help," he pledged, thinking of the unimaginable challenges before him.

Bishop Huntington dipped his middle and forefinger into a chalice of water and made the sign of a cross on Jian Chen's forehead.

"Robin Jian Chen, I baptize you in the name of the Father, the Son, and the Holy Spirit."

Bishop Huntington gently placed his hand on top of Jian Chen's bowed head and said, "Go in peace!"

In that moment, now baptized, Jian Chen assumed his new Christian name and shed his Confucian boyhood. An elderly Chinese lady began to play a hymn on an even older upright piano brought from America by one of the early missionaries. The piano, like many things foreign, bore deep scratches and scars from sword-wielding natives. The notes from this ebony survivor sounded thin and noticeably off-key—it could use a good tuning and a fresh coat of varnish—but the melody was played with vigor. The congregation sang with purity and passion, even though many did not know all the words.

Turning to face his parents, he grinned brightly and widely. This time they smiled back. He had no idea what was to transpire in the next few years, but he was ready to march to the strains of Christianity.

Robin commenced his new life as a servant of God and a soldier for Jesus Christ. There were wars going on in China, military and spiritual. Lives needed to be saved and lives would undoubtedly be lost.

Chapter 11

REVOLUTIONS

AND REBELS

Within a few months of establishing the Republic of China, Dr. Sun abdicated the presidency to General Yuan Shih-kai, a powerful warlord and head of the dominant Beiyang Army. Yuan had ascended to a position of great favor within the Ching government when he supported its suppression of the Boxer Rebellion against predominantly Christian foreign countries. As the Chinese people became disenchanted with the imperial state, the well-regarded Yuan mediated a settlement between the Ching court and Sun's revolutionary coalition. Killing two birds with one stroke of the ink brush, he brokered away the beleaguered Ching's dynastic rule through the abdication of the last Emperor, the five-year-old Pu-i, in favor of Sun and his Republic. Then, in exchange for Sun's subsequent resignation, Yuan assumed the presidency within the Republic he had cleverly secured.

Yuan was more conservative than Sun. Advocating for the traditional Confucian idea of an autocratic monarchy, he revived the possibility of a new empire with himself as Emperor. During this fight for the Republic, Yuan's chief rival was assassinated in March of 1913. Of course, Yuan was a prime suspect in the unsolved murder.

Sun's party lost the challenge to Yuan, and Sun fled to Japan in exile in November. Yuan then dissolved the Parliament in January 1914. After numerous political maneuverings, backed by a military force, Yuan declared himself the new Emperor of the Chinese Empire at the end of the following year.

Yuan's audacious, self-serving act shocked the world. After intense local and international outcry, Yuan retired as Emperor and died within a few months. Without an Emperor and without a Republic, the decentralized country became a fertile battleground for diverse provincial warlords eager to make forays into the power vacuum.

During these three years of post-revolution strife, Robin continued his education at St. James. Mr. Lund granted him a full scholarship, despite his father's proud protests. At his graduation ceremony, Robin took Hsiao Wang aside.

"You will serve our people. I will serve God," he told his friend. "We both will serve China."

Hsiao Wang was on his way to Union Medical College in Peking, with Mr. Lund's endorsement. The Rockefeller Foundation had taken its first steps toward investing in Western-style medical education by purchasing the school from the London Missionary Society. Hsiao Wang's parents had recently died from tuberculosis, despite the novel treatment at Wuhu General Hospital of artificial pneumothorax, the surgical collapse of the affected lung. This personal experience whetted his interest in surgery. He would no longer worry about planting rice, but neither would he be baptized.

After the ceremony, as they were about to go their separate ways, Robin held out a box. Hsiao Wang immediately grinned when he saw the familiar container. It was Sister Louise's chess set. Robin passed it to his friend.

Hsiao Wang opened the box, immediately picked up the bishop, and showed it to Robin. He grinned widely.

"This is you!" he said.

They both laughed and hugged each other like brothers.

ROBIN WENT ON TO BOONE UNIVERSITY, AN ANGLICAN SCHOOL in Wuhan located along the Yangtse River in the interior of China; his predecessor, Lindel, had done the same. Boone University began in 1871 as one of the first Episcopalian boarding schools for boys and, with its divinity and medical school, was now a premier breeding ground for Christian leaders, along with St. John's University in Shanghai. The school was named after the first Episcopal bishop in China, William Jones Boone, who, when informed that China was not open to outsiders, replied, "If by going to China and staying for the whole term of my natural life I could but oil the hinges of the door so the next man who comes would be able to get in, I would be glad to go."

Soon after Robin began his liberal arts studies, foreign powers took advantage of China's weakness to advance their own self-interest. Japan invaded the important coastal city of Tsingtao, which Germany had invaded and occupied since the end of the last century. In January 1915, Japan extracted a host of concessions from the Yuan-led Chinese government, called the Twenty-one Demands. This occupation, following the preceding hundred years of foreign intimidation, began to foment renewed Chinese nationalism and hostility against other foreigners, including Americans and Brits. This animosity spilled over to foreign Christians, many of whom had been persecuted and slaughtered in the Boxer Rebellion two decades earlier.

To add insult to injury, once World War I was over, the Big Five power-broker nations of Great Britain, France, Italy, the United States, and Japan designed the Versailles Treaty in Paris. Over the objections of China and the United States, German-occupied established countries were liberated back to their own self-governance. The spoils of independent German territories were awarded predominantly to the colonial superpowers, France and Great Britain. But in an egregiously damning scheme, the power brokers decided not to return the foreign concessions in Shantung to their rightful mother country, China. Instead, they consigned these territories, including Tsingtao, back to the foreign occupier, Japan.

Robin finished his degree in theology at the Boone divinity school. It seemed to him that the whole world had its weight firmly on China's throat. By himself, he was impotent. With the community and strength of the Christian church, he thought, he might be able to do some good.

THROUGHOUT CHINA, OTHER BOLD INDIVIDUALS WERE LOOKing for opportunities to wield influence in a central government vacuum. Dozens of warlords reigned, often brutally, over various regions—some extensive, covering many provinces, and some smaller. Armies grew, sometimes without adequate equipment or pay. Loyalties were tested and betrayals plotted. Skirmishes and major battles took place frequently, as each warlord tried to gain territory and influence while defending his empire from another's ambitions. Local bandits preyed on the vulnerable, whether Christian, foreigner, peasant, landlord, or shop owner. Individuals who tried to directly oppose the warlords were slaughtered like animals—sliced, dismembered, burned, beheaded, and disemboweled. China had had thousands of years to perfect gruesome ways of disposing of enemies. And thousands of expired humans were mere specks in a country with hundreds of millions of citizens, their weak and damaged bodies a universal testament to the belief that lives in China were cheaper than dirt.

University students, reacting against the insulting but yet-to-be-signed Versailles Treaty, demonstrated by the thousands in Peking, stoking nationalistic sentiment into the May Fourth Movement of 1919. The reigning Beiyang government, originally led by Yuan Shi-kai, was self-interested and weak following his death. It was too busy trying to consolidate power from competing warlords to be concerned with foreign influence in China. As such, it incurred the wrath of these students, who sought a new type of government, one that would restore national pride and protect their native interests over those of foreign powers.

In this slushy porridge of piecemeal politics and power-grabbing, a history teacher in Changsha, originally a peasant from Hunan, self-taught in political theories, set about organizing students and publishing radical articles. His goal was to rally peasants to overthrow a regional commander, a corrupt and vicious warlord. Previously a member and soldier with Sun Yat-sen's Kuomintang (KMT) party, the teacher called for organizing peasants, students, and workers into strong unions to be forces of social change. Having rebelled against his own arranged marriage at age fourteen, he, like many forward-looking thinkers and writers, advocated for women's equality. A dedicated anti-monarchist and anti-imperialist, especially in the condemnation of the United States, this son of a peasant transformed himself into a thoughtful, socially conscious intellectual. Like Robin, he wanted to change China and improve the lives of its masses. He, too, saw need and opportunity. When he began his political life, the unassuming Mao Tse-tung was just a year older than Robin.

Chapter 12

THE CONSTANT

B oone's sister school was St. Hilda's Girls School. One of the most important objectives of the Episcopal community in China was to increase educational opportunities, not only for the sons of China but also for its daughters. During the early days of the missionary movement, schools were created only for boys. Few girls went to school, and most who did went to government schools. Those attending the missionary schools that sprang up in the new Republic of China often did not complete their education or married immediately after graduating.

With the defeat of the Boxers earlier in the new century and the decline of the Ching government, the progressive idea of schooling China's women came to fruition. More young girls sought formal education. Parents began to believe and act on the concept of equality of the sexes. The Anglican Church took the lead and established schools for girls from Christian families: St. Hilda's in Wuhan, St. Agnes in Anking, and St. Lioba's in Wuhu. Boarding schools that only covered the early primary school years began to extend through to lower and upper middle, or high, school, just like the boys'. The three women's universities were all foreign missionary schools until two women broke tradition and entered the government-sponsored Peking University in 1920.

Reuben W.C. Nieh's daughter, Constance, was one of these lucky girls, although initially it might not have seemed so. Nieh was a progressive thinker and among the first deacons ordained into the ministry by Bishop

Huntington. He baptized Constance when she was one and adopted many Western ideas during his exposure to missionary life. But since his life bridged Old and New China, he still tolerated customs of the old society; one was foot-binding. Like petite waists in 16th century France, formed by molding ribs using tight corsets, the deformation of a young girl's pliable feet was viewed as similarly attractive. Peer pressure prompted the young minister to put his daughter through the painful process.

Every day, beginning when Constance was five years old, her mother wrapped her feet tightly with gauze, nearly squeezing out all the blood. The bindings bent the toes under the forefoot and the forefoot toward the hindfoot. The goal was to produce feet three or four inches in length, to fit into doll-sized lotus shoes. By forcing girls to walk with a short, shuffling gait as if on stumps, the effect was thought exotic enough to attract eligible husbands. Because it was difficult to walk, and thus to do heavy labor, it was assumed that women with lotus feet were wealthy enough to afford servants. Their deformed feet were tickets to a better life.

"Ma, it hurts too much," Constance whined as she fought back the tears. She wanted to chop off her feet with the cleaver her mother used in the kitchen.

"Shhh, shhh. Do not cry. Only for a short time," her mother replied as she pulled the canvas strip tighter.

Constance squealed, gritting her teeth. She would have to bear the pain.

Constance's first luck was having a mother who was more progressive than her father. After only three months of her crying in pain, her mother relented and, in covert opposition to her father, unbound her feet at night. Her father did not pay much attention; he was preoccupied with his work as one of a handful of Chinese priests. Constance developed "half big feet"—large enough to have the local grocery merchant scold her for ruining his store floor with her ugly feet, yet stunted enough to have difficulty walking. Her father looked the other way and never addressed her mother's act of sabotage.

Constance's second luck was having a father who, though not as progressive as his wife, believed girls were equal to boys. Constance became one of the first graduates of St. Hilda's School. She was smart, well-liked, and, indeed, pretty. Most of all, she was direct and straightforward. She was not afraid to speak her mind, unlike many Chinese women of the day who obeyed the adage: *men never talk inside; women never talk outside.*

Arranged, not necessarily forced, marriages were still the order of the day—a leftover from feudal China. While it ensured a family legacy, this form of marriage created a lot of anxiety in young men and women. Couples often did not see what their prospective life-mates looked like until the wedding day, when the bride's face, hidden behind a red veil, was revealed after the marriage ceremony. Those who could not tolerate the idea of a marriage with someone they had not seen often contemplated suicide.

The family go-between believed that Constance and Robin were perfectly matched. They both were well-educated and from respectable families. Most important of all, they believed in the same God.

"He is most eligible. Smart. Good family," the go-between reported to the Niehs.

How can I live with someone I am not in love with? Constance wondered. *How can I conceive a child if I do not find him attractive?*

Boys from Boone and girls from St. Hilda's went to services at the same church. The two schools had no other interaction or contact with each other. There was a physical wall between the campuses, and it was almost impossible for them to meet in church, where girls and boys were separated by a curtain. But church service was the best chance to catch a glimpse of her match.

One Sunday, Constance sat in the girls' section of the church, knowing that Robin was somewhere on the other side of the curtain. She shook nervously as she thought about the possibility of spending her life with a man she had never met. She knew he was a good man; her parents would not allow it any other way. Chinese men traditionally married women who were less educated, so he was probably quite intelligent. But since she was more educated than most girls, her marriage prospects were also less. She was about to graduate, so she had to marry soon; she did not want to be a leftover woman. If her parents approved, she would have to say yes.

But was he good-looking? Was he sociable, like her? Would he find her attractive?

She knew her American teachers did not marry like this; they thought it strange, even primitive. Should she just trust God and the go-between? Her head spun, and she prayed that she should just see!

One of her friends knew of her dilemma and found out where Robin was sitting. All she had to do was look. How could she?

During the prayers and Bible lessons, Constance could only think of what her match was like. Was he tall? Was his skin smooth? Did he look kind? She could not concentrate and fidgeted through the service. After the sermon, the congregation stood to sing a hymn. It was at this exact time, as the worshippers fumbled to find the song in the program, that her friend stooped and raised the curtain just enough for Constance to bend down and peek.

"*Kuai le! Kuai le!*" Hurry! Hurry! her friend whispered in her ear as Constance stole a glance at the rows of boys across the room.

"*Chien mien. Hao kan de!*" At the front. The handsome one!

Constance quickly set her eye upon the boy. Just as quickly, her friend dropped the curtain. But she had seen enough to be pleased. She would not say she was in love yet, but he was sufficiently good-looking. Besides, he was a good man, according to the go-between. And smart.

She felt her heart open and her face break into a smile. Yes, she felt quite lucky today.

UPON THEIR GRADUATION, ROBIN AND CONSTANCE WERE MAR-ried in that same church. It was a modern, but simple, Christian wedding. Red banners to ward off evil spirits prevailed, wishing them good fortune and double happiness. Friends brought monetary gifts in red envelopes, *hong bao.* Everything was in good-fortune red.

Neither Robin nor Constance cared about money or wealth. Both were eager to help the church in its mission. That drew them together, as much as the go-between. As Anglicans, they were in the smallest of the small group of Chinese Christians; Presbyterians and Methodists outnumbered Anglicans nearly four to one. Despite all the red surrounding them with promises of a happy future, China was descending into an uncertain chaos. The only stable haven for Christians was the church itself.

As the country floundered rudderless through rough waters, the Anglican Church continued to look to the future. It consecrated the first native Chinese bishop, Rev. Tsae-seng Sing, the Archdeacon from Ningpo, whose own father had been the first Anglican clergyman in Chekiang

Province. Sing, whose chosen name meant "born again," was an engaging, practical man with a hearty sense of humor, a healthy dose of humility, and the reputation of a clear thinker. He became the assistant bishop of the Chekiang diocese in Shanghai. Suddenly, there was real hope for a native church that had been imagined but never actualized. A new era of optimism arrived with the energetic Bishop Sing, an era that church leaders expected would lead to a flood of Chinese fishermen. But with all the agitation in the country, casting a wide net might not promise a bountiful catch. They would need lots of good luck, patience, and, most important, gentler currents.

THE YEAR AFTER HIS GRADUATION FROM BOONE, ROBIN WAS ordained a deacon by Bishop Huntington. He and Constance moved to Wuhu to begin his work and training. He would become and live the spirit of the Word. It seemed so clear; love and self-sacrifice for others made Christianity ideal for China. The chaos in China begged the need for a grounding belief in something beyond survival, even as survival itself was aided by the church's social services.

A year later, Constance gave birth to their first child, Chen Yu, whom they christened Paul. Two years after that, on September 28, 1923, their first daughter, Chen I, was born and given the name Grace.

As Robin was starting his family and ministerial work, Mao Tse-tung was organizing the Chinese Communist Party (CCP). He, too, saw the peasants' suffering and advocated for a "great union of the popular masses." He railed against foreign powers and, particularly, the foreign-mandated prohibition of Chinese taxation of British and American cigarettes. Everywhere he looked, he saw the same injustices against the Chinese people that Robin saw. There was a stark difference between the peasant-turned-political activist and the new Christian deacon.

One was an atheist.

Chapter 13

THE ANTIS

C onditions in China during the years following World War I were dire. Families accepted employment wherever they could. Individuals who found work tolerated conditions to the point of intolerance. As inflation outstripped wage growth among urban factory workers, strikes for higher pay and demands for payment in silver dollars, as opposed to the progressively devalued copper coins, were widespread and frequent. One successful strike in one factory in one major city emboldened other workers in other factories in other cities. Further strikes in 1925 were often supported by both the nascent CCP, which saw an opportunity to attract new members among the working class, and the more established, nationalistic KMT, which was in search of a rallying point to reinvigorate the party after the death of Dr. Sun. Strikers protested poor housing, safety issues, excessive working hours especially for women, unfair pay in the prevailing foreign currency of the day (as low as five to ten Mexican cents for a twelve-hour shift), abusive treatment that included beatings and sexual harassment, and, eventually, the sensitive issue of child employment.

While there was a general feeling, particularly among the British and Japanese, that children should be prohibited from employment, Chinese families often wanted the maximum number of revenue-producing offspring and relatives; they *needed* children to work in order to survive. A Child Employment Bill arose out of a Child Labor Commission of the Shanghai Municipal Court, prohibiting children under twelve from working in factories or other industrial settings. This well-meant effort to protect juveniles directly threatened their very subsistence.

Underlying all these labor disagreements was the Chinese resentment towards foreign ownership and the exploitation by these foreign owners. Why should foreigners have control over Chinese lives? Why were non-Chinese even here?

Pushing back, Japanese factory owners saw that relenting on wage demands simply encouraged more demands. They began to prohibit or dissolve unions. They sacked older workers so they could hire younger workers at lower wages. They substituted higher-paid men with lower-paid women. Lunch breaks were pared from an hour down to fifteen minutes in some instances. Some factories closed without notice, claiming lack of raw materials, putting many families under even more financial pressure. They had workers fined or arrested for damaging property during strikes. They twisted the arm of local authorities to look the other way when abuses occurred and to decline prosecution of foreign perpetrators of those abuses.

On May 15, 1925, workers at Japanese cotton mill factory No. 8, having had their demands for improved working conditions rejected, showed up for the night shift only to find the factory closed. They broke in and were confronted by Sikh police and Japanese foremen. The workers' anger, frustration, and desperation were at a point of no retreat. A violent exchange ensued, resulting in the Japanese foremen shooting ten Chinese workers. It was the foremen's misfortune that one of these wounded workers died two days later.

This event initiated a cascading series of maneuvers among various parties. Sympathetic factory workers began to strike in protest. Japanese factory owners threatened local courts and police to arrest striking workers. They warned local news publications against reporting stories favorable to the strikers; controlling the media controlled the truth. Political groups met among themselves to discuss how to use this local conflict to advance their national goals. Chinese factory owners saw an opportunity to gain from the troubles of the foreign-owned factories and supported the strikers, even though it raised the risk of repercussions in their own factories, which had equally deplorable working conditions. The group that had the most impact was a coalition of young university students backed by both political parties.

These students from local universities, incensed at the death of the cotton mill worker and upset at the lack of honest press coverage, organized rallies and protests demanding a transparent investigation into the deadly events. Two students were arrested. A few days later, further protests occurred at the memorial service for the slain worker.

"Down with Japan! Support the workers!" exhorted the student leaders.

"Kick out the foreigners! Throw them out!" responded the crowd.

More arrests of students from Shanghai University followed. Students who could not afford the $100 bail were held in jail. The trial for the protesters was set for May 30. It was to be held in the Mixed Court that had jurisdiction in the International Settlements. Chinese students protesting abuses by foreign owners in their own homeland were arrested by foreign law enforcement to be brought before a foreign court system. The students would not stand a chance.

The stage was set for a well-organized demonstration on May 30 to bring attention to the plight and mistreatment of factory employees, striking workers, and student protesters. While it was organized by Shanghai University students demanding the release of their schoolmates, students from other local universities joined in. Behind this overt scene played out on the streets of Shanghai, strategizing by more powerful national organizations made the demonstrations a referendum on anti-foreign and anti-imperialist attitudes.

Various factions of demonstrators marched down Nanking Road and through the international settlements, carrying anti-Japanese and anti-imperialist posters. Some ended up at the Japanese consulate and others in front of the Mixed Court, which was presided over by a Japanese assessor. Anger and fervor fed off each other. French, American, and British residents of the settlements watched curiously, although some scurried to the safety of their homes or shops.

"Kill all the foreigners!" shouted the students.

"Free the students!" echoed their compatriots.

Some students handed out pamphlets to foreigners. A few bold British and American residents engaged in purposeful conversations with students. Even though demonstrations were outlawed in the international settlements and dozens of demonstrators were arrested, most of the English-speaking foreigners did not feel threatened. The students were not there to commit violence, though their chants were not very encouraging. Most of their vitriol was aimed at the Japanese.

"Shanghai for Shanghainese!"

"Shanghai is the Shanghai for the Chinese people!"

"Kill the Japanese!"

As the British later colorfully characterized the incident, the crowd, or the "mob," descended on the Laozha Police Station. Demonstrators, numbering about two thousand, demanded the release of the arrested students, the "ringleaders." Suspiciously, despite receiving advance warning of the protest plan, none of the men in charge prepared for anything extraordinary: neither the American head of the Shanghai Municipal Council, Stirling Fessenden, described in a telegram from the British legation in Peking as a "feeble creature," nor Police Chief K.J. McKuen, characterized as "a notoriously incompetent loafer" by the British Consul in Tsinan, was present during the confrontation. In fact, McKuen ignored all signs of trouble and left the city that morning. When he returned later in the day, he hightailed it to the Shanghai Race Club.

McKuen's absence left Inspector Edward Everson, a Brit, as the highest-ranking officer at the station. Backed by a woefully outnumbered force of less than twenty Sikh, British, and Chinese policemen, the inexperienced Everson repelled the demonstrators using his fashionable and very sturdy, but insufficient, malacca walking cane and some wooden office stools. The demonstrators fought back with banner poles. The policemen succeeded in repelling the "mob" back out into the street. But the demonstrators, enraged at the sight of crimson flowing from their compatriots' beaten heads, rushed the policemen, sending them into retreat again.

The mob forced its way towards the front gate of the police station. Everson and his forces shouted at them but could not be heard above the rising commotion. They had to defend the station. Munitions inside the station were at risk. They could not let the demonstrators get access to the firearms. Mostly, they were afraid for their own lives.

"Stop! Stop! Or I'll shoot!" yelled Everson in Chinese.

Everson raised his pistol, and the other policemen reached for their rifles.

"Stop, or I will shoot!" he warned, this time in English, raising his pistol higher. "I *will* shoot!"

Seeing no reaction, either because the crowd could not hear the Chinese or could not understand his English—or were too angry to heed either—Everson did the only thing he could think of. He fired into the air.

Everson did not intend the shot to kill. He merely wanted to scare the mob and cause them to disperse. Had his men more correctly interpreted his benign intent, the course of China's history might have changed. But taking his shot as a cue, or miscue, policemen unloaded their firearms into the crowd in a barrage of bullets. The crowd panicked and ran, leaving behind four dead and numerous wounded; seven were so severely injured, they later died as well.

The aftermath of the May 30 incident was a tidal wave of protests, demonstrations, and boycotts of British and Japanese products. Martial law was declared in Shanghai. Tense hastily arranged meetings were coordinated among government, business, political, religious, and international entities. An international investigation eventually found the shootings lawful and justified, but Everson and McKuen were forced to resign. Strikes spread to twenty-eight cities and crippled the Chinese economy. Chinese citizens were beaten, arrested, and killed, and Christians became prime targets as the country's number one imperialistic foreign enemy.

The year prior to this incident—the bloody event that marked the beginning of what was known as the May 30 Movement—Robin had been ordained a minister, the second order in the Anglican Church. He and his young family were sent by Bishop Huntington to work in the mission at Nanling, in the mountainous county south of Wuhu. He followed Lindel, the rector there for seven years until 1921, when he went to work as general secretary of the Board of Missions. With two children in tow and a third on the way, he and Constance were responsible for the largest outpost in the Anking diocese. But even in remote Nanling, there would be a ripple effect to the violent anti-foreign, anti-imperialist, anti-Christian wave of urban nationalism.

Chapter 14

SIGNS OF TROUBLE

Bishop Huntington, like Mr. Lund, saw great potential in Robin, who seemed to be cast in the same mold as his predecessor, Lindel. Huntington foresaw the day when he and his foreign friends would relinquish governance over the church in China and be marginalized. In fact, he worked for that day. But the wave of anti-foreignism that rolled out of Shanghai presaged an uneasy future. He needed sincere, able Chinese to administer the workings of the church and minister to the native people. Without clergymen like Robin and Lindel, the Christian church in China would die a lonely death, beset by more powerful forces in society.

Nanling, a town of about twenty thousand people directly south of Wuhu, was a growing outstation. Located halfway between Wuhu and the smaller outstation in Maolin, it was nestled at the foot of a mountain range spanning the southern border of the Yangtse valley.

Lindel had done an excellent job of recruiting students, so the primary and middle school were in much demand. Like Robin's father, many parents worried about their children's future and wanted them to have an education the government just could not provide. Though it had made great strides in converting the old imperial educational system, based on Chinese classical learning, to a modern one based on science and math, government schools could not compete with missionary schools funded by American dollars. Out went Confucian-based superstitions of the earth's sweat and dragon's breath. In came understanding of the water cycle and wind currents.

Mission schools had the added attribute of providing a moral and ethical foundation based on their religious teachings.

Whereas most teachers previously were from the finest institutions in Europe and America, the majority were now Chinese. But providing education was not the only function Robin saw in his work. He wanted to make an impact in the quality of students' lives. That meant changing society itself.

The church had to walk a fine line. Parents valued the education and the medical clinics, and the church offered students tools and a path for a better life. But the Chinese as a group were still wary of Western ideas and of straying too far from Chinese traditions. The church symbolized decades of foreign intrusion, imperialistic subjugation, and national shame. Importing too much Western thought might produce a backlash, potentially squashing Christianity, as in the past.

Robin felt obligated to support the nationalistic movement with local merchants and peasant organizations in the mountain region. The difficulty was how to do it without cutting the church's own throat and financial lifeline. He did advocate the boycott of British goods such as cigarettes and textiles. This helped the local merchants with their business and sent a message to the English authorities that their privileged status, as well as that of the Japanese, in the case of Japanese goods, was no longer acceptable to the Chinese.

All up and down the treaty ports of China, from Peking to Hong Kong, boycotts brought trade to a standstill. Strikes in foreign-owned factories left the economy so crippled that the British government injected millions of dollars in loans to keep businesses afloat. But this did not satisfy the Chinese quest for freedom from foreign influence. In fact, it was just being whetted. Nationalism swept the country, claiming diverse victims along the way.

Robin was ready to assume more responsibility and looked forward to the challenge of overseeing the mission at Nanling. He was thirty years old and one of the more experienced of the post-revolution Chinese clergy. It was his own family and belief in God that would be tested first.

Constance bore her first two children without much difficulty in Wuhu. There had been experienced Western-trained Chinese and foreign doctors practicing there for years, since the Methodist-sponsored Wuhu General Hospital was built in the late 1880s. But in such a small town as Nanling, no such luxury was available. Soon after they arrived, Constance and Robin welcomed their third child into the world—their number two son. He was robust, with chubby cheeks, always smiling. Everyone at the mission loved his giggles.

Around his first birthday, he came down with fever and sweats. He felt hot to the touch and coughed incessantly. He would not feed and cried throughout the night. Without any doctor for miles around, Robin called a local herbalist. The healer took the baby's pulse, looked at his tongue, and felt his chest.

He told Constance to buy some fresh ginger, which he ground into a brown, soupy slurry. He fed this to the baby for three nights. The fever and the crying continued. The coughing got deeper and noisier. But the baby was too ill to travel back to Wuhu.

More ginger, the herbalist ordered. Constance ground more ginger.

Constance and Robin prayed every night for God to cure their child.

On the fourth day, the baby stopped breathing.

The next day, Robin and Constance laid their baby's cold body in a simple wooden coffin. At the gravesite inside the mission compound, the couple, accompanied by Paul and Grace, gathered with the staff to bury their third-born. Before they closed the coffin, Constance clasped a silver cross necklace around the baby's neck. She laid a kiss on his forehead and squeezed her eyes tight, forcing her tears back. The workers closed the coffin, lowered it into the freshly dug earth, and shoveled dirt into the shallow hole.

Robin tried to push aside his thoughts: *It is too easy to lose one's family.* Grace, barely three, stared as her young brother disappeared into the open ground. As the grave filled up and the coffin was covered over, no one spoke a word. The only sound was the wailing from the mission's mourners. Paul, standing quietly by Grace, took her tiny hands into his. She began to cry.

"*Bu ku!*" Do not cry! Robin gently commanded. "He is with God."

Grace swallowed her tears, reached out, and clung to her father's leg as Paul stared straight into the hole.

"*The mission is coming along but we are still in the very early stages. The school has attracted many young people thirsting for education and a*

*moral foundation. But that most unfortunate occurrence in Shanghai
has almost upset everything. Unquestionably, our boys are anti-foreign,
but it is only fortunate that they are not entirely anti-Christian. I hope
the Shanghai problem soon comes to its final settlement, otherwise a
foreigner cannot but expect trouble. I pray that friends of China will
soon advise all the Powers to abolish or revise the Unequal Treaties
which are the root of the anti-foreign troubles."*

Robin wrote his assessment to Bishop Huntington. He did not have time
to think about his deceased son. He was worried about the crosscurrents in the
community after the May 30 incident. The education of young boys was one
of the church's most important mandates and most praised accomplishments.
Every day, the clamor of excited children learning English in the classrooms—
sounds so familiar to him—brought a smile to his face. Their practice was
music to his ears. Any interruption would be upsetting to the mission.

A knock on the door to his study broke his concentration. He rose from
his desk. Alice Gregg, his American colleague, her brown hair cropped short
to resemble a bonnet, greeted him. The brows of her soft, square face were
furrowed and her lips tensed.

"Reverend Chen, I think you should come out to *see* this," she stated.

Alice was a missionary from Ohio, who, like Sister Louise, had given up
her own family eight years prior. She oversaw the educational system in the
diocese. Her voice emphasized *see,* not *think*; it was not at all a suggestion.

Robin reached for his scarf and his American felt topper hat that he wore
when the weather was cool. He hurried out into the autumn air, with Alice
close behind. He had gotten to know the serious-minded young educator
and trusted her judgment. They walked briskly across the grounds towards
the front gate of the courtyard. He could already hear the boys chanting
in the distance. The words were unclear, but they were certainly not verses
from Psalms.

As they drew closer, he saw his students had formed a circle around two
older boys who were taking turns yelling slogans.

"Down with foreigners!"

"Down with foreigners!" parroted the students.

"Foreigners prevent the liberation of China!"

"Foreigners prevent the liberation of China!"

Robin strode through the crowd. His students gave him a path but didn't stop their protest.

"Send the white devils home!"

"Send the white devils home!"

"Why are you here?" he interrupted the older boys.

He estimated they were in their early twenties. They were well-dressed, not like local peasants. It was the tallest and older-looking of the students who spoke first, his voice slashing through the air.

"We are the Nanchang National Student Union. You are an imperialist tool!"

The dialect was not Mandarin but a local one from the Nanchang region of Kiangsi Province. Because of his work in the region, Robin was able to understand the disrupters.

"Where did you hear that?" he asked politely.

"Students are traitors. You are a spy for foreigners."

Spy. Had he not believed they were serious, he would have been amused. But he knew that many Chinese thought that of him and his Western colleagues. Beliefs, like superstitions, were rooted in ignorance but fertilized with rumors and nurtured by self-interest.

"What are your names?" asked Robin.

"My surname is Wu," answered the older student boldly.

"I am called Wang Ming," mimicked the younger one.

"Mr. Wu, Mr. Wang Ming, students are not traitors. I am not a spy," Robin answered calmly, more bemused than angry at the absurdity. But he knew it was no joke to the boys. Wu and Wang were passionate about their misguided prejudices. Propaganda was easily formed to serve one's purpose and manipulate the public. Some Chinese thought that was what Christianity was: propaganda.

"You destroy Confucius. Force students to worship your god," accused the younger college student.

"Take money from rich American devils and foreign capitalists," stated Wu.

"Students are not forced to worship God," Robin explained.

"You pollute the minds of Chinese youths," retorted Wang Ming, growing bolder.

Wu spat on the ground, then pointed to Robin's hat.

"You, not Chinese! *Ni mao tzu!*" Your hat! shouted Wu with some vehemence. "Traitor!"

Robin took off his hat and showed it to Wu.

"*Mao tzu bu shi mao tzu,*" My hat is not a foreigner, he said, using a rather obscure homonymous pun.

He offered his hat to the intruders to inspect. It was made in Shanghai.

"What I wear does not make me less Chinese."

Wu faced the younger boys.

"Do you want to be American?"

"No!" they shouted, raising their fists.

"Do you want to serve the English?"

"No!" they shouted even louder.

Now a small crowd of local people gathered to watch this spectacle. They peered curiously at Wu and Wang Ming, then at Robin, then at the young boys, as if trying to decide whom to root for. Wu reached into his inside coat pocket and pulled out a sheet of paper. He handed it to Robin. It was a pamphlet from some organization with official-looking seals embossed on the front.

"We represent the Anti-Christian Student Federation," announced Wu.

"Anti-Christmas week?" asked Robin, reading the document. He had heard about anti-Christian organizations springing up throughout the country, first in Shanghai in 1922. This was in reaction to Christian organizations on campuses as the anti-imperialism campaigns over the last few years took on collateral victims. Still, he was incredulous that the nationalistic students would demand an end to Christmas. It went beyond Christianity as some sort of offensive, superstitious belief that damaged Chinese culture and traditions. It was treating Christianity as if it were an American or British import, the same as cigarettes or Western garments—a commodity to be banned or boycotted. It was absurd; Christmas marked the birth of Christ and was as central to Christianity as National Day was to the post-imperialist China republic. How can one ban Christmas? He wanted to laugh, but it was hardly a trivial matter.

Wu turned to the boys.

"Do not celebrate Christmas. Do not go to church."

Wang Ming chimed in.

"Leave devil's school. Go to government school. Support China!"

"*Chungkuo! Chungkuo! Chungkuo!*" they all chanted. China! China! China!

Just then, a group of KMT soldiers wandered into the courtyard. They were dressed in street garb stolen from local vendors and carrying various weapons: rifles, revolvers, swords. The young men pushed through the onlookers and students without much regard and casually sat down against the building walls. Some closed their eyes and napped, while others lit cigarettes and watched the confrontation.

"Comrades! The place is yours!" proclaimed Wu to the rather disinterested soldiers.

"This mission belongs to the church," Robin said to the soldiers. "But you may rest."

He placed his hands on some of the schoolboys and gently, but without ambiguity, directed them toward the mission buildings. He gave Wu and Wang Ming a sharp glance and waved his arms, making his intent clear.

"Go back to Nanchang. Do not make trouble here."

He herded the boys back into the compound, hoping Wu and Wang Ming would leave them in peace. Part of him thought they were right to oppose the church. As an extension of the Church of England and the American Episcopal Church, it was a foreign product—*the devil's dream,* as some referred to it—foisted upon the country by way of privileges granted to foreign missions in the Unequal Treaties. Perhaps it *was* the same as British cigarettes and American felt hats. Why shouldn't they want to drive it out of the country? He could not blame them, but he could not allow them to succeed. His homeland needed Christianity. He was not certain of much, but he was sure of that.

Chapter 15

FLAMES OF FURY

By the following morning, soldiers had filled the dining hall; some were smoking cigarettes, some sleeping on the floor or wooden benches, others filling their stomachs with hot food. One soldier spat casually onto the floor while a pair laughed conspiratorially at one of the young nuns. They could not have been more than eighteen or twenty years old, on average. A few looked as young as the mission's primary school students, perhaps thirteen or fourteen years old. Some had been conscripted via the village quota system; others enlisted out of necessity or under threat of death.

Robin helped the staff serve rice porridge, *hsi fan*, dotted with a few pieces of vegetables and some shredded dry beef, *jou sung*. He thought little of soldiers resting in the mission yesterday. The church had often given sanctuary to those without a place to sleep, but Alice was not convinced.

"Why are they here?" she asked.

"The local commander ran out of money," he answered. "When he couldn't pay, they deserted."

It was not an uncommon occurrence since the death of Dr. Sun Yat-sen earlier in the year from cancer. His passing left a void and disorder in the KMT, with various subordinates vying for power. The left wing of the party, dominated by Mao's Communists, also jockeyed for influence. The country was truly in a state of disarray. Providing hard cash to poor soldiers in a remote mountainous region a thousand miles from the central government was not an easy task. Loyalty to the army was only as sticky as the pay.

"Surely they have homes to go to."

"Miss Gregg, they are soldiers *because* they have nothing. If we do not let them in, if we do not feed them, they will simply take what they want."

"There are so many," she replied, wide-eyed, staring at their guns.

"What will you have me do? Turn them away? They are sheep without shepherds."

Alice sighed.

"Reverend Chen, you cannot save everyone."

"Miss Gregg, they are just boys, not yet men. Let them stay and rest." He smiled back as he spooned more porridge into a young soldier's tin bowl. "They will soon find their way out. For now, we do what we can."

That afternoon, after all the classes were finished for the day and the boys were relaxing in the courtyard, the two Nanchang college students returned and began to stir things up. They had recruited a few of the local people to join in.

"Down with Christians! British out of China! American devils go home!" they railed.

Robin heard the commotion and found Alice. They called the mission staff together.

"Send the older boys home," he instructed. "They will be trouble."

"What about the soldiers?" asked Alice.

Even if he wanted to, he could not forcibly remove the soldiers. The local police would not act, either. No one would go against soldiers of the KMT except forces of the local warlord or the leftist faction. Exerting authority over the soldiers, no matter which command they were under, would not help the church's cause. Any day, they could be swept up in the furor and driven out of their mission. Nothing could stop the soldiers from occupying or overrunning the mission. Dozens of Christian schools across the country had already closed under the growing accusations of imperialism and the real threat of violence.

"Let them stay," he answered. "They will soon tire of church life."

の ⊕ の

AS IT TURNED OUT, HE WAS RIGHT. THAT EVENING, WU AND Wang Ming returned with a much larger contingent of students from the local chapter of the Anti-Christian Federation. They also convinced some of the older mission students of their just cause and arranged for a demonstration in front of the mission church. They started out like the previous protest, with all the usual chants. Wu and Wang Ming were passionate and well-practiced in their propaganda. The older mission students, sympathetic to their cause, opened the gate to the courtyard.

"Reject the foreigners. China is for Chinese people."

"Christianity is imperialism."

"No more Chinese traitors."

One college student threw a stone at the church. A second student flung another. Emboldened by the older boys' brashness, one of the mission schoolboys joined in. That was all that was needed to provoke a shower of missiles aimed at the office building. A chorus of cheers went up that echoed throughout the courtyard. Soon, soldiers and workers streamed out from the various buildings, but by then it was too late.

Someone—no one knew who, even when all the boys were later questioned—lit a match meant for a Chinese cigarette, the very kind that benefited from the boycott of British brands. It started with a single butt that ignited a pamphlet, brandished as a torch, that lit a bush, and soon the courtyard side of the church, built from local wood, was on fire. The flames raced up the façade, voraciously consuming the dry timber. It did not take long for the entire face of the church to be engulfed in flames shooting high into the darkening sky. Another cheer erupted as the students raised their arms in exhilaration.

A mission worker grabbed a hose, while others rushed to a building that housed gardening tools to search for buckets. As the flames grew taller, more and more workers, teachers, and church staff, in diverse stages of dress, poured out of the offices and dormitories. The younger boys gathered to watch in fascination. The mission worker hauling the hose attached it to the water spigot and turned it on full.

The water stream, weak as it was and aimed at the center of the church wall, caused a hissing sound as it hit the flaming façade. Black whorls of smoke twirled into the night sky, as if painted by vigorous strokes of an artist's brush. The boys gave another shout as yellow flames reached their apex, rising side by side with the dark smoke. Barely reaching the middle of the wall, the feeble spray of water seemed inadequate and the firefighting effort futile.

Rocks flew again as the protesters pelted the workers who had lined up, passing buckets of water from the kitchen to the church. The hose was briefly turned away from the church and onto the rock-throwing protesters, causing them to scatter. Everyone was yelling insults at each other. Robin angrily ordered his students away from the burning building.

The soldiers reluctantly entered the contest by helping on the bucket line. Some roughly pushed the college students towards the gate. The college students, sensing their purpose was accomplished, retreated to the streets, unleashing a final volley of stones. One crashed through the mission office window where Alice and Constance and her two children stood watching the melee. Alice let out a scream as fragments of glass sprayed around her and the two children began to cry.

As the instigators retreated in triumph, Constance said a prayer. Robin, a dozen soldiers, and a host of workers furiously manned the hose and bucket line. The flames were unrelenting, the defense too weak. Prayers went unanswered and the wooden structure finally collapsed with a spray of embers, like a swarm of fireflies desperately trying to escape their demise.

IN THE MORNING, ROBIN, ACCOMPANIED BY THE REST OF THE missionaries, gave the blackened house of God its last rites. Robin stood by the smoldering ruins and thanked God that, unlike many other attacks on Christians that were occurring daily in myriad places throughout China, only a building was lost. One worker had suffered bruising from the stoning, and another had his hair singed from flying ashes, but, thankfully, no lives were lost.

Later that same day, after questioning those who had participated in burning down the church, the church staff led the upper-class boys out of the compound and deposited them into their parents' custody. There was little outcry and no protest by either the students or their parents after Robin explained his decision. It was clear to everyone that what had happened was wrong and that the older boys were at fault.

Rather than looking at expulsion as a punishment, for which they were certainly deserving, Robin removed the boys for their own benefit. He could not prevent the presence or influence of the anti-imperialism movement; he understood the mission and the church would be targets for that activity. He could only try to shield the older, impressionable boys from the hatred directed towards Christians. They, like he, were caught between their attachment to the mission and their innate loyalties to national Chinese interests. Of course, they would want to defend their country against outsiders, especially at the urging of older students. It would be too much for them to handle. They would be unable to stand fast against the tide of protest; better to remove them from the constant waves of propaganda. The violent nature of demonstrations was unacceptable, but perhaps inevitable and contagious.

The younger boys were too immature to fully understand the movement and were permitted to stay and continue their studies. The anti-Christian leaders would not care to target them. They instead would turn their activities against the foreign missionaries.

The level of animosity and the degree to which the Nationalist movement expressed that animosity were rising since the incident in Shanghai. Robin understood the people's outrage; his church and the missionaries existed here only because of privileges granted under the Unequal Treaties. It was natural and easy for him to show his patriotic side by speaking out against the Unequal Treaties and support the boycott of foreign goods. Some leaders in the church called for Chinese like him to become even more politically minded. Others believed in the strict separation of church and state. But his American and British friends had no place to hide, no way to convince the anti-imperialist and anti-Christian Nationalists of their alliance. To many Chinese, foreigners were clearly the enemy, identified by the fairness of their skin and the roundness of their eyes. Christians were guilty of not being Chinese.

Bishop Huntington called Robin back to Wuhu for a meeting of clergy from throughout the diocese to discuss the issue of rising demonstrations against the church. Robin summoned Alice to his room as Constance packed their belongings.

"We are returning to Wuhu, Miss Gregg. You and the others can leave from there."

Alice looked stunned.

"China is too dangerous. All the big cities are experiencing trouble, even here in the remote mountains. You see what is happening."

"I have been in China since I was twenty-two," Alice protested.

"It will only get worse. Boycotts show foreigners are not welcome. Things must change."

"China is my home, Reverend Chen."

"Sentiments towards us will improve, but it will take time. Now it will be worse, much worse, for Americans like you. Passions in one's youth can be ignited with a single spark. When a crowd is hot in its head, it is hard to stop the fire."

Throughout China, there were many stories of violence—and not only from student demonstrators or striking workers, although they were the most fervent and idealistic. Reports circulated of Christians being attacked, even murdered, by bandits and Communists. A few months earlier, a Chinese layman had been ambushed and killed by local bandits. British concessions in large cities, like Hangchow and Kiukiang, were in varying states of unrest, forcing foreigners to evacuate or repatriate to their home countries.

The still-smoldering remains of their church were a reminder of the hazards Christians faced. In some ways, it was not a new thing in the almost one hundred years since missionaries had come to China; martyrs were always created in foreign environs. And lives in China, a land of four hundred million people, were like grains of sand. A handful lost to the winds and rainstorms did not matter. The church was constantly assessing when enough was enough—when it was too dangerous, too difficult, too futile to continue.

"Reverend Chen, thank you for your concern, but I will stay," answered Alice. "I am in China *because* I am Christian."

BEFORE THEY LEFT FOR WUHU THE FOLLOWING MORNING, THE Chen family walked to the gravesite of their deceased son. It had been only a few days since the burial. They wanted to pray for the boy one last time before they left his body behind.

As they approached the freshly dug gravesite, toward the back of the compound, it was obvious that something was amiss. The ground was no longer flat and smooth. The dirt had been disturbed around the grave. Alarmed, they hurried forward. When they reached the gravesite, they saw the grave had been completely uncovered. A pile of dirt lay at the head of the site. Paul and Grace ran to look in the fresh hole. The tiny coffin that held the body of their younger brother was open. The silver necklace that Constance had placed around his neck was gone. In fact, the coffin was completely empty.

Robin's mind went blank. When Constance, and then Grace, began to cry, he did not protest. For the next two days, his family's grief did not dissipate. Robin felt something he had never felt before—a burning anger within. Not at his life. Not at the grave robbers after the silver necklace. Not at non-believers who persecuted his beliefs and fellow Christians. But at God.

Praying alone at night, he shook his fist at the sky.

Why did You let my son die? Why not let his young body lie in peace? Why punish those who believed in You? What do You want from me?

By the time Robin, Constance, and their two children arrived in Wuhu two days later, their tears were spent. What more could they do? Life had to continue, and they believed their son was in that place called heaven.

Chapter 16

THE DILEMMA

Sister Louise welcomed Robin and his family back to his familiar surroundings. It had been only two years since he left for Nanling, but the compound already felt different. He had left Wuhu as a newly ordained minister. The country was paralyzed by boycotts fueled by anti-imperialism and fragmentation caused by competing provincial warlords. Now it had a newly inspired leader in General Chiang Kai-shek, who was rallying citizens against the destructive warlords. A spirit of revival was percolating through the country, and people were hopeful that the country could get back on its feet. Unfortunately, the KMT was not the only party with aspirations. The fledgling CCP had grown since its birth and, with the backing of the Russian Soviets, had inserted itself into the left-wing faction of the KMT.

As he and Constance greeted Sister Louise, Lindel, and Lloyd Craighill, Robin noticed there were more foreign church workers and female students. The church had continued to grow, despite all the political turmoil. It fulfilled its commitment to gender equality by bringing up the standard of its St. Lioba's School for Girls to that of the boys school. Admissions to its primary school nearly rivaled that of St. James. Parents welcomed the educational opportunities for their daughters. Where there previously were few women teachers, there was now a growing, replenishing crop of educated women matriculating through mission schools.

"Dear Sister Louise," Robin whispered gently as he embraced her warmly. "It is good to be home."

"Robin, Constance, your loss is our loss," offered Sister Louise.

"It is God's will," he replied.

Accepting condolences from friends was easy. But God's will? That would take time. Was this the love Sister Louise had taught him? Was this the sacrifice and suffering he needed to endure? Perhaps Hsiao Wang was right, he thought: *God's will is not always easy to follow.*

As they walked toward the main office building, Sister Louise leaned toward Constance. "We now have twice as many women. Paul and Grace will have more amahs."

They both smiled as they locked arms.

Since just before the end of the Ching dynasty, the number of Protestant missionaries in China had quadrupled to eight thousand. Missions like Wuhu were the beneficiaries. But converts were not growing as rapidly as expected; their numbers simply matched the growth rate of the missionaries. Communicants in the Protestant church also quadrupled, from less than a hundred thousand at the time of the Boxer Rebellion to just under four hundred thousand. Anglicans under the independent umbrellas of the Church of England and the American Episcopal Church comprised just six percent of the Protestant community. Compared to the size of China, their numbers were minuscule.

Bishop Huntington and his fellow British and American bishops knew the slow growth had much to do with the cultural gulf between the Chinese people and the foreign hierarchy within the church. That needed to change. Foreigners were not the future; Chinese bishops, Chinese ministers, and Chinese women were.

"The only way China will gain is if women become equal to men, in opportunities and responsibilities," Robin stated to Sister Louise. "We cannot ignore half the population."

"I will do my part," assured Constance, as Sister Louise placed her arm around her and led her into the building.

"There is much to do here," assured Sister Louise.

ROBIN GOT RIGHT TO WORK WITH LINDEL AND LLOYD, PREPAR-
ing for the arrival of the other ministers in the diocese. While the main topic
of discussion was how to prepare the church for the future in the changing
landscape of the country, there was no escaping the political issue of continued and intensifying persecution of Christians for their link to foreign
imperialism. More and more leaders, both foreign and native, were calling
for direct political activism by Christian organizations. The call for the
church to formally condemn the Unequal Treaties privileges grew louder.

"We have to tread cautiously, or our door will close," warned Lloyd.

"Even within this mission are teachers who lean quite definitely towards
Communist ideas," reported Lindel. "They are more vocal, more active. We
cannot openly support them. But the church cannot ignore them."

"Who are they?" demanded Lloyd.

Lindel remained silent on this point.

Lloyd understood the undercurrent of political thinking within the
church. Like most of his fellow missionaries, he had great sympathy for the
Chinese and their plight. He was committed to helping them in their lives.
This traditionally meant building schools, medical clinics, even hospitals.
But choosing sides in international disputes, actively supporting strikers
or boycotts, or choosing between the CCP and KMT was not his mandate
and certainly not what funds from the American churches were intended for.
Sympathizing with Chinese anti-foreign sentiments put his American and
British friends and their businesses at risk.

"Our colleagues will be getting an earful," Lloyd stated uncomfortably.

"What would you do? Lock them up? Dismiss them?" asked Lindel.

It was Lloyd's turn to be silent. He did not have a good answer. He was
caught in the middle.

"The church can have little say in your own disputes. We cannot choose
sides. Our hands are tied," he finally answered.

"Students and teachers, both must be able to speak freely," suggested
Robin.

"Freely, but also carefully," warned Lindel.

Lindel was responsible for raising funds from overseas organizations
for the Board of Missions in Shanghai and was sensitive to the church's
association with political causes, especially with the Communists. He had

just returned from three years of study at the Virginia Theological Seminary and the Divinity School of the Episcopal Church in Philadelphia. He earned a master's degree in sociology at the University of Pennsylvania and was acutely in tune with the practical forces that influenced people's behavior. Despite the parallels he saw with Communism, he knew that an alliance would not sit well with church officials in the United States, and the church and its missions were still dependent on money from overseas. If the church in China was seen as leaning too far left in accommodating the Communist thinking, its lifeline could be severely limited. It was a tricky predicament.

OVERNIGHT, THE MISSION COURTYARD WAS TRANSFORMED INTO a political arena. Large "big character" posters drawn on long rice paper draped over walls and flapped in the gentle breeze. When Robin, Lloyd, and Lindel gathered in the morning to greet the arrival of the other clergy accompanying Bishop Huntington, they were understandably nervous about the display.

> *Down with slaves of foreigners.*
> *Down with Western culture.*
> *Down with American imperialism.*

As Bishop Huntington stepped out of one of the rickshaws that had carried him and other foreign clergy from the railroad station, he could not help but be perplexed by the protest without protestors.

"Are they our students?"

"Teachers," Robin answered. "A small compromise."

He explained that he and Lindel decided to allow the signs to prevent a larger, more vocal, disturbance by a small group of teachers. They were determined to avoid an all-out confrontation within their mission.

"The local authorities … they approve?" asked Bishop Huntington as he strolled to the office while perusing the banners.

No one said anything. Each already knew the answer. This would not be good for anyone.

IN A CLASSROOM THE FOLLOWING AFTERNOON, THE CLERGY
representing various churches of the Anking diocese crowded together in
front of Bishop Huntington. They passed around bowls of figs and oranges.
Of the thirty clergymen attending, less than half were foreigners, mainly
American and British. The rest were native Chinese.

"A hundred years here, and our mission is a breeze in a terrible hailstorm,"
stated Bishop Huntington.

"Without support from overseas, our mission would collapse," lamented Lloyd.

"The word of God is often accepted not because it is the word of God, but
because it brings food and medicine," explained Lindel.

One of the American missionaries spoke up.

"They are rice Christians."

A low-toned murmur rippled among the foreigners. It was not a com-
pliment nor meant as a criticism, but they all knew it was true. The church
brought the promise of a better life through schools and hospitals that were
built from foreign generosity. Commitment of faith or belief in Jesus Christ
as the son of God were not prerequisites nor optimistically expected. In
the beginning of the church's history, people were enticed to attend church
on Sundays with free tickets to hear a stimulating talk by the local pastor.
Specific groups or factories were often targeted. Once there, they were
introduced to the benefits and teachings of Christianity. Few understood.
Even fewer were interested. And nearly none would believe. Children with
bamboo poles on the banks of the Yangtse were luckier than the early missionaries. But occasionally luck would strike someone's soul. It was a wide
net cast for a handful of converts; only ten accepted the faith in the first
twenty-seven years. The same was true in Christian colleges, where students
were exposed to Christianity and theological principles but not obligated to
convert or even become believers.

"But they *are* Christian," Bishop Huntington reminded him.

The American simply shrugged.

"Most know nothing," he said.

"Now they are caught in the crossfire of anti-imperialism," continued

Bishop Huntington. "Any commitment to Christ pales in comparison to their commitment to China, except for the brave and truly faithful."

"Our students do not oppose foreigners because they hunger less for faith," chimed Robin, "but because they hunger more for freedom."

"Freedom? Freedom from what?" Bishop Huntington asked.

"From influence. Dominance. Persecution in their own country," Robin answered. He did not intend to sound accusatory.

Bishop Huntington and Lloyd as well as the other Americans nodded in agreement.

"We also come from a history of persecution," said Lloyd, sympathetically.

"Chinese are no different. We want freedom from ... inferiority," added Robin thoughtfully. "We want to exist ... as equals."

The room fell silent. Lindel turned to the Chinese to translate *inferiority*.

"The church must be for, by, and of the people. *Your* people. We all agree. We will never succeed here until it is your own. *Chinese!*" Lloyd declared.

"Our goal must be to shift the structure of the church," added Bishop Huntington. "To serve your needs, not ours. Support from America may come to a trickle, and then we foreigners will go home."

"Are our needs not the same? To grow the church?" queried a young man. He was one of the newest ministers to come from America.

"They should be. But they are not. And the Chinese are suspicious ... the ones that do not sincerely know us," answered Bishop Huntington. He turned to the Chinese clergymen. "What can the church offer?"

The Chinese in the room looked at each other. They were in friendly territory but, as was their temperament, still too timid to speak.

"Come, my boys, speak your mind," encouraged Bishop Huntington.

The Chinese exchanged glances, but the room remained quiet.

Robin rose from his chair.

"Assistance in land reform, to rise above the daily toil of poverty," Robin opined as he turned to face the room. "Education, away from the ancient classics and toward modern thinking. Science. Mathematics. Healthcare that tends to the sick throughout the countryside, not only in cities."

"This is why the Communists are favored," noted Lloyd bluntly.

Everyone in the room nodded in agreement.

"And why we must be cautious," warned Lindel.

Chapter 17

THE RAID

The raid that evening occurred without any forewarning, despite the excellent relationship between the mission and local police. Bishop Huntington was hosting a gathering at the rectory on Lion's Hill built by Mr. Lund two decades earlier. The large house was somewhat removed from the main compound farther down the hill. The group, including Robin, Lindel, Lloyd, Sister Louise, Constance, and the other diocesan ministers, had no indication anything was amiss until their conversation was abruptly interrupted by frantic beating on the front door.

"Reverend Chen! Reverend Tsen!" cried a desperate voice.

Robin opened the door to a trembling young man. Tang was a recent graduate of Wesley University, one of the nearly twenty Christian universities in China at the time and a hotbed for the CCP in Wuhan. The new teacher's wide eyes and the sweat on his elevated brow were no false alarm. His hands, moist with perspiration, were shaking as he latched onto Robin's forearm.

"Please. Police ... they are here!"

Tang explained in rapid-fire Mandarin that the local police, aided by the KMT commander, had burst into the compound, raising a ruckus as they charged through the offices and dormitory. They hunted down the three teachers who had hung the offensive banners and corralled them into the courtyard. After a few hard blows to the body with a baton, one of the teachers confessed that they had been secretly attending CCP meetings in the evening and were recruited to bring protests to the mission. The police threatened them with arrest unless they revealed other conspirators.

Tang's hands were clasped so tight the tips of his fingers were pink with engorged blood.

Robin glanced quickly at Bishop Huntington and Lloyd. Hiding a person wanted by the local police authorities was a major crime, but hiding a Communist from the KMT commander could be fatal for them all. Foreign missionaries interfering with local Chinese affairs was the ultimate transgression to patriotic enforcers. The teacher would be imprisoned, or worse.

British and American clergy, granted privileges under the Unequal Treaty, were immune from prosecution and had some jurisdiction and discretion in their mission. But this was the exact complaint the Chinese had that fostered such intense nationalistic animosity. Foreign church workers recognized this impediment to their work and sought to formally rescind privileged status for foreign missionaries. To submit to Chinese jurisdiction in legal matters would go a long way toward reversing the stain of the Unequal Treaty. It would be bad enough to claim immunity from wrongdoing as foreigners. To claim it on behalf of the mission in the protection of a fellow Chinese for the benefit of a revolutionary, anti-government Communist group would be intolerable.

"We cannot allow the authorities to arrest him on our property," Bishop Huntington told the group. He had a duty to protect his teachers, but a Communist was an entirely different matter.

"Nor risk confrontation," added Lloyd.

Robin could not leave Tang to face the police alone and gestured for him to come in. The teacher was no older than twenty-four or twenty-five. Robin did not recognize him, so he assumed he had come to St. James while he was in Nanling. He could see he was an earnest man, probably idealistic and patriotic to a fault, like many Communist students were. Robin did not hold it against him. They were all there to help China. Everyone was a patriot, and everyone was someone's enemy.

He motioned for Tang to hide in the kitchen at the rear of the rectory. While the young teacher made his way through the back corridor, Robin stood outside the front door and waited for the authorities. He really did not know what he would tell the police, but he could not stand by and surrender the teacher.

The police rounded up the three teachers and led them out the mission gates. The courtyard was filled with curious students and nervous teachers. A group of police made their way up the long incline to the rectory.

"Where is the traitor?" demanded one of the policemen.

"Please, sir. We ask you to not disturb our people. If they have committed a crime, let us talk to them," Bishop Huntington said.

"They are Chinese and must answer to Chinese authority."

"What are they accused of? This is property of the American church," interjected Lloyd.

"They are traitors, Communist sympathizers, seeking to create trouble. We demand you give us the last traitor. His name is Tang, from Wuhan."

The policemen, six in number, pushed their way into the foyer and began to search the first floor. Robin quickly stepped in and bowed to the leader of the squad.

"We are here to teach children. No one is a traitor. This is our issue, within our mission, not yours. Reverend Tsen and I can talk to your commander in the morning and resolve any problem with our teachers."

The leader looked at him blankly as if he had never confronted a fellow Chinese like Robin, a member of the foreign religion. Robin suddenly suspected that perhaps the policemen thought *he*, too, was a traitor.

The police pressed them about the missing teacher.

"When did you last see Tang?"

"Does Tang live at the mission?"

"Did you know he is a Communist?"

As Robin continued to make his case, Tang, terrified and hiding in the kitchen, snuck out into the dark night. The police searched the house and left with a harsh warning for Bishop Huntington but without their last prey.

Later that night, Robin and Lindel left the now-somber gathering at Lion's Hill and made their way to the police station to see what was to become of their teachers. The two managed to get as far as the front desk. They inquired about the teachers, but no one would engage them—they were met only by stony faces. In the end, they were politely escorted out of the station.

The teachers never returned to the mission. Two days later, they were executed by the KMT commander, along with other ordinary criminals. With that, Robin and the Christians at St. James were initiated into the early internal purge of the KMT's left-wing Communist faction. Judgment was swift and non-negotiable. Generalissimo Chiang was consolidating his power, and no further anti-government protests occurred at St. James.

Tang was never heard from again.

NOT ALL THINGS WERE SO GRIM FOR ROBIN. HIS FATHER, WHO had moved to Peking with his younger brother a year earlier, saw God's blessings in the success that Robin achieved; his son had made something of himself. Robin was a teacher respected by important men, including foreigners, and, most significantly, spoke English perfectly. Being grateful and impressed by the effect of Christianity on his sons, Robin's father professed his Christian faith and was baptized in Peking in 1926.

Constance and Robin added to their family with the birth of another daughter. She was named Hsiung. Like her brother and sister before her, the number two daughter was christened with a Western name, Helen, in her first year of life.

Chapter 18

THREE SELFS,
TWO PARTIES,
ONE IDEA

In February 1929, Lindel Tsen became the second native consecrated bishop in the Anglican Church in China, after Bishop T.S. Sing. As assistant to Canadian Bishop William Charles White, Lindel was at the head of the indigenous line to one day inherit charge of an entire diocese. The House of Bishops, composed entirely of foreigners, saw the great promise and necessity of the highly educated crop of young Chinese ministers—graduates from Christian colleges like Boone College, St. John's University in Shanghai, and Nanking Theological Seminary.

Robin watched this with interest, and restlessness. China had not changed much for the good since the end of World War I. In 1924, with the assistance of the Soviet Russia-led Comintern, Sun's KMT and Mao's CCP established the Whampoa Military Academy and Chiang Kai-shek was appointed its first chief commandant. The death of President Sun Yat-sen in early 1925 created a leadership void. After some internal struggles, Chiang emerged as Sun's heir apparent and thus secured both political power and military authority within the Republic. But China was still fragmented. There was infighting between the Nationalists and the left-wing Communists. At one point, there were three different capitals in China, at Peking, Wuhan, and Nanking. The end of the world war brought peace to the rest of the world, but not to China.

While the Three-Self principles—self-support, self-governance, and self-propagation—was an idea advanced by English and American missionaries to apply generally to any foreign mission, it had roots especially in China in the 19th century, albeit in a very ineffectual way. The foreign leadership understood the necessity of a native church because of pervasive anti-foreignism and anti-imperialism. But those leaders also recognized the challenges in attaining those goals because of the poverty of their communicants, the lack of educated and theologically trained native leaders, and the cultural resistance to Christianity in the face of persistent Confucian beliefs. The central administrative headquarters of missions, located worlds away in England and the United States, could never really appreciate the lives of the people in China. Famine, to the English and Americans, was a human tragedy that required money and donations of food and aid. But to the Chinese, it meant millions of deaths, untold suffering, and decimation of entire families and geographic regions, without any promise of hope for the future. Robin himself had witnessed this growing up in Anhwei. Money itself was a necessity but not an antidote to poverty. Solutions went far beyond that which foreign missions could provide.

The commitment to a Chinese church led a diverse collection of American and English Anglican bishops, clergy, and laypersons to form the Chinese Holy Catholic Church (CHSKH) immediately after the formation of the Republic. A Board of Missions was later established as a wholly Chinese entity sympathetic with the Three-Self principles. The intent was to see the institutional church in China evolve into one financially supported by its Chinese congregation, governed by indigenous ministers and bishops, and sustained by the intrinsic growth of local workers and worshipers. Foreigners would be obsolete. By the mid-1920s, the number of Chinese clergy nearly equaled that of non-Chinese, but the church was still nowhere near its goal. National events made progress even more difficult.

Chiang successfully led the Northern Expedition that effectively rid China of numerous warlord strongholds. Nearly every major province throughout the entire eastern half of China—from Manchuria in the north to Guangzhou in the south, and from Changan in the west to Shanghai in the east—was affected by the military campaign. By its conclusion in 1928, hundreds of thousands of soldiers and civilians had been killed, but China was free of major warlords, at least temporarily. Chiang was able to form a tenuous central government with its capital in Nanking.

The Western world viewed Chiang as allied with Communism because of the support the Soviets provided in money, munitions, and intelligence, and because of the acceptance of the CCP into the KMT encouraged by Soviet leader Josef Stalin. Because of this perception, Chiang was given the maligning moniker, the Red General. What those in the West, viewing things from afar, did not appreciate was that he was, in fact, ruthlessly purging the KMT of its Communist elements. Murders, executions, and mysterious disappearances decimated the Communist ranks and forced them to withdraw from the KMT. The CCP set up their own capital in Wuhan. Other casualties in Chiang's nationalistic ambition were foreign missionaries, many of whom were set upon by fiercely patriotic citizens and soldiers.

The church and Robin's ability to help China were at a standstill. Many schools had to close during vacillating military occupations. Mission schools, often required to be registered with the central government, were also directly affected by a new law that prohibited mandatory classes in religion. Some missions were turned over completely to the government for military use. St. James was overrun by soldiers and refugees, who at one point broke out into mutiny between factions of Chiang's army. The school courageously continued until it was impossible, as expatriates fled to Shanghai or were furloughed back home to America. Even staunch missionaries like Miss Gregg left; she returned to the United States to study for her master's degree, her previous resolve succumbing to the hostilities.

The objectives of the Three-Self principles seemed unattainable. While the surviving schools thrived and could collect reasonable tuition from more wealthy westernized Chinese, the masses were still hard to reach. Compared to the vast population of four hundred million, the number of Christians was still insignificant.

The House of Bishops felt it was important for ministers like Robin to seek additional education in the United States. As much as China's problems could only be appreciated by those in China, some solutions might well be found outside of the country. The experience Lindel gained in his years in the United States reinforced that view.

Robin was enthused to follow a similar path, encouraged by Bishop Huntington. The church was willing to send him to the United States, especially with the mission in dysfunction and the country in disarray. But Robin was in his mid-thirties, with a wife and three young children growing up quite happily in China. Uprooting his family to a strange country ten thousand miles away seemed impossible and unwise.

CONSTANCE WAS BUSY TEACHING ENGLISH AND VOLUNTEERING at the St. Lioba's School for Girls. She helped the Women's Auxiliary with their True Light Industrial Work Mission, whose products, such as clothes and toy dolls, helped finance the dispensary and provide income for the poor. The Auxiliary also ran a day care center, an orphanage, and a shelter offering a temporary resting place and medical care for two thousand coolies, rickshaw drivers, and heavy field laborers.

Paul was in his second year at St. James Primary School, Grace was starting at St. Lioba's, and Helen was barely learning to run when Constance found out that she was pregnant for the fifth time. She and Robin hoped it was a boy, to balance out their family.

Robin pondered Bishop Huntington's suggestion of studies in the United States. Everything told him that this opportunity was the right path for himself, the church, and for his congregation. There were capable young ministers who could support the church while he was gone. The Sisters of the Transfiguration were doing wonderful work for the church, helping sustain the mission and its schools. But he would still have to convince Constance.

"STUDYING IN AMERICA WILL HELP SERVE OUR PEOPLE BETTER," Robin said during a rare quiet time with Constance.

"Where would you go?" asked Constance.

"Southern Ohio. To learn about social services," he answered.

"For how long?"

"Two, maybe three years. I would study at the Divinity School in Philadelphia, then go to the University of Pennsylvania."

"Like Lindel," she said pensively.

He nodded, looking at her earnestly.

"It is important to connect with Americans, establish relations for the future, learn from them," he continued.

"America is far away."

"Perhaps the time is not right?" suggested Robin, sensing some reluctance.

"Everyone agrees?" Constance asked in her small voice.

"Yes," he replied tentatively. He knew the church's calling put her in a difficult position. "Bishop Huntington. Lloyd. Lindel."

"Then you need to go."

Her reply came without hesitation. Neither saw what they did as real sacrifice; others gave up even more. The animosity towards foreigners promised no peace, and life often hinged on the whims of nature. They had to do whatever it took to make a better China, not only for their own children, but for as many other children as they could. If it meant going to America and leaving his family, so be it. He could always return home.

Chapter 19

AMERICA AND
THE GREAT FLOOD

T he new child arrived too quickly. Eager to emerge into the world, she was delivered at home under urgent circumstances by her capable father. It was not a boy, as her parents had hoped, but she was nonetheless loved. Just before Robin boarded the ship from Shanghai to San Francisco, the girl was christened Mary. The family called her Hui.

Funds were collected in the United States and from the local diocese, and Robin's itinerary was set by church administrators in New York. The discriminatory Chinese Exclusion Act of 1882, prohibiting the immigration of ethnic Chinese laborers, was in effect. But a clergyman, with the wheels of bureaucracy greased by the sponsorship of the Episcopal Church, was allowed into the country without issue. He rode the train from San Francisco to Ohio on the very tracks built by coolies from Southern China whose presence had triggered prejudice against the Chinese and passage of the abhorrent Act.

During the first few months, Robin visited parishes along the East Coast. In invited talks and sermons, he spoke about the conditions in China and the goals of a Chinese church. The public and the Episcopal clergy were curious about his country. To them, he was an alien. It was a rare person who had met a Chinese from China and an even rarer one to have personally set foot on Chinese soil. His exoticism drew a circus-like fascination at each gathering. He was all too happy to oblige his audience with a raw picture of China and often brought out, to great effect, his traditional, full-length blue tunic for formal gatherings.

"Confucian standards of relationships are breaking down and people are seeking a new standard of religion," he reported to delegates at the annual Episcopal diocesan conference in Southern Ohio. He was given the opportunity to address the convention and explained that long-standing filial bonds were not sufficient to advance China. Not only were loyalties being tested by civil conflicts, but concern for others beyond family members and the subjects of the imperial ruler was necessary to unify the country.

"It is time for the Christian Church to go into China," he stated, part suggestion and part plea, following the exodus of missionaries the previous decade.

When he attended the Cincinnati Summer Program for Social Services, sponsored by the Southern Ohio Diocese, Robin was in the friendly and familiar company of other ministers. Although he was one of only two from China, the group of nearly thirty clergymen had the single-minded purpose of learning organizational techniques for social programs. Robin was convinced that organized social service was the medicine China needed, and that Christianity would need to compete favorably for the hearts and souls of the masses against the growing Communist movement.

"Communism is a definite problem and a peril because of the overwhelming poverty of the lower classes and their lack of education. Communism is the Christian church's greatest challenge," he warned his audiences.

He was cornered by reporters after one such talk.

"Why are you here?" came a voice from the pack. "China is hostile to the United States."

"Our nation's self-interest is mistakenly interpreted as hostility towards foreigners," he answered.

"You deny the hostilities?" the reporter retorted.

Robin paused, wondering if he was encountering a confrontation of ideas or only a persistent American reporter doing his job to elicit a printable quote. He was unsure of how he would come across.

"China has many problems, particularly poverty and education. Only the Chinese people can solve them. We only seem hostile if you do not respect us. We can learn from your successful programs. That is why I am here," he answered. "People may seem foreign, but ideas can be allies."

The reporter nodded in a friendly enough way as he scribbled down the quote. Robin welcomed the next question, relieved to find an open ear.

"What are China's biggest problems?" the reporter demanded.

"Poverty, lack of medical clinics, illiteracy, warlords, civil conflicts, Japanese aggression ..." Robin was quick to reply.

"Slower!" the reporter interrupted as he wrote furiously.

The group of clergymen and reporters laughed.

"I prefer to think about the possibilities of the human spirit," Robin continued as he leaned more confidently toward the gaggle of newsmen, as if imparting a treasured secret. "I have always thought the gift of American missionaries is not monetary, but spiritual. Foreign assistance helps our people survive, but it is belief in the Gospel and the works of God that gives infinite hope for the future."

There was a gentle murmur of agreement that percolated through the crowd. Heads nodded. Robin watched as the reporters dutifully took down his thoughts to disseminate to the American public. Relieved, he wondered if it would mean anything in the end.

IN NEARLY TWO AND A HALF YEARS, ROBIN CRISSCROSSED THE continent from Los Angeles to Boston, and from Canada to Texas and Florida. He found the American spirit willing but the body weak; the economic depression following the stock market crash had emptied the pocketbooks of many of the previous sources of missionary funds. Per capita contributions to charitable endeavors fell, as did the number of people willing and able to offer themselves to foreign missions. This was particularly true for China, where the report card for a hundred years of mission work showed good grades for social programs, including many hundreds of schools and hospitals, but poor marks for actual conversion. Some in the church talked about abandoning the missionary program in China.

But Robin, like many others in the church community, felt that America could not abandon China, and China should not forget America. Some Chinese were already resigned to the inevitability of being governed by a foreign power and were merely debating among themselves which foreign power, other than Japan, was preferred. In fact, Russia had shown itself to be an important influence in China, with its advisors and support of both Chiang Kai-shek and the CCP. Germany was also showing some interest. America could not afford to lose its influence over China to other countries.

The general consensus was that China and America would be better off as allies, mutually supportive of each other. For all its anti-imperialist concerns, China, vis-à-vis the ruling KMT, was wary of being controlled by its Soviet neighbor. While Robin was not at all a politician, he knew these forces were impacting his pastoral duties. Chinese Christians were tied to American Christians by the pocketbook. American funds would have to sustain the church in China until the Three-Self principles could be applied in a viable manner. That, he felt, might optimistically take a whole generation.

Conditions in the United States were dire. The economic crisis in America that came to be known as the Great Depression ruined fortunes, destroyed businesses, decimated the ranks of the employed, forced a tragic westward migration to a mirage of opportunity in the Golden State, and eventually drained the American people of their will. Things were no better in China, where a drought in a vast region of northern provinces, aligned with military campaigns that sucked up national economic assets, left millions of Chinese citizens destitute and starving. If the drought did not wipe out food crops, then their replacement with cash-generating opium for the military did. Severe hunger tortured their stomachs, driving people to peel bark off trees and dig into soil for insects to eat. It also ravaged the mind, with shocking rumors of cannibalism leaking out from some of the remote northern regions.

Robin was in Philadelphia, at the Divinity School, when news of the great floods broke in the summer of 1931. The brutal cold of the winter the preceding year produced an enormous buildup of snow and ice in mountainous northern China. He read the newspaper reports of the nonstop deluge that accompanied the late-spring melting of the frozen mass.

The cataclysmic summer downpour caused an overflow of the Yellow, Yangtse, and Huai Rivers into the lowlands of China. Many dykes, maintenance of which had been deferred in favor of military investments for the Northern Expedition, slowly eroded. Hundreds of doomed people sought refuge along their high points. Thinking they were safe, they perished when the dykes finally collapsed. Other dykes burst more suddenly, immediately drowning thousands of people as they slept in villages below. Survivors desperately retreated to rooftops merely a few feet above water that rose fifty to a hundred feet above normal levels. Some superstitious Chinese refused to be rescued from their homes. They surrendered resignedly to the predictable fate of periodic natural calamity and stubbornly clung to their ancestral homes. Imprisoned by rising water and traditional beliefs, they perished by the hundreds.

Grace and her family huddled with other mission families in the school building. They gathered on the first floor as the muddy river seeped into the school. The children commandeered a raft fashioned from a barn door to negotiate the neighborhood. To them, it was like being on vacation in the countryside. As the river rapidly rose, everyone ascended to the second floor. Within days, they were on the third floor.

Looking out from a window at the flooded school ground below, Grace saw a corpse floating face down across the schoolyard. She could not help but stare at it, wondering who it was. She had nightmares for days. After that, rafting was no longer for fun; it was for survival.

She and Paul ventured out together, looking for food for the family. Paul directed them around Wuhu, which was almost completely submerged. The unbearable stench from sewage in certain places made them vomit.

When they returned from their excursion, Grace would help her mother care for her two younger sisters. She made rice for them on a small coal cooker while waiting patiently on the third floor for the water to recede. When they became anxious and started to cry, she comforted them.

"*Bu ku!*" Paul, barely ten, ordered them.

Do not cry, she would echo more gently. She knew Paul was just trying to be like their father, and it was during these bad times she missed him the most.

The inundation eventually submerged scores of villages and cities, wiping out a hundred thousand Chinese in a matter of days and forcing mass evacuations into surrounding provinces. Crops were destroyed. Bloated carcasses of cattle, horses, and dogs lay floating near the riverbed, along with the lifeless bodies of thousands of peasants. Without dry land in which to bury them, decomposing corpses were pulled into the swollen river for unceremonious, murky burials or stacked high in wooden coffins.

Col. Charles Lindbergh, flying survey missions for the National Flood Relief Commission, reported that everywhere he looked, for hundreds of square miles, land and buildings were underwater. In one *Philadelphia Inquirer* article, Lindbergh said he did not see any high land for twenty-five miles south of one walled city. Of the districts east of the Yangtse River, the city that Lindbergh claimed suffered the worst damage was Wuhu.

Robin inquired about returning to China but was reassured that his entire family was safe. There was little he could do for them.

As the floods receded, government and international relief, with food and monetary donations from America and other Western countries, poured in, although not as timely or as universally requested by the League of Nations. Initially, the Japanese government sent supplies and personnel to help, but this assistance, tainted by Japan's aggressive occupation, was rejected by the Chinese. Refugee camps were set up, manned by nearly all the missionary denominations, as well as the nondenominational and influential Red Cross. Medicines were dispensed as rapidly as they were obtained. Hundreds of inoculations against cholera were performed in one camp alone, but that was not nearly enough to prevent the disease. Myriad maladies, including cholera, dysentery, and subsequent famine, killed millions of Chinese. Tens of millions of people were rendered refugees, and millions of dollars' worth of missionary property destroyed. But wherever they could, Christian missions opened their doors and welcomed wearied and emaciated refugees, often housing hundreds of people in facilities meant for a dozen. St. James Mission was no different.

While southern China struggled with the disastrous aftermath of the flood, the army of the Japanese Empire was quietly, but steadily—without approval from the Emperor— marching through city after city in northeast China, homeland to the former imperial rulers. Within a few months, Japan would secure possession of the natural resource–rich area known to the West as Manchuria. Soon after, Japan installed Puyi as ruler of the puppet government it called Manchukuo.

It was to this disorganized, suffering China that Robin returned home in late 1931.

Chapter 20

LESSONS OF
CHILDREN

By the time Robin traversed the United States and his ship reached China, flood relief efforts were well underway. His children accompanied Constance to greet him at the port in Shanghai. But the first words out of Hui's mouth when she saw him come off the ship surprised them all.

"Ma, who is that man?" Hui asked, squeezing Grace's hand, and tucking her tiny face behind her mother's coat.

"Shh!" scolded Grace. "He is our father!"

It took a week before Hui stopped staring at her father.

Robin was transferred to the Diocese's headquarters in the provincial capital city of Anking as the dean of the Cathedral of the Holy Savior. This was the exact path that Lindel followed upon his own return from Philadelphia. Given the economic effects of the devastating deluge, there was no possibility that the Chinese could financially support the church on their own, but self-governance was potentially achievable and necessary.

The Chen family, now six members strong, moved into the mission in Anking, located on the Yangtse waterway, six hundred li—about two hundred miles—inland from Wuhu. The compound was spread over eighteen acres. They lived with their amah and manservant in a house provided by the church, adjacent to the impressive landmark Cathedral.

The Gothic-style church, constructed from black bricks with limestone pointing, sat on a small hill so that its tower could be visible for miles around. It was built in a typical cruciform design, with fourteen pillars in the main section, and could ambitiously seat a thousand worshippers. It was a local source of pride that such a stately structure was constructed with native labor and craftsmanship at a bargain price of $10,000. The Cathedral was consecrated in 1912, with Bishop Huntington, Lindel Tsen, and Mr. Lund in attendance. At that time, there were seven Chinese ministers and seven foreign clergy, with about one thousand communicants. When Robin arrived almost two decades later, there were twenty-nine Chinese ministers in the diocese, only one foreigner, and twenty-three hundred confirmed worshipers.

Their house was two stories tall, with basement storage and a rear balcony on the second floor overlooking a small backyard. Paul had his own bedroom, while the three girls shared a room with twin-sized beds in a row. Paul kept to himself, reading books and playing his harmonica and violin. He rarely caroused with his sisters and said very little at family gatherings. The two younger girls were as rambunctious as rabbits, chasing each other in circles in the yard. Indoors, they scrambled onto the beds and vaulted after each other from mattress to mattress, leaping like frogs on lily pads. They would not stop until one of them fell, often injuring herself, or one of the parents chastised them for making too much noise.

Hui was the most energetic of the children, darting through the house, chasing pigeons and butterflies in the backyard, and scampering up a tree like a squirrel. Her naughty spirit often got her into trouble. Once, she attached a nail to the cone of a paper airplane. She tossed it into the air at a schoolmate, striking his forehead squarely in the middle. The screaming boy yanked the nail out of his skin. When questioned by her mother at the boy's parents' urging, Hui promptly confessed her prank.

"I am sorry. It was my fault. I promise not to do that stupid thing again," Hui pleaded to her father.

"It is good that you confessed. But that is not enough," Robin said with a stern look.

"But I am sorry," whimpered Hui.

"You must apologize to the boy and his parents. What if he had been blinded?"

"He is not blinded!" she protested through tears.

"You must apologize. Ask for forgiveness!"

Forgiveness? Hui knew what she did was wrong, but it was an accident. She wanted to hide and make it all go away, but what could she do?

That evening, Hui went with her father to the boy's house.

"I am sorry. Please forgive me," said Hui sheepishly as she faced the boy and his parents.

The parents pushed their son forward. He bowed to Hui, who stared at the ground and then to Robin. The boy had no ill effects from the homemade missile, except for a small wound on his forehead. His parents bowed. The boy and his parents forgave Hui. Everyone was appeased.

Hui, nearly five, learned about errors, and that one must also apologize to those injured by errors. It was not easy to ask for forgiveness. She felt ashamed. But the boy did forgive, and she felt such relief. With one small poke from a nail taped to a paper airplane, Hui experienced justice and forgiveness.

One morning, Hui found an injured bird in the garden. She was afraid of it, so she asked her house servant to pick it up. He said it was a blackbird, but Robin later told her it was a type of parrot. The servant made a cage, and her father showed her how to feed and care for the bird. She splinted its broken wing for two weeks and taught it a few words while it recovered. She bought sunflower and watermelon seeds and fed them to the parrot. When she removed the splint, the bird flew in circles in her room, but it did not fly away. Hui adopted the bird as her constant companion.

Grace was both studious, like Paul, and fun-loving, like Helen and Hui. As such, she was different from them as well. Within the neighborhood, she was known as the most disciplined and focused student at St. Agnes Girls Middle School.

"Chen I is so smart," one teacher told Robin.

"Your sister is so friendly," classmates said to Helen.

"Number one daughter is so pretty," a mission worker said, complimenting Constance.

When Grace made up her mind to do something, her sisters saw her put all her attention into it. She was quiet but exuded an inner self-confidence. She was assertive but gracious and graceful; she never yelled at her siblings. She had her own cubicle right next to her father's study in the front of the house. While she was a good athlete and loved to play badminton, Grace often buried herself in books as Hui and Helen played shuttlecock in the backyard.

Robin and Constance believed that boys and girls were equal. Because Hui liked to play with the boys, Constance cut her hair short and, in the summer, dressed her in a boy's vest and shorts. She could kick a soccer ball as far and hard as any of the boys and could run as fast as them, too.

But to Hui and her siblings, it was obvious that Grace was their parents' favorite child. And to Grace, being number one daughter was as important as being number one son.

GRACE FELT COMPELLED TO SET A GOOD EXAMPLE. SHE HELPED her mother with kitchen chores and, by seven, had learned how to wash and cook rice. Her father's father often ignored her and favored Paul, the only son. This slight annoyed Grace, so she studied even harder to keep up with Paul and other boys.

"I'll show the old man I am as smart as Paul," she thought.

She wished she could just have fun and play games with her friends— like mah-jongg, which adults often played for money. Her father strictly forbade gambling, since he associated it with the corruption of old China. Many who became addicted gambled away family fortunes or neglected their work and children. It was certainly not what a truly Christian family would do, so playing mah-jongg was frowned upon.

One night during the lunar New Year, when people were giddy with celebration, Grace asked her father to let her friends play. He refused, but she begged all evening.

"Ba, please, it is one time in the year," she pleaded.

He finally consented. He warned them not to gamble, so she and her friends played a friendly game without gambling, not even for candy.

A few days later, a rumor went around the neighborhood that the respected Reverend Chen was playing mah-jongg at his home. When her father heard of the rumor, he took the ivory playing pieces and threw them angrily into the hot stove. Grace apologized to her father. She stayed inside for two weeks, unable to show her face. All she did was study.

Because she was a top student and excelled in a predominantly male world, her light shined brighter in her parents' eyes. The mah-jongg incident was soon forgotten. But after that, Grace rarely played any mindless games. They were merely a waste of time.

Chapter 21

REAL RICE
CHRISTIANS

When the Chens settled in Anking, the CCP had already broken from the KMT and was taking hold in poor rural provinces like Anhwei and Kiangsi. Communism was growing rapidly with Mao as chairman. He formed the Red Army to counter the military forces of the KMT while Stalin sent instructions to organize the peasants and workers into units and institute land reform. As a result, Communists occupied many cities in Anhwei and Hubei, confiscating land from landlords, often by force and with loss of life. Peasants were then rewarded with redistributed plots to farm.

The success of the Communist land reform in winning the loyalty of rural peasants was not lost on the KMT leadership. Aiming to counter this Communist strategy, a rural reconstruction program administered by a newly formed Kiangsi Christian Rural Service Union was organized through a joint commitment from Generalissimo Chiang, the KMT, the National Christian Council, and the League of Nations. Land reform was not its only ambitious goal, but also education and healthcare. George Shepherd, a New Zealand-born Congregational missionary from America, was tasked with organizing the venture, including finding workers, funding, and a Chinese general secretary to run the program. Bishop Huntington, along with Dr. Y.Y. Tsu, representing the Council, met to discuss the endeavor with Madame Chiang Kai-shek, the project's champion. Although he was fifty miles away, putting down a Communist insurgency, Generalissimo Chiang was so interested in the program that he broke in the middle of a heated military conflict and invited the group to brief him during lunch.

"This program can bring peasants to our side," noted the Generalissimo.

"And consolidate many of our social organizations," added Shepherd.

"If the Communists gain a foothold, it will make things harder and cost more lives," continued the Generalissimo. "We need a strong leader."

Madame Chiang was listening carefully when the Generalissimo turned to her, sitting at his right side. She took her cue.

"A Chinese," she emphasized coolly.

"Of course! He *must* be Chinese," echoed Shepherd.

"A *strong* Christian," Madame Chiang added.

Everyone sitting around the Generalissimo nodded in agreement and began to eat. The issue was settled; Madame Chiang had that effect. Even the Generalissimo had nothing further to say.

Shepherd took his responsibility very seriously. It was imperative to counter the Communist movement. The Christian leadership across multiple denominations could be a worthy challenger, as a genuine force of good for the rural poor without the brutality of an armed force. Despite the stigma of anti-foreignism and anti-imperialism, peasants understood the practical benefits of Christian social services. It was clear that the Chinese were looking for saviors amid their hopeless, cyclical plight of poverty, deadly natural disasters, and armed conflict. The fortunes of the KMT and the nation might ride to a large extent on the success of the program.

THE PROGRAM WAS NOT ONLY IMPORTANT TO SHEPHERD AND other Christians, but it was personally and politically important to Generalissimo Chiang. Chiang, born to a Buddhist mother, had been raised in the Confucian tradition, much like his mentor, Dr. Sun Yat-sen. After two failed marriages, he fell in love with a devout Christian, Mei-ling Soong, the number three, youngest daughter of Methodist missionary and American-educated businessman Charlie Soong. Having promised Mei-ling's mother that he would consider Christianity as his personal faith, he studied the Bible daily and was granted permission to marry Mei-ling as a non-Christian in

1927. This Soong marriage changed China like the other Soong marriages: number one daughter, Ai-ling, married H.H. Kung, the finance minister and China's richest man, and the number two daughter, Ching-ling, married Chiang's predecessor and late brother-in-law, Dr. Sun Yat-sen.

Chiang kept his promise by religiously reading his Bible but continued to waver until a military engagement hastened his conversion. According to reports, while trapped with his troops without an escape route and fearing defeat by enemy forces near Kaifeng, he desperately prayed to God for a sign. He promised, if saved, he would profess Jesus Christ as his savior. A sudden snowstorm swept in and stymied the opposing army long enough for reinforcements to rescue Chiang and his army. Chiang kept his promise to Madame Soong to continue studying the Bible with an open mind, and on October 23, 1930, the ruthless, battle-tested Generalissimo was baptized as a Methodist.

The Japanese incursion into Manchuria successfully diverted anti-foreign animus and hostilities away from Westerners, particularly the Christian community, and towards the Japanese invaders. Even so, Chiang kept a low profile within the Christian community. As the civil unrest in southern and eastern China centered on the to-and-fro of Communist capture and Nationalist recapture of various regions, the Christian social agenda appealed to the Chiangs as a viable ally against Communist popularity. Fear of Soviet-backed communism was as much a motivating force as the desire to help the peasants. The American-supported, Christian-based, Chinese-led rural reconstruction program seemed to be a perfect foil. Rice Christians might indeed be crucial to China.

"We need a dedicated Christian with a strong will and clear head who can bring various groups of seculars, Christians, foreigners, and indigenous Chinese together," Madame Chiang astutely declared to Shepherd. "The person you choose must have knowledge of social service reform, an affinity for the plight of the rural poor, and an understanding of politics. He must be skilled at communications, *especially* in English. He must have the respect of overseas Chinese donors and American supporters."

Shepherd and the other organizers agreed wholeheartedly with the very articulate and observant Madame Chiang, the real strength and driving force behind the Generalissimo. They knew it would take someone special to bridge many groups.

"He also must be physically robust, able to endure the hardness of a good soldier of Jesus Christ ... clean in mind and body," added Shepherd. "He must be willing to sacrifice personal ambition for the higher value of team-work ... and be devoted to the welfare of the worker and farmer."

"That person will be central to our success in winning the masses," acknowledged Madame Chiang.

"Yes, he must be Christian in motivation yet scientific in method," Shepherd summed up.

"This may prove to be one of the most monumental rural enterprises of our time. We must not fail this opportunity," Madame Chiang emphasized.

With these numerous qualifications agreed upon, the countrywide search narrowed quickly and unanimously. There were only a handful of Christian Chinese that fit the description, and one name would arise in nomination for the position of the Chinese general secretary that had the resounding approval of everyone involved, especially Madame Chiang.

The Chinese candidate whom Shepherd found to be most ideally suited was Rev. Robin Chen.

That a Christian Chinese was to lead such an ambitious project, one that seemed so vital to this part of the Communist-dominated region of China, would go a long way, both for the KMT government and the Christian com-munity. A foreigner certainly would not do. Nor would anyone backed by Borodin, the Soviet advisor whom Chiang detested. The tenuous symbiosis of the KMT party with the American-supported Christian missionaries as an antidote to the atheistic Communists would signal a rejection of Soviet support. Chiang believed the Soviets had been injurious to the soul of Sun Yat-sen's early Republic, yet vital to the present Communist radicalism he was committed to erase. The situation seemed like a game of chess on a huge three-dimensional field with six differently colored sets of playing pieces.

Since his employment in the diocese was controlled by the American Episcopal Church, Robin's application was sent to the mission board in New York for official approval. Shepherd, so deeply vested in this monumental project, proceeded with his other major task of securing volunteers who would be willing to work only for expenses and not a salary. This self-sacrific-ing arrangement was similar to the one for Communist recruits. Enthusiasm for the project was running high.

But then the word came from New York. The mission board vetoed Robin's nomination. The rejection shocked everyone. It had nothing to do with Robin's qualification or the project itself. It was leadership's objection to a broad-based, ecumenical project that might be perceived as violating the well-founded American ideal of the separation of church and state.

Shepherd blew up.

"I hang my head in shame. It is utter suicide for the Christian leadership to miss this opportunity!" he complained to Madame Chiang. "Farmers may as well have good government as bad, one that guarantees freedom of thought and worship. Communism has no place in China.

"This narrow-minded stupidity ... this lack of vision," he railed, "will lead to opportunities for others who might take advantage of the peasants' plight in China and the instability of the Chinese political landscape."

It was recently, in 1933, that the Nazis had gained control of Germany and were looking to repair relations with China after losing Tsingtao. German advisers were assisting Generalissimo Chiang in his encircle-ment-and-annihilation strategy to exterminate Communist forces. Later in 1934, an agreement was signed between Germany and the KMT to supply Germany with raw materials for industrial products. Aware of this reawak-ening of German interest in China, Shepherd was specifically thinking of the outside threat from its supreme leader. He was fearful of the German Führer's aggressive expansionism. He knew that the last thing China needed was a German foothold in rural reconstruction. Above all else, what he could not tolerate was the idea of Adolf Hitler in China.

The failure of the Service Union to land Robin was a huge blow to the program and a personal disappointment for Madame Chiang. Shepherd spent the subsequent months in search of a substitute to salvage the effort.

But it was Bishop Huntington himself who expressed reservations about the KMT and sounded warnings against such a risky ecumenical partnership. He was wary that the tenuous state of the church and its long-sought goal of freedom from foreign governance would entangle it with, and obligate it to, China's own unstable political landscape. He had worked so diligently for the church's independence and was fearful the church might side with the losing ideology and wrong political party.

He was not the only person losing faith in the KMT.

Chapter 22

TWO FAMILIES

Following the rural reconstruction debacle, Robin and Constance settled into a comfortable flow, focusing on the needs of their congregation. The multidimensional chess game playing throughout China was something they could not control. They had two families to raise—their own and the church's. With their children in mission schools, their paramount focus was growing, educating, and nurturing the Christian community.

The rural reconstruction program did finally get off the ground, but essentially without American participation. It struggled to sustain the initial enthusiasm and aspirations Madame Chiang had engendered. The obstacles were the same as those Robin had identified years ago: illiteracy, profound poverty, intrinsic suspicion of a foreign church, and a paucity of well-trained volunteers willing to work not for money but for the people.

"Communism is the problem but shows us the solution," Robin explained to Constance one night as they lay in bed. "Without people, there is no church."

"No church?" Constance wondered out loud.

Robin lay silently, staring at the ceiling. No church? What would he do?

He was reminded of what one of his colleagues had observed: *Communism crushes the life out of organized Christianity.* While it succeeds in fighting for the dignity and livelihood of the common worker and peasant, Communism carries on the fight in the most indiscriminate and brutal of ways. *No church?* China *needed* the church. *He* needed the church.

In fact, it was the terrible destruction that rebel forces wrought on his adopted city in Fukien that had led Shepherd, in the first place, to believe that a Christian, rather than Communist, rural reconstruction could save China. Robin agreed that while the spirituality of Christian teachings might ultimately, and necessarily, lead China into the future, it was the practical improvement in the common man's life that would allow Christianity to do that. Without the church, Communism might fill the people's stomach, but eventually kill their souls.

Robin stared at Constance; he knew she believed what he believed.

"That cannot happen," he finally answered.

ROBIN UNDERSTOOD THE MISSION BOARD'S RELUCTANCE TO embrace a government that was questionable in many eyes and that might ultimately prove to be the weaker contestant for control of the common man. But he began to question the wisdom of separating the church too much from state politics and their caution in choosing sides in the economic policy battle.

Had the Anglican Church missed a golden opportunity to change China's course? Would Christianity truly be crushed by the passion of the agnostic youth who seemed to flock incessantly towards Mao's party? Every time Generalissimo's army gained a Communist-controlled city, the Communists would spring up again like tulips in the spring. What would become of Christianity in a Communist China? All these questions worried him.

One thing that was clear to Robin was Generalissimo and Madame Chiang's commitment to China. While many had questioned the depth of the Generalissimo's spiritual adoption of Christianity because of his less than evangelical demeanor in public and his ruthlessness on the battlefield, no one doubted his patriotic priority of country over self. Some, especially in America, cynically thought he was merely China's most prominent rice Christian, trying to curry favor from the Americans against the Communists with his conversion. Few, except for his closest Christian friends and Madame herself, knew that his Spartan lifestyle derived from his pledge to live in a Christ-like way, not from a spiritual perspective, but from a practical one; he wanted to win the loyalty and respect of his disciples and subjects. In this Christian construct, he justified the cold-blooded destruction of the Communists by equating them with the enemies of the chosen people in the Old Testament—the Philistines, the Egyptians, and the Assyrians. These were the heathens that God's heroes, like Joshua and Moses, righteously battled.

Robin found himself questioning his interpretation of the Bible within the morass of life in China. How much would he, if pressured, compromise Christian beliefs in pursuit of patriotic service to China? If attacked, could he turn the other cheek? If accused of being a disciple of Christ under threat of execution, would he deny Him three times before the cock crowed? Perhaps Hsiao Wang chose wisely when he shied from ministerial life.

He sensed an impending conflagration threatening to ignite the many forces in China. Life was uncertain and fragile. No one was truly in charge. For that, he feared for both his families.

CONSTANT THREATS BY MAO-LED AND OTHER LEFTIST FORCES suddenly subsided as Generalissimo Chiang aggressively cleared large areas of Communist influence in Anhwei and Kiangsi provinces. Church leaders tried to remain philosophically neutral in China's internal affairs, only speaking out when it affected their ability to do their work.

"The sooner we can transition to a Chinese church, the brighter your future will be," Bishop Huntington told him. "To flourish, you must be free."

Foreign missionaries tended to side with the Nationalists, since their leaders, Dr. Sun, Generalissimo Chiang, and many of the top officials were Christians. Although money from American and England had dwindled drastically, financial support, both private and organizational, was still predominantly from overseas and more aligned with the Western-connected Nationalists than the Communists. But native clergy like Robin found commonality with the communist end-product of land redistribution, its championing of the lower class, and the principle of equality. It was their methodology and atheism that were objectionable.

Corruption within the KMT was commonplace, tolerated and over-looked by Chiang. As their acts of brutality increased, evidenced by the daylight spectacles of public executions, the common person's sentiments easily drifted toward Mao's peasant-centric principles. Robin and the church were at a crossroads. A choice would have to be made if American and British treaties dissolved, putting Christians and their churches at risk.

After Chiang's army liberated Anking for the last time, Mao's Red Army and the majority of their allied forces began a retreat from the south and headed west and north—a march that eventually ranged nearly 6,000 miles, crossed eighteen mountain ranges and twenty-four rivers, at a cost of ninety percent of the troops, and spanned twelve brutal months. But this respite from Communist agitation did not last long. After only a couple of years of quiet, Robin and his family had to face the reality of another challenge more terrifying than the Communists, drought-induced famine, or unrelenting floods.

It was late 1937, and news came to Anking that Japan was attacking Shanghai.

Chapter 23

WARTIME PLEDGES

T he incident at Marco Polo Bridge in July outside Peking was a mis-
understanding between Japanese and Chinese troops, which led
to a full-scale assault by the Japanese and lit the flames of war. In reality,
both China and Japan were primed for bloodletting. Japan had taken over
Manchuria and had designs on China's natural resources. For its part, China
was still gripped by anti-foreign sentiments, and Generalissimo Chiang was
fed up with the Japanese presence in China.

Despite this, Chiang had to be convinced of Japan's mortal threat to
China. He spent three years pursuing the Communists, vowing to destroy
them with his encirclement and annihilation strategy. The Communists
defied all odds and overcame one military campaign or blockade after
another until they were forced on their long march to the north.

Chiang's single-minded pursuit of his fellow Chinese had been turned
on its head only after he was kidnapped in Sian by his own generals the
previous summer. He was finally released on Christmas Day 1936, after
the generals, dismissing the option of execution, forced him to negotiate
with Chou En-lai. Talks dragged out for months but led to a truce with the
Communists, incumbent on their joint collaboration against Japan, which
was seen as the greater threat to China. Convinced that only a unified
China could save itself from foreign domination, the Communists acqui-
esced and agreed to be subject to Chiang's command. They relented on
their forcible confiscation of land and agreed to the democratic principles

of the San Min Chu I. Mao's Red Army was subsequently absorbed into the Nationalist military.

Chiang sent his conjoined army and planes to attack Japanese marines living in Shanghai. Japan in turn sent in her naval forces and bombed Shanghai from the air and the sea. Another two hundred thousand Japanese soldiers were deployed to confront Chiang's army. Robin and his staff hoped the conflict would not spread their way—a hope short-lived.

The first air raid sirens broke the calmness of an autumn day. They started with a slow drone, crescendoing to a high-pitched scream. The crowded streets in Anking came to a standstill before people scampered to all four directions of the compass. After a few suspenseful minutes, a phalanx of propeller fighter planes bearing the unmistakable red Rising Sun on the underbelly of their wings came into view. Hysteria spread as rapidly as sound could travel, creating a chaotic wave of frightened humanity.

Thankfully, this was just a reconnaissance mission, and the low-flying planes soon disappeared into the horizon. But the arrival of Japanese planes was the only topic of discussion into the evening.

THAT NIGHT, GRACE COULD NOT SLEEP BECAUSE OF THE EARlier air raids and made her way through the darkened house. Paul, Helen, and Hui were asleep, and her parents' bedroom was empty. She headed stealthily towards the light coming through the church office windows in the adjacent building. She reached the office and stood motionless outside the door. She did not want to startle her parents, nor did she want to get into trouble.

She leaned her ear towards the room. The shortwave radio and muted voices speaking Chinese filtered through the cracked door. Her father abruptly turned the radio off.

"Maintain the people's spirit. Keep their hopes up," she heard him say. "*Yung gan chi lai.*"

Be brave.

Constance, a few church workers, and some teachers were gathered with Robin to hear the latest report on the Japanese advances and the carpet bombing of Shanghai. Grace watched as Robin prayed with them. She pushed herself in a bit further as his voice dropped.

"Be not afraid of their faces. I am with thee. I will deliver thee," he prayed.

Robin spied Grace through the crack in the office door. He dismissed the group and asked them to reconvene in the morning. He gestured for Grace to come in.

"Why are you awake?" he asked with concern.

"I could not sleep," Grace replied. "What is happening?"

"Shanghai is getting worse. We have to prepare for trouble."

"Why do Japanese hate us?"

Her father motioned for her to sit.

"They do not hate us." It was an optimistic half-truth. "Japan needs things that China has. China is weak and Japan knows that," he explained. "A divided house cannot stand."

"You taught that."

"The Bible teaches the truth. China is divided. We are fighting ourselves. Japan is united and their people will follow the emperor wherever he wants."

"What should we do?"

Her father looked at her for what she felt was a long time. It seemed as if he was not going to answer.

Her father placed his arm around her shoulder and walked her towards the door. "Stay together," he said. "A family stays together."

A WEEK LATER, AT 5:30 THE MORNING OF AUGUST 24, JAPANESE planes bombed the Anking airport. Fearing the same fate as Shanghai, the city quickly emptied. As was their historic habit, people scattered into the countryside like panicked prey.

Robin organized the Anking Special Times Emergency Committee to prepare members of the congregation who remained. He called a general meeting of all the mission staff, teachers, and clergy. They convened in one of the classrooms.

Dr. Harry Taylor sat at the front desk with Robin. The energetic, short-statured surgeon with a tall forehead, piercing eyes, and a sharp tongue ran the mission hospital. Affectionately known as China Taylor, the intrepid American had garnered a reputation throughout China since he first set foot there as a missionary in 1905. During the fall of the Manchus, he helped a local governor escape a mutinous group of revolutionary soldiers. After providing refuge to the governor in the hospital, at great risk of personal retaliation, he helped the heavy-set official sneak over the city wall in the dead of night hidden within a twine bosun's chair. With a band of angry soldiers in hot pursuit, he guided the governor through the bankside underbrush to a hired junk that safely ferried him to an awaiting Japanese gunboat.

Earlier in his missionary days, he was called from Anking to treat a priest in Kiukiang and was put up in an apartment above a rat-infested warehouse. The next morning, having paid the pesky pests little mind, he awoke on a pillow stained with blood. He had slept unperturbed through the night as one of the more curious, and obviously hungry, rodents nibbled on the tip of his nose. Just as unflappable in surgery, Taylor had a portfolio of patients with every imaginable injury: chests pierced by bayonets; livers cleaved by long swords; heads riddled with bullets; and mouths torn apart by lard-covered explosives mistaken for candy.

Peter Hill, the mission's accountant, flanked Robin on the right, along with Alice Gregg, who had returned to Anhwei after earning her master's and PhD degrees in America. Blanche Myers, another American missionary who worked as the hospital treasurer, sat next to Alice. Constance was positioned at the end of the front row with one of the young ministers. There was nervous chatter in the room about the unfolding events: an expansion of the Japanese incursion into China in an unambiguous act of hostility, clashing with Generalissimo Chiang's defiant defense. This could only mean a great deal of pain and bloodshed for everyone along the Yangtse River.

"Shanghai is in a terrible state," Robin stated. "The Japanese have brought in reinforcements. Their commitment to taking Shanghai is total."

"Our army can't withstand the Japs' air power," Dr. Taylor opined. He was an astute, no-nonsense missionary befitting his surgical decisiveness. "Prepare for the possibility of retreat. The Japs are ferocious, and the bastards will slither through China like snakes in the grass."

"What can we do?" asked Miss Myers.

"If the body is weak, the spirit must be strong. We need prayer books, Bibles, bandages, medical supplies, stockpiles of food—" answered Robin.

"Reverend Chen, last week, eggs were one yuan. Now they are three. Our treasury is almost depleted," complained Hill.

Rising uncertainty among the populace had created a rapid inflation of prices on foodstuffs of one hundred, two hundred, even three hundred percent in less than a week or two. With shrinking foreign donations and complex banking arrangements, finances were severely tested. It took extraordinary diligence on Hill's part to keep salaries, expense accounts, credit, and payments current. He was constantly juggling monies and pleading with bank officials to keep accounts liquid.

Miss Myers was the first to respond.

"Reverend Chen, I wish to contribute ten percent of my monthly wages."

The room fell quiet as everyone looked at her. Then they looked at each other. As it dawned on them what she had done, a worker in the back of the classroom shouted out.

"I will also give ten percent!"

Alice immediately chimed in.

"Twenty per cent for me! No, twenty-five percent!"

"Okay! Twenty-five percent for me, too!"

It was Miss Myers again.

Alice stood up and turned to the gathering, her hands firmly on her hips.

Dr. Taylor quickly declared, "Fifty. Make mine fifty!"

"Fifty for me as well," echoed Alice.

"Okay, fifty!" said Miss Myers cheerfully.

"I guess that makes mine seventy-five," grunted Dr. Taylor, his lower lip thrust forward like a pouting schoolboy.

Soon the room was filled with yelling, as if at an auction for a valuable painting. Most had no idea if they could afford their pledge. But they pledged, nonetheless. As the room echoed with numbers from fifty to ninety percent, Mr. Hill pulled out a notebook and began to scribble.

"Get all this down, Mr. Hill!" Alice instructed with a smile. She hugged Miss Myers as the room erupted in applause.

Robin looked proudly at Constance, who smiled back. He could not imagine ebullience in the face of such peril. These foreigners had so little but willingly gave of themselves. He had no earthly desires, no needs for his family that the church did not help provide for him—a room to sleep in, food to eat, and opportunities for his children's education. Anything else was a bonus.

"All of it, Mr. Hill," he said to the accountant. "Take all of mine this month."

He said it in a whisper, as if a secret. This small triumph was a necessary blessing in what might be a prolonged and trying time for his congregation. He could not fool himself into thinking that this extraordinary gesture by his people, though spiritually and financially significant, was in any way going to affect the eventual outcome—not with two hundred thousand Japanese forces and their superior naval and air power knocking on the mission doors.

It would not be nearly enough, but it *was* something.

Chapter 24

END OF GLORY DAYS

The next morning, Mr. Hill set up a collection table in front of the Cathedral. A line of people flowed steadily by. Each person placed bills and coins into a bamboo basket, while Mr. Hill wrote down the amount and name of the donors. One day, the church might reimburse them, though no one asked.

Throughout the rest of the compound and proximate neighborhood, workers teamed with nearby residents to build dugouts reinforced with wooden slats and sandbags supplied from an assembly line of laborers. Some entered the church basement and stocked the shelves with food supplies.

The work continued uninterrupted for days. Even children pitched in to help. With the donations from the mission's employees, Mr. Hill was able to procure medical supplies, prayer books, and Bibles that he and Miss Myers distributed to the congregation, along with Red Cross first-aid pamphlets. Robin continued to lead parishioners in prayer in the Cathedral.

After a few weeks of relative quiet without further bombing, residents trickled back from the countryside. The city filled again, and life was restored to its usual tempo. The air raid sirens sounded every now and then. But without any actual bombings, they did not revisit the previous panic. By now, the city had a protocol when the warnings went off; there was a more orderly procession into the shelters and dugouts. The mission workers headed to the cathedral basement, with its padded walls and shelves stocked with cans of food, dried meats, preserved fruits, and candy. They even had a small altar for worship services.

In early October, morning sirens screamed as before. But this time, a dozen Japanese planes were seen humming ominously along the horizon. As they approached the city limits, the planes fanned out in various directions. People hurried into surrounding buildings as bombs dropped outside the city. Drivers with their rickshaws sprinted down alleys with their fares. As if on command, the planes disgorged dozens of packages the size of small missiles. Instead of hurtling into the city with a telltale whistle, the packages burst into tens of thousands of pieces that descended gently onto the fleeing masses like giant, wounded butterflies. The items cast a kaleidoscope of ever-changing shadows on the ground. People grasped at the fluttering objects within their reach; the pieces of paper were half the size of a newspaper.

The message was bold, written in Chinese characters:

"Chinese Nationalist Government Most Glorious Day,
October 10, 1911. End of Glory Days, October 1937."

It was as clear as the sky was blue. A stark warning. The Japanese were coming.

Soon after, word came that their army was marching toward Nanking. Wuhu would be next, then Anking. Chiang's army was in retreat, despite a three-month stand against overwhelming Japanese forces. Robin knew Anking would inevitably be targeted.

St. James Hospital received the last shipments of supplies: bandages, bottles of saline and alcohol, surgical needles and packets of sutures, morphine, casting material, and crutches. Dr. Taylor and the staff taught the mission workers how to splint limbs, apply pressure bandages, clean and close wounds. Their students practiced with deliberate intent but also with a cheerful attitude. As terrified as everyone might have been, their work was governed not by fear, but by a sense of commonality. They faced the threat of Japanese hostility as an army led by Jesus Christ, their Lord and Savior. There was righteousness in their preparation for the battle that soon reached their doorsteps.

First, it was a trickle of civilians from Shanghai. These were the early refugees: normal, everyday Chinese individuals and families, fleeing out of fear. Most dispersed into the mountainous countryside. But then came the soldiers, initially in small numbers, then in larger groups. They came not because they were afraid, although they might have been that as well. They came because they were losing the battle.

The city was bombed continuously on October 22 and 23. The medical staff was ready to receive the wounded. But once the first, slow stream of vehicles began emptying bloodied passengers onto the hospital doorsteps, it continued relentlessly.

"Where are they coming from?" asked an incredulous nurse.

"Shanghai," answered a hospital worker. The word fell off his lips like he was dispossessing the thought. A regrettable fact—knowing it was true but wishing it were not. The unthinkable had happened, and the worst was yet to come.

Shanghai was the heart and soul of China—the international center-piece of the nation—and it was being overrun. Soldiers escaped Shanghai on ships by way of the Yangtse River. The wounded were offloaded on the riverbank and transported to the hospital by whatever means possible.

Within a few hours, the hallways were full of bodies and cries of agony. Dr. Taylor had his hand knuckle-deep in a soldier's thigh, his forefinger the only difference between life and fatal exsanguination. A nurse gave the young boy an injection of morphine into his other thigh to ease his pain and quiet him.

A soldier with a shattered ankle nearly fainted on a nurse's shoulder. She managed to find space on a bench, where she laid him down.

Another American nurse ran up to Dr. Taylor. Her uniform was stained with the color of half a dozen Chinese.

"Dr. Taylor, we can't take care of all of them. There are hundreds more outside."

Dr. Taylor had no idea if she was exaggerating but had no patience for complaints. He was only interested in results.

"Don't count! If you cannot save them, move on! Take care of those you can. Get me a clamp. Move those bodies. Clamp! Clamp! Somebody get me a damn clamp!"

So, it went, late into the night. Fractures were set and splinted, sometimes without the benefit of an x-ray. Wounds were cleaned and bandaged. Dr. Taylor, Dr. Sung, and the other Chinese surgeons each performed dozens of operations, removing pieces of shrapnel, stitching up gaping holes, amputating mangled limbs. It was not pretty, but it was effective. An amputation took barely ten minutes. The staff could set and splint an arm in under five. The hospital staff saved a lot of lives but was helpless against others. The workers could only do what they could do. The dead began to pile up. The nurses and doctors did not have time to ponder their work that night.

By the next morning, no one felt good. Wounded soldiers and civilians continued to arrive in motor vehicles, bicycle carts, even odd contraptions called human wheelbarrows—pushcarts with a single wheel centered through a wooden platform. Everyone worked without complaint.

Soldiers reported on the massacre that had taken place in Shanghai. Generalissimo Chiang was losing; half his men were dead. Regiments were decimated or in disarray. Without means of communication, troops dispersed haphazardly to the west. Some of the intact regiments were called to Nanking, where Chiang planned to defend the capital, knowing that this was the prized jewel of the Japanese incursion. Some fell back to Wuhu. Others ended up in Anking.

Robin kept the schedule as normal as he could. Church services and schools continued. It was important to hold the congregation together, to feed and bolster their spirit and morale. Hope and salvation had to triumph over despair. People sought solace in the cathedral. For the missionaries, it was their home away from home. For the Chinese and the refugees, it was their sanctuary, a place to gather as one.

"In wartime, it is easy to answer, 'Who is our enemy?'" Robin posed in his sermon one Sunday morning. "It is harder to answer how to defeat them."

Robin stood at the cathedral pulpit. The sunlight poured through the glass of the side windows. The nave was only a quarter full, with two hundred of his Chinese congregation and twenty foreign missionaries. Reverend Wu, a young, newly ordained minister, helped translate for the Chinese audience. He flinched as a bomb landed near the neighborhood, causing the church to tremble. Miss Myers and Alice held each other's hands as Constance wrapped her arms around her children.

"Our enemy is *not* the Japanese with their bombers. It is *not* the British or the Americans," he preached. "Our enemy is ignorance. Our foe, intolerance."

He paused after every word to allow Reverend Wu to carefully translate them into Chinese. Each word reverberated throughout the vast cathedral space. Each word made its effect and died out before the next was uttered. He forced the people to consider the meaning of each word.

"Poverty."

"*Ping chiung!*"

He saw heads nod after Dr. Wu's translation.

"Fear."

"*Kung chu!*"

The cathedral fell silent.

"Hatred."

Reverend Wu glanced at Robin, who nodded affirmatively.

"*Tseng hen!*"

Robin said the words quietly, but forcefully, without hatred. But Reverend Wu summoned the sounds from deep within his gut, expelling them from his throat like phlegm, as if to exorcise them from the cathedral. They were words everyone understood. They cascaded over the congregation and dissipated into the open space.

"Do not come to this cross," Robin admonished them, "without forgiveness in your heart!"

He looked out over his congregation. He could not blame them for their fear and their hatred. But that would not save them. It would imprison and doom them.

"For there you will find one who was crucified, who prayed—" he paused for even greater effect.

Robin was convinced of the truthfulness of his words. Perhaps not now, not even tomorrow, but in the end. He had to. What else was there?

"Father, forgive them ... for they know not what they do."

As if on cue, a huge explosion rocked the cathedral rafters, causing dust to shower onto the people's heads. But no one screamed. The entire church was stoically quiet, contemplating Robin's last few words.

In a letter to a friend later that night, Alice recalled her astonishment at Robin's powerful message of forgiveness. No one else could comprehend such a thought. It was natural that conflict bred war, and war always bred hatred, but she wrote, *Picture a clergyman in one of the Allied countries during 1914-1918 saying, 'Tomorrow night we will pray especially for the German soldiers."*

Her friend later replied: *I cannot imagine it.*

Such sentiment seemed inconceivable at times such as this.

Chapter 25

THE MASSACRE
AND THE PROMISE

Following the attack, the city experienced a few weeks of calm. Although the Japanese had not forgotten Anking, they were focused on final efforts to push out the last of the resistant Nationalist troops from Shanghai. Then, the beginning of December—more exactly, the 7th—brought one air sortie after another, with bombs raining down on the city in indiscriminate fashion. Word circulated that Wuhu had been attacked and the Japanese were planning the destruction of Anking on the 11th. The city evacuated again.

As it turned out, Anking was not destroyed on the 11th. The Japanese were too busy elsewhere. The Christmas month was progressing toward the traditional holiday season when news trickled out of the Nanking battle zone, telling in the most horrific and graphic detail of a thoroughly barbaric massacre. Soldiers and civilians who passed through the mission hospital described first-person accounts of mass murder and torture: Japanese infantry practicing bayoneting skills on hog-tied civilians, even infants; Chinese soldiers and unarmed citizens hunted in the streets for sport and amusement, like pesky pests; live group burials and mass executions hundreds at a time; gang rapes of defenseless children, women, and elderly; spontaneous and orchestrated public decapitations, resulting in piles of severed heads displayed on city steps like ceramic wares for sale or impaled on bamboo poles as if they were decorative lanterns. The catalogue of atrocities was truly unimaginable to all who witnessed them.

Dr. Taylor, hardly containing his rage, channeled anger into healing. He focused on the anatomy in front of him, blocking out as much emotion as he could. But when he opened an abdomen to clean out an infection, he replayed the report of a rape victim—barely a teenager—whose grandmother's belly was sliced open by a Japanese *kuei tzu bing*. A devil soldier.

"Damn bastards!" he spat into his mask as he hovered over an open abdomen. In the next breath, he prayed, "Lord, bless this poor soul. Damn it!"

Missionaries could hold back neither tears nor curious gossip. *Was it true, or were people stretching the truth? Did the similarities in their stories mean the inhumanity was real? Could people harbor so much hatred as to do such unspeakable things?*

A Japanese newspaper told of the competition between two Japanese officers vying for the most Chinese beheadings. Each strove to be the first to reach one hundred executions during their campaign into Nanking. The daily serials were complete with scoreboards, as if it were a sporting match. The gruesome contest was so close that towards the end it was mutually agreed upon to extend the winning tally to one hundred and fifty heads.

Another told of the partial beheading of a Chinese truck driver who was kicked about the head with his neck sliced open. While still gasping for air, he was mercifully killed with a few more awkward hacks of a sword, only to have his loose, bloodied head punted along the ground between his killers, like some warped soccer ball.

No one knew exactly how many Chinese were massacred, certainly tens, if not hundreds, of thousands.

The foreign missionaries knew Japan would be careful with Westerners, who were still privileged and protected within China. Japanese soldiers broke into foreigners' homes; American, British, German, and French embassies; and offices of major American companies like Standard Oil and the Texas Corporation. They ransacked and looted the premises, and yet, following the specific orders of the army's commander-in-chief, left the foreigners unharmed. But Chinese were a different matter. Weary, under-provisioned soldiers, as well as unarmed, vulnerable citizens, both were easy prey.

Over the next few days, as most Chinese emptied out of Anking, Robin went with Alice and Reverend Wu to inspect the damage done to the immediate neighborhood around the cathedral. A few buildings were destroyed.

Rubble and an occasional corpse lay scattered about the streets. None could imagine what Shanghai or Nanking looked like.

The trio ended back at the cathedral that had been converted into a first-aid station. Dr. Taylor, still wearing his blood-stained gown from the previous night, helped Grace wrap a soldier's arm. Helen and Hui gave candy to the children who sobbed by their parents' side. No one had bathed or changed clothes for days. A suffocating mustiness prevailed. A hundred parishioners and patients rested in the cool air of the December evening, which seeped through the doorways and helped dilute the offensive odor. The voluminous cathedral was filled with a chaotic din of chatter and whimpering. As Robin walked among the congregants, he placed a reassuring hand on a head or shoulder, stopping to offer a word of comfort or prayer.

"How long can we possibly hold out?" Alice whispered conspiratorially as she followed close behind.

"The army is retreating farther west," Robin answered. "Perhaps not long," he added.

"The Japs will follow," said Dr. Taylor bluntly as he chewed on a cigar. "From Nanking, two days. Maybe three. Our supplies are already low."

He spat out a vein from a tobacco leaf.

"The Japs won't touch us, but Robin, you need to go!" he concluded.

Taylor was a straight shooter and right, as usual. It was time for Robin and his congregation to leave. There was no telling what mood the Japanese would be in when they hit the city and what they would do to any Chinese they found. Would they be spent or still blood-thirsty and riled up by victory? As foreigners, Taylor and the other missionaries would probably be safe, but they could not protect their Chinese friends.

"Most of the city has already left," reasoned Dr. Taylor. He drew Robin aside, away from the rest of the group, and lowered his voice but not its urgency. "Robin, listen! Get your people out!"

THEIR CHILDREN SAT ON THE BED IN ROBIN AND CONSTANCE'S room that evening, waiting to hear of their parents' plans for evacuation. They were not unlike many children who fought to survive. As much as

Robin and Constance wanted to shield them from life's most cruel realities, the truth was, they could not. There was a reason why they sat through class in a Christian school and went to services on Sunday. But in order to understand the meaning of God's love, they also had to understand and see life's evil, all of man's naked ugliness and wickedness. Only then could they really grasp the concept of love—what was at risk and what was to be gained. The enemy was coming, but they could not show fear in the very face of fear. They could not succumb to hatred in the very face of hatred.

"When it is safe, we will return."

"Where are we going?" Paul, now fifteen, asked.

Robin and Constance looked at each other. Like most of the refugees, they really had no idea where they would end up. There might be camps and shelters set up by the various mission organizations, as well as government and military safe zones, but they would not yet be well-organized. Robin had a few contacts from the church, but a rabbit would have to run wherever it could to escape the fox. That is what they would do; they would become rabbits.

"The important thing is that we are together," he said. He turned to Paul. "Help your sisters. We leave in the morning."

"How long will we be gone?" asked Paul.

"Time does not matter," Robin answered tersely. A few days was too optimistic, but forever was unthinkable. "Go."

"Yes, *ba*." Paul nodded dutifully.

Once Robin let the congregation know that he recommended evacuating the city, they took little time preparing for their exodus. Since the majority would need to walk, they could only take what they could manage on their backs or in their hands. Some fortunate ones had bicycles, but most had only their two legs.

The bank had warned that communication lines were being interrupted and accounts might not be accessible if the conflict reached the city. It advised withdrawing as much money as possible, which Robin arranged to do. It was not much, but it would help for the next few days.

～ ✤ ～

IN THE MORNING, ROBIN HAD THE GROUP GATHER OUTSIDE THE
Cathedral. He came out with Dr. Taylor, Mr. Hill, Alice, Misses Browne,
Myers, and Sherman, and the foreign staff after a short service.

Robin, Reverend Wu, the headmaster of the St. James Boys School,
and Reverend Wang, the assistant pastor, shook hands with the foreigners.
Outside the Cathedral were two hundred Chinese of all ages. Each person was holding bags and knapsacks with necessary possessions. Hui and
Constance stood with Helen, while Paul and Grace were with other teenage
children. Families clustered together, waiting patiently and calmly. Some
children played in the road, kicking up dust.

"When all this passes, we will welcome you back," said Dr. Taylor, grasping Robin's right hand with both of his. His gesture was firm and reassuring.

"Yes. At Christmas. I promise to celebrate Christmas with you," Robin
said convincingly, but he knew it was only half a promise. No one could pre-
dict when the crisis would pass.

"Godspeed, Robin," offered Mr. Hill.

"Don't worry. They won't touch us!" Dr. Taylor stated emphatically.

Robin knew the truth of Dr. Taylor's statement. Japan was at war with
China, not the Western powers; foreigners were off-limits. It was hard for
him to ignore the fact that, in some incomprehensible, perverse way, it was
still better to be an American in China than a Chinese.

With their final goodbyes, Robin led his congregation out of the mission,
heading northwest. The farther away from the city, the better.

"Christmas!" shouted Dr. Taylor as he waved at Robin.

"Christmas!" Robin promised, waving back, as he and his flock descended
the hill away from the cathedral. As the tower receded from his view, Robin
wondered what might remain of the Gothic cathedral when it was finally
safe to return.

Chapter 26

REFUGEES

The congregation started out clinging tightly to each other like a single organism. The Chinese teachers helped keep the younger students corralled and entertained with songs and playful banter. A few hoisted the smaller ones on their shoulders when they tired. Some of the elders sat on bicycles pushed by their adult children; others were hardy enough to walk on their own. The group began to stretch out as they progressed down the road and the day wore on. By late afternoon, they were strung out like an army of ants instinctively following the leader, very orderly, without any sense of panic.

Along the way, they intermixed with other refugees, their lines coalescing into one long column flowing north away from floodplains of the Yangtse. Their goal was to get into the countryside, as far away as possible from the river. Japanese gunboats would be patrolling the riverbanks, attacking the heavily populated waterway cities.

The tangle of city streets became wide-open swaths of farmland, where people lived in villages with a few animals and limited possessions. Living conditions had not changed for decades. The peasants seemed oblivious to the dangers of the conflict because they lacked the literacy to read newspapers. News by mouth, taken as rumor, might take days to reach a farmer toiling single-mindedly in the fields. The first telltale sign of trouble in the cities was often a swell of refugees showing up in the villages.

The group walked northwards for two days. They sang Chinese folk songs, and when inspired, Christian hymns. Their favorite as they marched was "Onward Christian Soldiers." A good marching song with a strong beat, it helped them continue on when they felt the most exhausted. Their voices fertilized the countryside with a contagious spirit, coaxing smiles and hand-waving from peasants laboring in the fields.

Paul trailed leisurely behind his father. He preferred to be alone, not mixing with his sisters, sometimes blowing on his harmonica, at other times eavesdropping on Robin's discussion with the other ministers. His father periodically invited him to walk with them, putting his arms around his youthful shoulders.

"We serve God by serving others," the young Reverend Wu said to him.

"You can only serve people by becoming selfless," Robin responded. "That is the most difficult challenge, to lose one's own self."

Paul did not say anything. He could not help but weigh those words, and stared at the road ahead overrun with refugees.

ONCE FAR ENOUGH AWAY FROM ANKING AND THE YANGTSE, the congregation split off into smaller groups in a village whose name, translated into English, was Tang Family Bend. Here, they were in a quiet and serene setting among lush, green hills; houses lined both sides of a gentle, clear river that flowed towards the nearby lake. There was even a small waterfall at the base of one of the taller mountains. The air was crisp and cool, with the sweet and pungent scents of burning wood, roasted yams, and coal.

As it was soon past dusk, the congregation divided up, with one or two families going into separate farmhouses. Peasants understood their plight because conflicts over the years had produced one group of refugees after another. If people were not fleeing the Japanese, they were fleeing the Communists, and if they were not fleeing from the Communists, they were fleeing from local bandits, and if not bandits, then warlords. Once the peasants heard that the group was from a church, they warmly welcomed them into their homes. Christians were known to be different; they were resilient, humble, and well-mannered, as kind to the peasants as the peasants were to them.

One of the villagers invited Robin's family into his farmhouse and gave them two rooms on the second floor. The family, dusty and tired from their journey, wasted no time in throwing themselves on the bare floor and were soon fast asleep. Hui's parrot kept them company, chattering familiarly in its cage.

THE PEOPLE IN THE CONGREGATIONAL CARAVAN WERE GRATEFUL to the farmers, who had so little for themselves. Robin wanted to acknowledge the goodwill between the two groups and show his gratitude. He told Constance to plan a meal for the whole village.

Constance took the girls with some of the women to the local market. There, Hui noticed that many of the villagers had a large mass in their necks. She pointed to the tumor the size of a small sweet potato in front of their throats.

"Ma, what is that?" she inquired in a loud voice.

"Shh. Don't be impolite," Constance admonished her, gently slapping her pointed finger. "They are poor and live far from the sea."

"It is ugly," stated Hui as she wrinkled her face.

"Why do you say that?" scolded Helen, mimicking her mother. She, too, scowled disapprovingly at Hui who clutched her neck protectively.

"Do not worry," Constance assured her. "You cannot catch it."

Constance organized the women and prepared a feast, to the villagers' delight. Robin watched the group enjoy themselves and felt great satisfaction. It was a minor and brief moment when everyone he saw was smiling.

This gesture paid off a few nights later, when Hui and Helen were awakened by a sudden staccato of gunfire that crackled out of the darkness. The two sisters clung to each other as they went to rouse their mother. Constance instructed them to stay calm. After a few more gunshots, the whole household was awake.

"Bandits!" exclaimed the landlord in a hushed voice as he pushed the family into a large closet and closed the door. He left to see what was happening.

After a few minutes—and more gunshots and voices yelling in the distance—the landlord returned and led Robin and his family out the back door. Once outside, he motioned them to hide amid the thick foliage of the nearby woods.

"Be quiet!" he whispered and left.

As soon as the gunshots died down, the landlord returned and ushered them back into the house.

"Bandits gone," the landlord declared. "No good! What do we have? We have nothing!"

He lamented that bandits were a constant problem. They had heard of the church people's arrival and thought they were easy targets.

"We chased them away. They only want money. Rascal troublemakers!"

Constance and Robin thanked the landlord. It took a while for the children to quiet down. They all huddled together on the floor beside their parents in the larger room. No one said a word and it became quiet again. The only things the children heard were the rhythmic to-and-fro of each other's breath, intermixed with the familiar singing of crickets in the background. Crickets were always good luck. They were soon asleep.

AFTER A FEW DAYS IN TANG FAMILY BEND, ROBIN DECIDED THAT they had taken advantage of the landlord's hospitality long enough and perhaps even put his family in harm's way. The group was running out of money and needed to get to a city with bank connections. The incident with the bandits made the people uncomfortable. The next larger city away from Anking was Tongcheng. Rev. Wu stayed behind with some of the people who were content with their current location, while the rest of the congregation packed up, thanked the villagers, and continued north.

"That the villagers welcomed us is hopeful," commented Reverend Wang as they walked together. "It was not long ago that the Communists were here."

"Farming their own land gives them dignity," Robin remarked. "Tenancy is a problem. Landlords care only about their rent. Farmers do not produce enough even for themselves."

"Perhaps the Communists are right," Reverend Wang suggested.

"Self-determination is good for man's soul," concurred Robin. "The Communists mean well, but they are ungodly. You cannot serve two masters."

Robin again thought of Hsiao Wang, whose family had been slaves to the soil. They had nothing else. The church had helped Hsiao Wang break free, but the dilemma still bothered him. He wondered where his friend was and whether either of them would really ever have enough *yung ch'i* to make a difference.

"It is hard to win their souls when they worry about their bellies. That their hearts are still open, that is very good," Reverend Wang added as they walked.

Robin felt a twinge of satisfaction to hear his junior colleague speak so optimistically about the peasants, who had opened their doors when everything should have made them close them. He had felt the same way at his age. So much hope. When hope is lost, so is the war.

Once they reached Tongcheng, the group found lodging and were able to access the church bank account. Robin's family passed the time together, waiting for word on the Japanese progress. It felt like angry, dark clouds were blowing through the land, threatening to eclipse the sun. But for now, they were safe and together. All they could do was wait.

Chapter 27

A CHRISTMAS GIFT

It had been nearly a week since Robin and the group left Anking. The Japanese bombed the city randomly, without any strategic targets, but they did not advance troops into the city. Dr. Taylor and other missionaries worked diligently to care for the incoming refugees and soldiers. The hospital was over capacity, but new patients slowed to a trickle. The worst of the threat seemed to be over—for now.

The staff prepared the dining room for their Christmas Eve celebration the following day. They were tired, but this was the most joyful time of the Christian calendar. Bombings were infrequent. Instead, the air was dense with a torrential downpour. When the wind blew hard, the night became chilly—almost freezing. But it would keep the planes away.

Miss Myers and Miss Browne lined the room with strings of colored lights and were decorating a small evergreen tree with handmade ornaments: colorful paper cutouts, wooden crosses, stars molded from aluminum foil, and straw figurines. A Victrola played Christmas carols, filling the room with holiday cheer. The cook who stayed behind to serve the missionaries was busy rustling up a feast befitting an American holiday: roasted duck, sweet potatoes, boiled cabbage, long green beans, and steamed buns. The live duck had been procured the previous morning from a poultry dealer. Alice took it upon herself to bake an apple pie flavored with anise and cassia buds.

Dr. Taylor strolled in, puffing on a cigar. Mr. Hill opened a bottle of Chinese wine he had purchased for the occasion from a local wine shop frequented by foreigners, and Miss Sherman and Alice were decorating the table. A few of the missionaries sang along with the Victrola, a bit off-key but with true holiday spirit. A metallic clang sounded outside the main door, and within a few seconds the door opened, with a spray of cold rain.

"Reverend Wu! Merry Christmas!" called out Alice enthusiastically as the young minister stumbled into the room. He was breathing hard and soaking wet.

Everyone clapped and gathered around the young minister. Miss Sherman grabbed a towel and started to dry his hair. Dr. Taylor took his overcoat and waterlogged hat, shaking off the excess rainwater onto the floor.

"Where did you come from?" asked an astonished Miss Myers.

"North. Hundred li," answered Reverend Wu, in short gasps.

"My Lord!" exclaimed Miss Sherman.

"Reverend Chen?" someone asked.

"He is in Tongcheng. One hundred fifty li."

"Fifty miles," Dr. Taylor calculated for the group. A few groaned. For even the most venturesome and fit person, it would be a challenge. Dr. Taylor turned back to Reverend Wu. "The Japs took Nanking. But things are quiet here."

"Yes, yes," Rev Wu acknowledged sadly.

"Bloody mess!" swore Mr. Hill.

The thought quieted the room. The group shared somber glances, then looked at Reverend Wu.

"No worry," stated Reverend Wu resolutely, as if reading their minds. He rubbed his hands and went to stand by the warmth of the coal-burning stove in the corner of the room. "He promises. Christmas evening."

The next day was quiet. There were no bombings, although the rain was still coming down steadily. Reverend Wu recovered from his journey and was washed and dressed. He performed a simple Eucharist service for the foreigners. They continued to prepare for the festivities.

The cook had wrung the neck of the doomed duck in expert fashion, then plucked, scalded, and gutted it. After seasoning the skin with salt, the cook hung the duck in the kitchen, where it was now drying from the previous night. He prepared the rest of the meal, including the dough and filling for the steamed buns. There was a lot of chopping, mincing, and mixing. Dr. Taylor came in to inspect his work and patted his back with approval.

As each person drifted in, they placed a present under the small Christmas tree. The room filled up throughout the afternoon as the missionaries settled into idle chat and sipped Chinese rice wine. The rain and the wind continued as they waited; their worry grew with each hour that ticked by.

"It would be foolish to come. He should wait for the weather to clear," said Alice to no one in particular.

Miss Myers reached under the Christmas tree and took a small package wrapped in red, handing it to Dr. Taylor.

"Merry Christmas, Dr. Taylor."

"Thank you, Miss Myers."

He, in turn, took a long flat box and handed it to Alice.

Each person exchanged a gift for another. They unwrapped their packages: a silk scarf for Alice, cigarettes for Reverend Wu, a pipe for Dr. Taylor, a souvenir jade perfume bottle for Miss Browne.

The door blew open again. The rain was still coming down in sheets, and a Chinese worker stumbled in. He shook his head, throwing off streams of moisture. The Victrola stopped playing and Alice went over to put on some Christmas hymns. No one said a word as the muted, soulful melody of "Silent Night" drifted throughout the rooms. They continued to wait.

MR. HILL GLANCED AT HIS WATCH. IT WAS AFTER SIX AND GET-ting dark outside. Dr. Taylor looked at his own pocket timepiece and suddenly clapped impatiently.

"Come on! It's Christmas!" his voice boomed. He nodded to Reverend Wu, who motioned for the cook to start warming the meal. The group gradually made its way to the large table.

"Time for grace, Reverend Wu," announced Dr. Taylor.

The missionaries, now about twenty in number, distributed themselves behind the seats. The table sparkled with bright flames from fragrant candles. The guests stood with bowed heads.

"Heavenly Father, we give thanks this joyous season," began Reverend Wu. "In times of conflict and suffering, you have blessed us with your love in the glorious coming of your Son, Jesus Chri—"

The door flew open with a bang, causing the flames to dance, and another Chinese worker rushed in, startling everyone. He was dripping wet.

"Chen *Mushi*!" gasped the man, pointing to the Cathedral. "*Ta lai le!*" He has arrived!

Miss Myers let out a delighted, high-pitched squeal. The group ran out after the worker without bothering with rain gear; the windblown droplets hit them like a cold slap to the face. They continued sprinting toward the Cathedral's front door. It was Mr. Hill who was first to the bike leaning against the cathedral gate. He immediately recognized it and opened the heavy wooden doors.

They piled into the church. The cold cavernous space was dry, dark, and quiet—a perfect sanctuary. They saw Robin kneeling at the altar. He turned his head as they approached and rose quickly to greet them. He smiled broadly at his friends. The solemnity of the house of God broke into a loud cheer and the heavy rain landing on the roof of the Cathedral sounded like voices that filled the room.

The giddy group returned to the dining room with Robin's trusted bike in tow. Alice turned up the Victrola volume as the group's cheerful chitter-chatter increased and the feasting began in earnest. Throughout the evening, word spread of Robin's return. He had kept his promise. More and more people showed up at the mission to celebrate the holiday spirit. Miss Monteiro scrounged up food among the surprise attendees and, by the end of the evening, the count exceeded an astounding one hundred and twenty mouths: missionaries, ministers, refugees, patients, and hospital and mission workers. Everyone pitched in and everyone was sated.

With war brewing all around them, they were intent on celebrating the everlasting joy brought into the world that night. Jesus Christ was born! Friends had returned safely! They could not ask for more.

OVER THE NEXT WEEK OR TWO, THE CITY RETURNED TO A SEM-
blance of normality. Thousands of refugees returned to their homes, like
white-naped cranes and swan geese migrating to their winter nests. Seeing
the city was not being attacked, Robin sent for his family and the rest of the
congregation. His family moved into Dr. Sung's house when the hospital's
superintendent and surgeon left for Chungking with government officials.
Businesses reopened and church services were resumed.

Robin gathered his staff in the church office to discuss the ever-shifting
situation.

"Thanks to God, everyone is safe," Robin stated. "We must get back to as
normal a life as possible."

He spoke to Lloyd in Wuhu by phone and received details of the conditions there.

"The Japanese have occupied the city," Lloyd reported. "They tore down
our flag at the church."

"They'll be reprimanded for that!" spat Dr. Taylor upon hearing of the
incident.

Robin relayed that the Wuhu mission was safe, and the Japanese had
left the compound. But the flag incident was not the worst of it; before the
soldiers withdrew, they raped three women. He did not go into any more
details. There was only so much they could handle.

"We must reopen the school," he said, the heavy tone of his voice reflecting urgency. "We cannot waste time. Our children's education *must* continue."

St. Agnes and St. James schools opened their doors again, and students
returned to classes. The clinic continued to treat refugees and soldiers. Over
six hundred refugees were offered shelter, but soldiers were turned away for
fear of creating a target for the Japanese.

Robin worked to maintain a calm and normal routine within the mission, but on the outside that was not at all so easy.

Chapter 28

THE WATCH

Generalissimo Chiang and his government retreated west to Chung-king, leaving remnants of his army scattered from Wuhu to Anking and Wuhan. The police force in Anking was debilitated and ineffectual. As a result, crime was rampant. People scrambled for what they could find to survive to the next day. Robberies became a daily occurrence, and thieves were rarely apprehended, leaving them to steal another day.

While preparing for services at the Cathedral, Robin noticed he had forgotten his watch. He sent a young acolyte with Constance to retrieve it at Dr. Sung's house, where his family was staying.

He was typically organized and returned things to their proper place so Constance looked for the watch on top of the bedroom bureau. Not finding it, she immediately remembered what had happened the previous night.

While asleep in their bed on the second floor, she had been awakened by a noise she thought came from the dining room. She and Robin lay still, listening for any further disturbance.

"*Da shu!*" Robin muttered sleepily. Rats.

"Hui left food for the silkworms," suggested Constance.

Mulberry leaves were the sole diet for the worms but a favorite feast for rats as well.

"They will go away," Robin suggested.

Hearing nothing further, they went back to sleep.

The rattling soon began anew, and Constance sent Robin to investigate.

The basket of silkworms and mulberry leaves was undisturbed. Nothing else was amiss and he retired to bed.

Constance now realized the noise the night before was from a thief going through their belongings. The intruder had brazenly stolen the watch from beside their sleeping heads.

Constance brought the unfortunate news back to Robin. He went on with the Sunday service, recalling for the congregation the brutal destruction of Nanking. He chose not to dwell on the commonplace crime involving his stolen watch.

"No demand for our services is greater than what we are witnessing," he preached. "We feel powerless to help our fellow man escape the mass butchery. But God has worked enough miracles throughout history to assure us that it is in Him, and only in Him, that we shall be triumphantly carried through the present cataclysms. When evils of the age are baptized by the blood of Christ and met by a growing Christian spirit among His children, we shall not only find salvation of the Chinese people, but also the final victory of the world!"

The detectives were called in after the morning service. Finding nothing except for a jimmied front door, there was little they could do except write a report. Tracking down a thief in the city would be like trying to find the rat that stole a silkworm's dinner.

"War brings such chaos," Constance lamented to the detectives.

"People are desperate," rationalized Robin. It was futile to expect the watch to be recovered.

Over the next few days, Dr. Taylor's house was robbed, as was Miss Browne's. Then Miss Monteiro's bicycle was stolen. She reported the description to the local police and dismissed the loss, with little confidence in its return. They all forgave these trespasses, as good Christians would. Mostly, they were inconveniences, which they had come to accept living in China, where desperation and hopelessness was often a way of life. To forgive and forget was necessary.

The conflict continued to bring wounded soldiers into the hospital. Dr. Taylor and his Chinese counterparts worked hard to keep up with the load imposed after Dr. Sung's departure. Robin was busy helping Mr. Hill straighten out the church's finances, which were in disarray from the recent diaspora. After a few weeks back, he was finally getting a handle on disbursing funds to cover expenses incurred over the last months of the year.

Robin decided to make the rounds of the primary school, clinic, and hospital with Alice, Reverend Wu, and a few other staff. They went to a classroom where young girls were doing math. He smiled, seeing the students studying seriously despite the siege.

The next classroom was completely different. It was crowded with dozens of refugees. One was a Shanghainese woman, sitting on the floor weeping. Robin stooped down next to her.

"Why are you crying?" he asked, placing a gentle hand on her shoulder.

The woman could not answer, her sobs causing her to gasp haltingly for air.

"She was separated from her husband on the way from Shanghai. Now she cannot find him," Alice explained.

Robin turned to one of the mission workers.

"Send word to refugee camps. See if they can locate him," he ordered. He turned back to reassure the woman. "*Bu ku.*"

"We will find your husband," Alice added as she hugged the distraught woman. Her gesture was adequate translation for the woman.

In a corner of the room was a soldier with a tear in his pants from a shrapnel wound to his leg. He had been transported by cart from the riverbank and left in the mission. Robin stooped over the soldier and gently pulled back the edges of the rent in the pants. Stripping the cloth from the skin caused the soldier to wince and released the fetid odor of putrid meat. Dark blood had congealed into a dull, gelatinous mass around the base of the wound, and a crusted crimson ribbon trailed down to his ankle. Robin peered into the fist-sized, gaping hole. The wound moved as if alive. He leaned closer. In the depths of the jagged crater was a layer of grey maggots, writhing and crawling over the liquefying tissue. A spicule of exposed bone jutted through the soft mass. He could see the squirming creatures devouring the necrotic flesh.

Robin quickly motioned to the mission worker and Reverend Wu as he grabbed the soldier's shoulders. They hoisted the soldier off the ground and carried him to the hospital. The worker summoned Dr. Taylor, who immediately ordered his nurses to transport the soldier to the operating theater.

In the hospital hallway, filled with wounded and sick patients, the stifling air reverberated with anguished cries and moans, as if it were the antechamber to purgatory. Robin spied a young soldier on the floor leaning against a wall. He could not have been more than seventeen or eighteen. *Perhaps a few years older than Paul,* Robin sadly thought. His uniform was muddied by battle and hung loosely on his fragile frame, as if life itself had been sucked from his being. He was slumped over, barely breathing. His body was shattered, far too injured to waste resources to try to save. He had been placed in the corner and his head and shoulders covered with a blanket to live out the last few minutes of his sorry, desiccated life.

Robin knelt down and took the young man's hand in his. He asked his name, but nothing came from his mouth. His jaw was askew, and his trembling lips were bruised and swollen. His breathing was too shallow to form words— not even the guttural gasping of a dying creature—and his glazed-over eyes sat motionless in their deep sockets, staring at Robin with the emptiness of the already dead. There was a hint of a flicker in his eyes upon hearing Robin's voice. Robin felt a slight pressure in his hand and nodded slowly to the boy. He fixed his gaze on the boy's eyes, holding onto them as if they were the only fragile connection left to tangible life. Robin began to pray for the boy's comfort and his soul—a private moment between the two of them and God. He prayed God would forgive his deeds as a soldier and redeem his soul.

Before he could finish, the boy's eyes went blank and his hand limp. Holding lifelessness, Robin felt weak and helpless. All around him was death and despair. They kept coming, and coming again, and there was nothing he could do to stem the pain. He felt the same as he had at the gravesite in Nanling. Another son was lost. He sensed tears beginning to weep out, and quickly forced them away.

Miss Gregg and Reverend Wu reached to pull Robin away from the boy. As Robin released his grip on the boy's hand, there was a loud commotion at the doorway. A rush of hospital personnel surrounded a man in green military garb. The man was tall, standing almost a head above the workers, and sported a neatly trimmed moustache. He had wide shoulders and a stocky build that showed through his tight uniform. The man easily shoved the workers aside.

"*Shei? Shei?*" Who? Who? the man demanded.

Weeks ago, General Yang had retreated with his men to Anking from Shanghai and been placed in charge of the city's defense. He now had a small, frightened girl, perhaps six or seven years old, in tow, along with two uniformed underlings.

"*Tsai na?*" Where? his voice boomed at the waiflike child.

The General's face contorted tensely. His lower lip pushed out disagreeably. He roughly pushed the girl in front. She looked at all the patients and timidly pointed to a soldier cowering in the corner. General Yang strode up to the man and jabbed a finger in his face.

"*Ta?*" Him? he asked.

The girl nodded as Robin rose quickly to confront the general. The general went for the soldier and grabbed his wrist.

"Steal a child's bicycle? *Gou shi!*" Dog shit! he yelled, spit flying from his mouth as he tore a watch from the terrified soldier's wrist.

"General Yang. *Dui bu shi!*" I am sorry! the soldier pleaded, as he shrank away from the wild-eyed general. "I beg ... !"

"You disgrace me! *Ni she!*" You snake! the general snarled, shoving the soldier hard against the wall.

"Please, please!" begged the soldier. He was near tears.

"General Yang, Please, forgive him!" pleaded Robin.

General Yang pulled out his pistol from his waist holster and pointed it at the soldier's forehead. Screams filled the room.

"*Bu shing!*" No! protested Robin.

"*Ching, ching!*" Please, please! the soldier continued to beg, his hands folded in supplication. Tears streamed down his face.

Robin grabbed the general's arm, but the officer was much too strong to be deterred. He yanked his arm away with ease.

"Disgrace! Dog! Snake! Thief!"

The insults shot out fast and loud. General Yang's eyes widened as if the globes were about to launch out of his face like missiles. Without warning, General Yang pulled the trigger. The soldier's head exploded as the bullet penetrated his forehead and shattered the back of his skull in a spray of bright red, splattering against the dingy wall. His body fell clumsily off the bed and onto the floor. The whole room screamed, and the little girl threw her hands over her eyes as she let out a shriek.

Without another word, General Yang handed the watch to Robin, plowed his way through the crowd, and stormed out of the room.

It was later learned that the soldier had been in the hospital for days, observing the comings and goings of the missionary personnel. At various times, he would sneak out of the hospital, enter their homes, and rob them. After the execution, crimes against church people ended.

Chapter 29

A KULING SUMMER

For most of the spring, Anking enjoyed a rest from Japanese threat, which was directed north in Kiangsu and Shandong provinces. The mission schools ran quite normally, and the refugee situation calmed down as the city activity resumed its regular tone and pace. Robin was determined to put on a good face. His people were being pulled in many directions. Any faltering, any indication of doubt, might cause his congregation to abandon the church—something it could not afford. Chinese leadership was beginning to take shape, requiring even more commitment from each minister. To lose ground now would be a grave blow to its goals.

As summer approached, the Japanese secured victories in Suchow and Tsingtao in the North. They pivoted strategies and resumed their march westward towards Anking and Kiukiang. After Nanking was overrun, it seemed inevitable that the war would progress inland, toward the new capital seat in Chungking. Robin and Lloyd both felt they were about to face another serious onslaught. Even against the conjoined armies of the Nationalists and Communists, the Japanese armored troops and air forces were far superior. America and other Western powers were reluctant to commit their military might towards China's defense.

It was a Protestant tradition to hold a summer conference in the mountaintop resort of Kuling, named by an English missionary, Edward Selby Little. Appreciative of the cool currents of mountain air that offered necessary relief from the "torrid heat" and heavy humidity of the lowlands,

Little called upon his British wit to immortalize the town's name with his humorous homophonic pun. At the end of the last century, he established a retreat for foreigners on the gentle slopes of a valley, high in these tranquil Lushan mountains southwest of Anking, thirty-four hundred feet above sea level. The European-style community featured hundreds of large villas, conference buildings, chapels, and the American School for the children of missionaries. Generalissimo Chiang used the center for summer vacations with his Methodist wife, Mei-ling, who knew of the place from its regular conferences. Only the previous year, Chou En-lai had met Chiang at Kuling to initiate the CCP's temporary and tenuous alliance with the KMT.

Robin agreed with Lloyd that holding the conference for mission workers would allow them an escape from the heat of battle in the cities and provide spiritual relief with study and prayer sessions. Bishop Huntington wanted to hear more of their plans and summoned Robin to Hankow. Aware that those in Anking and other diocesan stations would have to travel hundreds of miles to reach Kuling, he worried about the risk.

"Fear and concern for one's own safety is a prison," argued Robin. "When man surrenders his own self, he can venture for greater things in the Kingdom of God. We show strength and hope in our freedom."

Bishop Huntington let the words settle in.

"We should convene the program in Kuling," Robin continued, not waiting for a response. "The Japanese have no designs on the area."

"You think that wise? The situation can worsen at any moment."

"Lloyd agrees. We cannot let the conflict stop our work. People need constant feeding, or their spirit will fade."

"Our people do depend on us to push forward," mused Bishop Huntington.

"Especially in adversity," Robin added.

"Then you must give them hope," Bishop Huntington said with conviction.

"The mountain will do everyone good, and it is safer than in the cities," Robin concluded agreeably.

"I leave it in your hands," the bishop replied.

Bishop Huntington arranged for the use of the resort from the Presbyterians, who had been running it since the center's return from British control two years before. After they conferred with the ambassador, consul general, and regional army commander, invitations for the conference went out to mission workers and their families throughout the diocese.

⌒ ⊕ ⌒

ABOUT TWO HUNDRED PEOPLE WERE EXPECTED TO ATTEND, AS more and more church members weathered the damp June of 1938. Week after week, they came from every corner of the diocese until there were over four hundred Christians present. All made the difficult trek up the mountain. Some required sedan chairs carried by sure-footed coolies to negotiate the steep path, one stretch of which counted a thousand steps up a stone staircase. Homes lining the side streets that branched off the main route were apportioned. Robin, his family, and Hui's pet parrot settled into a hilltop house at the end of one of the roads.

The Craighills, Miss Clark, and Miss Sherman shared another house that had a wide veranda, where dozens of bags of rice and other dry and canned goods were stored. Food was already becoming scarce in the surrounding area. If nothing else, they had to have rice.

The meeting proved to be well-timed, as the Japanese captured Anking a few days later, on June 12. By then, ninety percent of the population had fled the doomed city. The conference took on more significance as the people sought something to shore up their spirits and to give them hope against what was looking like a bleak future. Rather than waste this opportunity, they were determined to turn the detritus of war into fruits of spirituality.

Earlier in the year, Generalissimo Chiang, with encouragement from his influential wife, lifted the ban on religious studies that had been in effect in all mission schools. Robin, who headed the Committee on Religious Life, poured ideas into activities for the group. There were classes for religious and secular learning, Sunday school for children, a Young People's Fellowship group, choir sessions, Altar Guild training, and instruction in singing for the general congregation. Committees were formed to take care of food, sanitation, security, health, and education. A vibrant Christian community was constructed at this edge of the growing conflict.

From the center's high perch overlooking the valley and river, they could keep an eye on the movement of Japanese forces. Most assumed the

Japanese would not have any interest in the mountainous retreat. As such, they all felt safe.

The center's population continued to grow with familiar faces. Bishop Huntington arrived towards the end of June with some of his staff. Reverend Wu and Reverend Wang came with their families. It seemed like the whole diocese had flocked to this hospitable hamlet of hope. No one was turned away. Every study class was filled. Bellies were satiated. People doubled up in the available beds at night. The mountain air echoed with the sounds of the choir. Only on a few occasions was their song and spirit broken by the thunder of bombs exploding in the distant valley.

Grace supervised the younger children as they chased after birds and hiked along the mountain streams, from whose crystal-clear, nature-filtered rivulets they drank to quench their summer thirst. The streams, cascading under stone bridges and down shiny rocks polished by endless time, produced miniature waterfalls. The cool water emptied into quiet, shallow pools where children could swim and playfully splash away any care for the woes of war.

Hui and Helen found wild chestnuts that their cook roasted. They hunted sweet strawberries in the underbrush of the verdant hillside. They ate the ripe fruit, freshly rinsed with morning dew, directly off the stems, impressing their young minds with memorably clean flavors of Kuling.

Grace and Paul hiked for whole days with a dozen of their friends and explored the dense mountain forest, discovering magical waterfalls and fields of stellate red tiger lilies and bright yellow dogwood shrubs. They played croquet and badminton on the lawn of the conference center. On warmer days, they would just sit under towering evergreen trees and consider their future. Despite their closeness in age, they exchanged little conversation. School was most important to them, and their dreams remained captive within their own heads. Like most Chinese brothers and sisters, they rarely pried into the other's thoughts. To them, Kuling was a fun-filled vacation, bursting with nature's colors and distracting laughter, not a dark hiding place from bloody conflict.

The adult leaders were not as optimistic. While they felt safe high above the valley, they were well aware of Japan's ultimate goal to occupy China. The presence of gunboats dotting the river surface was a constant reminder.

To ensure they would not suffer the same fate as Nanking, every road leading to the valley was marked prominently with an American flag. Every house owned by foreigners had an image of that flag painted on its door, like the protective mark of blood from a sacrificial lamb.

Every evening, foreigners surrounded one of the shortwave radios at the American School and listened anxiously to the progress of the war. Each time, more ominous reports trickled through; the Japanese forces were pushing further westward, upriver toward Kiukiang, just twenty miles north of the center. Refugees in the region were encouraged to seek out the numerous camps operated by the government, the Red Cross, and missionary organizations.

TOWARDS THE END OF SUMMER, ROBIN BECAME CONCERNED that Paul and Grace would miss the beginning of their high school year. The importance of school even during war was firmly ingrained in his thinking. Peasants comprised the vast majority of the population, but it would be the educated youth who would lead the country towards its future and an equal standing with the rest of the world.

Robin arranged for Paul and Grace to take a cargo barge four hundred and fifty li, or one hundred and fifty miles, to Wuhan. The night before they were to depart, Paul eagerly packed his belongings, including his harmonica and some Chinese novels, and climbed quickly into bed.

"Why must we leave again?" asked Grace. "What if the Japanese arrive while we are gone?"

"Father has prepared everything," Paul answered with a slight frown. "Why worry?"

"How can you not?" said Grace. She wished she had her brother's confidence; perhaps she might have felt differently if she were a boy.

Paul shrugged and turned on his side.

"Father believes school is important. *That* is what is certain. Anything else, I do not know."

"Do you want to go?" Grace asked.

There was a long silence.

"Of course, I should go," Paul answered.

"Do you *want* to go?" she persisted.

Another long silence.

"Father wants me to go."

"Because you are the son," Grace said, pointing out the obvious.

"He treats us the same," Paul said plainly.

"And the oldest," she added, knowing he meant that she should be the same as him.

"Get on the boat," he said, closing his eyes. "Everything will be good."

She should feel the same, even if she was not a son. She wished it were so easy. She should want to go. But she was still wide awake when Paul fell asleep.

THE NEXT MORNING, THE FAMILY WALKED DOWN THE MOUN-tain to the river docks and handed the luggage to the bargemen. Paul bounded onto the barge, as did a daughter of a family friend. Grace looked down at her feet, willing them to move across the small gap between the dock and the barge. She did not look at her parents, fearful she would break down and cry. She gingerly placed one foot on the edge of the barge, then shuffled across the space onto the gently rocking deck.

Robin and Constance, with Helen and Hui by their side, watched as bargemen threw off the lines and the boat began to drift away. Constance pressed her lips together, fighting back tears.

Suddenly, Grace began to cry. She turned to her parents. Tears flowed down her face. She knew her father wanted her to go; she did not want to disappoint him. But she could not leave. They had no home. They had nowhere to go. What if the Japanese came and swallowed her family while she was gone? What if she never saw her sisters again? She could hardly bear the thought.

"*Ma! Ba! Wo bu yao chu!*" she cried. I do not want to go!

Her hands reached out to touch her mother's. Tears leaked through her eyelids.

"*Bu chu!*" Do not go! her mother shouted. "You don't have to go!"

Constance's face dissolved into a palette of anguish upon seeing Grace cry.

Seeing her mother cry made Grace cry harder. She scolded herself: *Bu ku! Do not cry!*

As the boat separated from the dock, Grace lunged toward her mother and grabbed her hands tightly. Then she leaped onto the dock. For a brief moment, she teetered on the edge of the wooden planks, almost pulling her mother off her feet. They embraced, each saving the other, until Grace found solid footing.

Paul shot Grace a scowl and quickly tossed her luggage onto the docks. He waved to his family. Grace could tell he was upset. All she read on his face was disappointment.

Grace saw her father take a deep breath, let it out slowly, then quietly pick up her luggage. She wondered if he was as angry as Paul. For now, she would not worry. The barge was too far away and there was nothing more she could do. She was just relieved to be back on the dock with her family.

Chapter 30

KILL THE CHICKEN, SCARE THE MONKEY

rom the cragged cliffs looking towards the east, a keen eye or one with
a handy spyglass could observe the river connecting the Yangtse in the
north with Poyang Lake to the south. Lloyd had previously noted booms,
far off to the east, strung across the river to impede the progress of gunboats.

"They have breached the barrier," he announced grimly, as he handed the
spyglass to Alice. The booms were gone, and he could see half a dozen Japanese
gunboats pushing their way up the river. Small wakes trailed their bows,
making a pattern of white V's, like aquatic arrows aiming toward the retreat.

"They won't come here, will they?" Alice asked tentatively.

"There is nothing here for them," he answered reassuringly. But inside,
he was not so sure.

OVER THE NEXT FEW DAYS, THE PRICE OF EGGS INCREASED EXPO-
nentially until none could be had. Shopping expeditions returned with less
and less rice. Soon, villagers ventured up the mountain into the conference
center seeking food; the Protestant group were rumored to have more provi-
sions than any other organization on the mountain.

Miss Sherman was in charge of a brood of hens housed in a coop near
the dining hall. She complained to Robin that they had not been laying any
eggs for a number of weeks, despite a steady diet of boiled rice.

"Every day, nothing," she complained. "They eat but produce nothing."

"*Sha ji, jing hou,*" replied Robin.

Lloyd and Miss Sherman looked at him blankly.

"Kill the chicken, scare the monkey," Robin translated. "Enjoy one, others will pay attention."

He and Lloyd laughed at the joke. But he was quite serious. If the hens were not contributing …

That night, the cook efficiently slit the throat of one of the chickens, causing blood to squirt onto the ground until the fowl was still and completely drained. He cooked the chicken and served it to Robin and the other ministers. As they enjoyed the chicken, they noted that the sparse sounds of distant bombing were growing more frequent and louder. Whereas the noise had come predominantly from due east, they agreed that now, bombs were dropping to the northeast and southeast. They were being surrounded by the Japanese.

Word came that the Japanese had taken Kiukiang, north of Lushan. That meant Generalissimo Chiang's defenses were not holding. The local commander sent word to Bishop Huntington that he could not guarantee their safety any longer. While it was inevitable that Wuhan would be next on the way to the displaced capital of Chungking, Nanchang, the large capital of Kiangsi province to the south, was also a likely target. Lushan would be right in the middle of the Japanese army's southward path from Kiukiang.

The next morning, hundreds and hundreds of villagers arrived from the Kiukiang region, beginning at dawn. It was an extraordinary sight. It started as a trickle, until people were streaming in from the main road and the many side footpaths. Bishop Huntington, Miss Sherman, and Miss Clark were on the veranda, taking inventory. Bishop Huntington stared in disbelief as the first groups straggled up the road. They emerged from every path, swarming through the resort. Miss Sherman immediately signaled for one of the coolies to fetch Robin, who soon arrived with Lloyd.

"They have no place to stay," explained Miss Sherman, having questioned a few villagers. "No food."

"We have barely enough ourselves," reported Miss Clark.

Robin conferred with Bishop Huntington and Lloyd. This was not good. The center was already overcrowded. Their food supplies were low and not being adequately replenished. And the presence of the peasants from all sides of the mountain could only mean the Japanese were closing in from various directions.

By the time the logistics for housing and food were worked out in the late afternoon, there were nearly one thousand more stomachs to fill and a thousand more bodies to house. The designated refugee camps and safe zones in the area were filling up quickly, and word, however mistaken, had gotten out that the Protestants in Kuling had a healthy store of food. Unfortunately, that news was a couple of weeks old and hundreds of mouths earlier.

"We can feed them for a few days, but they cannot stay," announced Robin. It bothered him, but he had no choice. The center would run out of food within the month, and the conditions would only get worse. He wanted to feed them all. He wanted to give people hope and lift their spirits. But he could not work miracles.

The cook prepared *hsi fan*, the everyday porridge, using one part rice to twelve parts water. Add a few slivers of green vegetables, slices of fragrant ginger, some threads of dried meat floss mixed with saltiness from soy sauce, and a cup of rice could feed a dozen people. It was not much of a feast, but it did appease their growling bellies. None of the visitors complained. In fact, they were uniformly grateful. Some joined the missionaries in saying grace for the first time in their lives.

Robin and Miss Sherman went to check on the hens after the prior evening's chicken dinner. Miss Sherman entered the coop with a basket that had gone unfilled for weeks. She looked under the hens.

"Yay!" she squealed.

Two freshly laid eggs!

She gathered up the precious pair, placed them in her basket, and presented them to Robin as if they were jewels. Both laughed at their good fortune.

"God heard our prayers," said Miss Sherman with a smile.

"Perhaps the chickens *are* paying attention," Robin joked.

From that day on, Miss Sherman collected fresh eggs every morning. It was not much, but the daily treasures made her and the cook quite happy.

The new guests were divided up among the available houses. Rooms were utilized many times beyond their intended capacity. At night, church members lay head to head and feet to feet with strangers. Babies and children snuggled on their parents' or older siblings' bodies. Rooms meant for four or six were packed with fifty people covering every inch of the floor. Despite this, there was no trouble between any of the guests. The extraordinary communal spirit was heartening to everyone in this dark hour of their lives.

Some guests required medical treatment at one of two makeshift hospitals, converted from chapels and staffed by various church groups. The resort population quickly grew to over six thousand, including almost two hundred foreigners. The Catholics themselves housed over two thousand refugees.

As the week after the villagers arrived wore on, the food supply was seriously dwindling. Robin and Reverend Wu gave the bad news to their new guests and pointed them in the direction of the refugee camps to the south. The villagers packed up, thanked the missionaries, and descended back down the mountain without argument. They were fish caught between the net and the shore and found themselves back at sea. Robin did not know how much longer his own group could hold out; they certainly could not yet go back home.

Every night, foreigners hunched over the radio, listening to the enemy's progress towards the base of the mountain.

"Japanese are spotted heading south from Kiukiang as gunboats move inland. Generalissimo Chiang makes a stand with his forces at Wuhan, while refugees stream into camps near Tehan and Nanchang," crackled the English radio announcer.

"The noose is tightening," observed Bishop Huntington, stone-faced.

The conference pushed on with classes and prayer sessions, hoping that the mountain would be spared. Children continued to frolic on the colorful hillside and hike into the forest. Robin and the other ministers still led Bible discussion groups. But when the coolies returned from their shopping trips in the villages below with only one or two bags of rice and with reports that most of the homes were abandoned, decisions had to be made. Bishop Huntington conferred with the local commander, then called for a strategy session.

The conference leadership gathered in the dining room in the evening. A large map of the region was placed in the center of the table. Lloyd marked the map with a black pen.

"The local commander says they will not be able to hold off the approaching forces," reported Bishop Huntington. "He advises immediate evacuation and has agreed to send some protection from the Fourth Army."

"Fourth Army?" asked Lloyd skeptically.

The Fourth Army was a recent amalgam of guerrilla troops left over from the Red Army. Most of the Red Army was up north after the Long March, but the conjoined forces ended up with some of these soldiers south of the Yangtse—exactly where the Japanese were now heading. It was a strange coalition, as the Nationalists and the Communists had been hell-bent on mutual destruction. Many thought it uncomfortably ironic that, while previously focused as much on opposing Christians and foreigners as on destroying the Nationalists, the Red Army soldiers were now instructed to give protection to these same groups. Just as disconcerting was the stark realization that the Kuling congregation, both Chinese and Westerners, cut off from their homes, were now in fact not merely attendees at a religious conference, but refugees.

Robin and Bishop Huntington huddled over the map and pointed out escape routes. Lloyd leaned in and blacked out the main road that the commander reported was cut off by Japanese troops. Other exit routes were also eliminated. The map was soon scored with bold black slashes.

"This is the only way down," explained Lloyd as he showed a small trail to the group. "The Japanese are here ... here ... here."

"Are we ... too late?" asked one of the foreigners hesitantly.

"We will soon find out," Robin answered wryly. "South ... then west. Four groups ... to Nanchang. A hundred li to the camps at Tehan."

There were no objections. The congregation was organized into the four groups. The cook was instructed to boil all the remaining rice so it could be portioned out to each individual. They had finished off the last can of pumpkin the previous night; the center was completely out of food. When they would be able to procure food again was not at all certain.

Robin told Constance he would stay in the last group to leave the resort and assist Bishop Huntington, who had just turned 70. She was to go in the second group, with their three daughters. They told the girls to pack only what they could carry in their hands or on their backs and that, if they became separated, they would find each other in the government refugee camp near Nanchang. Nothing was valuable enough to keep, except the parrot. Hui could not abandon the pet she had so devotedly nursed back to health.

Chapter 31

FIELD OF DEATH

Groups of a hundred each were escorted down the lone narrow side trail each day. Fifty coolies shouldering rattan sedan chairs and carrying bamboo poles helped transport older members, small children, the sick and infirm, and some luggage. Constance, her three daughters, and their amahs went in the second group, while Robin was in the last with Bishop Huntington, Miss Clark, and Miss Sherman.

A handful of the Fourth Army guerrillas accompanied each group, as promised by the local commander. The soldiers donned coolie garments to disguise their presence and lurked inconspicuously at the periphery of columns of refugees. Each was armed with a Russian-made rifle and had a pair of pineapple and pear grenades tucked into outer vest pockets.

After an initial gradual descent, the path down the mountain became steeper. At one point, the trail devolved into a slippery mess, forcing people to slide down a mossy slope. This was fun for the children, but terrifying to less agile elders. The coolies were skillful at negotiating these challenges and carried their loads with ease. Without them, the exodus would have been impossible.

As those in the first group made their way through the lush forest, they caught glimpses of Japanese planes through breaks in the canopy overhead. The planes often flew quite low but never dropped any bombs. By the time the later groups embarked on their leg of the evacuation, machine-gun fire could be heard echoing through the trees.

Constance walked hand-in-hand with Hui for most of the trek. She shuffled slowly because of her half-bound feet but refused to ride in a sedan. There were other women whose deformed feet were half her size and needed to be carried. *Step by step, however slow,* Constance thought, *like a silkworm munching through a mulberry leaf.* Within a few hours, they lagged behind Helen and Grace.

On the journey down the mountain, almost every home was empty. Abandoned villages were void of any life. Shops were closed and stripped bare. There were more stray dogs than people. An eerie air of fear permeated the region like its oppressive humidity.

Hui and Constance walked past rows of empty stores; there was hardly anything to see. But suddenly, they came upon one shop where a crowd had gathered, chattering noisily in front of the window. They pushed forward for a peek.

Five bloodied heads were on prominent display, hanging like roasted pig carcasses in a butcher shop. Droplets of coagulated blood leaking from the open veins pooled beneath the heads into small, individual puddles. Constance smothered Hui so her eyes would not meet the empty gazes staring back. Around each head hung signs identifying the victims of misfortune: *traitor, Japanese, traitor, traitor, Japanese.* Constance pulled Hui tighter as she hurried by.

The soldiers left the group after they reached the lowlands and headed north to join the main forces outside Kiukiang and Wuhan. Constance and Hui entered the first refugee camp on the route to Nanchang. After receiving their identification tags, they immediately set out looking for Helen and Grace, who had arrived a few hours ahead. All three girls and their mother were quickly and tearfully reunited. The camp was teeming with refugees. The Japanese campaign had corralled everyone in their path.

The camp was a designated safe zone. For the most part, this convention was respected by all parties, even in Nanking, as long as it did not harbor enemy soldiers. The Japanese knew foreigners helped run these camps, and they were not eager to stir the international community against it, especially the United States.

After a supper of steamed buns, Constance and her daughters retired to a large tent and snuggled together for what sleep they could get. They still had a long day's hike ahead to reach the next camp, just outside of Nanchang.

The three sisters lay quietly with their mother. Their idyllic summer had been suddenly broken into fragments of memories—some peaceful and tranquil, others colorfully adventurous and happy, both interspersed with horrid, dark images. They were adrift like twigs on a swift-flowing river, moved by the will of strong currents and the whim of swirling winds. They clung together as twigs would in water.

"Where is father?" asked Hui, her voice small and innocent.

"Do not worry," answered Constance as she stroked Hui's head. "He will come soon," she promised.

The camp was quiet except for the crickets.

"You walk too fast," Hui complained to her older sisters, remembering their earlier separation.

"Aieee," squealed Helen as she and Grace playfully spanked their little sister's thighs.

"You are right, Hui. We should stay together," Grace said seriously. She wrapped her arms around both sisters.

No one had anything more to say. Physical exhaustion overtook the sisters' bodies. Entwined within each other's arms, they surrendered quickly to safe oblivion.

THE FIRST GROUP WOKE EARLY AND RECEIVED A BOWL OF *HSI FAN*. Rice was all that anyone had, for every meal—sometimes overcooked into a soupy mess, sometimes undercooked and chalky, with a few unsuspected mealworms mixed in. Each person was given a few cubes of rice cake to quiet their internal rumbling later in the day. Most only had the clothes they were wearing, having discarded their belongings along the way. Hui had thrown off her backpack and carried only her parrot's cage.

"*Chih! Chih!*" Eat! Eat! the parrot squawked. "*Chi lai! Chi lai!*" Get up! Get up!

The sisters burst out laughing and thought about their home in Anking.

They walked south the whole day, toward Nanchang, finally reaching a large, abandoned house at the base of a mountain, in front of a clearing. It was almost dark, and the people were worn out. Their feet were sore. They were all hungry and wanted only to get to the final camp. Those who had any food shared it, making sure the children had at least some hard candy or strands of dried beef to keep them quiet.

Reverend Wu and Mr. Hill gathered the group into the hallway of the mansion and carefully explained the next part of the trip. The instructions were critically important, as was the impossible task of imparting a sense of calm.

"The camp is across the field ahead. Everyone must be as quiet as possible. The enemy is on the mountain to the east," informed Reverend Wu, although the group was already well aware of the gunfire.

"Keep quiet. Don't stop," instructed Mr. Hill.

"Run as quickly as possible. Once you reach the camp, you will be safe," said Mr. Wu.

For the next few hours, they waited. Hui tried to quiet her mind, which conjured horrible images of headless torsos. The relative quiet was intermittently punctuated with flashes of machine-gun fire, which flickered on the mountainside like firecrackers at a lunar celebration. An explosion kicked up a cloud of dirt and smoke as it landed in the empty fields. It was meant to intimidate and taunt. To those watching the clearing in the moonlight, it had its desired effect.

A baby cried loudly, eliciting a nervous murmur through the group. The mother muffled the baby, but its muted whimpering could still be heard. The tired group waited as quietly as possible. Some started to doze off.

The night wore into the early morning, until Reverend Wu roused the congregation from their uneasy slumber. The group went outside the mansion, which was set back from the edge of the woods. They crouched at the clearing's perimeter. The night had been quiet; the enemy was either sleeping or readying its firepower. They would soon find out which.

Constance and Hui, gripping her parrot's cage tightly, stood together. Grace and Helen knelt shoulder to shoulder, right behind. The rest of the group were lined up two or three persons deep. They could see faint light from the lamps in the camp. Grace estimated that it was two hundred meters away. It would take her perhaps less than two minutes to reach the other side. But it might take her mother and Hui, and certainly many of the older people, twice as long. Easy targets.

Grace could see the faint outline of a wire fence and some posts about halfway across. The sky began to show some light from the sun still low behind the mountains to the east. Otherwise, the field was nearly black. The ground looked flat, but bombs probably left craters she would have to be careful not to fall into. The lowland humidity had brought some showers and the ground was moist. That could trip them up in their sandals. She whispered all these observations to her mother and sisters. In the end, all they could do was run as fast as they could—and pray.

"Get ready!" said Reverend Wu in a startling loud voice. "Don't stop!"

He looked at Mr. Hill, who nodded.

"Go, go, go!"

Everyone took off and began to sprint towards the camp lights. Hui squeezed her mother's hand and pulled her forward. Constance had endured six pregnancies and had no trouble staying with Hui. The ground was soft. It did not take more than a few yards before many lost one or both sandals in the mud. They kept pushing forward, running as fast as fear urged them.

Grace and Helen sprinted side by side. Halfway to the fence, Grace tripped over a log. Helen grabbed the log to throw it aside. It was not a log. It was a man's leg.

Hui fell. Her face landed on the face of a corpse, its mouth gaping open in a frozen scream. The cage flew out of her hand and tumbled onto the ground. Constance held tight and pulled Hui up quickly. Hui scrambled after the cage.

"Let it go!" Constance shouted, tugging on Hui's arm.

"No!" Hui shouted back.

She broke free and reached for the cage. She grabbed the handle and jerked it out of the mud. Then she and Constance took off towards the camp again, with the cage rattling noisily in her grasp. All around them, people stumbled over one corpse after another. It was a field of death, a graveyard for Chinese who had become target practice. Children shrieked as a barrage of gunfire whistled over their heads. They all kept running, head down and headlong toward the beckoning lights of the camp. Those who fell were pulled up by a companion. Others who were too slow were half-carried by more able people. Everyone helped someone.

Grace and Helen reached the fence. As they squirmed through the wire, they could now see the posts in the faint light of dawn. But they were not posts. They were lifeless bodies slumped over the wire.

"Hurry! *Pao kwai!*" Run fast, they yelled at their mother and Hui. "Don't look!"

No one could think of anything but *run*. And *pray*. Run and pray. Run and pray.

At the end of the field, the whole group stumbled through the camp's entrance—exhausted, muddied, crying. No one was injured. No one was shot.

The morning sun rose quickly to bring light to the obstacle they had just traversed. The field of death was fully revealed, with lifeless bodies strewn throughout. The congregation looked beaten. They had smelled death. But they all were alive and safe—all, except the parrot.

Hui's inseparable pet lay at the bottom of its crushed cage. It was, miraculously, the group's sole casualty. Hui opened the crooked cage door, picked up the parrot in her small, soiled hands, and began to cry.

Chapter 32

SPIRIT OF BIRTH

The final group of one hundred was halfway down the mountain from Kuling when a church worker ran up, pulled on Robin's arm, and frantically gestured toward the trail ahead.

"*Lai! Kwai le!*" Come! Quickly!

Robin ran with the man and came upon a young woman lying by the side of the narrow path. She was writhing in pain, with a moist patch of ground between her legs. It was obvious she was about to give birth. Robin spied an abandoned mud hut amongst some trees. The front door had been torn from its frame. With the worker's help, he picked up the woman and carried her inside the thatched-roof hut. Other people followed, crowding curiously around the open doorway. Miss Clark went in as Robin and the worker laid the woman down on the dry ground and positioned her to deliver her baby.

Without any medical personnel in his group, Robin's memory went back to Hui's home birth, nearly a decade ago but still vivid. He squatted and placed his hands on the woman's pelvis. Miss Clark tore a broad strip from the bottom of her skirt to swaddle the baby. The woman grimaced but did not scream. She pushed harder and harder. Sweat ran down her forehead and cheeks. The hut was eerily quiet except for the woman's heavy panting and the muted whispers from the onlookers poking their heads through the open entrance. Bishop Huntington slowly shouldered his way through the crowd and into the hut. He knelt down beside the woman and grasped her hand.

Robin saw the top of the baby's head present itself between the woman's legs. He reached in and gently but firmly pulled on the head, guiding it through the birth canal. It seemed to go smoothly but then abruptly stopped, with the baby's shoulders stuck inside the woman's bony frame. Robin knew he had to pull to help the baby come out but was wary of pulling too hard. He waited patiently, feeling for the woman's contractions. He thought about the births he and Hsiao Wang had witnessed in the clinic, and the discourse between doctor and nurses. Pull too softly and the baby would not come out. Too hard and it could be paralyzed ... or worse. But no help would be coming today.

Despite the contractions, the baby remained stuck. Many minutes passed. The mother seemed exhausted. She was drenched in sweat, suffocating in the dank heaviness of the enclosure. Miss Clark used her skirt to wipe the mother's brow and gave Robin a worried glance. Robin continued to gently coax the mother on as Bishop Huntington peered over her shoulder.

"*Tui! Tui!*" Robin urged. Push! Push!

The mother obediently bowed her head and pushed down with her remaining energy. Her face puffed out as if it were going to explode and her skin color darkened.

"*Tsai ts'u! Tsai ts'u!*" Again! Again!

Summoning all her strength, the woman forced the baby's shoulders out. Robin pulled on the arm, and the body followed easily. It was a boy. Robin only had to grasp the slippery newborn and hand him to Miss Clark. She cleaned and wrapped the baby with her skirt's remnant. Robin took a thin strip of Miss Clark's skirt and tied off the umbilical cord, separating the baby from its mother with a knife one of the soldiers handed him. He pulled out the placenta afterbirth, which was followed by a gush of blood.

Miss Clark gave the swaddled newborn to Robin. He raised the bundle high, presenting the baby to the crowd, like a baptism. There was a celebratory cry from the onlookers, who began to clap spontaneously. He handed the baby to the smiling mother. All around the miserable, dark mud hut, with the occasional sound of explosions in the distance, the Spirit of their God was felt; a new life had been given to them. Word of the birth flew from the hut like a strong wave propagating down a stream from the great river. The good news rippled throughout the congregation strung out along the narrow escape routes leading down from their mountain sanctuary.

For a brief moment, Robin felt their worries disappear and life's good fortune lift their spirits. He saw his congregation rejoice as if their tide had turned. He could not help but smile. Perhaps the church would be all right.

NEAR THE BOTTOM OF THE MOUNTAIN PATH, JUST BEFORE IT fanned out into the flat plains of the fertile lowlands, Robin's group was met with a barrage of missiles from the Japanese Imperial Army Air Force. Although the bombs landed some distance away, the reverberations shook people out of their afternoon weariness. Coolies dropped their cargo, including the sedan chair carrying Bishop Huntington. They ran back into the forest, leaving Bishop Huntington stranded in his chair in the middle of the path.

"*Hui lai!*" Come back! he shouted in Mandarin. "Where are you going?"

"Too dangerous!" came the protest from the faceless forest.

"It is dangerous there!" retorted Bishop Huntington into the dark thicket. "The trees will protect us."

"The trees will fall on your heads," he shouted back. "Don't be afraid. They are only trying to scare us."

There was no reply. Bishop Huntington did not know if they were thinking it was true or were secretly laughing at his innocence.

"Why am I paying you one hundred and thirty dollars? I should give you nothing!"

Again, there was no answer. But just as he was about to plead again, the coolies emerged from the forest, looking as if nothing had happened. They were laughing among themselves and at him. Was it all just a joke to them, to see how scared he would get? It did not matter, as long as they picked up the sedan chairs and got the group to the refugee camp. The able coolies went back to work without further protest.

THE NEW MOTHER WAS UNABLE TO CONTINUE DOWN THE unfriendly path, with its loose stones, moist moss, and steep pitch. She had lost blood and was dehydrated and weak from the delivery. The swaddled baby was placed in a basket with the mother's belongings and attached to a bamboo yoke, which one of the coolies slung over his shoulders. The other basket of the tandem was already carrying a toddler, expertly balanced by the coolie. Once a rhythm was established, the flex of the yoke made the coolie's task easier.

Robin hoisted the mother onto his back and couriered her down the rest of the way. He was one of few people who had no family with him and was strong enough to bear the load, unlike the baby's father, who was as small as a schoolboy. Some men offered to relieve him, but Robin refused. If no one else was complaining, how could he? He reached the lowlands without mishap, at which point Bishop Huntington gave the new mother his sedan chair, against her protests.

WHEN ROBIN'S GROUP REACHED THE REFUGEE CAMP, ROBIN AND Bishop Huntington were assigned a small hut to share and given the usual ration of porridge. They were fortunate to have boiled water with which to wash the grime off their face and bodies. There were a couple of cots and a blanket, which were also a welcome sight. Bishop Huntington took to the cot while Robin cleaned the sweat and mud off his neck.

"Quite an ending to our conference," remarked Bishop Huntington.

"Ministry is a mission of improvisation," answered Robin with a smile.

"Hmmm. At any rate, well done. Our people might have lost hope long ago."

"Bishop Huntington, your presence was greatly appreciated by all. Our people see your commitment to them."

The bishop stared at the ceiling. He let out a long sigh and closed his eyes.

"Thirty years ... and still a foreigner. *Wai guo ren,*" he mused. He had come to China, like so many, to spread Christianity, to convert a foreign people to a foreign belief. He meant well. But whether it had been folly, naivete, or arrogance, the goal seemed far off. He had come to love and respect the Chinese, with their humility, humor, and sincerity, and despite their stubbornness, occasional hostilities, and insufferable indifferences. He understood why they were reluctant to embrace his beliefs, why they might welcome him as a friend or colleague—a teacher, of sorts—but still not as one of them. Through the decades, he had learned to reconcile his personal expectations with the necessary goals of his church.

"It is our nature," Robin explained. "We cannot help being Chinese."

"We can only do so much for your country," said Bishop Huntington. He had seen missionaries come and go. They were both welcomed and despised. They came with hope on their minds and left with frustration and longing in their hearts. He often wondered how to instill hope when he himself saw the future so barren of it.

"In your country, all Americans are Americans," noted Robin, as he settled into his cot. "Foreigners, even Chinese, can become American."

"It is what we are most proud of," replied Bishop Huntington. Perhaps that was the church's early mistake—to assume that Christians in China could be like Christians in America.

"Yes," Robin replied as he, too, closed his eyes. "Here in China, it is different."

Truth fell like gloom onto Bishop Huntington's ears; a foreigner will forever be a foreigner in China. To his friend, Robin, no matter his belief in Father, Son, and Holy Ghost, China would always be his irreplaceable mother. The night was dark and quiet, and they still had a dangerous tomorrow to face.

"Robin, you will need to give birth to your own future."

With those final words, Bishop Huntington slipped into a much-needed slumber.

Chapter 33

ON THE RUN

All groups faced the same trials on their way towards Nanchang. Resources, including food and fuel, were diverted to the conflict. Few motorized vehicles, except for military ones, were on the road due to scarcity of gasoline. Some people were fortunate enough to beg or cajole their way onto fuel-carrying army trucks, the sympathetic driver risking punishment for transporting civilians. Constance and her girls persuaded a driver to take pity on them. At one checkpoint, they huddled together in the cargo space, behind stacks of highly explosive barrels, as an inspector peered in. They could hear the driver nervously lie to the inspector.

"*Mei ren!*" No people! stated the driver. "Only gas. *Ni kan!*" You look!

The inspector gave a disinterested glance into the back of the truck and impatiently waved the truck on. As the truck crawled through the checkpoint, a loud commotion ensued at the side of the road. The girls could hear shouting and screaming outside.

"What is happening?" whispered Constance to the driver.

She could not see soldiers beating a group of men with long wooden rods and the butts of their rifles. She could only hear the bone-crushing blows and desperate screams. Within a few minutes, the screaming abruptly stopped.

"*Pan t'u,*" Traitors, the driver muttered nervously into the cargo space as he continued past the limp bodies, swaying from trees like the day's dirty laundry. He stared straight ahead and did not look back.

Except for their short stint in the fuel truck, most of the remaining nearly hundred-mile trip to the Gan River was accomplished on foot. Many of the coolies were long gone since descending from Lushan. Women, children, and elderly had to walk, frequently under cover of darkness in an attempt to avoid the daytime patrols and bombing missions of the Japanese Imperial Army Air Force.

On one occasion, the group was walking along the riverbed at dusk when planes came screaming from the north. Dirt kicked up from the hail of bullets, prompting some people to dive into the river. Constance pushed Hui tight against the edge of the riverbed. Pressing her head into the mud, Hui shut her eyes as tightly as she could. All around her, people were screaming.

The planes flew out of sight, but within minutes they returned with the same menacing drone, and again the ground came alive with a sheet of whistling bullets. No one was injured except for Reverend Wei, who had a piece of shrapnel lodged in his thigh. It seemed like a miracle. They asked each other, were the Japanese were being uncharacteristically merciful or simply toying with them, like crickets in a cage?

ROBIN'S GROUP REJOINED THE REST OF THE CONGREGATION IN Nanchang, where the diocese had built a leprosarium a decade ago. They soon discovered the city was in the eye of a deadly military storm. Air raids were frequent, and bombs dropped with increasing frequency and intensity. They were staying near the hospital in the Methodist mission. When sirens sounded, everyone in the area fled to the hospital basement, the safest place in the city, where the walls were reinforced with concrete.

One day, Bishop Huntington was getting a haircut in a small shop on a main boulevard, accompanied by Miss Clark, Robin, and Mr. Hill. Despite the wailing of sirens as the raid began, the old barber acted as if nothing was wrong. Bishop Huntington admonished him to hurry, but the barber persisted in a maddeningly deliberate manner. He wondered, was the old man deaf?

"Finish quickly!" Bishop Huntington urged.

The barber continued unperturbed.

"Do you not hear?" asked Mr. Hill, his voice rising higher than Bishop Huntington's. He was halfway out the back door.

The old man smiled like a curious cat and kept clipping away, even as the street erupted with a shower of gravel.

Without another word, Bishop Huntington bolted from his seat, leaving the old barber with his scissors perched in the air. He ran with Robin and the other two out the back door towards the hospital a block away. They took cover behind a concrete wall in front of the hospital as planes emerged from the clouds and dropped their loads. A few seconds later, concrete exploded not more than twenty feet away, collapsing the wall in a plume of dust.

As soon as the planes passed, the group sprinted unhurt into the hospital. At that point, it was decided that Nanchang was too dangerous, and the group moved again.

OVER THE NEXT FEW MONTHS, ROBIN, LLOYD, AND VARIOUS contingents of the congregation were constantly moving—to Jian, Anfu, and Wanfuchiao, or poetically, Ten Thousand Blessings Bridge. Bishop Huntington returned to Shanghai, which adapted to the Japanese occupation with refugee camps inside the international settlements. Each time they moved, Robin and his congregation organized study and prayer sessions, held Sunday church services, and even established makeshift schools for their children and those of the local communities.

At Anfu, the congregation set up a chapel for wounded soldiers, staffed by one of the church members who was a doctor. In Wanfuchiao, they took over an abandoned Confucian temple and, over an intense ten-day period, scrubbed it clean, evened the floor, swept the roof, and painted and papered the walls, converting the temple into a church and school. Jian was large enough that Grace, Helen, and Hui were able to attend local schools that had moved their campuses from Nanchang. The farther west they went, the safer they were, but the fewer resources were available. By the time Robin and his family settled in the westernmost part of Kiangsi province, the girls were free from any formal schooling and spent most of their days at leisure.

Life was chaotic and uncertain in 1939, but everywhere they went, Robin and the church members tried their best to create order and do good deeds. They strove to maintain a level of education for their children and instill a spirit of community among their members. They tended to the wounded, the sick, and the dying. Along the way, they gained recognition and respect from local citizens. In their hearts, they believed they were serving China and planting Christian seeds for its future, even as they were running for their lives. They did this without any thought for their own glory.

In the spring of the prior year, Robin had been awarded an honorary Doctor of Divinity degree, in absentia, from the Philadelphia Divinity School. But now, the only reward that mattered was life itself, and the belief that what he was doing was good for China.

Chapter 34

UNDER OCCUPATION

The Japanese finally took Wuhan in October 1938. They invaded Nanchang in May 1939, forcing one hundred and forty inmates of the leprosarium back onto the streets. The whole eastern half of China was occupied territory, from west of Wuhan in Hubei province all along the Yangtse River to Shanghai, and from the northern half of Chekiang and Kiangsi provinces to Manchuria. Everyday life returned under Japanese authority; schools started up again; hospitals were staffed and restocked with medical supplies; shops opened and banks reestablished financial markets. People returned to their homes, but there was no mistaking who was in charge.

Japan assumed control of major cities, delegating some policing duties to deputized Chinese personnel. In certain areas, weak puppet governments were established, and authority given to Chinese under the heavy hand of Japanese commanders. Some opportunistic Chinese were very willing to acquiesce to the militarily more powerful Japanese. Uncertain of China's future, they gambled on gaining favor and fortune once peace was inevitably established under the new banner of the Rising Sun. Japanese soldiers were ubiquitous in all areas of the occupied cities and required subservience and obedience from their Chinese subjects. Missions and churches generally remained free of their influence because of the implied protection afforded by their Western connections.

Robin and his congregation began to filter back to Anhwei from various regions of Kiangsi province; many of them ended up in the Maolin outstation. This relatively minor enclave had been reinvigorated by refugee church members from the Wuhu region who had opted out of the Kuling conference due to travel concerns. The town had a church and three chapels. Schools were re-established. The older Chen girls went to middle school, while Hui attended primary school. Alice welcomed Constance home and immediately put her to work as an English teacher.

Maolin was too remote for the active front, but the Japanese army was still very engaged in stamping out pockets of resistance. The atrocities they committed in Suchow, Shanghai, and, especially, Nanking, were fresh in people's minds. Parents were fearful for their daughters; females were known to be raped or used as sex slaves across the occupied territories. Some were systematically whisked away as "comfort women" in military stations to satisfy the sexual drives of Japanese soldiers before battle. This was instituted in the naïve belief that these sanctioned outlets could reduce sexually transmitted diseases and sexual assaults in the battle theater.

Chinese men were obligated to show submissiveness to their Japanese superiors, who traditionally looked upon their Asian neighbors as culturally inferior. They were expected to bow when passing Japanese soldiers, and failure to do so often incurred verbal insults, slaps to the face, sword whippings, or worse. Images of public beheadings and other forms of execution or humiliation for minor acts of disobedience served as effective deterrents to civil unrest or disrespect.

It was in the cold, early weeks of winter that Robin received a request to travel to Wuhu. Bishop Huntington had moved the main center of activity there because of the destruction in Anking. Work was begun to renovate some of the damaged compound, which had accommodated the presence of nearly two thousand refugees at one time. A diocesan business meeting required Robin's presence. As senior Chinese clergy, his advice on church matters was highly valued. With the country effectively under foreign rule and the church nearly cut off from their Western sponsors, the Anglican mission in China was at a critical crossroad.

Gossamer morning fog drifted up through the valley as Robin looked at the mountain ranges rising up on all sides of the Maolin mission. The rays of the sun peeking over the tops of the mountains created a dawning luminescence that infused the landscape. In the distance, he heard a solitary voice singing a Chinese folk tune, breaking the tranquility of the valley. It was a mystical atmosphere as he contemplated his trip to Wuhu. Alice came out to join Robin and stood next to him, enjoying the picturesque scenery.

"Magical," she whispered as she drew in a deep breath of air that smelled of the rich earth.

"This is my China, Miss Gregg," said Robin with unfeigned pride. "The China we love. More beautiful in stillness."

Alice turned towards him with a nod and soft smile. It was a rare moment of peace.

They took a moment together in the amber mist.

"Tomorrow I leave for Wuhu."

"Impossible!" Alice protested, her eyes widening with surprise. "The roads are sealed!"

"Bishop Huntington requires me to attend."

"It is occupied territory," she said, looking at him in disbelief. "Surely you will not travel alone."

"Who will care about a lone prophet wandering through the wilderness?" Robin replied with a slightly mischievous smile.

"But you will have to pass through the front lines," she protested.

"God will protect," Robin said, as he patted her forearm reassuringly.

"Reverend Chen, you take the good book too literally."

Robin laughed good-naturedly. Alice shook her head helplessly. Robin started back to the mission compound but then stopped and turned to his colleague, his smile now gone.

"Miss Gregg. Please ... look after my family."

ROBIN SAID GOODBYE TO CONSTANCE THE NEXT MORNING AND gave each daughter a hug. The clergy and staff came out at the mission entrance to send him off. Many had offered, even insisted on accompanying him on his trip, both for companionship and protection. But Robin knew it was a risky venture having to pass both no man's land and the front lines. He insisted on traveling alone; putting another person in harm's way was unthinkable. Traveling solo would make him appear less suspicious and threatening to any Japanese troops, who were always on the lookout for spies. It would also be faster.

Robin wore his traditional, full-length blue clerical tunic with a white collar, black cloth shoes, and his ever-present black topper hat and scarf. He brought a wool jacket for warmth during the cool winter nights. With a backpack carrying some food, a change of clothes, and his Bible, Robin set off into the mountain range.

Small fields of crops and rice paddies led up to the first set of hills. As Robin trekked along the narrow dirt path running between the fields, farmers whose children were learning English in the mission school waved to him. Robin cheerfully waved back.

The road continued at a gradual incline. Robin's gait was steady and rhythmic as he paced himself up to the ridge leading across the first range. He passed an occasional house: one- or two-room huts for goat herders and farmers who tended the terraced fields. After walking for half a day, he was invited into a farmer's hut for lunch. He sat in the tiny, all-purpose room and said a prayer for the family. After eating and a short rest, Robin was on his way.

The sun rose high over the mountains as he resumed his hike, passing a herd of goats and their tender. The higher he climbed, the fewer people he encountered. By the end of the afternoon, he was all alone. He found a soft bed of moss under some tall evergreen pines. He lay down and wrapped himself with his wool jacket under a canopy of sparkling stars. In the quiet of the night, he could hear the rhythmic chirping of crickets breaking the silence, like the constant curiosity of his childhood at St. James.

Chapter 35

SIZZLING
STRING BEANS

Alice took Robin's request to heart. She knew Constance as a respected woman of strong constitution and inestimable capabilities, but imagined being married to such a singularly minded, spiritually focused man as Robin could be difficult. She was well aware that Constance worried about her four children and, that having lost another, wanted them to have good fortune and long, happy lives. That was not an Oriental cliché heard in America; the constant turmoil in China made those desires tenuous. Long life was not merely a polite blessing, but a hopeful wish engendered by the common calamities that befell many Chinese. Long life in China was not often achieved; neither was a long marriage. Alice knew from her study of social conditions that Chinese people would be lucky to live past their forties, and many children faced their future with only one parent—and some with none.

After Robin left, Alice visited Constance to see if she could be of help to her. Constance invited her to stay for dinner. The cook assigned to the Chens was off duty, so she gladly agreed. She found herself assisting Constance in preparing the family meal. After a moment of courteous small talk, her curiosity became too strong.

"How do you bear this?" she asked bluntly as she snipped the tips of a long green bean.

Constance peered up from her mound of beans with a quizzical look. Miss Gregg met her gaze.

"Running ... from mission to mission ... village to village."

"What choice do we have?" Constance replied, with a shrug of her shoulders.

"America. You can live in America."

Constance picked up a string bean, pinched off the tips, and expertly stripped the fibrous spine in one smooth motion. She tossed the tips and spine into a bag of waste and the bright green bean into a bamboo basket.

"Christ already suffered on the cross for you," added Alice.

Constance stopped what she was doing, looked at Alice bemused, and responded, "China is all about suffering. We cannot escape it."

Constance resumed her peeling. She was smiling now.

"Christ showed us *how* to suffer," she continued. "Life for us is not about the present, but the future, our hope for what *will* come. Suffering is just part of the journey."

With both of them expertly peeling the beans, the basket was filling quickly. Alice was listening with interest.

"Until then, we do our best," Constance added. She looked up from her task. "Why do *you* stay?"

"I can do more here than at home," replied Alice with a shrug.

"You sacrifice a lot for us. You do not need to be here."

"Some left when we did not feel welcomed, and some were frustrated and returned home. Life here is not easy," answered Alice, her attention focused on the last few beans. "We will eventually all go home when our time is done. We always have that choice. You may not."

"If we do not stay, then you will have failed. What would we do in America?" Constance reasoned as she put the last pod in the basket and then washed her hands. "China is our home. We can never leave. If we leave, we would not be going home."

Alice sat back in her chair as Constance dried her hands with a towel. She looked at this diminutive figure with admiration. She wanted to feel sorry for her—this poor Chinese woman—but she did not.

"It is true. Our mission is dependent on people like Reverend Chen. He is our rod and our staff," she said. "You must miss him when he is gone."

She immediately realized it was a silly statement—perhaps, too personal. Constance picked up the basket of peeled green beans and dumped them into the hot pan. The beans immediately crackled, spraying droplets of oil into the air that caused Alice to jump back. Constance laughed. Alice did not know if the laugh was because of her comment or her reaction to the sizzling beans.

"Miss Gregg, we suffer not for ourselves, but for others. See, the oil must be hot. Cook quick, not long," she explained, stirring the beans as the droplets of oil leapt off the bottom of the deep pan. "In the end, our lives are really quite delicious."

Constance looked at Alice with a humorous sparkle in her eyes, then broke out in laughter.

"Come. Do not worry about us," she said, placing a reassuring hand lightly on Alice's shoulder. "Eat."

Chapter 36

THE LORD IS
MY SHEPHERD

Grey clouds, pregnant with moisture, loomed over the valley as Robin continued his trek along a roadside stream bordering the forest. A faint rumble of thunder on the other side of the range foretold a more difficult northward leg of his trip, and the morning winter air urged him to draw his jacket tighter. He pulled his hat lower against his ears as a light wind kicked up.

The road was pockmarked by bullet holes and an occasional crater left by some sort of explosive. He approached a grove of willow trees stretching their fluid branches over the stream, like verdant arms seducing him to a more hospitable side; a dozen or so soldiers dressed in the uniform of the Nationalist Revolutionary Army rested in its shade.

"*Wai!*" Hello! he called out, announcing his presence so as not to startle them.

The soldiers waved half-heartedly. They seemed stunned by the sight of a minister walking through this military zone.

Robin sat down and explained that he was on his way to Wuhu.

"How do you go?" one asked incredulously.

"*Zou lu.*" Walk, he answered.

"*Chi kwai!*" Strange! one snickered.

"*Sha kua!*" Fool! another muttered, his head resting on a comrade's lap.

Did he know that there were Japanese units surrounding Wuhu, they asked. Did he know that the Japanese pilots were still patrolling the roads?

Didn't he know planes would drop a bomb just to scare the locals? The soldiers peppered him with questions sprinkled with various timbre of derisive chortle.

Yes, but he had to get to Wuhu. Did they see any vehicles traveling toward the city?

They snorted at his ignorance. The only vehicles were Japanese, they explained as they pointed up the road. They themselves were heading south, away from the city.

"Crazy one," snickered one soldier as others joined the laughter.

"Watch out! *Jih pen kuei tzu*," another warned.

Japanese devils.

Robin thanked them and told them to be safe. One of them handed him a walking stick. They laughed again and shook their heads as Robin continued up the road. The gloomy skies lit up with a bolt of lightning, followed a half-minute later by the muffled growl of thunder. Robin was soon alone, following the small stream towards the mighty Yangtse.

THERE WAS NOT MUCH LEFT OF THE BOMBED-OUT MISSION compound at Nanling. Most of the buildings were damaged, and burnt vehicles lay scattered by the roadside. Robin saw few farmers as he passed through the town and into expanses of farmland.

He felt drops of rain and quickened his pace with the help of his new walking stick. He hoped to get through the lowlands and into the next collection of trees, where he might find shelter in a pine forest or abandoned hut.

His thoughts were on his children, where to send Grace and Helen for schooling. They should go to college, of course, but how to patch together middle school was a problem. The war had disrupted many colleges, which moved their campuses farther and farther west—or were shuttered altogether. Primary and middle schools suffered the same fate. Government schools were in complete disarray as financial resources and personnel were siphoned into the war effort. Foreign support was virtually nonexistent, so the mission school persisted only because of pure will, dedication, and local contributions. Some schools, like St. James in Maolin, reopened with no laboratory supplies, a few hand-copied textbooks, and nominal fees afforded by the students' families. And yet, they still prospered; St. James had nearly five hundred students.

He thought about what the church could do to survive during the occupation. Assistant Bishop Sing of Chekiang had retired in 1931, due to poor health, and Lindel was consecrated as the first Chinese bishop of Honan by Bishop Huntington in 1935. Lindel had gone to the Canadian General Synod in 1937 and became friendly with Bishop Paul Sasaki from Japan. He established good relations with Japanese Christians in subsequent visits to Japan, instilling hope for the future. But these interactions came to an abrupt halt as the Japanese invasion of China intensified. Still, Robin thought the presence of Christians, especially among military leaders, had some good influence, sparing church properties during certain military campaigns. One day, he hoped the world could worship and live peacefully together—one church, one God. Christians, even in the midst of political and military conflict, could still act as a universal force of goodness. He would certainly not live to see that, but he believed it was possible.

Having become weary of his wandering thoughts, he began to say the 23rd Psalm, one of his favorites. Walking along in this war-damaged countryside, he thought the verses quite familiar and timely.

"The Lord is my shepherd. I shall not want. He maketh me to lie down in green pastures. He leadeth me beside the still waters."

He glanced at the widening stream.

"He restoreth my soul. He leadeth me in the paths of righteousness for his name's sake. Yea, though I walk through the valley of the shadow of death ..." he said, pausing to look up at the menacing clouds hanging over the mountaintop.

"I will fear no evil!"

He said it loudly to the peaks above and imagined an echo from above. *Fear no evil ...*

It was at that very moment when his eyes drifted down and he spotted the first Japanese soldier coming around a curve in the road. As the soldier came into view, another appeared immediately behind him, then another. In the time it took Robin to walk twenty feet, there were close to a hundred Japanese soldiers, some carrying flags marked in the center with the blazing red sun. The men certainly spied him—a solitary Chinese, neatly clothed in priestly garb.

He kept walking without hesitation. He continued reciting. The heavens answered by opening up with torrential sheets of driving water.

"... for thou art with me. Thy rod and thy staff, they comfort me. Thou preparest a table for me in the presence of mine enemies. Thou anointest mine head with oil."

Heaven's oil, he thought, as he watched the sea of red banners and soldiers part before him. Rain ran off the brim of his hat.

"My cup runneth over."

As he walked between them, the soldiers pulled on their rain gear. Their faces were expressionless, and their skin was deep brown—harsh and leathery. They looked fit and energetic, not like the battle-weary Chinese soldiers he had encountered. Only a few of the soldiers gave him anything more than a curt glance. Their eyes were clearly trained on the road ahead of them.

"Surely goodness and mercy shall follow me all the days of my life. And I will dwell in the house of the Lord forever."

The orderly ranks of Japanese soldiers, stomping their boots in unison, closed behind him as if he were a lonely goat in the road. They showed him no fear, no hatred, no animosity. He forgot to bow, as the Chinese had been instructed to do, but the Japanese soldiers paid him little mind; he looked the part of a harmless priest. Perhaps they thought him weak in the head—a lonely man talking to himself.

As he left sight of the Japanese forces, he felt the power of his faith, but also the sad and ominous truth, having seen troops on both sides, that China's resistance was no match for Japan's resolve.

Chapter 37

SURVEY WEST

Robin walked and walked, through rice paddies, up and down undulating trails, across streams that turned into small rivers, until he reached the outskirts of Wuhu. He endured lightning storms, slept on wet ground, and sheltered in the modest comfort of a peasant's home. His damp clothes dried by the iron stove at night and by the radiant winter sun by day. He did not eat full meals every day, but neither did he go hungry. His feet were swollen, his shoes worn, and his hair unkempt. A light beard had grown scruffy, like the moss on the sunny side of a tree. The cold night air had given him a small cough.

He still carried his walking stick, leaning on it more and more for support, as he limped up the old road to the St. James mission compound. It had taken him six days, walking ten to twenty miles a day, but he reached his destination unscathed—tired, yet filled with internal vigor. He passed a group of Japanese soldiers lounging on the side of the road. They looked at him amusedly, but none said a word. As he approached the gate, he smiled at the surprised gatekeeper.

"Chen *mushi!* Chen *mushi lai le!*" Reverend Chen! Reverend Chen has arrived! the gatekeeper sang loudly. "I did not recognize you!"

Another worker inside the compound repeated the announcement, and soon the courtyard was full of familiar faces.

Upon seeing his colleagues, Robin suddenly let his guard down and buckled at his knees. The gatekeeper and Lloyd lifted him as he was surrounded by Bishop Huntington, Reverend Lee, Reverend Yen, Miss Clark, and Sister Louise Magdalena—one of three young Sisters of the Transfiguration from Ohio recently recruited by Bishop Huntington. More than twenty people escorted him through the compound.

He was just glad to be home.

ROBIN SAT WITH HIS FEET SOAKING IN A BASIN OF WARM TEA while the other leaders of the diocese gathered in the mission office. The water was murky with swirls of fresh blood leaking from his blisters. A nurse sat waiting with a towel and a jar of Vaseline sent from America.

"We cannot count on America or England," began Bishop Huntington. "Survival of the church will only come with the Three-Selfs."

The vision had been clear for a while, but progress was limited. Half the diocese had been staffed by foreign clergy when Bishop Huntington was consecrated. Now, after the mass exodus of missionaries during the anti-foreign movement, nearly all the ministers were Chinese. But the church was still not financially self-sufficient, and war the past four years had not helped in recruiting new converts. No one realistically saw this changing any time soon.

Robin lifted his feet out of the opaque water, and the nurse took them into the towel, drying them gently and thoroughly. She took a dab of Vaseline, rubbed her hands with it, and began to carefully massage Robin's sore feet. He waved her away and finished applying the ointment. Miss Clarke came in with a pot to offer the group some hot tea, like that earlier used to soak Robin's feet.

"The Council has entrusted us with an important task," announced Bishop Huntington. The National Christian Council in China was the leading organization that sought to coordinate activities of Western missionary societies with native Protestant church groups. "A survey of every diocese of every province in Western China. We cannot grow without knowing whom we serve."

"It is a Herculean task," remarked Lloyd.

"It will require at least a few months," Robin suggested.

Bishop Huntington sipped his tea and continued, "Perhaps half a year. The Japanese occupiers will relent. They will not wish to stir up sentiments from America or England."

"They will look the other way only if the US remains neutral. If the situation changes, so will they," Robin reminded the group. "What does the Council propose?"

"He must be a native," replied Bishop Huntington.

Bishop Huntington looked at Robin without saying another word. In their silence, Robin realized that Bishop Huntington and Lloyd were directing their comments at him, not the others. They had already discussed the Council's task, and he had been chosen.

"When do I leave?"

"Two weeks. First to Shanghai, then to Chengtu," answered Bishop Huntington.

Robin did not say anything as he put on his slippers. He stood up gingerly and slowly limped to the door. His legs felt achy and weak, but he forced his body to stand erect.

"Time enough for wounds to heal," he declared, then left the room to rest.

AFTER HIS FEET AND BODY RECOVERED, ROBIN DEPARTED WUHU by train to meet the Council administrators in Shanghai. Two important events took place in his absence.

Bishop Huntington decided it was time to retire. He would be turning 72 years old in the summer. He had accomplished his main task of ordaining a generation of Chinese ministers and consecrating the first Chinese bishops of the Anglican church. The next phase of the transformation had to come from younger leaders. With his impending vacancy as the primate of Anking, Bishop Huntington and the House of Bishops of the CHSKH nominated Lloyd Craighill as his successor. Lloyd's position was then ratified by the House of Bishops of the American Episcopal Church.

Just as significant was the election of a Chinese counterpart to be assistant bishop, the first time in the diocese's history. It signaled the changing order of the church. Bishop Huntington placed Robin's name in nomination before the House of Bishops and the Standing Committee of the other Chinese dioceses.

"We need natives like you to lead, sacrifice, and put their lives on the line," explained Bishop Huntington by phone.

Robin relayed the news to Constance, who had returned to Wuhu with their children. He explained that, if confirmed, he would need to travel more than usual.

Constance had mixed feelings. Their family had been split apart so many times. With Robin constantly working for the church, their children were growing up fast. It was rare to have a moment of true peace with her family. Being bishop would mean even more sacrifices.

"It is your dream," she conceded.

"We can do great things when the war ends," he posited.

"We need to survive."

She remembered what Alice had told her. *There is always America.*

ROBIN EMBARKED ON HIS MISSION USING CHUNGKING AS HIS base, a thousand miles from Shanghai, in Szechuan province. From there, he traveled by truck, sedan chair, rickshaw, and airplane from one village to another in the remote westernmost region of China. He spoke to local officials, attended church services in small chapels, discussed the needs of the local citizens, preached sermons, and met with local ministers. It was long, tiring, and often lonely work. He was inspired by the devotion of the local ministers and missionaries amid the spotty enthusiasm for the Gospel by citizens. But he was frequently dispirited by the slow progress of the church, due to lack of funding and experienced personnel.

After four months of travel, Robin returned to Shanghai to give his report. The Council representatives and officers met to hear of his experiences and observations.

"You surpassed our expectations," said Ronald Rees, the secretary.

"Your assessment of the local government signals an opportune time for us," added Edward Hume, a subcommittee secretary.

"They are ill-equipped, preoccupied with foreign invasion and the

Communist uprising," Robin elaborated. "Large regions have no schools, no medical care. The best hospitals, the best schools, they are all Christian."

Wu Yi-fang, the respected president of the prestigious Christian school for girls, Ginling College, spoke up.

"The church is indispensable to ecumenical services. We could not exist without it."

Wu was also a converted Christian, educated in the United States. Robin had high regard for this soft-spoken, clear-headed champion of women's rights and education. He often held her up to his daughters as an ideal role model who overcame a childhood marred by her father's, brother's, and sister's suicides.

"The government is unresponsive to the needs of the people, and the Communists are driven by their suppression of the individual. Our colleges and universities will not survive their system," she added.

"This country *needs* the church," reaffirmed Hume.

Robin nodded in agreement. There seemed to be no dispute about the problem or the challenges.

"It cries out for our involvement," he stated. "But there is growing resentment between the immigrant refugees from the east and the indigenous people in the west. Our own citizens can feel like foreigners. They do not understand each other. They have different experiences, different needs."

"Your experience is well-suited for this task," said Hume. "Bishop Huntington has approved another three months."

"For the southern provinces," clarified Cressy, the secretary for the commission on Christian education.

"Bishop Lacy will join you," Rees explained, mentioning that the Methodist missionary from Foochow would meet Robin in the southern coastal province of Fukien.

Robin suddenly felt weary and slumped ever so slightly in his chair. He had just spent four lonely months away from Constance and his family. Now he was being asked to travel extensively for another three months. He was exhausted and a bit overwhelmed by the task. He knew the Council was right to request the survey, and he knew the work was important, even crucial to the future of Christianity, but could he refuse? Were they asking too much of him?

"Your family will be safe," reassured Wu, as if reading his mind. She knew Robin was known among the foreigners as the most capable, energetic, and articulate of the Chinese clergy.

"You have a month before you begin," stated Cressy.

Robin stood to leave. He needed to talk to Constance, although his path was evidently already decided for him. She had always been supportive of his career and decisions, but he could not help but wonder if this was yet another one of the moments Hsiao Wang had been thinking about.

ROBIN TOOK THE TRAIN FROM SHANGHAI AND RETURNED TO Wuhu. It was all clear now. Bishop Huntington's retirement was a matter of formality. Lloyd would become the new bishop and Robin, if he accepted, would become the first Chinese assistant bishop of Anking. The uneven wheels of progress towards an independent, self-governed Chinese Church were slowly lurching forward. While there were only two Chinese bishops in the thirteen dioceses of the Anglican Church—Lindel Tsen in Honan and T.K. Shen in Shansi—there were now seven assistant bishops of Chinese background waiting to take over in the following years. All they, and the church, had to do was survive.

One bishop assessed the situation succinctly, "When life presents an opportunity, the Lord throws us a challenge."

THE FIRST TIME THEY HAD A CHANCE, ROBIN AND CONSTANCE walked around the St. James compound. They went into the small chapel that first inspired him to the Christian faith, recalling his curiosity about the symbolism of the simple cross. After a prayer together, they strolled among the plants and flowers in the garden he and his classmates had planted and tended thirty years ago. Some of the original trees and shrubbery were still there.

"The Council needs me," Robin began.

"How long?" Constance asked.

"Three months."

They walked in silence. Paul was in Kunming. Helen and Grace had studied at St. James Middle School in Maolin, but then came back to Wuhu and were sent to St. Mary's Girls Middle School, an Episcopal boarding school in Shanghai. Soon, they would be off to college.

"There is only Hui," said Constance.

Constance took his arm. Their arms wrapped themselves around each other as if a single limb.

"Why do you hesitate? I will care for the children," she said. "You … take care of God's."

Nothing more needed to be said. Two weeks went by quickly. There was a lot of preparation and planning to be done, but, in due time, Constance was alone again. Robin hired a sedan chair out of Wuhu, then a small boat on the Yangtse, then another chair. Four days later, he arrived back in Maolin.

Chapter 38

WAIT PATIENTLY

Robin was elated with the reception he received in Maolin, now the most important and active outstation of the diocese. The first Sunday there, a homecoming of sorts, he gave a rousing sermon to three hundred rapt churchgoers. But the next day, he was on his way again.

As with his travels in Western China, Robin met with various ministers, theological students, and representatives of the local government and Christian organizations: the China Inland Mission, the Methodist Church, the Roman Catholic Mission, and the influential YMCA. Every few days he visited another village or city: Taiping, Tunchi, Lanchi, Kinghwa, Yingtan. Some places were virtual ghost towns. Others were severely damaged, with early evidence of rebuilding. The more he travelled, the more he appreciated the plight and pride of the people he met.

"If bombs once more destroy our city, we will build it over again," promised one resident as he and Robin hid in a renovated missionary hospital during an air raid. He added, with fervor and optimism in his unwavering voice, "If they tear our fields, it will be easier to plant crops."

In Taiping, Robin wrote to a church magazine:

This is a difficult area to preach the gospel, as relative wealth and isolation encourage complacency. The new life which has come with the outsiders now flocking into the area makes for a more hopeful future, and even these new arrivals are asking for more teachers of

Christianity. The interest which is shown in large areas of China for the Christian gospel is due in part to physical suffering and hardship, which have led many people to seek anew for spiritual comfort and for the eternal values of life, and, in part, to an appreciation of the assistance of Britain and America during their time of struggle.

The journey was not without adventures. He travelled by a charcoal bus that frequently broke down, at one time necessitating his assistance in extracting the unreliable vehicle from a ditch. He took a train that was forced to stop to lay new rails, replacing those sabotaged by explosives. Once, he enlisted a friend's connections to hitch a ride in a convoy of eight trucks, a deal lubricated with a few Mexican dollars to the drivers. Along the way, the convoy was blocked by a bus, broken down in the middle of the road, with a Kuomintang general perched on its hood. The general refused to move the bus and demanded one of the trucks give him a ride to Tunchi, a detour from the convoy's intended destination. The drivers of the trucks refused until Robin negotiated an agreeable settlement. The general was appeased and the other seven trucks, with Robin aboard one of them, went on their planned route to Lanchi.

He was due to meet Rev. Carlton Lacy in Chungchun, but when his bus broke down and could not be repaired, he hired a rickshaw driver and rode it one hundred and twenty li over uneven roads to Lichwan. He spent the night at a Methodist church before walking another twenty li to Chungchun.

"Carlton, my good friend! I am sorry I am late," Robin said, extending his hand in greeting as he arrived. His excursion was two days behind schedule because of the mishaps.

"Robin, welcome! I am myself a day late. How was your travel?" asked Carlton.

Carlton was born in Foochow, the son of American Methodist missionaries. All of his siblings, three brothers and a sister, were missionaries in China. He had been schooled in Foochow and Shanghai prior to college in America and was one of those devoted Americans who saw China as his own native country.

"Uneventful. Rather uneventful," Robin replied, with a gleeful glint in his eye.

Carlton spied the grime on Robin's shirt, shoes, and hands. Knowing China well, he laughed.

ROBIN AND CARLTON WERE NO LUCKIER OVER THE NEXT FEW days as they headed southwest, traversing mountain ranges and navigating a dilapidated transportation system. As in his previous experience, Robin's first bus ride with Carlton ended in a ditch. The accident subsequently forced them to hire rickshaws and sedan chairs. They passed through Hwangchan, reaching Yutu just as storm clouds were gathering in the surrounding mountains. They were in the southernmost region of Kiangsi province, deep in what used to be Communist territory. Yutu was where the Long March began, leading to the solidification of Mao Tse-tung's leadership of the CCP and its Red Army.

The area was in the heart of the Kiangsi Christian Rural Service Center, which programs were diligently led by a small group of Anglican clergy and local workers: reclaiming land for individual peasants from landlords; building schools for the children of refugees from the east; arranging refugee camps; instituting mass literacy and education projects; developing a light industry of craftworks, like weaving, to help the people support themselves. It never seemed to be enough. Peasants still struggled to provide for their families, and the program had difficulty recruiting workers.

They had scheduled a meeting with local officials and students in the missionary Baldwin School for Girls in Nanchang. Since they were two days late, the meeting was canceled. When they finally arrived, they were greeted by Rev. Daniel Liu and ushered to a building in the school compound.

Reverend Liu, young and energetic, took Carlton and Robin's bags and led them up to the second story of the damaged building. They entered a bare room with an attached bathroom but no doors. The ceiling was missing in large sections. There were gaping holes in the roof. All the windows were blown out. Against the wall were four chairs and two detached doors. Carlton put the bag down on one of the doors that Reverend Liu laid across the seats of two chairs facing each other. The other "bed" was a wooden table.

"It is a beautiful door," commented Robin as he tested the sturdiness of his bed.

Carlton laughed.

"That it is," he said.

"So, so sorry. We are honored to have you, but this is all we have. Japanese planes passed through here and we have yet to rebuild," Reverend Liu said, appearing very embarrassed. "We are poor but have enthusiasm!"

"I have laid my head on much worse," confessed Robin.

He and Carlton both slept rather well under the open roof and were thankful it didn't rain.

THEY TOURED THE SCHOOL THE FOLLOWING DAY AND PLANS were made for a meeting that evening. Robin and Carlton had no expectations that the previous meeting could be successfully rescheduled on such short notice, but they did not want to squander the opportunity to learn about the region. They had decided to stay the extra day and hoped it would not be a wasted effort. At dinner, they were guests of the local magistrate and were joined by Reverend Liu and local government officials.

"We have announced your arrival and hope people will come to the meeting," explained the local magistrate.

"I am sure our students will be interested," said Reverend Liu hopefully.

But by the end of dinner, it had already started to rain. As they walked to the meeting room, the sky opened up with a fury and the area was drenched with a summer thunderstorm. The winds picked up and a howling sound reverberated through the empty campus. Because of limited electricity, the area was quite dark, bathed only by the faint light of the nearly full moon peeking desperately from behind the dense clouds.

"You are quite famous here, Reverend Chen!" shouted Reverend Liu over the wind as he shielded Robin with an umbrella.

"So is your weather!" replied Robin, just as loudly.

"We are honored by your presence and by your interest in our situation," said the magistrate as he walked with Carlton.

"Our students respect the work of the church," Reverend Liu declared.

"But foreigners ..." Carlton finished the thought.

Reverend Liu gave Carlton a nervous glance.

"I am sorry about the weather," he said apologetically.

"If we touch just one, many may follow," interjected Robin with optimism. He hoped there would be more than a few present.

As the group approached the assembly building, there was light filtering out through the windows. Shadows moved against the lit backdrop and voices emanated from the room. It was evident that there were a lot of people inside; others were outside, pressing against the window, straining to look in. The entrance was blocked by throngs pushing from behind.

Reverend Liu's heart raced. The turnout was beyond any expectations. Everyone was soaked from the rain. The room had few chairs, and the wet floor was crowded with teachers, students, parents, and government officials sitting or squatting shoulder to shoulder. As Robin and Carlton entered the room, making their way through the crowd, the room erupted in spontaneous applause. The clapping in the room became rhythmic, in unison, louder and faster, until it drowned out the sound of the rain on the ceramic roof. Carlton and Robin exchanged glances as they made their way to the front and wore full smiles by the time they faced the audience.

The magistrate gave a welcoming statement; then Reverend Liu introduced the guests. Carlton offered a short comment on the purpose of their visit, but the hushed audience glanced around warily, well aware that he was the only foreigner in the room. His Mandarin elicited suitably polite applause and a few giggles.

When Robin finally made his way to the front, the room was quieted. He was the guest everyone had heard about. Students were eager to be inspired, teachers eager to learn, and officials eager to be informed. But he did not talk about education in the classroom. He was not an expert on land reform. He did not have ideas about planting crops or growing the local economy. He did not know what the future of China would be or what the political solution was for the military or ideological conflict.

"Death. Destruction." He paused. It was a bleak, hate-filled world they all lived in. "People against people. Nations against nations."

He stared at the crowd sitting at his feet, their faces looking up to him, drenched with the evening's precipitation.

How much more difficult could their lives be? How much more danger could they withstand?

"But love … love conquers all!"

He raised his arms to embrace his audience.

"Love of knowledge conquers ignorance."

He moved his eyes over the audience, looking directly at each person he encountered.

"Love of fellow man conquers war. Love of God conquers evil."

His words were absorbed by his audience like rainwater into the ground after a drought. They clung to each phrase, contemplated each sentence. He spoke from his own life. His words held hope, as if wine in the offertory cup of his oration.

"His presence saves me. He lifts me out of the pit of despair, out of the mud and the mire. He sets my feet on solid ground and steadies me as I walk along."

His voice got louder and louder, steadier and steadier. Hope started as a sprinkle and slowly grew to a torrent anointing their spirit.

"Wait patiently for the Lord!"

His voice rang out clear and forceful.

"Be brave. Be courageous! Yea, wait patiently for the Lord! Wait patiently!"

The sound of his voice died out. The room seemed to wait obediently, as if expecting God to descend from the heavens.

Someone clapped. Then another. Like the raindrops dancing irrepressibly on the roof, the listeners leaped to their feet and erupted into applause.

Within minutes, Carlton and Robin were immersed in a clamorous sea of four hundred admirers.

Chapter 39

REFUSES

The survey team moved progressively in a southerly, then westerly, direction, utilizing every means of transportation available in the country: railroad cars, charcoal buses, military vehicles, rickshaws, two- and four-man sedan chairs, bicycles, planes, small river boats, and their own two-legged human power. They even rode horses. Wherever they needed to go, to meet whomever they needed to meet, they found a way. Once, they sat in sedan chairs for two days from Yutu to Hsinkuo. Another time they took three buses, including one that broke down, to go from Kian in Kiangsi province to Kukong in southern Kwangtung province. About the only thing they didn't ride was a donkey. By the end of their assignment, they were experts in China's variegated transportation system.

In Kwangtung, they inspected a large, wildly understaffed, and under-supplied camp for displaced orphans. Female infanticide was a known antidote to the problem of unwanted births, and laws enacted by the Nationalist government in 1927 and 1935 punished abortive mothers with imprisonment. But the war with Japan disrupted core families, producing a long trail of children without families to rear them. Orphanages sup-ported by Christian organizations, as well as by the Soong sisters, sprang up throughout the country. Over time, these facilities filled with tens of thousands of the children Madame Chiang had nicknamed "warphans."

"They are the refuse of war," lamented Carlton as his eyes settled upon the hundreds of children dressed in their uniforms of white shirts and blue cotton sacks for pants.

"No," Robin retorted quickly, laying his hands on some of the many toddlers that came out to greet them. "They are our future."

They made detailed notes to be passed along to the diocese of Hong Kong.

From Kwangtung, they went to Hunan and the large city of Henyang. Taking a train and then a houseboat on the Shiangjiang River, they entered Kwangsi Province, making slow progress through the gorges, riverbeds, and stone peaks of the countryside, ending up in Lingling. They stopped in homes located far removed from any major city. Schools were nearly nonexistent and every peasant was illiterate. Medical professionals were predominantly herbalists, acupuncturists, and local Taoist-based personnel, dispensing questionable and superstitious remedies: bear claws for sexual potency and snake bile for fevers and convulsions.

They happened upon a father caring for his daughter in his isolated mountain hut. The child appeared three or four years old, lying in bed with a high fever and a rash. Her father described her gripping bouts of abdominal pain. Robin immediately recollected his son's tragic day, fifteen years ago. Carlton placed his hand on her forehead and glanced knowingly at Robin.

"Typhoid," he said to Robin.

"*Yiyuan?*" asked Robin of the father. Surely there was no hospital of any worth in this remote region.

"Kweilin," the father answered, with a timid voice.

He looked at Carlton and shook his head in resignation.

"A hundred miles," muttered Carlton.

The father's eyes were pleading for a miracle. There was a reason why he was alone with his young daughter, without a wife or other children. He gripped Robin's hand as if there was nothing else to hold on to.

"Give her tea. Every hour," Robin instructed the father.

That was all he could think of. Then he took the girl's hands with the father's and said a prayer. There was nothing more they could do. They promised the father they would send medicine when they reached Kweilin.

"Prayer gives hope," said Robin as they left the pair. "But it is medicine that cures."

When they arrived in Kweilin, they hired a local guide. They went straight to the pharmacy and procured a bottle of tonic. They paid a coolie to take the medicine back to the sick girl, explaining carefully how to find the father's hut.

"*Liang tian*," said the coolie, holding up two fingers. Two days.

Even that was optimistic, but Robin sent him on his way.

"A fifty-fifty proposition," guessed Carlton.

"At most," answered Robin, nodding in agreement.

As they walked out of the shop, Carlton pulled on Robin's arm.

"Robin, the guide wants to show us something interesting."

Within the city limits, beside the banks of the Li River, the guide brought Carlton and Robin to a series of caves with large, luminous, limestone pillars. The guide explained that the vast local attraction—tens of meters high and tens of meters in width—could hold thousands of people and were used as a refuge when Japan flew air missions into Vietnam. While the city itself was not invaded or significantly bombed, Japan was actively attacking Vietnam to the south. Taking advantage of Hitler's triumph over a weakened France, it sought to secure Indochina's border and its southern access into China. With their conquest of Manchuria in the north and occupation of the eastern seaboard provinces, the Japanese were close to sequestering China from the rest of the world.

Carlton and Robin walked along the colorful walls, illuminated by a network of electrical lights, and marveled at the cavern's beauty—a majestic palace of God's miraculous creation, fashioned inexorably over millions of years. But the guide pointed out areas that housed sleeping cots and medical equipment; others hid printing presses to publish newspapers.

"When planes come, we hide," explained the guide.

"Locals use it as shelter," added Carlton. "They can survive for weeks, even months."

"But these caves cannot protect them from mustard gas," Robin remarked solemnly.

The caves were death traps—prisons of fear—like the catacombs he had read about. People were not meant to be confined, cowering in a dark hole in the earth, awaiting death or deliverance. They were meant to be free.

The two left Kweilin and backtracked to Kukong. They flew to Hong Kong and promptly returned to Shanghai to give their report.

∽ ❀ ∾

"CHURCH WORKERS ARE DOING EXTRAORDINARY WORK UNDER extraordinary circumstances."

Carlton's critique of the situation was not intended to be entirely negative. In fact, much of it was indeed quite extraordinary—even inspiring. The Chinese were resourceful and resilient. They all felt a loyalty to their country, expressed however differently. People were grateful, though they harbored resentment towards foreigners. That was not something so easily erased. But the overriding problems had persisted for hundreds, if not thousands, of years, and missionaries could not expect to change that.

"Areas have an unrequited thirst for spiritual leadership but a severe lack of trained workers," concluded Robin.

Their task was to identify problems and offer tangible solutions. Savings souls was a lofty goal. Providing food, medicine, and education was what really counted; those things opened the door for the church. Serve the people's needs, and their spirit and souls will follow.

"Support is getting more difficult. Missionaries are staying home. Many of our colleges are closed ... or destroyed," noted Bishop Scott.

"If we do not persist, if we retreat, then the void will be filled by the grassroots appeal of the Communists. Christianity will be lost ... forever!" argued Robin.

Carlton and Robin laid out their recommendations: more church leaders and parish programs; coordination and cooperation between church groups; more Bibles and devotional materials; improved transportation (maybe Ford Motor Company can help, they mused); a clear purpose for missions once peace is restored and refugees no longer a focus. But there was a keen awareness of looming incompatibilities.

There was conflict between church and state, between theology and politics, between God and country. The lines were drawn. The prize and the purpose were the same, although the methods and the loyalties were not. It was Christianity or Communism. They both could unify. They both could serve the people. They both could modernize the country. But it seemed something had to give—they could not co-exist.

One would have to become the country's refuse.

Chapter 40

REFUGEES AGAIN

"You are the beginning."

Those words fell upon Robin's ears on St. Andrew's Day, November 30, 1940. His consecration as the first Chinese assistant bishop of Anking was one of two events that foreshadowed major changes to his life and the future of China. He was now well-known throughout his country, as well as within the international Christian community, as the brightest and most dynamic of the handful of Chinese bishops—and yet everything seemed unsettled.

In the months preceding his consecration, there were indications of the impending second event.

Robin was in Shanghai, working in the central office. Constance and Hui went to the station in Wuhu to take a train to visit him. Crowds were squeezing into the cars while Japanese soldiers, perched on the roof, screamed orders at them.

"Hurry!" yelled the soldiers in Japanese. "Move!"

The soldiers flailed at them with whipping sticks and the butts of their rifles, as if they were herding pigs into slaughter pens. Constance raised her arms to shield Hui. The end of a bamboo cane whistled through the air and caught Hui on her upper arm. She winced.

"Are you hurt?" Constance asked Hui as she glowered at the soldier.

Hui bit her lower lip and shook her head as she fought the sting.

"Scum!" spat the soldier.

"China pig!" yelled another.

"Why are you so impatient?" Constance shot back.

"Move!"

Neither understood what the other was saying, although the message of the cane swishing over her head was unmistakable. Constance ushered Hui quickly into the car and, for the whole trip, tried to understand why the soldiers were lately so agitated.

AFTER THE FAMILY'S RETURN TO WUHU AND THE CELEBRATION of Robin and Lloyd's consecration, Japanese presence intensified. Soldiers forced Chinese to kneel before them, often lashing at them with canes. Farmers were coerced to plant poppies around the orphanage.

As Hui witnessed these cruelties and grew more frightened, Robin took time to lie with her at night, reading tales from *One Thousand and One Nights* and telling stories about happier days at St. James. He told her about Hsiao Wang and how this poor, timid boy became a doctor somewhere in the vast country. They prayed together for better days ahead, and she would fall asleep with her head in his arms.

In late November, the son of the American missionary and mission school principal, B.W. Lanphear, was arrested and detained by the Japanese. While in custody, he overheard talk of a plot against the Christians and its new Chinese bishop. When the American was released, he warned Sister Louise that the Japanese local commander was wary of Robin and was plotting a move against Chinese Christians. The situation was serious. What had changed after three years of stable occupation? Why were the Japanese acting so aggressively?

The answer came on December 8, 1941, when the second, more monumental, event took place. The Empire of Japan attacked the soil of the United States of America with over three hundred and fifty aircraft, sinking or damaging every American battleship docked at Pearl Harbor. The preemptive strike took the world by surprise and was intended to prevent an intervention in a more forceful and widespread Japanese campaign into China, Singapore, Malaya, Hong Kong, and the Philippines. Japan was going all-out in Asia and wanted America neutralized.

The following day, in a dramatic address to the United States Congress and the American people, President Franklin D. Roosevelt officially declared war on Japan. Japanese soldiers who had previously respected the boundaries of the mission suddenly swarmed in and rounded up foreigners; clergy, teachers, workers, and medical personnel were all swept up.

"Have faith, my good friend," Lloyd told Robin as he was surrounded by the soldiers.

One by one, the missionaries gathered and said goodbye.

"It is time for me to go," Alice said fatefully, as she gave Robin a hug.

Sister Louise, now in her mid-fifties, couldn't get words out. Robin spoke first as he cupped her hands in both of his.

"I can never repay you," he said.

Sister Louise pulled him close, so the soldiers wouldn't hear.

"America can no longer protect you. You must get out!" she said in her familiar schoolteacher tone.

Lloyd shook hands with Robin and was whisked off to be interned at the rectory. Word from the Episcopal Church in the United States urged Robin to leave Wuhu. With no means of support, the dispersion and incarceration of the missionaries, and the rapid escalation of hostilities, it was clear that the mission was doomed and that the Japanese commander was suspicious of Robin's position with their newly declared enemies.

THE NEXT PRIORITY WAS THE DISPOSITION OF ORPHANS THE convent had accumulated. Dozens of babies had been brought to the convent during the earlier years of conflict, either abandoned in fields to be fortuitously discovered, or left anonymously, as if they were secret offerings. Sliding drawers were built into the church doors to avoid the donor's embarrassment.

One by one, the accumulated children were given away to sympathetic families. A toddler with a big head, wide eyes, and fair skin caught Robin's attention. The little child, about two, smiled constantly and enjoyed vigorously kicking her feet while lying in her carriage. Robin and Constance took easily to the child. They named her Hsiun and christened her Little Constance. This last "warphan" became their fourth daughter.

WHEN THE JAPANESE STORMED THROUGH THE COMPOUND, looting it of furniture, tools, and medical supplies, Robin knew it was time to leave. With the United States formally at war, Chinese Christians previously shielded by the West were at risk. He heeded Sister Louise's warning and stole away with Grace in the middle of the night. They made their way through the front lines back to Maolin.

Constance, Helen, Hui, and Little Constance followed a few days later, along with many of the remaining Chinese workers and most of the congregation. American personnel were repatriated or interned at Lion Hill. Eventually, foreigners were transferred to one of the nearly two hundred crowded settlement camps in Shanghai. Within a few months, the mission was completely occupied by the Japanese army, and its chapel and classrooms filled with office and communications equipment. The garden and surrounding hillside were replanted with poppies, reviving the time-honored practice of producing opium cakes to help Japan finance the war at Chinese expense. Church services were allowed to continue for those who remained, but little else of mission life survived.

In retaliation for the internment of Japanese-Americans by the United States government, Japan swiftly detained Western missionaries in major cities, including Anking. Dr. Taylor and other foreigners were placed under house arrest, and the Japanese military occupied the hospital and mission compound. The church in China was under siege and the Chen family was on its own. Again.

MAOLIN HAD BEEN THE SITE OF THE NEW FOURTH ARMY INCIdent in January 1941, when the KMT government forces wiped out remnants of the Red Army. As more refugees flowed into Maolin, what was once a quiet, relatively inactive outstation for the diocese burst into an active center for church work. Besides the St. James Primary and Middle School, regular Sunday services were performed for hundreds of parishioners. A clinic was organized not only for the usual minor injuries but also for eye diseases and malaria, which were rampant in the area. Supplies of quinine were donated by the International Red Cross. That they would undertake the arduous trek up the mountain to access the clinic was a testament to the value local farmers placed on its medical care.

A small commercial enterprise was started to help the local people develop skills in handicrafts and weaving. Ingenuity and resourcefulness were at a premium. Old newspapers and magazines were cut up and fashioned into decorative paper lanterns. Wild bamboo was carved into hundreds of swab sticks for the clinic. Local wheat straw was woven into sandals and fans. The money earned provided minor, but welcome, financial assistance as the inflation rate exploded over the following months. Prices for necessary items such as soap, fuel, eggs, and rice increased three- to tenfold as more and more basic resources were diverted to military uses.

Reverend Kimber Den, a contemporary of Robin, followed a line of succession after George Shepherd. He led the land reform program that began in Kiangsi province and expanded to southern Anhwei. New mission stations, fostered by Carlton and Robin's report, were established in Tunchi and Kanhsien. An added activity for the church and school—a somber sign of the times—was a military training program where students, including the Chen girls, dressed in military uniforms and learned how to use a rifle and throw hand grenades.

Grace and her sisters liked to go to church services and sing in the choir. Both Helen and Grace were excellent singers, with voices that soared above all the others. Everyone could tell when the two sisters were present. All they had to do was close their eyes and listen to their clear-pitched voices.

Grace rarely went out to play but spent most of her time at home, studying and reading. During the summer she was the principal of the Bible study program. She also volunteered in the medical clinic. This made her parents very happy. Her teachers encouraged her to go to the best college.

As the war continued to intensify, China aligned with the Allies in both the European and Asian theaters. More support arrived from America. Generalissimo Chiang was named commander-in-chief of the Allied forces in Asia, elevating China's stature to that of the Soviet Union, Great Britain, and the United States. Investment in the country's military goal had a detrimental effect on the missions.

Inflation, diversion of resources, and the breakdown of communication and banking facilities placed enormous financial stress on the mission workers. New Chinese teachers and workers from Peking and other areas of occupied China could only be hired at bare subsistence salary. No allowance was given for clothes, shoes, medicine, or personal pleasures. Because of the meager pay, well-educated young workers were hard to come by. Many members of the congregation were malnourished. Robin's salary was barely enough to provide anything extra for his four daughters. But no one complained. In fact, Robin contributed part of his salary to help students attend St. James.

Food shortage was a severe problem, as Robin's salary was reduced even further. Constance often went into the mountains to hunt for bamboo and edible wild plants. She took Hui and Grace to the highlands to find lemon grass. They would cut the stalks of grass, wrap them in bundles, and carry them down the mountain.

Once, when they had completed their foraging and were walking back home, they saw Miss Smith approach them. She was one of six foreign missionaries, along with Miss Browne and Miss Monteiro, who had chosen to stay at Maolin after Lloyd and others in Wuhu had been interned.

"Throw your grass away!" ordered Constance as she dropped her bundle by the side of the road, and Hui and Grace quickly threw theirs into the gutter. "Hui, play with your sister!"

Hui started to chase Grace. They ran around, pretending to play tag, as Miss Smith walked up the road. After exchanging pleasantries with Constance, Miss Smith continued on her way. As she disappeared from view, Constance, Grace, and Hui retrieved the bundles of grass and resumed their walk home.

"Are you ashamed to be cutting grass?" Hui asked her mother. "Is that why you told us to throw away the grass?"

"It is not shameful to be poor," Constance replied quietly. "We all must do the things necessary to survive."

"Then why did you want us to throw away the grass and play with each other?"

"Miss Smith and the other Americans are kind and generous people. They have given their lives to help us. They should not feel sorry for us. If we must struggle, do not show it."

They continued on home, where Hui cut the grass and crushed the base of the stalks to boil for soup. As Constance worked over the stove, stirring the large, steaming kettle of water, Grace looked at her with admiration. She slowly walked over and stood behind her mother. She wrapped her arms not so familiarly around her tiny waist. Grace felt the warmth of her mother's body against hers. The heat rising from the stove embraced their faces pressed close together. Together, they peered into the kettle and watched the grass swirl as a tangled mass, disappearing into the agitated broth to become their dinner.

Chapter 41

A TREK TO
THE DENTIST

By the middle of 1943, most of the Western missionaries, including Bishop Craighill, Dr. Taylor, and Mr. Hill had been repatriated or interned in settlement camps. Bishop Huntington retired and returned to America. His vision of "building up one church to save the world" seemed a distant dream. The Wuhu mission was completely overrun by the Japanese. The properties in the Nanling outstation, including the church, rectory, school, and offices were destroyed. The Anking buildings were damaged beyond use or occupied by the Japanese army. Even the hospital closed. But church life throughout the diocese continued in some way, even if it meant moving into old, open-roofed houses, with dirt floors and infestations of bed bugs, mosquitos, and fleas. Every day brought new adventures as the world raged with war.

The Maolin area was rife with disease, mainly malaria, and medical facilities were as scarce as they had been decades ago. There was no dental care available, so Robin organized an excursion to Tunchi, where the diocese had a new outstation, about two hundred and fifty li from Maolin. The group included Reverend Wang, his assistant, Miss Smith, Miss Browne, a few other church members, and seven coolies. He asked Grace to accompany him. He rarely saw Paul, who was off to college in Kunming, and Grace would also soon be gone the following year.

They began crossing the mountain range from Maolin over narrow stony footpaths. Out of sight from any village, the solitude of the summer scenery, where rocky peaks jutted from a sea of greenery stretching for miles around, afforded a necessary respite from the nightmares of war. The simple act of putting one foot in front of the other was a welcome exercise.

They traveled leisurely and stopped for tea every few hours. Their first night's rest was in a small inn, high in the mountains, where beds were hard planks set on wooden benches and a thin quilt for a mattress. Sleep came in fits and starts, a battle between weariness and discomfort.

The next day was glorious, and their group started out afresh along a small stream. The flowers along the banks were in full bloom, a botanical bonanza of clematis, wild roses, honeysuckles, lilies, orchids, and irises. Grace stopped to observe the different flowers and plants, sketching in a notebook she carried. She studied each detail, reproduced it as true as possible with her pencil—then erased it and tried again. She showed her drawings to her father.

"How beautiful!" he said, then added, "Practice more!"

Every time they rested, she sketched. Her sketchbook filled up quickly. She showed new drawings to her father, who examined each picture. Every time the answer was the same: Practice more.

One time, a baby deer crossed their path. The group stopped to watch it feed just as a flash summer storm dropped buckets of rain on their heads. They took refuge under coffin-tile shelters that the local people had built for this occasion. Once the storm broke, they continued along the mountain stream to the base of Huangshan Mountain. These were China's most famous mountains, with distinctive rock formations towering over seven thousand feet. They visited the nearby hot springs that evening, then bedded down at the Huangshan Travel Service Hotel.

The summer storm resumed the following day, preventing further progress, but they were able to set off again the fourth day. Grace cherished this time with her father—a rare stretch of quiet, personal time. Because of the war activities the previous year, she had not been able to go to college. They had talked about her education for years and recently settled on the best college for women in China, Ginling College. The missionary school was established in 1915. It was supported by its sister school, Smith College in Boston. Eight missionary boards of various denominations, the YWCA, and the China Medical Board all provided aid. Originally founded in Nanking, the college was forced under the Japanese occupation to relocate farther west, in Chengtu, in 1937. Its original campus was converted into a refugee camp for ten thousand people, but Smith College continued to support the school, both financially and academically.

"China will emerge from this conflict. Your opportunities will be great," Robin said to her as they walked.

"Do not waste them."

Grace absorbed her father's words, feeling their weight. She dared not say anything.

"Many obstacles may come before you. See how the Lord has provided?" he finished and lightly placed his hand on her head. "Trust Him."

She knew he meant well.

THE FOURTH DAY BROUGHT THEM TO THE LOWLANDS, WHERE a paved road cut through tea fields. Armies of tea pickers hunched over the plants, their straw cone hats bobbing and swaying like flowers floating on a carpet of waterlilies. Coolies carried empty baskets to the pickers and returned loaded down with the leaves, bringing the harvest to the city to be processed and marketed. Robin and Grace loved meeting the farmers and the pickers who performed the back-breaking work without complaint.

"Working together for everyone's benefit. That is the Christian way," he observed as they hiked through the fields.

Grace listened to the tea pickers sing of their harvest. She didn't know the song but began to hum along, imitating the melody. After a few verses, she sang the words as if she had known them her whole life. The laborers she passed smiled and waved, and for a brief moment they would sing in chorus. She became bolder and her voice rose above the tea pickers', and when she did not know the words she simply sang "*la la la.*" Robin and the others in the group laughed at her, but Grace ignored them. Walking through the green tea fields with her father made her feel happy. She sang to the clouds and forgot about the Japanese.

That evening, the group rented a room in a small inn just thirty li outside of Tunchi. The group had little money, but the proprietor was happy for what came her way. After a brief period of haggling, a deal was struck. The inn was not much to look at and seemed to shake with each small breeze; at least it was a roof over their heads in case the rain reappeared.

"I think a small gust of wind will topple this house," one of the missionary women whispered to Grace, "like Joshua's horn and the walls of Jericho."

Grace smiled at her humor.

Two older women and two children lived in the inn. There were seventeen travelers, including seven coolies, for a total of twenty-one people.

That evening, Robin and Reverend Wang slept on two tables in the corner of the room. A stranger who also happened by took another table opposite them. The two women and two children claimed a small alcove off the room. The rest of the group, including the women missionaries and Grace, spread out on the floor, separated by a curtain from the coolies, who huddled together in the other half of the room.

"I am happy to say there are no bed bugs or lice here," boasted one of the proprietors.

"Of that we are very glad," answered Miss Smith.

"But other than that, nothing is guaranteed."

Miss Smith and Miss Browne looked at each other, bemused, and shrugged their shoulders. The crowded room fell silent and they retired for the evening.

Although the wind blew throughout the night and the walls shivered, in the morning, the inn was still standing.

THE GROUP MADE THE LAST LEG OF THE TRIP TO TUNCHI IN A torrential storm. The rare passenger bus traveling in that direction was overcrowded, leaving their group without transportation. Everyone kept their good spirit, even joking about their technique of keeping dry by dashing into the roadside underbrush and squatting under their opened umbrellas. Robin laughingly compared them to clustered troops of large-cap mountain mushrooms.

In Tunchi, they took turns going to the dentist. Teeth were pulled, cavities filled, and enamel scraped and cleaned. It was five days of hiking but well worth the trouble. When they finished, they made the five-day hike back to Maolin. These were the last few intimate moments Grace had with her father. She knew the next few years would be difficult. Japan's occupation had been going on for seven years. It couldn't last forever. Someone would win. But how? Who? When? She had no idea.

As fall arrived, Grace, now twenty, left her family to attend Ginling College in Chengtu, in the far western reaches of Sichuan Province. She could see her future as a doctor in China. All she needed to do was study hard; that was all she had done her whole life. One day, perhaps not soon, but one day, China would have peace. When that day came, she would be ready to make her parents proud. Perhaps then, she thought, people would not have to travel five days over mountain ranges just to clean their teeth.

Chapter 42

WAR'S END

The following year, Japan made an aggressive push farther into China, particularly south of the Yangtse. The renewed military offensive forced the church and its congregation to scatter from Maolin. Robin, fearing for the safety of the American missionaries, sent Miss Browne, Miss Montiero, and Sister Louise to the interior of China. They first walked forty miles, crisscrossing and backtracking across Anhwei and Kiangsi provinces, ahead of the Japanese. With Robin's connections, they ended up in Kanhsien, in southernmost Kiangsi, and then caught a flight that took them another eight hundred miles west, to Kunming.

Robin returned to Wuhu, which had settled down under Japanese occupation, while Constance and her three daughters set off on a river floater heading south. As this was now the dead of summer, the floater was a welcome method of travel. The living quarters were above the waterline and dry. But the partially submerged lower deck of the barge allowed them to sit with their feet dangling in the cool river.

In the middle of one still night, river pirates stealthily boarded and robbed the floater of one of their luggage boxes. Despite Constance's complaint to the local police in the morning, nothing could be done. The pirates were long gone and the floater soon on its way again.

After one whole month on the floater, traveling south into Kiangsi, they headed toward Kanhsien, near Kanchow. The area was also rife with bandits, who at one point invaded a local official's home where they were staying.

They spent the night huddled together in an attic. At dawn's break, they emerged from their hiding place to find the wife of the official murdered.

It was too dangerous to continue to Kanhsien; the Japanese were about to capture nearby Kanchow, effectively cutting them off from any western route. They detoured east, but the jeep a friend hired for them broke down. They continued on foot, passing wounded soldiers and pedestrians injured by the hectic traffic on the unpoliced roads. American soldiers supporting the KMT seemed indifferent to the chaos and drove recklessly toward their self-designated mission, causing accidents and altercations often solved by impatient gunfire. Everyone seemed on edge, running from one trouble spot to the next.

The KMT soldiers continued to give up ground to the Japanese. To Constance, it was not hard to see that their government forces were demoralized, disorganized, and defeated as they continued to lose one battle after another. The more area that was surrendered, the farther they had to run.

Constance never had enough money in her pocket to feel at ease. Helen immediately set about looking for employment to help the family survive. She found work at a cafe run by the local YMCA. But the May Dragon Boat Festival brought so many people into the shop that the second floor collapsed, leaving Helen without a job. Constance resorted to selling some of their extra clothes by the roadside. With the money gained, she bought flour, some meat, and vegetables and turned them into dumplings.

She taught Hui how to make the dough, letting it sit in a warm place for a while. Hui would break off small pieces, roll them flat, delicately thin, then fill them with whatever Constance could find: vegetables, ginger, green onions. Pork, if money allowed. They would sit together folding the skin in half, pressing the ends to seal the filling, and pleating the edges. Sometimes, the filling was generous. But when money was wanting, so was the filling. If they had eggs, the white part served as a glue. When eggs were scarce, water would do. If the dough didn't stick together, the dumpling unraveled, and the filling would leak out. That would be bad luck, as if fortune were wasted. Hui became proficient enough to earn a few coins selling dumplings to soldiers.

Hui came down with chilblains, painful red spots brought on by cold weather. Constance washed her legs every day, applied a salve, and massaged her feet three times a day. No sooner had she healed than the Japanese pushed even closer. The family moved again further east, then north to Lichwan, near Foochow. Fleeing from each threat forced them to retreat in circles. At one point, they found an abandoned Buddhist temple, which they cleaned and made their home. They slept on the ground next to a giant reclining Buddha. The clay figure terrified Little Constance, although Hui found its appearance serene and soothing. If only they could be as peacefully as the Buddha. He alone seemed oblivious to the world's commotions.

Constance found neither rest nor peace. Helen and one of their ministers, Reverend Chou, developed typhus and head lice, and were quarantined in a house infested with free-roaming rodents. Constance brought Helen chrysanthemum tea and diligently de-liced her hair while mice watched from a corner of the room. Her routine required application of delousing medication and combing Helen's hair for two hours every day for two weeks. She did not miss a single day. Every stroke was methodical—slow and steady. Stroke after stroke. She never wavered.

Constance insisted Hui attend the local primary school. Hui had already missed much of her early education, and the war with Japan had consumed half her life. That Grace was able to gain entrance to Ginling and that Ginling still had the support of all the missionary organizations were miracles. Constance was determined to have her children more than survive. All she could do to that end was to keep going.

IN AUGUST 1945, THE UNITED STATES UNLEASHED TWO ATOMIC bombs that leveled the Japanese cities of Hiroshima and Nagasaki, killing hundreds of thousands of people. The world had never seen such immediate destruction.

A month later, with tens of millions of Chinese displaced throughout the country—some deep in limestone caves awaiting mustard gas—welcome words came to Constance at Lichwan. The Japanese emperor, Hirohito, had surrendered unconditionally to the American General Douglas MacArthur on the battleship USS *Missouri*. Constance gathered up her children and returned home to Wuhu. Their years of eluding the fox's claws were over. God had indeed protected their family.

But the church itself was falling apart. Missions and church buildings were damaged, occupied, or destroyed. Foreign administrators and bishops had been interned or repatriated out of China. Ministers had dispersed throughout the country. Church personnel were underpaid, under-rewarded, and difficult to recruit. Little if any foreign financial aid was coming into their coffers. Accessing hard currencies and disposing of accounts receivable were difficult at best, with financial institutions within the country beset by disrupted communications and runaway inflation. Congregations were decimated and concerned with survival on earth, not salvation in heaven. The church's intricate game of chess, with its strategic positioning of playing pieces, attempted forays forward, and careful defense of its most important assets, was upended by gusts of wind.

After a century in China, the church needed to start from scratch. Peace with Japan was not an opportunity to celebrate. The time had not yet come for China; life was not that simple. While people were eager to resume normal living, Generalissimo Chiang and Chairman Mao were not. Even before hostilities with Japan ended, Chiang and Mao were realigning forces and exerting influences to their advantage in expectation of a Japanese surrender and withdrawal from China. Soldiers from defeated armies defected to the opposition. Backroom bargaining took place between Chinese factions, the Soviet Union, the United States, and Japan. Double-dealing of alliances, bartering of land and military equipment, and manipulation of the Japanese withdrawal in Manchuria created great uncertainty in China's future.

For Robin and the rest of the Anglican and other Christian leaders, the long-sought Three-Self objectives were distant dreams. Self-governance was imposed with the wartime withdrawal of Western bishops, but self-support and self-propagation were yet to be solved. Success would depend on leaders like him, Lindel, and other Chinese clergy. No one could do it for them.

By the fall of the year following Japan's surrender, Grace was studying in Ginling College and Helen at its Middle School, Paul was finishing college in Kunming and planning to get married, and Little Constance was just beginning school. General Marshall's grand mission to unify China failed to bring Chiang and Mao together, and China was in the throes of full civil war.

With help from missionaries freshly discharged from internment camps, Robin set about to rehabilitate the mission. The Lion Hill rectory, school dormitories, office buildings, and church had been ravaged, ransacked, and gutted by the Japanese and later by swarms of pillaging government troops. Estimates for repairs soared impossibly into the tens of millions of Chinese dollars. The diocese could not afford that, but it had to be done. He sought assistance from the only place he could turn to— the place that he revered and appreciated almost as much as his homeland. He made his way back to America.

Chapter 43

AMERICA, AGAIN

"I thank the Women's Auxiliary and the Reconstructive and Advance Fund for all the help they have given China. The work of the Chinese Church has never stopped, not even in the worst days of the war."

Robin stood in front of over three hundred well-dressed ladies and gentlemen. A banner draped behind him announced the meeting of the Women's Auxiliary Club of the New York Episcopal Church. The group, attired in genteel finery, listened intently as they nibbled on their Waldorf salads and sipped their chardonnays. They had heard so much about this dynamic Chinese clergyman but knew so little about the true state of Christianity in China following the war. Repatriated church leaders like Bishops Craighill and Huntington had given personal accounts of the church's struggle and its triumphs. They both related how resilient and truly Christian the Chinese were. The Chinese were no longer just rice Christians, they claimed; Christian values flowed through their Chinese blood. In turn, China's culture and people were embedded in the missionaries' hearts. Neither could wash the other out of their lives. This mutual devotion compelled Lloyd, Bishop Roberts, and others to return to China following Japan's surrender. As with many other missionaries, not fully understood by their American friends, it felt as if they were going home.

"Our churches and other buildings were destroyed, and we were obligated to move many times," Robin recounted. "But we kept the work going."

The audience was rapt in its attention.

"Opportunities are greater than ever in history," he continued. "And a remarkable fact is that neither the Chinese Nationalists nor the Chinese Communists are against the church. Before I arrived here, I received letters from two Communist leaders saying the church was doing fine work and asked me to send church workers into their districts.

"What gives me great anxiety is whether we shall have the ability to meet the great and unique opportunities in China. We need material equipment. Spiritual equipment is needed even more. The Chinese are ready to do all they can. What they need most is training for the service of their own people. Clergy are needed, and so are teachers, doctors, nurses, and workers in every branch of church work."

A man in the audience raised his hand.

"Bishop Chen, what is your stance on the possibility of a Communist government, a party of atheists?" the man asked.

"We are not concerned with political struggles ... only with the people's well-being and moral spirituality," he answered.

"But what if that should come about? Is Christianity in China then not dead?" the man persisted.

Robin had long thought about this. It was true. Christianity, in fact any religion—the sigh of the oppressed creature, the heart of the heartless world, and the soul of soulless conditions, Marx's opium of the masses—was threatened by a Communist government. Church organizations would wear the translucent veil of imperialism, capitalism, and foreignism from their past, a veil to be torn and shredded at the earliest opportunity, destroying that which lay beneath. It was a frightful thought. But spirituality, belief in the teachings of Jesus Christ, acceptance of God's love: *How can that be expunged? How can truth be squashed by politics?*

"With God, all things are possible," he stated.

It took a few seconds for his answer to impact the audience. It was common opinion that China was a mess; that the church should simply give up. The financial support through the years left it with few missionaries and little to show. Even counting President Sun and Generalissimo Chiang as converts did not temper the bloodshed between fellow Chinese. Were the Chinese perhaps the primitives who could not be civilized, the wretched souls that could not be saved? The Communists were on the verge of victory and the church in China was surely soon extinguished. Instead, they heard from an eloquent orator the improbable possibility of Christian survival—even its necessity and permanence—as if it was an essential anatomical component of the Chinese nation.

"No government, communist or not, can suppress what is in a person's heart."

He was finished.

The audience took to the message from China. They stood as one body and applauded as one voice.

THE ENTHUSIASTIC AFFIRMATION IN NEW YORK WAS THE CUL-mination of a two-month speaking tour that began at the National Convention in Philadelphia. There, Robin was afforded the honor of addressing its delegates. They were from around the torn globe, few countries of which were left untouched by war. The world was attempting to heal, and China, represented by the Nationalist government, was placed on an equal level as one of the great powers of the world. Christian organizations were looked upon as a force of healing and reconstruction, and China needed their help.

"Your Church is mother to our Church. She knows best, but the child still may say what it needs. More youths to minister, more missionaries, more books. America, help us all you can!" Robin had implored.

Help did come, with $2.7 million of the $7 million annual budget of the Episcopal Church's National Council Reconstructive and Advance Fund going to assist China. Most of the funds went to schools and colleges and to assist in rebuilding facilities damaged or destroyed by the war. But a request for Chinese control of these funds in China was denied; the mother was still in control. Robin left the convention early as the only feasible expression of protest.

He was uncertain if his words at the convention would be heeded. Would they accept the church in China as equal but separate? Would they still be willing to assist one of their offspring, even as it sought its own freedom and independence?

The ovation at the Waldorf was reassuring.

GRACE WAS ELECTED CLASS PRESIDENT AT GINLING COLLEGE and had given the commencement speech at her graduation. She was selected to represent China as one of its student leaders at a youth conference in India. The conference was organized to coincide with the celebration of India's independence from British rule. During the conference, she met newly elected President Jawaharlal Nehru and the oddly ascetic, surprisingly influential, Mohandas Gandhi. Armed with a personal recommendation from her college president, Wu Yi-fang, she was on her way to the University of Pennsylvania as one of only three women in her medical school class, and the only Chinese.

Robin met Grace in Philadelphia to formally receive his honorary doctorate degree. It had been a full decade since the degree was bestowed upon him, and so much had occurred that it seemed almost a triviality from another lifetime.

The auditorium at the Divinity School was filled with students, teachers, and clergy as the dean walked to the microphone. Grace sat in the front row with her father, wide-eyed and transfixed. It was hard to believe she was finally in America.

"Bishop Chen has been a friend for years," the dean began. "He championed the education of many boys and girls and is a strong voice for Christian values. This honorary doctorate was conferred a decade ago, while he was fleeing with his flock from Japanese invaders. We are honored to see our friend again."

The dean gestured to Robin, who stood and walked to the stage, appreciative of the polite clapping. Robin shook the dean's hand as the dean read from the framed diploma.

"For his astounding mastery of Occidental learning and his rare ability to express himself in an acquired tongue," read the dean as he presented the diploma to Robin. "One of China's most gifted ministers, Bishop Robin Chen."

Applause came from all areas of the room as Robin ascended the stage. He looked at the plaque and its inscription, then glanced at the audience, setting his eyes on the row of young, bright-eyed divinity students sitting behind Grace.

"Despite the ubiquity of war and stubbornness of poverty, the spirit of Christians, that group of Chinese General Marshall called 'splendid liberals,' is inspiring," Robin began. "Christianity, the basis of democracy, peace, and unity, is up against a crisis, a dangerous opportunity which, should we miss it, might never come again."

Robin knew his history. The United States was built on Christian doctrines and beliefs. It would be unthinkable for Christianity not to exist there. But in China, Christianity was the *other* religion, the outsider's doctrine. To most Chinese, China could exist without Christianity, and among most Americans, China and its people were seen as heathen, so foreign as to not even exist as human. It was often posed to him: what use did one have for the other?

Off to the side, a hand shot up in the air. One of the divinity students stood up.

"Bishop Chen!" the young man called out.

The dean rose to cut off the interrupter, but Robin pointed to the student.

"Please," he invited the eager student.

"China was the first nation to sign the UN Charter to ensure against war and promote human rights and international justice. You are a confidante to Chiang Kai-shek. A *Christian* confidante. What did you advise him?" asked the student.

The young student had done his homework. The Charter was signed in 1945, prior to the end of the world war, and China was given the honor of being the first signatory as the initial victim of an Axis power. Chiang did often consult his Christian countrymen.

"Generalissimo Chiang is a Christian," acknowledged Robin. "But a leader acts for his country and its people without regard to personal beliefs. I offered my thoughts as a Chinese, *not* as a Christian. *All* Chinese are Chinese. All Chinese, Christian or Communist, want peace!"

"But is it true you have lost faith in the Generalissimo, that Christians in China are now Communist sympathizers, friendly to the Reds?" the student inquired.

That was the prevalent perception. The CCP *was* growing in strength because it fought for the peasants and workers. The KMT had forgotten the people of China. It had fostered corruption to which America turned a blind eye in its belief that Generalissimo Chiang, however flawed and accommodating to his party's criminality, was the only leader strong enough to unify China and quash the spread of Communism. It was a gamble they were forced to make. Christians were torn between their history with the Nationalists and their shared social values with the Communists. Were they doomed either way?

He looked the student in the eye, then cast his view over the audience, landing back on the student.

"God knows no politics. We want peace."

Robin glanced at Grace. Her eyes glistened with the pride one feels for a parent. Despite all they had been through, Grace, his number one daughter, was in the United States of America, studying to become the doctor China desperately needed. They had survived. They would all be all right. The future indeed looked bright.

Chapter 44

FINAL GOODBYES

Robin was scheduled to travel to various cities, as he did two decades ago. But before he left Philadelphia, he said goodbye to Grace. She would be in the United States for four years to complete medical school, and there was no telling when he would be back. He had met a wealthy Philadelphian family, the Perots, through his old Divinity School friend, Rev. James Gilbert, pastor of St. James Church of Kingsessing. Mrs. Perot's brother-in-law, Dr. Gummey, was the head of the Divinity School and taught both of the young students, who had lived together between 1928 and 1931. The Perots generously offered to look after Grace in their hometown.

The Perots were well-respected old money. They had owned a major brewing and malting company in Philadelphia since the early 1800s, and Mrs. Perot was from the Heublein family, whose company popularized premixed bottled cocktails. Heublein had diversified into Brand's A1 steak sauce and Smirnoff vodka. Just the previous year, they had acquired Grey Poupon mustard.

Like the Heubleins, the Perots were the epitome of American capitalism, and, as generous philanthropists and good Episcopalians, the finest example. The link between Bishop Chen and people like these families was emblematic of the strong ties between the Chinese Christians and the network of American missionary organizations. It was the Women's Auxiliary of the Diocese of North Carolina that had financially assisted Grace throughout college, and now medical school. Grace and her father were grateful for their

American sponsors; they were true lifesavers, without whom Grace could not afford to study in the United States.

"Never forget. Knowledge is intended not for your benefit, but for China's. Your people and your country need you," Robin reminded Grace as he stood outside the Divinity School auditorium.

How could she forget? It was all she had heard from him for years. She did not understand all the politics of China, but she knew China could not move forward without young people like her. The peasants might bring the Communists to power, but the educated would bring China prosperity. She wanted to be what her father called "the light and the salt."

"Robin, we will take good care of Grace," promised Mrs. Perot.

Robin put a comforting hand on Grace's shoulder as she willed her tears away. He gave her a fatherly hug and shook Mr. and Mrs. Perot's hands.

"Till we meet again," he said.

With that curt goodbye, he strode to the awaiting car and entered the back passenger seat.

As Grace watched the car drive off, she saw her father wave to her through the rear window. Grace's gaze followed the car down the long driveway and out into the street. Her father's smile continued to beam at her and she answered with a wave back.

Till we meet again, she thought as the car and her father faded out of view. She would see him home in four years.

ROBIN, THE ITINERANT PREACHER, TRAVELED AS HE DID BEFORE, up and down the States, informing and educating his American audiences, and seeking financial assistance. But Americans were more interested in the specter of Communism looming in Asia. Everywhere he went, he was questioned about China's politics. Suspicion was often second nature to those he met.

"For the first time, people in China are vitally concerned about the issues at stake," he reported at one gathering. "There is much talk of eventually resolving political differences into a united China. The Chinese people are— what is the term?—fed up with war."

"But are *you* a Communist?"

The local reporter had come to hear Robin speak at a church in Kentucky. It was such a direct question that it caused the others in the room to shift and murmur uncomfortably. But their voices quieted quickly and they leaned forward expectantly.

"My position is to minister to our people."

"Is that a yes or no?" persisted the reporter.

Of course, he was not a Communist. He never even considered the absurd idea. But to admit so would be to reject the common goals he felt Christians had with that political movement. How could he not stand with the impoverished and the weak? But to side with the KMT against the Communists would continue the tradition of elitism, corruption, and foreign ties that hampered the Christian church in China. Who was he? Could he be *for* something without being *against* another?

He remembered what John, the apostle, wrote: *He that loveth not his brother, whom he has seen, cannot love God, whom he has not.*

"Christ walked among the poor, the sick, and the persecuted. I follow his footsteps, except I do it in China," he said. "That is all."

The reporters chuckled as Robin walked out of the room. In the back of the room sat a couple of men in sunglasses. They weren't laughing at all. They were taking notes.

FROM KENTUCKY, ROBIN TRAVELED TO VIRGINIA AND MET WITH Reverend Wall and officials of the American Episcopal Church. The offering from the Sunday morning service was donated to Robin's diocese. Much of it was coins, but an American dollar went a long way in China; it showed that Americans still valued his work.

"The Anglican Church in China thanks you for your support. I am heartened by the desire of even the youngest and most humble of your congregation to help us. We are all one people under one God," Robin told Reverend Wall.

Reverend Wall handed Robin an envelope and replied, "We know that this small collection will be put to great use in China."

"One day we will be self-supporting. But that day is further into the future."

"Our own days in China are at an end," lamented Reverend Wall.

"Mao *is* gaining support," Robin responded frankly.

"I fear the writing is clear."

Reverend Wall took Robin's arm and pulled him close. They didn't know each other well. Forces larger than any one person or one church were at work. Anglicans were only a small fraction, perhaps no more than ten percent, of the Protestants in China. Communists were millions strong.

"You … your entire family will suffer. Consider the alternatives."

"Alternatives?"

"Join your children here in the States."

Robin heard this plea everywhere: Ohio, Pennsylvania, Massachusetts, even Toronto. Come to America, they said.

"America is always a sanctuary for the oppressed," he answered carefully. He thought of his conversations with Bishop Huntington. Their countries were different. America was always a beacon to him, he felt proud to say. His education in mission schools, his travels to so many states, and his two eldest children attending universities in America made him feel as if he was an adopted American. Were the college students in Nanling right when they said he was not truly Chinese? Did Christianity transform him into a cultural traitor? Could he betray his homeland?

"We will do all we can for you," promised Reverend Wall. "Nothing good for Christians is going to come from the civil war in China. And if the Communists win …"

Robin shook his head and put his arm around the minister's shoulders.

"Reverend Wall, thank you. China is my home."

With that, Robin said his final goodbye to America.

Chapter 45

NIGHTMARES
BECOME DREAMS

Upon his return to China, Robin immediately noticed the economic effects of the civil war, especially on his Western colleagues. The average monthly salary for American missionaries was $75. Robin's was $30, although his original contract with the church was for $100. But commodity prices had recently doubled. The Shanghai wholesale price index of 15 in 1941 was now 16,000,000. The KMT was printing money to finance their military activities, and inflation caused prices to double every week or two. In December 1941, a US dollar exchanged for 18.93 yuan on the black market. At the end of 1945, the yuan had fallen to 1,222 for the same dollar. A new Chinese yuan was issued by the government that converted to the old yuan at a ratio of one new to three *million* old. The money supply would increase twenty-fold in six months. A suitcase, even a wheelbarrow, was needed to haul the currency required for a ticket on a ship to America.

Robin's trip to America had been good for his overall health. Food was plentiful and nutritious. He was well-hosted in comfortable, sanitary housing and was able to rest between his travels to dozens of cities. He had gained weight and felt strong. But as soon as he landed in Wuhu, worry about the church, about finances, about the country's future caused an old ailment to act up. His chronic abdominal pain came back worse than ever. Surgery for a stomach ulcer was offered but ultimately rejected. There was too much for him to do.

In June, he was called to Shanghai on two days' notice. An unprecedented eleven bishops from China were to attend the Lambeth Conference of Anglican bishops in England. Constance reluctantly helped him pack.

"The others ... they will be enough!" she complained.

His stomach problems were worsening. He had lost all the weight gained in America.

They were constantly short of money, and Constance often could not buy much more than rice and some vegetables. Meat and eggs were much too expensive. She grew melons, green vegetables, and corn in their garden and was raising two pigs. Thankfully, their only hen hatched a dozen baby chicks. In a recent letter to Grace, she had complained that there was such a big gap in pay between the Western and Chinese ministers that her family had to rely on help from friends to make ends meet.

"You need to rest!" Constance argued.

"We must make a strong case. We *all* must go," he explained quietly. "It is our time."

China was first invited to the decennial conference as a fully recognized national church in 1938. Lindel Tsen was the sole Chinese at that initial meeting. Now, the church was preparing to send four Chinese bishops—Robin, Lindel, Y.Y. Tsu, and Michael Cheng—along with seven non-Chinese: Curtis, Bevan, Hall, Roberts, Wellington, White, and Halward. It would be a dramatically stronger showing, a statement that, despite being so remote from the center of influence, China was a significant province worthy of attention.

"It's too far ... too much for you," Constance continued to protest.

"We *must* show unity. If not, we will always be a child. The church will wither and die."

Hui walked into the room and interrupted them.

"*Ba. Lai, chi.*" Come, eat.

She had prepared dumplings. It was her going-away present to him; he would be gone nearly the entire summer. She spent the morning folding her tasty treasures and sealing them with water. It was something she could do with her eyes closed. Today, she boiled them into a soup.

Robin left Constance and went with Hui.

"As good as Mother's," Robin said as he sampled a piece.

"She taught me in the countryside," she said, beaming.

Her face suddenly dissolved into a look of anguish. Her thin voice cracked and her eyes began to tear.

"I had nightmares."

Robin ate slowly and nodded. He savored each bite, mindful of upsetting his stomach. Nightmares were common in China. Images of severed heads did that to children.

"*Bu ku,*" he said, gently this time. "When our country has peace, filling the mind will be as necessary as filling the stomach. You, Ge Ge, and Jie Jie will rebuild China. Your nightmares will become dreams."

THE NEXT DAY, ROBIN WENT TO THE SHANGHAI TRAIN STATION with hundreds of other travelers headed for Peking. Cars were filled to capacity, though he had a reserved seat in second-class. His stomach ached the whole trip, so that he was exhausted by the time he arrived. The real traveling then began. He and the ten bishops boarded a Pan Am flight for their trip to London. It took three days with many planned stops: Bangkok, Siam; Calcutta and New Delhi, India; Karachi, Pakistan; Damascus, Syria; Istanbul, Turkey; and Brussels, Belgium. They finally landed in London at half past three in the morning.

Robin, like his fellow bishops, had a full agenda of invitations to various parishes around England, speaking with ministers and congregations of China's plight and hopes. There were important delegate presentations and meetings, proposals to consider, and a presidential gala dinner. Robin had a personal invitation to stay with the Archbishop of Canterbury, Geoffrey Fisher, at his residence at the Old Palace, a 10th century medieval building next to Canterbury Cathedral.

China needed to attract church workers and young, educated clergy. The bishops brought an important resolution before the delegates: the proposal to allow deaconesses to ascend to the priesthood. This idea was decidedly against the usual tenets of both the Anglicans and the Roman Catholics. But China saw itself differently. Women were as capable, dedicated, and spiritual as men. And China, both the church and the country, needed women and was willing to challenge the rule of the mother church.

Robin knew Grace, as an American-trained medical doctor, could be one of the influential women to lead China into the modern era. For that, her time in the States would be worth it. She had been profiled in a new book, *Christian Voices in China,* as "representative of many young Chinese girls who come from good Christian homes and schools," who, with many complicated problems in the world, "faced reality with courage, sound judgment, and confidence." Immediately following her biography in the book was that of Madame Chiang Kai-shek.

He felt proud of Grace. But she had yet to accomplish everything she was capable of for her country.

Chapter 46

LAMBETH

The procession of bishops was held on a blustery, overcast English day. The walkway leading into the 11th century Gothic Canterbury Cathedral was lined by throngs of spectators wrapped in overcoats, occasionally grasping at their hats as the breeze threatened to snatch them away. It was a celebratory parade for such a religious event and many of the 300-plus primates smiled and waved to the crowd. The clergymen, some in the traditional dress of their homelands, walked behind wooden cross banners marked with the names of their countries. Leading at the front, the Archbishop of Canterbury, Geoffrey Fisher, garbed in his finest ceremonial regalia, stood tall with typical British aloofness. He wore glasses that seemed too small for his elongated, gourd-like face, with its jutting forehead and prominent chin. His wispy hair barely encircled the occiput of his otherwise bald head. It wasn't a glorious day, but the gloomy skies graciously held off on releasing their moisture onto the priestly procession.

The Cathedral was a massive stone structure whose interior was over five hundred feet long and eighty feet tall, richly embellished with colorful glass windows, bossed vaulted ceiling, and majestic arches. The bishops took their seats in the sanctuary and choir sections, with other ministers seated in the front of the nave. The rest of the capacious cathedral was filled with parishioners, guests, and spectators. After an invocation, Archbishop Fisher welcomed the audience.

"The Mother Church is overjoyed to greet delegates of the Lambeth Conference," Archbishop Fisher began. "Your duty and privilege is to represent the Church in all corners of the globe. It is indeed a heavy burden to lead the world away from the conflicts and politics of the Second Great War and the threat of turmoil in the distant land of Asia. We are a church of inclusion, love, and charity, not war. May we find unity and consensus in our honorable conference."

It was a hopeful time, Robin thought. The conference had been postponed eight years due to the great conflict. That men of the church could gather in, and speak of, unity was testament to the indestructible Christian capacity of forgiveness. The Japanese delegation had been subsidized by the British Army. They stood in the same church as the delegates from China, their former foe, and prayed in the same pews as the hundred bishops from their vanquisher, the United States. There was reason for optimism that the mother church would listen to his country's requests.

Later, the bishops gathered at Lambeth Palace, the residence of the Archbishop. Lindel, now Presiding Bishop, laid out the Chinese bishops' appeal.

"It is a great honor to represent our Chinese brothers and sisters. To be fully recognized as a separate but equal arm of the Anglican Church is an historic event. Florence Tim-Oi Li, ordained by Bishop Hall of the diocese of Hong Kong, should stand as a progressive example of the usefulness and necessity for women priests in China. China is fighting for its future, the result of which is uncertain. What is certain is that we must succeed in our self-governance, self-support, and self-propagation. Old traditions have stunted our effectiveness in the new world. This esteemed governing body must recognize the wisdom and inevitability of our autonomy."

It was bold and direct, with respect, but without ambiguity. China wanted autonomy, an end to foreign regulation, and the right to ordain women.

Women had never been allowed to rise to the priesthood; it was an unpopular idea. But China was too vast and large a nation to ignore half its population. To be of service to the church, it was proposed that women be required to have the same qualifications as the men; in addition, they had to be at least thirty years old and unmarried for the duration of their service. Was this demand going to cause a rift in the church? Would the mother church understand the needs of its child?

Robin applauded with the other bishops from China, impressing upon the Archbishop the unstilted support they gave to their application for women clergy. They would have to wait for the verdict.

The bishops were invited to a sumptuous garden party at Buckingham Palace to meet King George VI and his queen, Elizabeth. The king had famously ascended to the throne after his brother, Edward, abdicated to marry the American divorcee Wallis Simpson. Few in the Chinese delegation had ever been to such a magnificent building.

"You love your royals," remarked Lindel to his English counterpart, John Wellington, the British bishop for Shantung Province.

"Separation of church and state is, at best, tenuous and vexing," injected the American Bishop Roberts.

"Here, separation does not exist," explained Bishop Wellington. "We *are* a church of the state."

"But *we* carry the yoke of guilt by this royal association," Lindel lamented.

"It *is* a yoke," Robin agreed.

The three hundred and twenty-nine bishops were dressed in their official purple robes as they entered the majestic Reception Hall, which had been bedecked in red: red walls, red curtains, and red furniture. If the style were different, they could have been in China. Guests included the Shah of Iran, with his extensive entourage, regal Indian princes and bejeweled Indian princesses, and former Prime Minister and Mrs. Winston Churchill, he with his ever-present cigar.

It was after the receiving line and the party with King George VI was long over that Archbishop Fisher let it be known that China's resolution had met with rejection from the conference members.

"The General Synod of the Church in China having brought a proposal that for an experimental period of twenty years a deaconess might be ordained to the priesthood and, having referred the question whether such experiment would be in accordance with Anglican tradition and order, the Conference feels bound to reply that such an experiment is *against* the tradition and order and would gravely affect the internal and external relations of the Anglican Communion."

There it was: a clear rebuff of China's request. China, the child, would get neither help nor liberty from the mother church.

"We appreciate your efforts on behalf of our Church. Independence is a laudable goal, yet it is still not achievable. China is an extension of the Mother Church," explained the Archbishop to the Chinese.

"We beg reconsideration," Robin interjected. "England cannot comprehend the obstacles China alone faces."

"The autonomy you seek sets a precedent that can only hurt the Mother Church," answered the Archbishop.

"The Mother Church is only as strong as its children," replied Robin.

"Yes, but the Mother Church is, nonetheless, the mother," stated the Archbishop emphatically.

That was it. Unity within the church meant China was still the child. The conference also rejected the intercommunion of the newly formed church of South India, which had united diverse denominations of the Protestant faith. Loyalty to the catholic and conservative principles of the Mother Church was paramount. In that exact moment, the Three-Self principle moved from being a *better* road for China to a *necessary* one. Bitterness soured Robin's understanding of the Archbishop's reasoning.

"I am sorry we cannot do more," the Archbishop replied politely.

"Our church must be for China and its people," conceded Robin.

The Archbishop shook Robin's hand.

"Bishop Chen, you are a patriot in your homeland. The struggle between church and country is great, even here."

"Your Grace, God has no homeland. If the church does not serve the people, the people will not serve the church."

It seemed obvious, meant as premonition rather than a threat. The Chinese bishops' work in England was done. They went to the airport to return home, except for Lindel, who decided to visit his son in Philadelphia, and Bishop Tsu, who went to Holland for a conference.

The plane carrying the delegation departed the mother soil of England and ascended towards the darkened sky. It broke through the opaque nimbostratus, turgid with summer's moisture. Robin peered out the window and beheld the boundless, blindingly bright space above the dense clouds. It was as though he had ascended to heaven, where peace reigned. A heavy burden was lifted. He closed his eyes and thought: *God's will be done.*

The path ahead was clear to him as the saturated clouds finally relieved themselves onto the land below.

Chapter 47

HOUSES DIVIDED

Robin was still relatively young, not yet fifty-five years old, and there was still so much to do. The Nationalists were losing more and more cities to the Communists and, even though the United States unofficially supported Chiang with troops, equipment, and money, the international community largely treated the civil dispute as an internal affair. No one wanted another international war.

The American government, missionary organizations, and business corporations strongly advised mass evacuations of expatriates. Many dedicated American ministers and bishops chose to remain at their posts, but it was a financially tenuous position since transfer of international funds into Communist-held territories was uncertain. A request from Bishop Roberts for a $91,000 advance to pay for six months of salaries was hotly debated in a National Council meeting in America. The fear was that the monies would not reach the intended beneficiaries or would not be recoverable if unused. The request was rejected, and, because the Chinese church was not yet self-sufficient, missionaries dug into their own modest savings to keep mission activities and their own families viable.

Mission organizations were conflicted. They had a responsibility to their employees and volunteers, including financial obligations for evacuation out of China and travel back home. But they were reluctant to send money into China. This put an undue burden on the Chinese to support those foreigners who decided to stay when they could ill afford to do so. While all common sense indicated that evacuation was prudent, even obligatory, that action could understandably lead to a sense of abandonment among the Chinese. If the Chinese had to stay, why would not the foreigners who were bringing them this religion of salvation and hope in the first place? Loss of courage by the missionaries could be interpreted by the Chinese as a loss of trust, faith, and commitment. As a result, ninety percent of the missionaries volunteered to stay. Robin and his Chinese colleagues were appreciative of the foreigners' great sacrifice, which, in turn, gave greater resolve to their own faith.

Robin knew a dramatic event was about to occur. It was only a matter of when and how bloody it would be. Most of the people's sentiments were with Mao and his CCP. The Red Army was growing in strength, surpassing the KMT forces, which were deteriorating. Captured soldiers crossed over and joined the Red Army, as did millions of peasants who were promised land ownership.

In some areas, the Communists protected churches, schools, and mission buildings, as well as foreigners themselves. In others, they took possession of facilities, including hospitals, dismissed the personnel, and stripped clinics of supplies and equipment. In general, despite the uneven treatment, common people embraced the like-minded Communists and turned against the corrupt, cruel, and inattentive KMT.

Sensing their grip slipping, KMT army officers and China's elites funneled money and treasures out of the country. Generalissimo Chiang shipped thousands of crates of ancient artifacts, artworks, jade carvings, calligraphy, porcelain pieces, historical books, copperworks, and tons of gold to the island of Taiwan. Some called it safekeeping. Others referred to it as looting. Either way, Chiang was preparing for defeat and his own escape. The Marshall Mission to incorporate the CCP into the KMT government to form a united China was failing miserably.

Robin was glad Grace and Paul and his wife, Helene, were away in America. He was confident the rest of his family would be as safe in China as his oldest children were in America. The fighting and the fear were not as great as when the Japanese invaded; the country had surrendered to fatalism. The KMT had long lost the people's hearts, and Chinese citizens were tired of war. The form of government was not as important as peace itself. The people only wanted a side—any side—to win; if Communist, so be it.

After all, in the end, any government would be Chinese, not foreign. Once Grace and Paul completed their studies abroad, they could return to help rebuild the country. He could continue his church work, convinced there would still be religious freedom. Of that he was sure. Communist leaders had pledged as much to him.

THAT DECEMBER, AT AGE SIXTY-THREE, BISHOP LINDEL TSEN suffered a stroke while in the United States and was paralyzed. He remained in Philadelphia and submitted his resignation to the House of Bishops. The House rejected the resignation and appointed Robin as acting Presiding Bishop, with the hope that Lindel would eventually recover and return home. Lindel planned to retire in another year or two, and Robin was expected to succeed him as Presiding Bishop, but things were moving too fast. The country was in turmoil. The church was on unsteady ground, and foreign relations were breaking up. The economy was collapsing, and inflation was out of control.

Hui had not been admitted into college, an obvious disappointment to her and her parents but understandable, given her fragmented education. She went to Shanghai to help Robin in the central office of the CHSKH while he assumed responsibilities as the interim Presiding Bishop. She spent every day with her father, taking the bus from their rented room in a house owned by the dentist of one of his theology students. They ate every break-fast together, had lunch at a local restaurant, and then returned home to eat dinner. Every moment Hui was with her father, she could feel the pride he had in his country and the hope he had for peace. She listened closely to each of his carefully chosen words, memorizing their meaning and impact. Each conversation was like a valuable sermon.

"With peace will come prosperity. With prosperity we can defend against outsiders," he assured her. "The Kuomintang government has rotted, but the Communists have the people's welfare in mind. Perhaps they will be the dawn after the darkness we have experienced."

Robin kept Grace and Paul informed of what was happening in China. His letters were long and descriptive. Of the Communist takeover of Wuhu, he wrote:

Dear Grace, Shanghai might be out any moment. Enemy forces are nearer every day. Quite a few people were killed during the change of hands. One rich man was burned by the mob. Recently a search has been started to arrest the so-called "war criminals" and a number of leading citizens have fled for safety. I told Mother to sell some of our things when she needs more money.

Sometimes, he was the concerned father giving advice:

Pathology has so many medical terms entirely new to you. It will take time for you to build up your vocabulary to find it easy to study such a subject. But it will not be impossible. It simply means you have to spend more time on it.

At other times, encouraging his children to be of service:

We shall be ever more in need of well-trained social workers and first-class men and women in the gigantic task of social reconstruction. By "first-class," I mean not merely men and women of brilliant scholarship, practical ability, and high ideals, but also those who have true Christian hearts and vision, not of the average or even typical American type, but with the humility, compassion, and vicarious living of Jesus, the son of Man, who was always ready to live, to share, and to suffer with the poor, the depressed, and the underprivileged sinners and outcasts as well as the helpless children. There will be no way out for this country of ours unless everyone who has received a good education is wholeheartedly willing to live simply and vicariously for the good of the common people without pride and that feeling of superiority which we do find in the consciousness of many of our educated people and Western friends. Therefore, I earnestly hope that you will always bear in mind that you are not preparing yourselves to serve an American or Russian community, but to come back to your own chaotic country to serve your unfortunate brothers and sisters with the sympathetic understanding and with true Christian humility.

And ever the preacher:

China is desperately in need of help not from others, but from her own loyal and sacrificial sons and daughters. God will lead us to help her if we are willing to try our utmost to offer the whole of our lives for Him to do so. May God richly bless each and all of you so you may never fail the unprecedented opportunities of serving Him and our country and our world that are ahead of you.

Robin knew the world was about to change.

Chapter 48

THE LIBERATION
OF SHANGHAI

W hile the panic in Shanghai did not match the terror of the Japanese invasion, there was still panic. Market shelves were emptied of foodstuffs. Thousands of frantic foreigners waited anxiously as custom officials expedited far fewer visas than were demanded. Foreigners packed as many of their belongings as they could and headed for the Shanghai port, where officials tried to control the massive crowds. Travelers struggled to haul their own luggage up the crowded, steep plankway into the awaiting ships; foreign currency to hire help was worthless. The Whampoa riverway was filled with vessels tightly crammed, stern to bow and port to starboard, forming a floating mosaic of junks, sampans, and barges.

At the railway station, a crush of Chinese overwhelmed the offices. Tickets were quickly sold out and the buildings closed. Riots erupted as angry crowds tried futilely to break down the doors. Every flat surface of the train making its deliberate way out of Shanghai was occupied by desperate people clinging to any fixed structure. Bodies dangled out of the windows. Riders sat hip to hip and shoulder to shoulder on the roofs of the cars, even perching themselves precariously on the front of the locomotive—attached human appendages flaring like the horns of a water buffalo. The cars leaving the station were charged with the most basic instinct of humanity. Survival.

The main artery leading south, away from the Communist forces advancing into the city from the north, was congested with a steady flood of pedestrians and wheeled vehicles: motorcycles, bicycles, rickshaws, cars, buses, two-wheeled mule carts, and single-axle wheelbarrows loaded with tightly bound mounds of worldly possessions towering over their owners.

Street intersections were tangled messes of vehicles. Drivers shouted their way through the cross-currents of traffic that came to a standstill, like debris caught in a clogged drain. Those who made their way out of the city passed KMT reinforcements sent in as a doomed, last-ditch effort to defend the metropolis.

In the center of the city, individuals suspected of being communist sympathizers were rounded up, arms tethered helplessly to wooden boards behind their backs. They were forced down on their knees, then unceremoniously executed in the streets by local police and KMT officers. A few required a second bullet before they expired. Some went through impromptu shotgun proceedings on a convenient curbside. Others were spared this façade of formality and disposed of promptly without the charade of a judicial hearing. Thousands of citizens witnessed this purge, which turned sentiments against the KMT even more. The cold-blooded executions were brutal acts of vengeance and cowardice, proving futile as the Communist army moved virtually unopposed toward the heart of Shanghai. One more dead sympathizer would not stop the inevitable.

Days prior to this climactic exodus, Robin had come to a momentous decision. Sitting at his desk, writing a letter to Grace, he heard rapid knocking on his door that announced an eager visitor. He rose to open it, revealing a well-dressed man.

"Bishop Chen. Charles Clark, from the American Church Mission."

Robin invited Clark in. The man took off his hat and extended his arm. They shook hands as Robin indicated a chair. He noticed the man's face was tense with worry.

"I am sent by the directors," said Clark, sitting on the edge of the chair. "They implore you. Leave Shanghai. We have seats on our last boat tomorrow. Once the city falls, you will not be safe."

"Mr. Clark. All of my family, my co-workers, my parishioners, they are here in Shanghai."

"Parishioners will not matter. Let us be frank. There is no future here. The Communists will destroy the church. They will show you no mercy."

Robin was familiar with this reasoning: Communism and Christianity could not coexist. Their gentle treatment of missionaries was designed to gain the trust of the people; that was all—a calculated political ploy. Once in power, their beliefs would not allow religion to exist, certainly not a reactionary, foreign one. There could be only one authority. He, too, had firmly believed this.

"How can I leave?" Robin asked.

"We can assure safe passage to America, in the morning. We *all* must get out."

Robin meant his question to be rhetorical. He had suspected things would come to this, but he had never contemplated his own safety or leaving China. It was unthinkable. But now that the inevitable was at his doorstep, it was different. The foreign clergy for sure must leave. But the Chinese? His family?

"We cannot help you if you stay," warned Clark as he noted Robin's hesitation. "You will be on your own."

God's love had to prevail. Love so great.

"Mr. Clark, before I am Christian, I am Chinese."

"Please, we beg you. Think of your family. Come with us," urged Clark.

Robin stood up. He held out his hand. He couldn't fault this American for believing it would be better to leave China.

"Thank the directors for their kind offer."

Clark looked at him oddly, but then nodded resignedly.

"I am sorry, Reverend Chen," Clark said as he stood up to leave. "Good luck."

Once Clark left, Robin went back to his letter. He thought of Grace and tried to imagine what she was doing. He hadn't heard her voice for nearly two years. She would be wearing a white coat, learning how to listen to a patient's heart or how to take a medical history. She would be surrounded by other young doctors eager to learn. He hoped she had a social life. That would be important. She was about the same age as Constance when he had married her. Would she meet some nice Chinese man, perhaps another doctor? It was all rather unlikely, he thought. A father's selfish wish. She was one of three women, and not a single Chinese man in her class. Perhaps she would return home to serve the people and find a husband among her own kind. China needed doctors. It needed strong women. It needed good Christian patriots. It needed so much.

He felt tired from all the writing and dreaming and laid his head down to rest. He was soon fast asleep, oblivious to the distant sounds of gunfire and the commotion that was engulfing the city.

∽ 🌐 ∽

THIS TIME, IT WAS HUI WHO WOKE HIM FROM HIS DEEP SLUM-ber. Another visitor was rapping on the door, which Hui opened, and a man in full uniform strode into his study. Robin recognized Commander Liu of the Republic's Armed Forces 52nd Regiment. Four other soldiers were waiting outside.

"Commander Liu!" exclaimed Robin in surprise.

Robin quickly rose to greet the officer, who wore a stern face. The Commander removed his cap and reached out his hand. Robin indicated to a nervous Hui to fetch some tea as he grasped the commander's hand.

"Bishop Chen. The enemy is at our doorsteps. Generalissimo Chiang has instructed me to offer protected transport for you and your family."

"I am indebted to the Generalissimo." *A private request*, he thought. Chiang had officially given up the presidency earlier in the year and had effectively retired, fully expecting a change in government.

"The Generalissimo insists. Tomorrow, the port will belong to the opposition. Shanghai is destroyed!" Liu stated as if it had already occurred.

Robin had his connections to the Communist leadership and knew this last statement to be false. Or at least he believed it to be inaccurate. Chou En-lai was clear in instructing his troops to protect the people and to preserve buildings and important landmarks. The Communist victory had long been ensured by Mao, who had plans in place.

To destroy the most populated city in China would only force them to spend a fortune and time that they could ill afford to rebuild it. Preserving it would engender goodwill from the people. The gracious and generous victor would serve a much more persuasive purpose than a vengeful vanquisher. Mao and Chou were not stupid. They were clever, calculating, and dependent on the people's support.

"The Generalissimo and I share the same goal. Peace for China," replied Robin, unwilling to argue with the Commander about the questionable intentions and magnanimity of the Communist leadership. Hui returned with tea, which she poured into a cup for the Commander. He waited for her to leave before continuing.

"I have men ready to escort you before dawn," persisted the Commander as he blew on his tea to cool it. He took a sip as he waited for Robin's reply, which was deliberate and slow in coming.

It was well known that Madame Chiang admired Robin. The Generalissimo also respected Robin but was more interested in depriving the Communists, draining China of its valuable and important assets—that included personnel, which he thought of as if they were pieces of jade or porcelain.

"Commander, my entire life has known only war. Peace is a precious commodity we cannot sacrifice. Now, we will be done with war. It is time to rebuild our great nation."

"Bishop Chen—" the Commander began to protest.

"You ask to give up my country," Robin interrupted. "No. I cannot abandon it, or our people. My prayers are with Generalissimo and Madame Chiang. They are in great danger if the opposition succeeds. I believe I am not."

"You are mistaken."

"May you have safe passage."

The Commander put down the teacup, bowed, and began to walk out. Robin motioned for him to wait and went to his desk. He took the letter he had written, looked it over, then signed it.

"Commander Liu," he said, carefully folding, addressing, and sealing the letter. He handed the envelope to the officer. "Please, for my daughter."

The Commander looked at the letter and nodded when he saw it was addressed to the United States. He bowed again, this time a bit lower, with a softer look on his face, as if he understood the sacrifice. He turned and left with his guards.

Robin closed the door and went back to his desk. He did not envy the Commander or the Generalissimo; they were forced to leave China. They were without a future, without a home.

On the desk were photos of his family: Constance, Paul, Grace, Helen, Hui, and Little Constance. Paul had a young wife, Helene, and a new son, now almost two years old. Life marched on. Had he made the right decision for his family? Would life truly prosper in a peaceful China? He looked at Grace's photo from her Ginling College graduation. He saw China's future in her.

"Hui! Hui!" he called out.

Hui came running. She had been listening just outside the room.

Robin pointed to a chair. Hui sat down. He faced her as calmly as he could.

"Hui, the government has abandoned Shanghai. The last boat leaves at dawn."

He let his words sink in for Hui. They looked at each other. Robin took her hands in his. He had determined her fate and that of the whole family.

"Chou En-lai sent an emissary," he said.

"Emissary? When?"

"A week ago," he said, as Hui stared at him with wide eyes and an open mouth.

"Why?"

"The Nationalists will destroy Shanghai before the Communists arrive. They have already begun to loot the city. Terrible things are happening. But Chou promised to protect our city and our people."

"You believe him?" she asked incredulously.

"Chou is not stupid. He sees peace and prosperity for China. His side will be victorious, not because he has more troops, but because he has the people. He will not destroy their future."

"Why did he send *you* an emissary?" she asked again.

"He asked me to stay."

Hui stared at hm blankly, not understanding.

"To help rebuild."

"Why you?"

"He knows we are afraid of communism. He knows many will want to leave. He asked for my loyalty."

"Your loyalty?" Hui asked. "To Mao? To the party?"

Robin shook his head.

"To China. To our people. He knows our church people are good people. We respect the law. We help others. We believe in goodness and will help China succeed. He knows about our schools, our hospitals, our land reform. We are part of China and its future."

"What did you say?" she asked.

"I told him my loyalty is to my faith and to God."

He looked at Grace's photo again. Hui waited for him. His answer was for Grace. And Paul. For his whole family.

"My faith tells me ... rebuild."

It could be no other way. For, as many times as he had visited other countries, including America, he would never leave China. Just as he had thrown his lot in with God, he would see China through to its destined future.

"I will go make dumplings," Hui said abruptly and stood up.

They both heard explosions outside, growing louder and more frequent, and they knew what to expect. The Communists would soon be there.

Chapter 49

RECLAIMING CHINA

Hui lay in her bed on the second floor of the house she and her father shared. The morning sun was beginning to cast a smoky yellow hue through her window. She had gone to sleep to the punctuated crackle of gunfire and the distant thud of explosions. But now it was eerily quiet, as if the sounds of war were a radio broadcast that had ended while she slept. She rubbed her eyes and then her ears. Something had happened.

She jumped out of bed, quickly dressed, and ran down the stairs, out into the street. Her eyes met an extraordinary and unfamiliar sight.

People were smiling and walking towards the main boulevard, chatting excitedly with each other. She could see rows of soldiers sleeping on the sides of the streets. They wore the dull yellow-green uniform, not of the Nationalists, but of the People's Liberation Army. They had slipped into the city unopposed, careful not to alarm or disturb the residents. Some people offered them flowers, food, even warm towels. But the soldiers politely refused.

Once Hui saw other soldiers marching in orderly fashion through the streets, their firearms holstered or slung casually over their shoulders, she turned around and quickly sprinted home. She threw open the front door and ran through the house.

"Ba … Ba!"

Robin was up and dressed, and soon joined her. They walked together to the boulevard and watched the troops flow into the city by the thousands.

The crowd had also grown in size. Hundreds of people were laughing and waving to the soldiers. They cheered and danced freely.

Robin smiled and threw open his arms, embracing the world. *God brought China out of the darkness and the shadow of death, and He tore off their shackles,* he thought. The soldiers' feet reminded him of Hsiao Wang; thousands of pairs of straw sandals had come to save Shanghai. He wondered where his friend was at this great moment.

Hui and Robin hugged and cheered with the rest of the crowd.

HUI GLANCED AT HER FATHER AS HE WAVED TO THE YOUNG soldiers. His face was filled with the broadest of smiles. The morning rays reflected off his glistening cheeks, moist from the tearful twinkle in his eyes. She felt an unfamiliar calmness, a long time coming. She hadn't seen him this joyful. Ever.

Hui yelled as loud as she could and wiped shameless tears from her cheeks.

JUST THE NIGHT BEFORE, THE CITY HAD BEEN BEDECKED WITH banners praising the victorious Nationalist army, urging people to "Strike Down the Communist Bandits." There was even a spontaneous parade prematurely celebrating the triumph of the KMT army. The trappings and sham sentiments of those festivities evaporated overnight. The liberation of Shanghai grew from a gleeful welcoming of the Communists to the grateful community's purposeful interactions with polite soldiers. The troops swept the streets clean of broken glass and debris, fixed rickshaws and bicycles, and helped push overburdened carts across bridges.

The people, in turn, tended to the soldiers' wounds. They provided towels to clean their dirt-frosted faces. Women sewed buttons back onto tattered uniforms. They offered fresh, hot food, which the soldiers at first refused. Hui gave her dumplings to soldiers after convincing them that they would not be any less honorable for accepting. The soldiers were well-trained and maintained their discipline and reserve. Hui remembered seeing people run away from the Nationalist, American, and Japanese soldiers. But Shanghai people were running towards the PLA soldiers who embraced the embattled city.

The city returned to normal life in the following days. Shops gradually reopened. People went back to work. Repairs to buildings began. Businesses, presses, and banks resumed services.

"Hui, tell your friends we are going to the theater."

Hui looked at her father like he was crazy. Had he lost his mind? But she could see he was serious and went to fetch the three daughters of their friends, the Dengs.

Robin and the four girls walked to Shanghai's Grand Theatre—the ornate Deco-style movie house on West Nanjing Road, which featured first-run English movies: *Tarzan's Secret Treasure, Kismet,* and, more recently, *The Perils of Pauline.* Normally, ushers in natty uniforms, top hats, and white gloves greeted theatergoers dressed in fashionable clothes and seated them in comfortable, cushioned chairs equipped with individual headsets for translations. The cinema had high ceilings, wrought-iron railings, dazzling chandeliers, and seats for 1,900 patrons. But on this day, they were among only a handful of common people who braved the confusion and commotion to lose themselves in a tale from Hollywood.

As she watched the movie, Hui caught a glimpse of her father from the corner of her eye. He saw her looking at him. He smiled at her and her friends as the reflected images danced across their faces. She saw a glow twinkling from his eyes, and she smiled back. The eyes said they were safe. It hardly occurred to her that they were enjoying a rare moment of peace, sitting in the most opulent showpiece of colonial China, as the populist Communist government was taking over their city. None of that really mattered. In the comfort of the vast darkness, with father, daughter, and friends, hearing voices and seeing scenes telling a story born of imagination, life did seem grand.

The changing of the government guard progressed to a city-wide event, with a military parade featuring artillery armaments, new tanks, armored cars, and truckloads of soldiers waving to the massive crowd. The streets teemed with humanity. Trolley cars were decorated with glistening trim and large photos of Mao and Commander General Chu Teh. Banners, fluttering in the breeze, proclaimed, "Against Bureaucratic Capitalism, Feudalism, and Imperialism," and "Increase Production, Grow the Economy." The Communist propaganda machine was wasting no time.

There were colorful figures on stilts, dancing yellow and red lions, thousands of balloons, and fragrant bouquets tossed at the victorious soldiers. Some women were bold enough to place flowers in some of the soldiers' uniforms, helmets, and rifle barrels. The atmosphere was spirited and loud. Men banged enthusiastically on cymbals and drums. The staccato of exploding firecrackers startled the crowd, beckoning people into the streets instead of driving them underground. The noise and sparkles delighted the children. For the people of Shanghai who had remained, peace had finally come to the city.

Just as significant was the exodus of the foreigners. It completed the liberation of Shanghai and the end of imperialist colonialism. It was no wonder the people celebrated; Shanghai was on its way to becoming Chinese again.

WITH THE METROPOLIS SOLIDLY IN THE HANDS OF THE Communists, the missionaries' day of reckoning arrived. Those who wanted to fulfill their commitment found it increasingly hard to rationalize staying. More workers and ministers decided to return home. Mission hospitals continued to operate with remnants of a foreign staff until they could be safely turned over to the Chinese. Months before, Dr. Taylor had refused to repatriate and continued his work in Anking. Communist soldiers were impressed with the care and gentleness of the foreign doctors and nurses, who treated them with the same standard as they did the Nationalist soldiers.

"We do not know why you people are so kind to us," one Red Army soldier told Miss Myers.

She replied, "To us, you are the same." She meant it as a Christian.

Mission schools reopened with great enthusiasm, although the new government ruled that religion could not be taught and attendance at church services would not be mandatory. At St. John's University, some students were reluctant to choose elective courses in history and government because of the required study of Communist theory of dialectical materialism,

Marxist economics, and the New People's Democratic Principles. While other students had definite Communist leanings, many were either more practical-minded in their studies or were devout Christians. Theological schools saw similarly high levels of appeal but were naturally exempt from the prohibition on religious studies.

In the United States, there was intense debate among the Episcopal leadership about whether missionaries should be required to evacuate and how much, if any, financial support could be provided to those that chose to remain. Many were uncertain about the long-term prospect of continued American involvement, despite pleas from Robin and other bishops not to abandon China. Debate was serious and diverse.

"China is lost."

"They are atheists."

"Once a Communist, always a Communist."

"Only God can help them."

"If a person can become a Communist, can he not learn to become an anti-Communist?"

During this time, Lloyd decided to retire and return to the United States. He was sixty-three, and his wife, Marian, and children had already repatriated. The writing was on the wall. The only way any Christian church could survive was if it became wholly Chinese. There was no room for foreigners within the new political system, and Robin would become the first Chinese Bishop of Anking.

Lloyd said his goodbyes to Robin in Shanghai. He believed the diocese, however fragmented and war-torn, was in capable hands. He had helped prepare Robin for this day, just as Bishop Huntington had prepared Lindel. Other friends left as well. One gave Robin an American flag that had flown over the school in Wuhu. It seemed like an innocent gesture among friends.

THE FATE AND FUTURE OF THE COUNTRY WAS OFFICIALLY determined on October 1, 1949. After tens of millions of lives had been lost or damaged in forty years of war with the Manchus, the European powers, the warlords, Imperial Japan, and the country's own people, peace finally settled on China. In front of an audience of hundreds of thousands of cheering civilians, soldiers, and CCP members neatly arranged in Tian An Men Square, Mao Tse-tung, peasant scholar and militant Marxist, standing atop the towering front gate of the historic Forbidden City, definitively declared himself head of state.

"Fellow compatriots! China's People's Republic ... Central People's Government ... today ... is established!"

With those few defining words, Robin and the Chinese Church entered a new phase. More than anything else, it was a phase of uncertainty. And that uncertainty prompted certain actions.

Chapter 50

NEW FORCES

L loyd retired to Virginia, although he kept active in church affairs, attending national conventions and giving talks to groups about events unfolding in China. Most of the other bishops in China seriously contemplated leaving the country in face of the nationalistic government that was willing to accept Western help but not its authority or principles.

During this transition, a new force was moving unfettered within the fledgling government, and the Three-Self movement gathered an important ally within the Communist leadership. It began with a bold, open letter to Western mission boards outlining the stance of an informal, but respected, group of Chinese Christians. Spearheaded by Y.T. Wu, the short-statured, bespectacled, left-leaning head of China's secular but highly influential YMCA, the coalition's letter painted the mission's history with broad strokes. It noted the intentional, and advantageous, colonial privileges inherited from mainly British and American political policies and business involvement. It unequivocally rejected bureaucratic capitalism, feudalism, and imperialism. It forcefully identified the necessity of the church to transform itself into a native church based on the Three-Self principles.

"Mission funds are welcome, provided no strings are attached," read Reverend Wall from the letter to a group of clergy gathered at the American Episcopal Church offices.

"Bishop Chen. Robin Chen. Did he sign?" asked Lloyd anxiously.

Reverend Wall looked through the letter and shook his head.

"Robin is practical, but principled. He acknowledges the role of capitalism and false steps of early missions. But to condemn us for exploitation and feudalism ... that is not the friend I know," Lloyd stated, exhaling with relief.

Reverend Wall continued to read, "The Chinese church will not emerge from this historical change unaffected. It will suffer a purge. Many withered branches will be amputated."

"Amputated?" echoed a minister with disbelief.

"Religious freedom ... a constitutional right? Rights do not require purging!" scoffed another minister.

"Every clergy will be a tool of the central government. This letter is proof. They have crucified our faith!" said the first minister with dismay.

Lloyd shook his head in emphatic disagreement.

"A few have strayed, but our Chinese are true to faith, not politics. I've witnessed them for years," he countered.

"No one is free in China. Time will be the proof," argued the second minister.

Reverend Wall folded the letter that laid out the expectations of future missionaries and placed it carefully in his coat pocket. It was not that they couldn't be helpful, but they would be subservient to the Chinese leadership. They would need to learn to work under the current political climate, in disregard of the traditional separation of church and state. Most importantly, they would serve the Chinese; that meant subsistence under excessively low standards of living, without freedom of travel and a dependence on local funding. Any foreign funds would be dispensed at the discretion of the Chinese leadership. Dominance by foreigners in the church was at an end. The privileges of the century-old Unequal Treaties were revoked, and China was wresting back its authority. It would no longer be dependent on the West, nor inferior to it.

BY THE END OF 1949, THERE WAS NO UNCERTAINTY ABOUT WHO was in charge of China. Generalissimo Chiang and two million of his military and party members had left the mainland. In essence, they had invaded the small island of Taiwan, previously occupied by Japan until the end of the war. Chiang relinquished any command on the mainland and establishing a provisional government in exile under martial law as the Republic of China. Mao was the chairman of the ruling Communist Party and Chou En-lai was China's premier.

In the subsequent months, Western bishops quickly left China. Some retired permanently from their positions once back in their own countries. Only Bishop Roberts remained in Shanghai. Lindel showed no signs of recovery from his stroke and officially resigned as bishop of Honan. The House of Bishops gathered in Foochow for their annual meeting to select their new chairman.

"Foreign roots of a hundred years have withered. Self-governance, self-support, and self-propagation must come quickly!" declared Bishop Tsu. "Voices urging the church to stand with the new government against foreign imperialism and capitalism grow stronger, more forceful.

"Bishop Tsen submits his resignation as chairman of this House of Bishops. Our church needs a new Presiding Bishop, one with wisdom, energy, and foresight to guide us through treacherous waters. The nominating committee endorses Bishop Robin Chen."

The votes came in unanimously in favor of the nominee. Bishop Tsu and Robin warmly embraced as the appointment was announced to the public. New China with a new government and new political reality now had a new Presiding Bishop of the Holy Catholic Church of China (CHSKH). But the church, and its new leader, were not yet in the good graces of the new government.

Y.T. WU WAS MORE INTERESTED IN CHRISTIANITY'S SOCIAL impact on China and less with its spiritual influence. He was an early critic of the KMT during its period of nonresistance against the Japanese occupation and its aggressive annihilation campaign against the Communists. With his progressive political leanings and interest in Christianity as a force for social reform, he was a logical secular choice to lead cooperation between the Chinese Christians and the Communist government. The Communists and the YMCA had long supported each other during the early revolutionary years of the party, and Wu tried to broker an understanding between the CCP and the National Christian Council immediately after the liberation of Shanghai.

Wu saw the political and economic advantages that communism offered China, but he was still a Christian. He was concerned about maintaining universal love as a fundamental Christian principle, and Christ, the Son of God, as the centerpiece of Christian behavior and beliefs. One of his main concerns was that lower-level party members, in their fervor for the atheistic materialism of communism, would not understand the constitutional freedom of religious belief. He feared the widespread and uninhibited persecution of Christianity and its believers.

To reconcile his Christian beliefs with the principles of the new regime and to present his concerns about the rank-and-file cadres, he organized a group of Protestant leaders to hold discussions with Premier Chou. He asked for a clarification of the government's position on the function of church organizations. Instead, Chou, clever strategist, turned the table and entrusted the group with producing their own document that outlined the Christian relationship in the People's Republic of China. Rather than coerce the Christian community into obedience to the Party, he thought it more effective to arm them with their own self-determination. Chou believed they would self-destruct of their own free will. By insisting on their principle of self-support, the inability of Chinese congregations to financially support themselves would cause Christianity to wither away. Yet by this very gesture of permissiveness, Chou ensured the patriotic efforts of good Christians.

"We both believe *truth* will prevail," Premier Chou told Wu without sentiment.

"Truth *will* prevail," Wu concurred with equal directness.

"We think your beliefs untrue and false. If we are right, people will reject them. Your church will decay."

"What we believe is not a threat to China," reassured Wu.

"If we are wrong, you will thrive! We are prepared for that risk."

"That is all we ask. Allow us the risk to be right," answered Wu agreeably.

"If you are right, China will be stronger for it," Chou, ever the stateman, posed confidently. "But if you fail, it will simply prove your beliefs wrong. China will be even stronger."

They shook hands. Armed with Chou's shrewd blessings, Wu proceeded to gather support for the reorganization of the Christian Church under the Communist flag.

❧ ✦ ☙

HUANGPU PARK, AT THE END OF THE BUND NEAR THE WATER-front, was originally conceived for mainly foreigners to enjoy. Chinese, except for servants of the Western inhabitants of foreign settlements, were specifically excluded from using it, beginning a few years after its opening. Later, Chinese who could afford the high price of admission were permitted entry so as not to offend the well-to-do Shanghainese with whom the Westerners did business. But the average Chinese worker and coolie were prohibited—along with dogs and bicycles. With liberation, the park was open to everyone.

It was a sunny, early autumn day when Y.T. Wu invited Robin for a stroll in the popular park. The beautiful gardens and walkways surrounding the small, picturesque ponds were populated with all sorts of people: elders sat on benches playing *hsiang ch'i* or swayed rhythmically under willow trees practicing graceful *chi kung* or *tai chi chuan*; young women chatted with each other or sang folk songs; and small groups of musicians played traditional Chinese instruments.

"The Premier has accepted the revisions from the House of Bishops, but further changes are impossible," Wu said to Robin as they made their way through the grounds.

Wu and his group had come to Robin twice before to endorse the document they had created with Premier Chou. Twice, Robin refused.

"Anti-imperialism, especially against America, must be clear. The break *must* be clean," insisted Wu.

"Untruths cannot right the wrongs of the past. We cannot condemn all foreigners!" countered Robin. "And we do not know the path the government will truly take with regard to Christianity. How can we pledge loyalty to that which we do not know?"

"It is faith, Robin."

"My only faith is to God," Robin replied.

"The Premier was clear. We, as a nation, must form a united front against foreign aggression. Outsiders from the West *must* be seen as our common enemies."

That statement sent a chill into Robin's conscience. *Common enemy.* That was Japan for China. It was the Jews for the Germans and Nazis. Countries like the United States would be designated common enemies to unify the Chinese people, as were Hitler's Nazis for the Soviet Union and the United States. Designating a common enemy was a common ploy of unification.

"My friend, we have been treated in hospitals, educated in schools, and lived in buildings built by Americans," he argued.

Americans were his family. Bishop Huntington, who died early in the year, had been so influential in his career. Lloyd, now safely retired in Virginia, was a supportive colleague and good friend. Without Sister Louise, who knows where he might be. Grace, Paul, and Helene were sent to study in America because he admired that country's educational superiority. What repercussions would fall on their young, innocent heads if he should turn against America?

"The Premier has offered to work with us. The final draft acknowledges good deeds of past missions," Wu persisted.

He stopped and turned towards his colleague.

"Robin, we both want to preserve our faith and the church. Encourage the others to sign."

Around them, families were strolling together. Children were riding bicycles. China was at peace and rebuilding had begun.

"It is the only way," added Wu.

"We have friends ... colleagues ... in America ... in England," Robin protested.

"If friends, they will understand," Wu continued. "If not, it will not matter."

Robin continued to walk with his friend in silence. He did not feel right. There was only one authority and he knew they both understood what eventually needed to be done.

AFTER A TOTAL OF THREE MEETINGS WITH PREMIER CHOU, WU and his group completed a final draft of what they called the Christian Manifesto. It was a brief, but all-encompassing, declaration that condemned past misdeeds of the Church and its foreign missionaries. It criticized Christianity's association with foreign imperialism, specifically singling out American imperialism. It proposed the expulsion of missionaries and rejection of foreign financial aid. It avowed the church's loyalty to the country and the ruling party, ceded church organizations to the leadership of the government, and reaffirmed its acceptance of the Three-Self principles.

The Manifesto, essentially a pledge of allegiance, was published in the official mouthpiece of the government, *Ren Min Jih Bao*, the People's Daily newspaper. The goal was to have every Christian sign the Manifesto. Wu and Premier Chou wanted all the Anglican bishops to sign.

Within days after the Manifesto was published, Robin convened the House of Bishops to assess and counteract such an affirmation of obedience to the governing Communist Party. The party could not be the authority of the church, so he steadfastly refused to endorse the declaration. By not signing, he knew he would come under great pressure and scrutiny. Some might consider him a traitor. But he was uncertain about the intent and trustworthiness of the new Communist government. It was premature for the House of Bishops to throw in their entire lot with Mao and Chou. They had had a good relationship with the former KMT, among whose leadership were counted many Christians. One thing for certain, Mao and Chou were not Christian.

"No one can represent this holy body to sign the Manifesto," he began, addressing the bishops seated around the large table and holding a copy of the Manifesto for all to see. "Our values speak against the rich and powerful, and we cannot compromise with imperialism, capitalism, or bureaucratic feudalism. But the church cannot be an active arm of the new regime. To break the grip of foreign influence, only to imprison ourselves under a new master, will not achieve the independence we seek."

"Can we ignore that this document comes directly from the Premier?" queried Kimber Den, recently consecrated Bishop of Chekiang.

"The Premier had a hand in its creation, but the Manifesto is a statement from fellow Christians," Robin replied.

"Bishop Den is correct," noted Bishop Mao. "Christianity is a foreign religion. The Communist movement sides with indigenous beliefs against the foreigner. We are forced to follow the Party."

"They will root out anyone not aligned with its purpose. We will become enemies of our own country," added Den.

Bishop Mao stood and leaned across the table toward Robin. "We must renounce the West! It's the only way forward."

Robin did not immediately answer. The Church could not simply turn itself over to the government leadership and the CCP.

"Our congregations will follow in our footsteps, but once we surrender ourselves to those in political power, our beliefs will no longer matter," he explained.

"We must attain self-reliance as quickly as possible and only think about what is good for our people," he continued, standing up as Bishop Mao took his seat. "We welcome the new regime. Their cause is aligned with ours, to serve the poor and oppressed. But their authority comes from their leaders, their power from their army, not from the word of God. They have not yet proven themselves to be welcoming to Christianity or the church."

The members of the House nodded in reluctant agreement. It was a dilemma, not only of practicality with signing the Manifesto, but within the soul of Christians. Whom do they serve? When forced to choose, whom will they obey?

"Our support is not for their authority, but for our love of China and our fellow mankind," Robin declared as he dropped the Manifesto on the table.

Robin did not have all the answers, but he knew what he believed. He instructed Bishop Mao to draft a Pastoral Letter from the House of Bishops in response to the Manifesto.

The Pastoral Letter reiterated condemnation of bureaucratic capitalism, feudalism, and imperialism as anti-Christian. It repeated the Chinese Church's goal of self-reliance in the form of the Three-Selfs. It acknowledged the primacy of God as Lord of all the Universe and heartily supported the government's constitution, with emphasis on the guaranteed freedom of religious belief. But, most importantly, it omitted any pledge of allegiance to the Party, failed to directly link missionaries to imperialism, and did not mention America by name at all. In the battle between church and state, Robin and the House of Bishop sided with their church.

Chapter 51

CHOICES

One of the goals of the Communist government was to modernize thinking and to discard old, superstitious concepts and traditions. Political
science, philosophy, and sociology were common subjects offered in colleges.
Courses directly advantageous for the new government included studies in
patriotism and human development. Inserting mandatory courses in human
evolution into the school curriculum fit well with their modernization efforts
and their atheistic doctrine. It did not fit well into a bishop's household.

Hui finally matriculated to Ginling College, like her older sisters. The
concept of human evolution was eye-opening. She had never thought about
where man came from, except as a creation of God. Life was always about
the present and the future, not the past. It changed her view of the world and
elicited a call to her father from the college's deacon.

"How can she reject the church?" Robin asked Constance upon hearing
of the dilemma.

"Children must be allowed to choose," Constance reasoned.

"My whole life has been the church," lamented Robin.

"Education opens the mind. Hui believes what she believes," replied
Constance.

He was close to Hui because of their time together in Shanghai. She
should have adopted his way of thinking and incorporated his beliefs.
Evolution should not erase God. Science was not meant to replace faith. He
would have to clarify this rebellious thought when she returned home.

HUI ARRIVED HOME. SHE DUTIFULLY BOWED HER HEAD AS ROBIN said grace at dinner. Perhaps she hadn't rejected all her beliefs. Or was it only a habit? They dined in uncomfortable silence. *Let her enjoy her dinner,* he thought. He was glad she was home.

After dinner, they went to the living room. Robin settled in a soft armchair while Constance and Hui sat on the couch.

"All the teachers said Jie Jie was their best student," Hui said proudly.

Constance managed a smile, but Robin didn't react, except for a quick nod. He already knew Grace was an exceptional student. She had graduated at the top of her class. He didn't need to know that. He needed to know about Hui.

"Deacon Yu called," he interjected. "He said you don't go to services. You don't go to church meetings."

Hui sat in silence, her head bowed onto her chest.

"You are their bishop's daughter!"

His raised tone made Hui shake.

"Tell me!" he instructed sternly. "Why?"

"Ba, how do I believe in God? We come from monkeys!" she blurted. "That is modern teaching. Now it is in my head!"

"Your head? What is in your head?"

Robin got up to pick up his Bible, lying on the nearby desk. How could his own children not believe in God? He opened the well-read book, leafing through its worn pages. Bishop Huntington had given him the book when he was ordained. He had used God's words to learn English. They were in his head. Thirty years ago. A different time, a different world. But the Word is always the same.

"Where is your faith?" he asked, waving the Bible at her, making her grimace.

"What is the use to learn if all you care about is faith? We have evidence!" Hui stammered. "'How can man come from God and from monkeys?"

Robin felt his face get hot.

"Teachers show evidence, so you believe evolution."

"It is science."

"God shows evidence," he said, sitting next to her. "When I was born, we believed Confucian ideas. But I became a Christian because of faith. When your grandfather died, he was a Christian. Evidence was in front of his eyes. *I* am his evidence. Our family is evidence of God's goodness!

"Science did not save us," he declared as he stood up. "Faith did!"

Robin closed the Bible and put it back on the table. He went to sit in the chair. He had never spoken to any of his children like this. Perhaps it was a sign that Christianity was destined to lose. If he could not keep his own daughter in the fold, what about others? Can God's child come from monkeys? He glanced at Constance, who sat silently, her face calm.

They sat without saying anything more. They couldn't argue faith. He remembered Mr. Lund's words: *Faith will come later.*

In the evening, when all their heads cooled down and Hui was asleep, Robin went to his Bible. The pages were soft and pliable from years of learning and turning and searching. The sweat from his fingertips had marked the edges as evidence of his life. He went to 1 Corinthians 13:13. He knew it by heart, but he wanted to read it aloud as he had done so many times in sermons. The words of Paul the Apostle would guide and reassure him.

"So now faith, hope, and love abide. These three, but the greatest of these is love."

He closed the book.

How fortunate I am to have all three, he thought.

Hui was asleep, but Robin went to her side. She had gone to bed with tears in her eyes, and it bothered him. Anger would not resolve the dilemma in her head. He sat next to her and put his hand on her shoulder, as he had done with so many of his parishioners. She stirred and turned towards him.

"Ba, I do not know what to think. I do not know what to believe."

"Believe what is in your heart, Hui. Live what you believe. That is what matters."

Hui sat up and hugged her father tightly.

Robin was satisfied. He felt her body relax.

Life will change, he thought. *Truth will always find its home.*

MORE CHANGES CAME, AND THEY CAME QUICKLY. BECAUSE OF the Manifesto, missionaries who had stayed after the turnover in 1949 began to leave. *Expelled* was perhaps a more accurate term. China and the Church were beginning to isolate. They wanted their own identity and autonomy. They withdrew into their own universes.

Robin wrote to Grace, telling her of the changes:

> *Grace, funds from the foreign mission have stopped. Our treasury is about to be exhausted. Life will be very difficult, but as long as we are determined, we can overcome all difficulties.*
>
> *Do not worry about us. We have offered our whole life to God. Although I am at this time not strong physically or mentally, I still can work hard. I am willing to face hardship and work under the guidance of the Holy Spirit.*
>
> *I hope you will finish your studies and return to serve the people. No matter what happens to us, be sure to prepare yourself to become a modern Christian physician willing to serve the human race. Our future is hard to say …*

As Robin's salary decreased, Constance practiced the same frugality she did as a refugee. He would not accept money from foreign entities. Robin believed this was the proper and necessary road for the church and individuals to take. Everyone had to sacrifice for the country's future.

CHRISTIANS INDIVIDUALLY CONTINUED TO SIGN THE MANIFESTO, but the House of Bishops held off. Robin was still wary of the new government and refused to sign for the third time. Word of this disagreeable stance found its way to Beijing. A fourth time would be bad luck.

Premier Chou wanted the Anglican leadership to support the government. Having all the oxen pull together makes the plowing easier. Cooperation is better than coercion. Y.T. Wu had made good efforts on his behalf in that regard, but it was now time for personal intervention. The premier summoned Robin to China's capital.

"We do not wish to eradicate you. That would be foolish and serve no purpose but to create enemies here and outside," Chou explained as he sat side by side with Robin in the formal greeting hall. "Your church is small and cannot be a threat, but the new path of China needs all its citizens. You can help China succeed."

"Your goals and ours are not dissimilar. We are not so far apart. We both love our country, our people. We both have lived with conflict too long," Robin answered, frankly.

Chou was intelligent, if not clever, in politics. There was always a practical side to his argument.

"We do not wish to treat you like a mosquito, a pest of no use," Chou calmly stated.

"We do not think of ourselves in that way," Robin replied.

"But bees, their lives are orderly. When given a chance to work together, they produce honey from their hive. They provide great help to our farmers."

"Bees are necessary for life" Robin replied. "We prefer to be bees."

The two men stared at each other. They could have been brothers earlier in their lives, only four years apart in age. Today, they were just Chinese.

"Bishop Chen, China wants your assistance. You and your church have led China in many parts of our people's lives. But the foreign path is no longer the correct one. We support the Three-Self approach. We guarantee your right to religious beliefs. If we all agree to help serve our people, we will have no problem. We are stronger if we work together."

Chou did not talk about imperialism or religious spiritualism or allegiance to God. He talked about making China strong and the people prosperous. He acknowledged the great things Christians had accomplished, and he was right. The future required a different path. America and England no longer mattered. There was only China. Robin had an obvious choice. Give him a chance to give Christianity a chance, or be swatted away like mosquitos.

"Help us rebuild China," invited Chou as they parted.

"For *all* our people," answered Robin, matching Chou's grip.

"*Hao, hao!*" Good, good! replied Chou with a wide grin, returning Robin's deep bow.

Once Robin saw that the new government permitted the church to function and that Chou was committed to improving the standard of living for all citizens, he signed the Manifesto. The rest of the House of Bishops followed. In reality, they had no choice if they were to continue as an organized church. Mosquitoes are easily squashed.

In the end, over 400,000 signatures were collected. Of the 1 million Protestants in 1949, only 70,000 were Anglican. But they were the denomination best organized and prepared for changes. When the war forced Western clergymen back home or into settlement camps, most of the work of the Christian church was done by the highly educated Chinese Anglicans. With the commitment of the House of Bishops, the nondenominational, wholly native Three-Self Movement Church, sponsored by the CCP and headed by Y.T. Wu, was in complete control of organized Christianity. It was committed to moving forward with the new government's blessing.

BISHOP TSU, KNOWN AS THE BISHOP OF BURMA ROAD, SOUGHT permission to travel to the World Council of Churches convention to attend the meeting of its Central Committee, of which he was a member. The meeting was held in Toronto and, because of the uncertainty of the church's relationship with the new Communist government, he financed the trip himself so as not to be accused of profiting from his position.

Two weeks before Bishop Tsu traveled to Toronto in late June of 1950, North Korea—with blessings from Stalin and a pledge of provisional support by Mao—invaded South Korea. The Council's Central Committee drew up a resolution condemning the North Korean invasion that included 14,000 voluntary Korean soldiers from the Chinese PLA. Bishop Tsu signed the resolution, oblivious to its far-reaching implications. Both the Manifesto and the Pastoral Letter, drafted just days before, promoted peace as a Christian ideal and condemned killing associated with wartime aggression. There was no reason not to add his name to the resolution as a citizen of the Christian community.

Concerned with the spread of communism and the act of aggression towards its ally, the United States quickly sent troops to support South Korea. The combined United Nations forces, commanded by General Douglas MacArthur, breached the 38th Parallel dividing the Korean peninsula, Mao decided China itself was being threatened; the bloody chess game was being played according to Western, not Chinese, rules. He sent in troops at the request of his ally, President Kim Il Sung. By November 1950, the presence of 300,000 Chinese troops in North Korea took General MacArthur by surprise, forcing President Truman to formally launch a full-blown, multinational Korean War. China had miscalculated the United States' commitment to military support of South Korea, and the United States had underestimated China's appetite and capacity for another major war.

Bishop Tsu turned sixty-five and decided to step down, despite requests to delay his formal retirement until later in 1951. He had sons in college in the United States, and things had changed too much in China. China was for a new crop of leaders.

Having signed the Manifesto committing the church to the Three-Self Movement, Robin began to use his pulpit to encourage people to support the government in its effort in Korea. He encouraged his audience to contribute, both with monetary donations and as volunteers to the war effort. Many enlisted in the army or medical corps, including Little Constance, now a teenager. She sacrificed her schooling to train as a nurse for the army. As much as Bishop Tsu saw reason to support the Christian resolution against Chinese aggression, Robin saw reason to support patriotic efforts aiding North Korea. All Chinese should be supportive of their government and homeland, even if they were also peace-promoting Christians.

With the country now at war less than a year after the defeat of the KMT, unification of the country was paramount to its success. Only a unified country can wage a successful war. The Christians saw immediate effects of their alliance with the government in the closing of independent churches, consolidating them into a handful of state-sanctioned churches. This prompted many worshippers to attend non-sanctioned underground houses of worship. These operated outside of government oversight. But worshippers in the Three-Self community were more single-minded and organized under one umbrella organization. As the Korean conflict grew more serious, there was a drive to firm up support for the government from all sectors, Christians included.

In early 1951, when Robin was at the offices of the Three-Self Movement, officials from the central government paid an unannounced visit. The official in charge held a photograph of Robin with Bishop Tsu—the one taken at Robin's election as Presiding Bishop. Robin listened to their statement as he stared at the familiar photograph.

Loose ends need to be tidied up, he immediately thought.

"*Sha ji, jing hou!*" the official ordered. Kill the chicken, scare the monkey!

The official was respectful, but he was not smiling. He handed the photograph to Robin. Robin remembered that happy day. He was called upon to serve, and he answered the call. He knew he would be tested. One day it would prove hard to obey God—that day had come.

Robin shook his head in frustration. He could see blood spurting from the chicken's neck. Killing the chicken would serve the people and scare all the monkeys.

"*Sha ji, jing hou!*" the head official repeated, shaking a finger at him.

The officials didn't wait for a reply. They turned and walked away. Nothing more needed to be said. They all understood what needed to be done.

As soon as they left, Robin closed the door, clasped his hands, and dropped to his knees.

Chapter 52

BETRAYAL

" A man shows love through his sacrifice," Constance said.
She sat next to Robin on their bed and looked at the photo.

"It is what you believe," she added.

"A silly schoolboy. *Wo shenma dou bu zhidao!*" I knew nothing! he lamented as he held Constance's delicate hands. "I asked Sister Louise, what is God's love."

"What did she say?" she asked, coaxing him on.

"Giving what He loves the most."

"The cross and salvation do not come easy."

"We are only foot soldiers," he lamented. "Pawns to be sacrificed."

Constance put the photo aside and stood up.

"God will know what is in your heart," she said.

"And Yu Yu?" he asked, referring to Bishop Tsu.

Robin knew what he must do.

"He will also understand," said Constance gently.

Robin wasn't sure, but he had no choice.

THE GOVERNMENT CALLED ONE HUNDRED AND FIFTY CHURCH leaders to a conference in Beijing. The purpose was to discuss the problems in Chinese institutions and the state of their relationships caused by the sudden withdrawal of missionaries and ban on foreign financial support. These institutions included church organizations, hospitals, and mission schools, which the government began to appropriate. Robin had sent the last of his American colleagues, Dr. Taylor, off to America with a special communion service in Shanghai. The survival and fate of the church was now entirely in Chinese hands.

As delegates gathered, officials adorned the stage with large photos of three Western missionaries: Dr. Timothy Richards, Dr. Frank Price, and Edward Lockwood; and four Chinese: Dr. S.C. Leung, Bishop W.Y. Chen, Ku Jen-en, and Bishop Y.Y. Tsu.

Robin marched on stage under the watchful gaze of the party officials, one of whom handed him his declaration. He was well aware that it was as much his own trial, freedom dependent on this patriotic performance. He was a leader in the Three-Self Church, but felt he was a servant of the Party. He told himself he was a foot soldier for his Lord, that he loved his country and his fellow Christians. *Seek truth. Seek truth.*

"Bishop Tsu, of Kunming, has shown himself to be a heartless renegade, a running dog of American imperialism," he spoke, reading slowly and halt-ingly. "He escaped to America on a passport of the reactionary Kuomintang. He attended the World Council of Churches, which is a tool of American imperialism and which passed a resolution in support of American aggres-sion. He protested against support of our ally, North Korea."

Robin looked out over the delegates. The conference's agenda had been hijacked to one of accusations and criticism. He could hardly stand. His hands shook. He had made the sacrifice. But he made it not out of hatred. Not out of bitterness. But out of love for his country and for his beliefs. He believed Bishop Tsu would understand. He believed his friend would forgive him. He believed this was all good for the sake of China, and for the church.

"The Party must condemn his unpatriotic actions!"

With that, he was done. The party official clapped vigorously, and the delegates followed.

Then it was Methodist Bishop Z.T. Kiang who rose to speak out against his fellow Methodist, Bishop W.Y. Chen. One by one, over two days, the seven Christians were publicly denounced by their colleagues. One after the other, the seven Christians fell. The Westerners were accused of being "imperialist spies under the cloak of religion." The Chinese were called "renegades and enemies of the people."

The deed was done. The chickens were killed.

Robin committed wholly to the Three-Self Movement. Any reservation was expunged by his sense of patriotism. It was what was required of him and what he accepted. Like a servant, he was there to help his master. By serving his master, he kept his family alive—not only his own, but his whole Christian family. By serving the mortal master, he also was serving the Everlasting One. He believed that.

The denunciation meeting had been planned by party officials at the highest levels of government and orchestrated by Y.T. Wu, the key government liaison and head of the Three-Self Church, and Cora Deng, General Secretary of the YWCA. The organizers were careful to choose accusers who were close to the accused. This struck the loudest alarm. But they also chose the condemned to produce the least individual harm. One of the Westerners had been dead for over thirty years, and another was already out of the country. Bishop Tsu and Dr. Leung both had left China. The mainly symbolic denunciation was meant to exert pressure, not produce paranoia. It did both. The monkeys were scared.

That night, Robin went home and vomited. As he clutched his stomach, his face contorted. Constance stood by his side with her arms resting on his shoulders.

"He is safe. He will understand," she reassured.

It was not physical pain that hurt him. It was deeper, something he could not touch. It was not what he had done. He could not change that. It was the truth which was to come.

"It is only the beginning," Robin whispered with a grimace.

The meeting sent a chilling message throughout the Christian community. The red line was drawn. Believe in God but support the Party. Christians like Y.T. Wu and Robin did so with authentic passion and true patriotism. Self-criticism struggle sessions and denunciation rallies became the norm sweeping throughout the country. Calls to support the new government seeped into Sunday sermons. Others, distrusting of the government or unable to justify relinquishing their devotion to their God, were driven underground into small, unregistered, clandestine house churches. There, they prayed in fear of their lives.

It was soon starkly evident that the Christian house in China was deeply divided.

Chapter 53

GRACE

G race was taken into the Perots' Philadelphia home, but within two weeks contracted pneumonia. This caused her to fall behind in her studies, and she was forced to withdraw from classes. She resumed her studies a year later, in the fall of 1948.

Since moving to America, she had received letters from her parents on a regular basis. It was hard to truly comprehend what changes they were going through. First, it was the disruption of daily life, the uncertain future of the church, and the financial strain brought on by the Communist uprising during her freshman year. This was followed in her sophomore year by her father's guarded optimism about the new government. She hoped it would be better than the corrupt KMT.

She quickly learned that Communist China and its people were considered enemies of American democracy and capitalism. She was invited to a summer program for Chinese students in 1949. Unbeknownst to her, a topic of discussion was the similarities between the communist doctrine and Christian beliefs. Only later did she find out that the Chinese American Christian Association was one-fourth communist organizers, one-fourth communist sympathizers, one-fourth opportunists looking for connection to communist China, and only one-fourth anti-communist. When she discovered the true motivations, she stopped attending meetings.

Lately, her father had been writing more positively of the new government and how it appeared to care about the people, but she knew she had to read between the lines. American newspapers constantly reported on the

Communists' propaganda and their suppression of freedom. She began to wonder how much of what he wrote was true. Was he being brainwashed?

The loss of China to communism shook America. Pundits criticized the strategies used in handling Chiang and Mao. Whatever the direction of the arguments, the result was an innate fear of communism. Without even a full understanding of what communism really was, its mere mention conjured up an evil threat: imprisonment of citizens, suppression of truth, and dictatorship by party propaganda. This was not lost on students like Grace. Communism was bad. The enemy. A threat to America. And often, so were China and Chinese people.

Grace was part of a small group of elite, well-connected, English-speaking Chinese students, mostly schooled in Christian missions. They came to America for education. Most were welcomed because of their high achievement, good lineage, or future potential. They were kind, lawful, and, often, true Christians. In many respects, they were China's crème de la crème. They were the ideal immigrants and ideal candidates to become ideal citizens in a Christian United States. They did not feel like the enemy.

Most had intentions of returning home after graduating. But Mao changed all that. They were stranded. They might not have considered themselves refugees, but they were. America didn't know what to do with these friendly, educated people from a communist nation. In fact, because of the Korean conflict, China and the United States were nations at war, in practice, if not legally. Chinese students were viewed by some Americans with suspicion. Commie chinks.

Grace had little understanding of the conflict her father was facing back home. He had mentioned "bad elements" in the church when he became the Presiding Bishop. The Pastoral Letter he wrote with other bishops mentioned "rotten members" of the church whose "sins are condemned by the church." She did not know some were publicly shamed, arrested, jailed, or even executed. She did not know whom he was referring to, or who they were. She was simply studying medicine so she could return home and help China. That was difficult enough.

As a favor to Robin, the Perots generously supported her. They paid for her living expenses. They housed her in their attractive mansion, elegantly appointed with heavy mahogany furniture, silk curtains, majestic grandfather clocks, and antique collector plates lining the dining room wall. She was treated like their daughter.

Paul had come to study labor relations and social studies at Columbia University. His new wife, Helene, also was at Columbia, while their young son stayed in China with Constance. The couple would visit Grace, but Paul's solo visits at the Perots' house gradually became more distressing to her.

"They are capitalists! How can you sleep under their roof?" he muttered out loud in Chinese during one visit.

"They are good to me," countered Grace discreetly as they walked through the expansive landscaped gardens with their neatly trimmed hedges. "They are our father's friends."

"Do you know what is happening back home? What is happening to Father?" he asked.

"Why bother me about those things?" she lamented.

"The country belongs to the people now," he insisted, leaning into her. "Things are not the same."

"What should I do?" Grace shot back in frustration.

"Think about going home," he persisted in a loud voice that made the approaching Mrs. Perot raise her brows. "Father wants you to go back."

"After I finish," she replied quietly, while flashing an admonishing glance. She knew what her father wanted.

"Is everything all right?" asked Mrs. Perot from the veranda.

"Yes, yes!" Grace replied quickly.

"Then come in, you two. Lunch is served," Mrs. Perot said, gesturing to the house.

"You are Chinese," Paul whispered a bit too loudly to Grace as she walked away, "not American!"

Grace noticed Mrs. Perot barely looked at her brother, which she thought was uncomfortably dismissive, but she continued to smile. Mrs. Perot put her arm around her waist and led her back to the house. Paul trailed behind, hands in his pant pockets, frowning at his sister's back.

Later, Paul told her he was returning to China immediately after completing his master's degree. How could she live like a princess in the house of the American aristocrats? Did she not know that could be a death sentence back home?

Within a few months, after junior year and without much explanation, Grace left the Perots' home.

SOON AFTER MOVING INTO THE CITY, ON OCTOBER 12, 1951, A knock on the door of her new Philadelphia apartment that she shared with two other Chinese students woke her to America's realities. Her roommate opened the door. The two men in suits and ties were neatly groomed, stood ramrod straight, and wore fedora hats befitting serious men.

"Grace Chen?" inquired the taller one, with short brown hair, dark, deep-set eyes, and chiseled features.

"Yes?" the roommate questioned.

"FBI."

The roommate blinked a few times as the man introduced himself as Agent Jason-something and presented his badge and identification card.

"Grace!" she called out nervously.

"Wait outside," instructed Agent Phillip-something, the shorter one with black hair, also cropped short, wearing dark-rimmed eyeglasses. His face was round like a melon. He shut the door on the roommate.

The tall one perused the magazines on the small coffee table: *Harper's Bazaar*, Sears-Roebuck's catalogue, and *Time* magazine. He noticed a Bible on a crowded bookshelf. The short one peered down a hallway just as Grace came out of one of the bedrooms.

The men introduced themselves again. Like her roommate, Grace only heard "FBI."

"Just the two of you here?"

The tall one seemed to be the head interrogator.

"Three of us," she answered.

"I see. We'd like to ask you a few questions."

"What questions?" she asked innocently.

"You came here four years ago, in 1947?"

"Yes. Why are you here?" she asked politely, but she knew the US government was on special alert the last few months.

"Sorry, but *we* ask the questions," interjected the short one.

"Have I done anything wrong?" she asked deferentially.

"No, of course not," reassured the short one.

Grace did not know that police had ransacked an underground house church back home, confiscated Bibles, and arrested the worshippers. The worshippers were later released, having done nothing wrong, but Grace could not have known that in Philadelphia.

"Have you joined any groups while you are here?" asked the tall one.

"Clubs, organizations ... political parties?" clarified the short one.

"I am not interested in politics. I am studying medicine," explained Grace, still very polite.

"Yes, we know. Have you heard of the Chinese Association of Scientific Workers?" asked the tall one again. The official-sounding group was dedicated to the technical training of Chinese students to benefit Communist China on their return to the mainland.

"No."

"Never attended their meetings?"

"Never."

"Never?"

Grace didn't answer. *What was their point,* she asked herself.

"How about the Chinese American Christian Association?"

"I stopped going two years ago."

"Are you a member of the Communist party?"

"I have no interest in politics," she replied, slightly irritated.

The tall one picked up the Bible sitting on the coffee table. He began to leaf through it almost absentmindedly, as if it were a prop.

"Why do you want to become a doctor?"

"China needs doctors."

"You know any other women studying to be doctors?" the tall one continued, directing the question to his partner.

The short one, playing along, shook his head.

"We had three in my class!" blurted Grace.

"Had?"

"One had nerves. The other—" she caught herself. They did not need to know about the suicide.

"How many from China?" asked the tall one.

"Have I done something?" asked Grace, scowling at them now, her brows drawn tensely together.

"How many?" repeated the tall one.

"Just me," she answered.

"You plan to return to China?"

"Perhaps, when I graduate," she answered. "I *like* America."

Grace did not know that while the Immigration and Naturalization Service was trying to deport Chinese students for fear that they would somehow contaminate American culture with communist thought, the State Department had instructions to detain Chinese students, especially those with scientific or technical backgrounds. They feared students, like members of the CASW, might export valuable American secrets or technology. Chinese students were too risky to keep in America, and too risky to send home.

"To Grace. Love, Mom and Dad," read the tall one from the inside Bible cover. "Your father's a priest."

"Bishop."

"Hmm. A bishop from *Red* China?" He spat out "Red" like it was an expletive.

Grace did not know that some ministers who refused to join the Three-Self Movement were, perhaps at that very hour, being persecuted by the government. She did not know that Bishops Kimber Den and Quentin Huang had been incarcerated and Bishop Tsen placed under house arrest upon his return to China. She did not know that churches not registered with the Three-Self Movement were being torn down or that somewhere in China a minister climbed up a flight of stairs at his church, strolled out onto the roof, and after a short prayer, landed headfirst on the pavement three stories below. She only knew her father supported the new government.

While the tall one interviewed Grace, the short one slipped into the bedroom. He returned with a framed photo of Grace with a group of well-dressed students. It was labelled Christian Medical Society across the bottom of the frame. He showed the photo to his partner.

"Is it against the law to be Christian here?" she asked as she quickly reclaimed her photo.

"Not Christian, but Christian from Communist China?" The short one furrowed his brow.

"I am not communist!"

"Frankly, we don't care if you're a Jew or Buddhist, as long as you obey the laws," interrupted the tall one.

"Did I break the law? Are you going to arrest me for something?" Grace demanded.

"Do you talk to your father?" the tall one asked, ignoring Grace's question.

"He writes."

"Do you write back?"

"I am very busy," she replied. *What did they want? Why were they interested in her father?*

As the two men went through her apartment looking at photos, closets, and the magazines on the coffee table, Grace knew things were not right. She might be a foreigner, but they had no right to search her apartment.

"You need to leave!" she blurted out. She pointed to the door. Her mother had done the same when her father was traveling abroad. Standing less than five feet tall, her mother stood her ground against the Japanese soldiers. Go away! she scolded them to their faces. They obediently left.

The two men followed Grace to the front door. She opened it and let her roommate in.

"We'll be in touch," the tall one said as the two stepped out the door.

Grace did not reply and quickly slammed the door shut.

"What did they want?" asked the roommate.

Grace could not put her thoughts together. *What was going on?* She began to tidy the magazines, which lay askew on the coffee table, stacking *Harper's Bazaar* on top of the Sear-Roebuck catalogue. *Why were they talking to me?* She placed *Time* over the catalogue and made sure everything looked straight. She glanced at the *Time* cover. All she wanted to do was to study medicine. She had not had time to read the magazines. The dark eyebrows and piercing eyes stared at her.

What did the FBI want?

The face on the cover was not friendly. It did not say "Welcome to America." Its cold eyes bore into her: the heavy, brooding stare of Senator Joseph McCarthy.

Chapter 54

SUSPICION
AND LOVE

race felt much more comfortable around fellow Chinese students,
living in her own apartment. But it was hard for her to explain to Mrs.
Perot, who had been so kind and generous to her, why she left. She let her
calls go unanswered.

Grace did not knew the FBI had also paid a visit to Mrs. Perot.

MRS. PEROT EXPLAINED TO THE AGENTS THAT SHE FELT GRACE
was ungrateful for all her support. She had treated Grace like her own
daughter, then she disappeared. Perhaps she had misjudged her. And Paul,
that brother of hers, rubbed her the wrong way. He seemed arrogant and
aloof. He had a hold on his sister, she told the agent.

"I don't really know why she left. She seemed happy, but she just packed
up and moved into the city. Poor girl. It couldn't have been easy. All alone
here after her brother left." Mrs. Perot paused, huffing a bit. "I don't think he
was happy with Grace."

THE FBI PURSUED INFORMATION FROM OTHERS: REVEREND Gilbert, Dean Kennedy of the medical school, and nearly a dozen friends and teachers, even Bishops Roberts and Tsu.

"Bishop Chen is one of the finest Chinese Christians I know," Bishop Roberts confided to the investigators. "There is no doubt he is being forced to support the government. Criticizing America goes with the territory."

"And the denunciations?" asked the agent. "He openly condemned his own bishop."

Bishop Roberts drew in a deep breath and confessed, "The government was strangulating the church ... cutting off funds, confiscating properties. All of us left. Under these circumstances, I might have done the same. The pressure on him ... his son—"

He paused, carefully choosing the words before speculating, "There must be something wrong."

"With the son?" the agent asked.

"Bishop Chen wanted his children to return to China. Paul, his only son, heeded his father and is teaching at Shanghai University. It used to be a Baptist school," Bishop Roberts explained.

"And?" asked the agent.

"The teachers and students at Shanghai University are *all* Communists. But Bishop Chen, I assure you, is *not* a Communist!"

Bishop Tsu echoed these sentiments during his interview. "Anti-American? Never! He had no choice."

"You're sure? He called you a ... running dog," the agent pressed him as he checked his notes.

Bishop Tsu shrugged his shoulders. He closed his eyes and sighed deeply.

"So, you forgive him?" the agent asked.

"Forgive?" Bishop Tsu paused, pondering out loud. "There is nothing to forgive. The church and I are still standing."

He waved his hand dismissively.

"There are *many* sacrificial lambs in China."

Reverend Gilbert corroborated the bishops' testimonies. "Grace? A communist? *Impossible!* All she wants is to become a doctor. And her father? He is as American as a Chinese can be."

The federal agents seemed appeased—for now. Grace was clean. It seemed clear; no one had heard her speak of politics or communism.

In reality, it had little to do with the Perots or politics. Three years had been enough for Grace, and it was best not to burden her hosts with uncomfortable feelings brought on by Paul's visits. She just wanted to focus on her medical studies without any distractions, and the clinical rotations in the city hospital made living in the suburbs too inconvenient. That was all.

DURING HER JUNIOR YEAR, GRACE MET A HANDSOME YOUNG doctor who was also studying at the University of Pennsylvania School of Medicine. Robert Hsun-Piao Yuan was a dapper Shanghainese with a characteristic rectangular face and stylishly slick black hair combed straight back. He often dressed in a neat suit, saddle shoes, and white panama hat, looking very Westernized and worldly—like many who came from missionary colleges.

To prepare for the residency entrance exam, Robert was taking a surgical review course offered by Dr. Josiah McCracken, whom he met while attending St. John's Medical School. At that time, Dr. McCracken was serving as the dean of the medical school. Like Grace, Robert graduated at the top of his class and was president of his college and medical school classes. The young doctor's ambition to become a neurosurgeon came not because he had been inspired by neurosurgeons in Shanghai but because the whole country had only one, in Beijing. Seeing little opportunity in China, he sought it in America by borrowing $3,000, stuffed into a suitcase, from his generous brother-in-law.

The two students were introduced by Reverend Gilbert. They had much in common besides their medical school education, excellent scholarship, and personable nature. Similar to Grace, whose father was the current Presiding Bishop of the Anglican Church in China, Robert was the favorite grandson of Bishop T.S. Sing.

Because of Bishop Sing's unapologetic affection and attention, young Robert was jokingly, if not enviously, referred to by family members as his grandfather's *only* grandchild. This rubbed his seven older sisters, a younger half-brother, and dozens of cousins the wrong way. When the bishop wanted company on a trip outside the diocese, he would bring Robert for the long treks. When the family fled Ningpo in front of a rumored Japanese insurgency in 1937, it was Robert whom the bishop requested to be by his side.

Likewise, Grace was her parents' shining star, but, despite these similarities, there were two important differences. Robert spoke Shanghainese while she spoke Mandarin, so they conversed in English. And Robert had lost both his parents by the time he was five. His mother died of scarlet fever after childbirth, having contracted it from Robert, who recovered. Two years later, his father came down with dysentery after eating ice cream. He became dehydrated while his doctor, a family friend, was inopportunely out of town. By the time the doctor returned two days later, Robert's father was dead.

Robert was immediately smitten by Grace's lively eyes. Neither had met anyone else of interest. They were each other's first love, and there was no reason to look elsewhere. They were a smashingly handsome couple to their friends. Their courtship quickly led to engagement and designs to marry once Grace finished medical school.

Both originally planned to return to China. Now, they were stranded in the promised land of America while their own homeland was turned upside down by communists.

Robert felt nothing but respect from Americans he met. He spent a year working in a small hospital in a West Virginia coal-mining town to earn some money before getting married. The West Virginians welcomed him with open arms. They were excited to have a polite young doctor in their hospital and seemed genuinely proud that he was Chinese—the first of his kind many had ever seen. Everyone wanted to be his friend. The police offered him rides about town, civic groups wanted him to give talks on China, and the high school invited him to be their graduation speaker. He indulged them all. He enjoyed being a small-town celebrity. Later, the only other Chinese who came to town opened a laundry.

The young couple loved the self-determination of American life. Grace told friends that she would not return to China if she and Robert married. She really did not like anything she heard about communism and was thinking of becoming a naturalized citizen. America was beginning to feel like her home. Robert felt the same.

Chapter 55

STRANGE INSECTS

The hardline crackdown on Christians who did not demonstrate support for the revolution or join the Three-Self Movement had the unlikely effect of producing a more cohesive church. For the first time in their history in China, organized Protestants worked, prayed, and acted as a single, non-denominational body. As long as they were supportive of the government, the government supported them. It was a symbiosis of two species.

When Mao called for the country to "Resist America, Aid Korea," Robin felt a duty to support the effort, not so much an act of a communist—which he was not—but of a Christian Chinese. All of China supported the "Resist America, Aid Korea" message. For Robin it served both religious and patriotic ends; pray for peace and fight for an ally. There was no contradiction. It did put the Chinese at odds with their English counterparts.

At the 1948 Lambeth Conference, the Chinese bishops had met many important English people, from Archbishop Fisher and Winston Churchill to Prime Minister Clement Attlee and King George. Another figure who made an impression was Hewlett Johnson, Dean of Canterbury Cathedral. Dean Johnson was notorious in England because of his unabashed pro-Soviet, Marxist views. He was a headache to the Church of England; more so after he, along with Madame Sun Yat-sen, was awarded the Stalin International Peace Prize, which he accepted much to the chagrin of his countrymen and fellow Anglicans.

"England is too good for a Bolshevik," wrote an indignant Brit.

The Anglican hierarchy was eager to be rid of him, as he was often an embarrassment to the more respected Archbishop of Canterbury, for whom he was often mistaken. This was the product not only of his title but also of his similar height and facial features. His long face, large chin with elongated nose, and flaring occipital tufts bordering his otherwise balding head resembled features of the Archbishop—although more weirdly whimsical than weighty and wise.

Dean Johnson, having first visited China in 1932 to assist in Wuhu famine relief efforts, returned as a guest of China in the spring of 1952. He met with Chairman Mao and Premier Chou as well as Robin and Y.T. Wu. It was during these visits that he listened to an astounding story—a story so strange, outlandish, and sinister, he found it hard to believe.

Chinese military and civilian doctors had encountered a rash of infections near the North Korean border. Both North Koreans and Chinese soldiers were affected, along with local peasants. The doctors discovered that these diseases were uncommon in that region.

Villagers found satchels of insects and saw Chinese dressed in white coats, gloves, and masks descending on the area. Soldiers crawled on hands and knees in open fields, sweeping up thousands of insects. The locals claimed the unusually large insects were released from a variety of non-explosive canisters that, instead of detonating like bombs, ruptured upon hitting the ground. Some insects were black; some were yellow. Bigger than bees. No one could identify the strange insects. Soon after, residents in Mukden, just north of the North Korean capital, fell ill.

"People developed high fevers, became delirious and complained that their heads hurt. Their muscles ached and they had blisters on their lips. They groaned with pain and drifted in and out of consciousness. They couldn't eat anything and just kept asking for cold water," reported one villager.

After examining the cases, both government and medical experts came to the inevitable conclusion: the United States and their ally, Japan, were engaging in biological warfare. The insects were believed to have been dropped by American planes, carrying a variety of lethal organisms. The story was published in the *China Weekly Review*, a periodical founded in Shanghai by American John Benjamin Powell and run by his son, John

William Powell. Formal accusations were aired. The Chinese Commission to Investigate American Crimes of Biological Warfare led by Madame Li Dequan, the People's Republic of China's first minister of health and President of the Chinese Red Cross Society, corroborated the suspicions. Insects were collected, pathogens isolated and cultured, clinical histories of patients documented, and diagnostic autopsies performed. There was little doubt in the Chinese Christian leaders' minds.

"America will deny it," argued Dean Johnson, referring to the unthinkable, if not implausible, story.

"You *must* bring it to the West," urged Y.T. Wu.

The dean was a well-known advocate for world peace. He had gone to the United States on two occasions after the war and had spoken to tens of thousands of people at Madison Square Garden, campaigning for peace and a more accommodating posture towards the Soviet Union.

The dean knew this was a highly controversial and dangerous charge of international importance. The Chinese believed they had definitive proof, but none of the Allies would accept it. It was too heinous. Being a communist sympathizer, he was not viewed as a neutral observer. The Chinese would be accused of propagandizing, if not outwardly defrauding, the international community for purposes of mobilizing sentiment against the United States. The charges by the Chinese might also preemptively inhibit use of such weapons by the US. But they needed a strong spokesperson to advocate for the veracity of the story.

"How authentic is your information?" queried Dean Johnson.

"Our doctors and scientists found smallpox, cholera, anthrax, and bubonic plague. All unexplained," Wu reported.

"You will vouch for it?" pressed the dean.

"Our experts have. We cannot be silent on this. It is unacceptable," insisted Robin.

"It will not win me points back home," lamented the dean, well aware of the accusations that would be slung his way.

"We believe it is true," said Wu. "But it cannot only come from us."

The dean hesitated but took the letter. He read it once again, then folded it and put it in his briefcase. He was admittedly an unabashed Sinophile. He loved the Chinese; especially, of course, the Christians.

"The world will know, one way or another," the dean promised.

"Let truth fall where it may," declared Robin as he and Wu shook the dean's hand. "History will judge us as heroes or fools, but no one will be able to say that we stood by and did nothing while our countrymen died."

Dean Johnson took it upon himself to travel to Fushun and Mukden to confirm the evidence. When he returned to Beijing, he discussed the controversy with Chairman Mao, who, in turn, calmly instructed Premier Chou to offer the dean any assistance he needed. The dean informed the Chairman that he was prepared to bring the inflammatory complaints back to England. Taking a breath between puffs of his ubiquitous cigarette, Chairman Mao prophetically remarked, "You are brave!"

Chapter 56

GERM WARFARE

Dean Johnson did bravely bring up the issue before the British public, as guest speaker at a London Town Hall meeting sponsored by the Communist Party of Britain. It was a decidedly partisan and vocal audience, receptive to his passionate perspective.

"American aggressors would like nothing better than to increase the death rate in China. The Imperialist United States and its allies fear China. That China will be the leading power at the end of this century cannot be tolerated," he declared as he produced a collection of documents and waved them in the air. "This letter from China, signed by four hundred religious leaders, appeals for world peace."

The letter was disseminated in British publications, which referred to him as "the messenger of world peace." At the top of the list of signatories were Y.T. Wu and Liu Liang-mo, respectively chairman and secretary of the government's Christian Reform Committee. The third signature was Robin Chen, Presiding Bishop of the Anglican Church of China.

He lowered his reading spectacles to the tip of his substantial nose and read to his audience:

> *We Christians of China would like to report to you an inhumane and anti-Christian crime recently committed by American aggressors, which is bacteriologic warfare they have launched against the Chinese and Korean people. We Chinese Christians confirm that the crimes of*

the bacteriologic warfare committed by the American aggressors are
irrefutable and undeniable ....

Science should be used to cure people's disease, but the American
aggressors are making use of it in spreading disease, and the evils will
certainly be punished by God and condemned by the people of the
whole world ... For the sake of humanity, righteousness, and world
peace, we want to appeal to Christians throughout the world to raise
protest so as to put a stop to the atrocious deeds of the American
aggressors in massacring Chinese and Korean people with bacterio-
logic weapons."

The dean also produced a similar manifesto from the Chinese Roman
Catholics, whose collective signatures following the body of the message
ran on for an astounding thirty-four feet.

The dean railed against the United States, not about national politics,
but about Christian beliefs. Communism—champion for all people—was
Christianity incarnate. For that, Stalin was a saint. Peace, love, and equality were values both Christian and communist. What was so difficult to
see, he asked.

Dean Johnson concluded his address, "If the United States believed the
death rate would climb after these atrocities, they are mistaken. This warfare
perpetrated on innocent Chinese has stimulated their national health campaign. Their population has increased by leaps and bounds!"

The dean's impassioned speech brought the Londoners to their feet.
They clapped and cheered their support for China and the dean, and against
the criminal United States.

Across Britain and the United States, headlines shouted: "Germ
Warfare!" The public engaged in heated and divisive debate. In the publication *Fighting Talk*, sponsored by the British-China Friendship Association,
the dean published a response, titled *I Appeal.*

Here is the voice of millions of Chinese Christians.
It is a spontaneous voice. It is a passionate voice.
No longer can these allegations of germ warfare be dismissed as

*mere Communist propaganda, emerging from Moscow. Can we dare
we doubt the integrity of our Eastern Christian brethren?*

*That great Eastern body of Christians listens eagerly at the
response of their Western brethren. The Archbishop of York has
declared his Christian abhorrence of the use of germ warfare.*

I appeal to him. I appeal to the Archbishop of Canterbury.

*I appeal to the British people and the conscience of the Church not
to turn down this cry for help or dismiss it with calculated scepticism or
diplomatic phrases.*

*I appeal to all Christian leaders not to drive a wedge between us
and our Christian brethren in the East and make more difficult the
path of Christians who derive their teachings from the Churches of
the West.*

*I appeal to the decency, the honesty and courage of the whole
British people to insist that they will have no part or lot in this crime of
genocide, this crime of germ warfare.*

Right or wrong, impassionate or foolish, Dean Johnson proved himself
to be a brave voice for China.

Chapter 57

TRUTH ON TRIAL, ENGLAND

While the dean was making the rounds with his message, peasants in China and North Korea continued to suffer respiratory failure, grotesque red lesions, and the blackened, mummified fingers and toes of bubonic plague. As the war escalated, troops were captured on both sides. Pilots from downed American planes were paraded before cameras in North Korea POW camps and interrogated about claims of germ warfare.

"Something wasn't right," USAF pilot Lt. Paul Kniss told a cluster of microphones in a room full of reporters and officials. "Payload is prepped two hours ahead. This time was different. Bombs were loaded fifteen minutes before … by lab technicians."

He bowed his head.

"What we did … it was wrong!"

USAF reserve 2nd Lt. Floyd O'Neal, testifying before the International Scientific Commission headed by noted British biochemist and sinologist Joseph Needham, confessed, "I was the most nervous I had ever been in my life … I never wanted to participate in bacteriological warfare. I was coward enough to do what I was told … We were told not to discuss this with anyone else."

Both pilots ended their testimony with poetic remorse for their actions. Kniss repeated the remark he had voiced while showering with his fellow airmen after the mission.

"My soul will never be clean."

The unmarried O'Neal, imagining conversations with his future family and children, similarly repented. "How can I go back and face my family in a civilized world? I am a criminal in the eyes of humanity."

THE DEAN'S AUDACIOUS ACCUSATIONS—BACKED BY THESE AND other POW confessions and reports from Chinese scientific and medical experts—traveled far. The firm, united voices of the Chinese Christians echoed throughout the world, prompting the British Parliament to take up the challenge, not so much on the veracity of the claims, but on the politics and personality of the messenger, Dean Johnson. The politicians gathered with the hope and expectation of killing the messenger and, thus, the message.

"Can legal sanction be brought against Dean Johnson?" asked deputy speaker Lord Ammons. "He has committed libel against England while the world is sitting on a powder keg! He should be sanctioned for making more difficulties between nations!"

"The attorney general informs no charge of treason can be brought, but there is still question of criminal charges," answered Lord Simons, responding to the bill to be debated that July day.

A member of Parliament in the back row hollered, "We all know the dean is Communist!"

The chamber erupted in jeers and boos.

Lord Ammons, breaking in over the cacophony, shouted, "May we hear from the honorable Archbishop of Canterbury?"

The chamber quieted, and Archbishop Fisher strode to the lectern, his signature round glasses perched in a delicate balance over his brows far below his receding hairline.

"The dean's first and final duty is to the ecclesiastical office which he holds; and he must do nothing to misuse or compromise that office. The complaint is that over a long period of time he has seriously misused and compromised his office, and that he did this in two ways—first, by a degree of unreason and self-delusion, obvious to everybody but himself, which robs his judgment of the respect which is required of a holder of his office. He has lost all sense of the right proportion of things, and all the general controls of common sense. The dean is free to hold what views he likes, but he has made it his chief concern to advocate for them with all the fervor of fanaticism. He has become an active agent for their propaganda."

The room broke out in loud argument. The Archbishop raised his hands, and the room gradually settled down to a low-pitched rumbling.

"He proclaims that in China religion is free, and he believes it. My Lords, there are many people in England who know far more about the state of religious affairs in China than the dean does. Many of us have had words and messages passed to us from Chinese Christians, by strange and devious ways, that count for more than anything that the dean had heard. We have knowledge which he lacks, or ignores, as to what it means to be a Christian in China at the present time; what it means to be a deviationist from the appointed policy; what it means to decline to sign a document; and what it means not to respond sufficiently to 'ideological mouldings.'

"He has—although probably he does not realize it—allowed himself to be exploited by managers of a political system for their own ends."

The House loudly hooted their displeasure.

"The dean is no atheist and not officially a member of the Communist Party. Firmly and frankly, the Church has no power to proceed against him. He is not guilty of heresy in any legal sense.

"If he is guilty of self-delusion to a degree short of certifiable lunacy, this does not expose him to legal consequences, and it is unfortunate that it does not. The dean is not dangerous *yet* to public safety. He may be a public nuisance, and certainly a thorn in the flesh of all of us, but the Church of England has had, on many occasions, to put up with victims of insane folly, self-delusion, and blind partisanship."

A hysterical roar went up.

"We can put up with the dean," concluded the Archbishop.

The parliament hissed like a snake stealthily stalking its hapless prey.

Lord Teviot added, "It seems to me, from what has fallen from the Archbishop, that the dean is quite unfitted to occupy the great position he does within our Church. He has borne false witness not only against his neighbour but against his country and his country's friends.

"The Communism which he supports is the curse of the world, causing misery to millions, as we well know. Undoubtedly, there are millions, and the majority of the millions in the world who are longing for those who are against Communism—and I believe that this applies even in Russia—to stand up and destroy this pernicious creed. That must happen unless civilization based on the teachings of Christ is completely to be destroyed. The most reverend Primate has referred to atheism. We know that atheism is a brother to Communism."

The members debated the myriad entangled issues: ecclesiastical duties, the dean's public influence and persona, the sanctity of freedom of speech, state and church reputation, and the dichotomy between Christianity and Communism. The various Lords and Earls sparred with their witty phrases and well-mannered insults. From the impassioned debates, there was one voice that stood up for the dean and the Chinese.

The 12th Duke of Bedford was a complicated but fair-minded man, perhaps to a fault; at once a nature-loving pacifist and a cold-hearted loner. His nascent interest in politics began with liberal leanings towards socialism but later fell under the spell of fascist ideology and a misguided admiration for Hitler. He had acknowledged that his initial assessment of Nazi concentration camps was flawed, as was that by the Swiss Red Cross, which examined the camps and revealed—astoundingly so, in retrospect—there was nothing seemingly sinister to be exposed in the dressed-up ghettos. Thus, he now tended to be more circumspect in his oft-unpopular, and judgmental, opinion.

"Anybody who knows anything about churches in far-off lands is aware that there is no more honourable and respected body than the Christian Churches of China. It was suggested that these churches are being persecuted. Locally, I do not doubt that is true. But what one has to remember, and what people continually forget, is that in a country as large as China anything can be locally true. I am convinced, from information given me by reliable people, that today in China there is both persecution and freedom, side by side, no doubt depending largely on the character of the local Communist officials.

"No person who is not mentally perverse can read the list of the signatories to that protest, and see the positions which they occupy, without realizing that here the dean has something of considerable weight," continued the Duke, briefly stroking his aquiline nose in thought. "Moreover, this protest was not given to the dean under the instructions of the Chinese Communist government. It was quite a spontaneous affair, got up during the course of his visit within the space of a few days. And when he had a personal interview with Mao Tse-tung, the latter was unaware that this protest had been made."

Regarding the confessions from the captured pilots, he added, "It would have been perfectly easy for the Communist authorities to get intimidated airmen to say that they had dropped bombs carrying germ-laden insects and other things on different places. But it would not have been so easy for them to invent and forge the immense amount of technical detail, given in an extraordinarily natural way, which those airmen are claimed to have given when they described 'hush-hush' lectures which they attended on germ warfare. The United States claims that confessions by their airmen were fakes. If so, they were uncommonly clever ones.

"Let it be known that the reason why I left the Church of England was that I believe it is a state church, and a war-mongering one at that!

"Already we and the Americans have given our blessing to the use of atomic and napalm bombs, instruments of war as devilish as—in my opinion more devilish than—germ warfare. More, we and they have departments investigating germ warfare, and presumably they do not work for fun."

This bold soliloquy brought the house to competing cheers and jeers. Had the Members of Parliament been carrying swords, as in days of yore, blood might have been spilled in contradiction to the great tradition of peaceful resolution.

In the rancorous debate that followed, Earl Winterton seconded Lord Teviot's sentiment, adding, "I would venture to demur from one statement made by the Archbishop, that the dean had never denied any Christian doctrine. This man has borne palpable false witness against his neighbour."

To temper such an impeachable charge, the Archbishop stated, "The noble Lord has not proved that the dean has 'wittingly' published false witness, although in fact he has published false witness. That is really the issue. Does one deal with a man by his acts or by his intentions in a matter? I beseech the House not to silence Dean Johnson. He should be endured ... a small price to pay ... for freedom of speech!"

"Hear, hear! Freedom of speech! Freedom of speech!" the members shouted.

Lord Hailsham jumped up and shouted with evocative emphasis, "The Red Dean is a serious scandal for the Church of England, not because he is a Communist but because he is a clown!"

"The Dean is a joke, but he is not regarded as a joke behind the Iron Curtain," interjected Earl Winterton.

Another round of laughter exploded from the boisterous members, and the Marquis of Salisbury had a moment to add his observations.

"The Duke of Bedford appeared to me to be just a gramophone repeating ordinary propaganda that comes out to us day after day from Moscow. We know the noble Duke. We are used to him. He dearly loves to be a minority of one. We cannot believe that the regime which the Duke seems quite happy in supporting is compatible with the teachings of Christ.

"The Dean has not been drunk in the pulpit, he has not pawned the church vessels, he has not been guilty of flagrant immorality. To regard the Dean as a serious menace is to lose our sense of proportion. He is merely a foolish old man, puffed up with conceit, hankering after publicity—not an attractive sight, but not a threat to our institutions!" said the Marquis.

"Hear, hear. Yea, yea!" they crowed.

With final words of gravity, the Marquis ended the session by saying, "The real truth is that the Dean is not dangerous: he is merely contemptible. And the course most consistent with the dignity of this House and of this country is to treat him with the contempt he most surely deserves."

It was settled. The Red Dean, the charismatic and controversial cockatoo of Canterbury, could not be muzzled or impeached, but only ridiculed and criticized mercilessly, patriotically, even sanctimoniously.

The dean did not surrender quietly to the very public poking and persisted in advocating for the Chinese Christians. A letter was sent to Archbishop Fisher in which the Red Dean appealed yet again:

These Chinese Christians have entrusted to me the most serious message I have ever carried in my life. I enclose their statement with its long list of signatures, and I would ask your Grace to study this list with care, to note the signatures of such of those who attended the

*last Lambeth Conference. We live, Your Grace, in critical days—days
which can determine so much for good or ill. The judgments of all
of us are, no doubt, fallible, but there is one simple rule which we
clergy have always taught to our congregations, and by which we
ourselves stand. That is, to tell the truth as we see it without fear of
consequences. Only this can save our Church and do justice to our
Christian conscience.*

The Archbishop ignored the Dean's appeal, and Churchill, despite
admiring the dean's brash independence, called on politicians and the press
to turn a deaf ear to the dean so as to snuff out his celebrity. Hewlett Johnson,
the Red Dean, could neither be censured nor impeached, but the messenger
might be quarantined.

The aftermath of the Parliamentary airing of the Red Dean's outra-
geous conduct and support of the germ warfare theory was emblematic
of the battle, both ideological and pragmatic, being waged between the
self-righteousness of Western dominance and the suppression of freedom
in a Communist utopia. The public was polarized on the issue. American
officials cried "brainwashing" and "coercion" when commenting on the
American pilots' confessions under torture, duress, and threats of death.
They claimed it was all Soviet and Chinese propaganda. Facts were disputed.
Commission reports were damned on both sides as biased. Opinions clashed
across oceans. Accusations were lobbed back and forth about cover-ups and
fabrications. Robin and the other Christian leaders were simultaneously
hailed as champions of peace and humanity, and condemned as traitors to
the truth.

"Mr. Johnson is one of the most sincere, courageous Christians I know,"
commented Jessie Street, the wife of Laurence Street, Chief Justice of New
South Wales—and the dean's ally—when interviewed about the allegations
against the United States. "He and the Chinese who exposed these issues
should be applauded. They performed a great service, standing up for the
truth against the United States."

"You are a Communist, aren't you?" asked the television reporter.

"Red Jessie," like the Red Dean, was a Soviet sympathizer and human
rights and peace activist. She relished the notoriety of her moniker.

Without flinching or consenting, Mrs. Street answered sharply, "If so, what of it? A Communist cannot tell the truth?"

The Archbishop of Canterbury editorialized on truth in his Parliamentary speech, saying, "It is to be said that one of our greatest glories, which serve to keep us in the way of living truth, is this right of members, short of heresy, to speak the truth *as each sees it.*"

THE TRUTH ROBIN SAW WAS THAT COMMUNISM IN CHINA WAS beneficial to its people. Others saw it as imprisonment. To the West, the signatories to the Manifestos were, right or wrong, solidly pro-communist, like the Red Dean and Red Jessie. Archbishop Fisher's failure to support their claims further exacerbated the schism between the Mother Church and its faraway child. It was the final signal to the Chinese that they must stand on their own. It pushed their church closer to its own sponsor, the Chinese Communist Party.

In the United States, in late 1953 after the end of the war, the American pilots, to a man, officially recanted their confessions, stating emphatically that they were coerced into falsifying their statements and that they were ill-treated in violation of every one of the Geneva regulations. They claimed they were beaten, forced to stand or squat for hours, placed in solitary confinement in unheated three-by-seven-foot hovels, forced to "wallow in filth and dirt," and subjected to psychological trauma, frostbite, starvation, and threats of death. Yet, even these recantations were procured only as an alternative to court martial.

John Powell and his co-editors were threatened with charges of treason and sedition for publishing false accusations of germ warfare. China and the United States faced off on the world stage.

Truth was on trial, patriotism was being tested, and anti-communism raged within America.

Chapter 58

TRUTH ON TRIAL, AMERICA

" John Powell, Sylvia Campbell, Julian Schuman, do you swear to tell the truth, the whole truth, and nothing but the truth …"

William Jenner, the square-jawed Republican senator from Indiana, listened to the swearing-in of the publisher of the *China Monthly Review*, his wife, and his editor. Jenner was chairman of the Senate Internal Security Subcommittee, and animosity was running high, both in America and in Senate chambers. Senator McCarthy had put America on edge, redefining what America and being American should be. Supporters, like Jenner, bolstered by Truman's Loyalty Program, were flushing out anyone who did not exhibit absolute loyalty to American democracy. Any scent of communist ideology, organizations, or practices brought on the hunt for treason and sedition.

Earlier on September 27, 1954, Jenner had promised to interrogate Americans who would give "aid and comfort to the bloody cause of Red China." John Powell and his associates now sat before his subcommittee for that very reason.

"… so help you God?"

"I do," the trio pledged.

But nothing more than that, thought Powell.

"Mr. Powell, you were the publisher of *China Weekly Review*," began Senator Jenner.

"I was," answered Powell.

Powell had previously written that America, "long the champion of the oppressed and long the world's leading exponent of national self-determination, had shifted course and had become the most powerful force of reaction throughout the world." In commenting about the American military strategy of "aggressive interventionism" in Korea to turn back the threat of communism from China, he had said, "Truman is wrong."

The weekly periodical's last few years had been rough, and it was renamed the *China Monthly Review*. Its demise was inevitable following flagging sales—in a country devoid of English-speaking foreigners and another country hostile towards publications sympathetic to Red China. It had finally shut down its presses the previous year. The magazine had published articles from a Chinese perspective, seen as favorable to the Communist government. It was accused of brainwashing and indoctrinating American POWs forced to read its issues.

"In 1952, your magazine accused the United States of germ warfare against China and North Korea, saying the evidence is overwhelming. You fabricated this tale with religious leaders from Red China. They enlisted Dr. Hewlett Johnson, Dean of Canterbury, to spread these lies," stated Jenner, his steely eyes boring into Powell's. "You are aware that Dean Johnson is known as the Red Dean?"

"Yes."

"Your allegations are serious, based solely on statements by members of a government-controlled organization," Jenner said sternly.

"I am not aware that these claims are fabricated or that these Christian voices are government-controlled," asserted Powell.

"Don't be naïve! The Communists shut all churches, consolidated them into a state front, and persecute those who stray outside this façade ... to the point of imprisonment, torture, even death!"

"Of these, I have no first-hand knowledge," Powell retorted.

Jenner leaned over to confer with another senator. After a brief conversation, Jenner continued.

"Mr. Powell, have you first-hand knowledge of the use of biological weapons?"

Powell bent towards his attorney to ask a question. Receiving an agreeable answer, he replied, "Invoking my journalist's right to confidentiality, I decline to answer."

"This committee believes there are individuals supporting propaganda on behalf of these brainwashing, soul-killing Red Chinese. You are aware that you and your associates face potential charges of sedition and treason, the penalty of which includes personal imprisonment ... up to twenty years."

The corner of Jenner's mouth twitched uncontrollably.

"I am," answered Powell.

Jenner again conferred with his colleague. He turned back to Powell and glared.

"Are you a communist?"

Jenner gripped the microphone and continued to stare down Powell.

"I'm not called upon to reveal if I am a Democrat, Republican, or Communist!" Powell countered coolly.

"Have you ever been a member of the Communist Party of China?"

Powell leaned toward his attorney for advice.

"I do not care to answer and invoke my rights under the Fifth Amendment."

"Does the Communist Party of China advocate the overthrow of the government of the United States?"

Again, Powell conferred with his attorney.

"I do not care to answer and invoke my rights under the Fifth Amendment."

A restless murmur rippled through the room.

"Why do you risk your own freedom?" asked Jenner.

"I believe the Chinese ... these Christians, Red or not—they are trustworthy and honorable ... willing to risk their own lives and reputations for the truth."

Powell and his associates did not give in. They held fast to their journalistic tradition and prerogative. They continued to defend their accusations against the United States government.

The ball was now in the Senate's court. Charge them or shut up.

Chapter 59

CHINA NEEDS
THE WORLD

After the Red Dean faced calls for sanctions, even excommunication, and the Powells and Schuman invited indictments for sedition and treason, Robin became firmly entrenched in the Three-Self Movement. He was elected to the National People's Congress as the first vice-chairman of the church, along with its chairman, Y.T. Wu, who was referred to by Western bishops as the "Pope of China." Though not Party members, he and Wu occupied seats at the political table of influence. Lindel had died in Shanghai in 1954, and Robin was now the most senior voice for Chinese Christians.

The church was renamed the Three-Self *Patriotic* Movement, but, rather than being a church in captivity, China was eager to have it sit at the same table as the free world powers. A love- and peace-based religious institution that non-communist countries could relate to was a very powerful messenger for Premier Chou.

The country's fortunes took a dramatic turn following the Korean War, reaping record crops to feed its millions, stamping out corruption and vice, and rebuilding the country with roads, bridges, railways, and dams. It was time to rejoin the non-communist world.

In the spring of 1956, Robin, as Presiding Bishop, took a bold step and extended an official invitation to his colleague, Bishop Howard Mowll, Archbishop of Australia, writing, "Such contacts made in the form of inter-Church delegations will not only help to promote mutual understanding and friendship between peoples in the cause of world peace, but also strengthen the genuine spiritual fellowship between national Churches in the interest of Christian unity."

Mowll, a tall, outspoken Englishman from Dover, grew sympathetic to the Chinese people after his initial travels throughout China in 1923. He had married Dorothy Anne Martin, an Anglican missionary, in Chengtu. After serving as assistant bishop, he was consecrated Bishop of West China, championing the independence of the Chinese Church. He was critical of the oft-autocratic missionaries and helped prepare the church for autonomy by consecrating two native assistant bishops.

Acceptance of the invitation was vociferously attacked by the Australian Anglican establishment. Some clergy understandably granted Bishop Mowll latitude for a nostalgic visit to his former diocese. But others viewed it as an inappropriate, ill-advised play into Red China's hand, since Australia had no official relations with China. The visit could give the seemingly subservient Chinese Anglicans a setting to propagandize for their oppressive regime and its illusory state of religious freedom. But Bishop Mowll knew Robin was an open-minded, fair person, and the intent was truly collegial—though perhaps naïve—even if others read it as opportunistic.

The Bishop of Hong Kong defended Bishop Mowll's decision. "Some will never be persuaded that an Australian delegation will not be hoodwinked by the Machiavellian Chinese and 'used' for nefarious purposes. There has been almost universal praise from the widely representative groups who have visited the country."

After much debate and criticism, Bishop Mowll led an eight-member party to China, the first Western clergy to bear witness to the country's political and social transformation. The Australians were forewarned about the glare of publicity and the fear that "world Communism was going 'all out' to foster the myth that Christianity and Communism can co-exist."

In a caravan of shiny black limousines, the kind of reception usually reserved for top diplomats, Bishop Mowll and his companions were chauffeured from their quarters in Shanghai's old French Concession to Robin's compound. They passed through a student demonstration protesting the "wicked British and French imperialists" for their invasion of Egypt after President Nasser had expelled the colonialists and nationalized the Suez Canal. Although the crowd was noisy, there were no police present with rifles and bamboo canes. The caravan slowed as it weaved its way through the well-behaved demonstrators.

"Before liberation, I would not have dared meet you at the railway station. It would not have been safe," Robin noted.

"Should we reroute?" asked Bishop Mowll anxiously, not wishing to incite further trouble.

"Now, everything is changed," answered Robin with a reassuring wave of his hand.

Robin pointed out that, prior to the new government, it would have been impossible to bring his friend through such an event. The unruliness prevalent in pre-liberation society would have instigated a violent anti-imperialist reaction, with a good possibility of bloodshed. Now demonstrations were measured and peaceful.

"You see, the students are orderly, very proper," he explained with a wide smile as the motorcade pulled away. "If they knew who you were, they would treat you with every courtesy. We have a new attitude."

Much indeed had changed since Mowll first arrived in Szechuan province. One of the Englishman's first experiences was coming upon forty soldiers wounded by bandits and infected with smallpox, cholera, and dysentery. The men were left to die in two old temples while "lying on the hard ground amid indescribable filth and stench," as he would later describe. The frontier was so wild and untamed that within two years, he, along with seven others and a child, were kidnapped and taken hostage by roving bandits. Only after a ransom was paid by the local magistrate were they released unharmed. In the few years after liberation, China had completely turned itself around. Bandits did not exist. They and counterrevolutionaries had been eradicated.

Robin spoke glowingly of the vibrancy of the church and the optimistic openness of the new society. As the demonstration scene receded behind them, neither he nor Bishop Mowll were aware they were early witnesses to China's next chapter.

THE AUSTRALIANS WERE AMONG THE FIRST FOREIGNERS TO participate in a communion service hosted by the new Chinese Church. The audience packed the cathedral to standing-room-only capacity. The organist, Margaret Yuan, the best of all of Shanghai and another of Bishop T.S. Sing's grandchildren, played the processional music with the vigor of a resurrected church. Bishop Mowll was eager to give the guest sermon; he was well aware of the impact of his remarks. The world was wondering: Can Christianity exist in a Communist state?

Mowll was not there to create problems for the church but to support it. His task was to thread the needle of ecclesiastical and political diplomacy.

"Christ spoke little in regard to social conditions, although he was vividly conscious of them," Mowll preached. "He evaded political questions. He did not condemn.

"Everyone who accepts the advantages of the rule of the State is bound to discharge his just obligations to the State," he went on, contemplating the competing loyalties of Chinese Christians. "Render unto Caesar the things that are Caesar's and unto God the things that are God's. If we seek first the Kingdom of God and His righteousness, then everyone else will receive his due."

Robin beseeched Mowll at his departure, "The Church here is still in a period of reconstruction. We need very much the advice and help of others. We realize there are still many defects in our work and ask you not to hesitate to tell us what our defects are. We know it is only by being humble, listening to the advice of others, that we can progress."

Upon his return to Australia, Bishop Mowll gave glowing reviews of the church, which he assessed was growing and free from religious persecution. He did not address the curious fact that, prior to the visit, Bishop Kimber Den, who had been arrested and imprisoned for four years without explanation, was unceremoniously released from prison—also without explanation. It was perhaps a gesture of international goodwill, and the official who had made false accusations against Den was himself later imprisoned. Instead, Bishop Mowll, motivated to build bridges of friendship, noted that factories were being constructed and railroad lines laid down. Gambling, petty crimes, and prostitution had been eliminated. Farms, cultivated like variously colored terraced chessboards across the countryside, were efficiently tilled for maximum productivity. Most importantly, people seemed genuinely happy and free to worship. What he saw was a sincere church thriving under the new government, exercising its constitutional right of religious belief.

Launching a counterargument, a minister of the Scottish Church in Sydney called the Church in China a "tiger in a cage (who) has so come to enjoy his cage that it has lost its tiger-like qualities and become a more domestic cat." Of Mowll's effusive praise, he called it "high treason in the ideological war."

A group of American students also reported favorably on their visit. But as the trip was not approved by the State Department, upon their return home, some had their passports confiscated. The ideological war within Christian communities and the political war between communism and democracy was not so easily resolved. Suspicion and mistrust were pervasive.

As the various denominations of Christianity disappeared in China, communion among different congregations was expedited. Whereas Anglicans previously comprised less than 10 percent of all Protestants, the Chinese Church now had no interdenominational conflicts or distinctions. Methodists, Lutherans, Congregationalists, Baptists, and Presbyterians came together under one literal roof. The Anglican goal of a unified, self-governing Chinese church—one church, one God—was becoming a reality, while the Catholics—in a similar, complete break from the Pope and the Vatican—were organized separately under the Chinese Catholic Patriotic Association.

Along with this independence, foreign funding came to a standstill. Self-support, the second pillar of the Three-Self principle—the pillar that Premier Chou had bet would collapse—was a practical focus.

Lloyd, now retired, petitioned the American Episcopal Church to neither forget nor write off China. But the West was skeptical of China's religious freedom. The disappearance of Chinese Christian leaders from the world stage and the withdrawal of the Chinese church from the international community fostered a perception that Christians were persecuted and the church suppressed by the government. For many, Christianity and the church in China did not even exist. Criticism of the Three-Self Movement as a functional puppet arm of the Communist Party was understandably harsh. Others spoke out in favor of reasserting communication with Chinese Christians. But while the ecclesiastical estrangement seemed to have no end in sight, Robin remained determined to open the church to the outside world.

He entertained clergy from India and Japan. He forged conversations with Buddhists and Muslims. When former British Prime Minister Attlee was invited to China, Robin made a point of inviting him to a family dinner, a gesture openly praised by Premier Chou.

Another old friend of China, Dean Johnson, returned for his third visit after surviving the still-unsettled germ warfare controversies. Robin met him in Beijing with a retinue of church representatives, who reported on the progress and growth of the church. One clergyman recited the goals of Christians: achieve the Three-Selfs; construct a socialistic, Christian-like society; and work for world peace. A student leader related the enthusiasm of a recent conference of 1,700 students studying to be good Christian workers. Another bishop commented on his inspection of prisons, where prisoners, mainly counterrevolutionaries, worked in spotless factories making clothes, shoes, and matches, and received medical care, plentiful food, and recreational programs. Comparison with the deplorable conditions of incarceration before liberation was dramatic. He explained that all citizens were organized into collectives or neighborhood groups, which ensured each member's well-being. No one was alone. The dean was duly impressed with these dramatic changes.

Later, they joined half a million people celebrating China's National Day with a four-hour rain-soaked parade in Tian An Men Square. Wave after wave of military personnel and armament equipment, youth groups, religious organizations, and battalions of marchers representing all segments of society passed triumphantly in front of Chairman Mao's viewing stand.

That evening, as the skies cleared, the Red Dean and the Red Bishop sat with other guests atop the Great Gate of Heavenly Peace as people frolicked in the square below. Tables laden with food and drinks were arranged around a dance floor, and a band played music, making for a jovial gathering. Suddenly, the night erupted with spectacular fireworks, accompanied by rockets and cannons bursting in a semi-circle around the square. Bright military spotlights choreographed swaying columns of pink, white, and blue, sending the colorful lights into infinite space. Then, as if on cue, first Premier Chou, then Chairman Mao, appeared, walking freely among the guests. The clergymen were among the dignitaries, who included an English Nobel laureate, the Indonesian president, the Rumanian ambassador, Canadian politicians, Indian officials, Italian literati, and high-ranking PLA generals.

Christians were a small but important element in China's re-emergence onto the international scene and were in the good graces of the central government—for now. China wanted and needed friends, even Christian ones, on its own terms. Seven years after the Communist takeover, with three recent consecrations, including that of K.H. Ting of Chekiang, all seventeen bishops were natives. Vestiges of Western oversight were expunged, and the CHSKH was truly a Chinese church, standing on its own for the first time in history.

As an important link between the government and the church, Robin received favorable treatment, including a driver and car to attend meetings, a private telephone in his home, financial support, special health coverage, and, most importantly, a coal supplement for the winter. As the financial stability of the church improved with its steadily growing membership, so did Robin's. He used his own funds to help less-fortunate children attend school.

"Finances from outside have been interrupted, but life on earth always has a door to victory," Robin wrote to Grace with his inimitable optimism. "Faithfulness, truthfulness, light, salt of the earth. These are good words all preachers want to use."

"Grace, do you have a date to return home?" lamented Constance. "Will we ever see each other again in this life?"

Robin and Constance had loaned Grace to America and wanted her back. China was no longer a land from which to escape but a land to cultivate. It was a nation awash with hope and prosperity. The whole country was fertilized with Chairman Mao's thoughts, and Robin believed the church and its members were crucial to its harvest.

"I have one important principle," Robin wrote with uncompromising directness. "No matter how great the burden to study medicine, when you finish, surrender your freedom. Contribute to the people."

Chapter 60

DELUSIONS OF
DREAMS

Immediately after her graduation, Grace married Robert, in Philadelphia in June of 1952. Her father's friend, Reverend Gilbert, officiated the wedding, which was attended by the Perots, Dr. Gummey, Bishop Roberts, his wife, Dorothy, Alice Gregg, Sister Louise Magdalena, and, to Grace's chagrin, nearly forty of Robert's classmates, friends, and spouses, including his former dean, Dr. Josiah McCracken, his half-brother, his sister, and brother-in-law—but none of her own family.

When asked by friends why they married, Robert quipped rather practically, "Grace was charming, beautiful, very agreeable. We were perfectly matched. Grace was very much just like me. We were both from good Christian homes and were both interested in medicine. It was like a fairy tale story, written and directed by God."

It was quite simple to him.

Grace also gave a practical explanation, revealing only half-jokingly, "He said he had no parents, no home. I felt sorry for him."

Their friends laughed at the answer. To her, it was just as simple.

Following an unlikely honeymoon at a dude ranch in the Poconos, the couple moved to Boston, where Robert accepted a position in the neurosurgical residency program at the New England Medical Center.

Boston was the world's medical mecca, with its renowned Harvard Medical School. The surgery training programs at the NEMC and its affiliated hospital, the Boston Floating Hospital for Children, the Massachusetts

General Hospital, commonly known as the MGH, and the Peter Bent Brigham Hospital, where the world's first human kidney transplant had been performed two years earlier, were top-tier.

Boston would be their home and their future.

TO ROBIN, GRACE WAS ALWAYS COMING BACK—IT WAS ONLY A matter of when. China was dramatically better than when she left. Mao encouraged party members to consider reasonable, alternative views from foreigners and non-party members with which to openly criticize the government and its leaders. Demonstrations like that witnessed by Bishop Mowll were encouraged. Posters criticizing the Communist Party adorned a "Democratic Wall" at Beijing University. Letters by the millions were sent to Premier Chou offering constructive criticism but also calls for resignations and disempowerment of the Party. This new chapter gave people a voice and the appearance that leaders were receptive of new ways to improve life. The "Let a Hundred Flowers Bloom and a Hundred Schools of Thought Contend" campaign was intended to stimulate new ideas in arts and more progress in science. But newfound freedom led to excessive criticism of the government and its policies. Mao responded with a reactive, vicious crackdown on exposed, outspoken activists, writers, military leaders, politicians, and intellectuals. This Anti-Rightist Movement—what amounted to a country-wide purge—did not rattle the patriotism of the Christian leadership. It strengthened its resolve. Anything that promoted frank discussion leading to corrections in behavior was encouraged.

Some members of the church were deemed to need "re-thinking" in their loyalty to the government and to the goals of social reform. They were sent to camps in Harbin in Northern China, where winter was hell frozen over. Cleansing of the soul—the casting-out of bad elements—was a necessary act in the Church, in the government, and throughout society. With the armistice of the Korean War and the heavy hand of re-education, China was at relative peace, and patriotism was of paramount importance.

The conclusion of the Hundred Flowers campaign brought the official end of the CHSKH. The transformation of the missionary-based,

Western-modeled Christian Church into the Communist government-sanctioned Three-Self Church was complete. The CHSKH was replaced entirely by the Three-Self Patriotic Movement. Although they were not party members, Christians, like all Chinese citizens, were expected to be loyal to the Chinese Communist Party.

Robin was instrumental in this re-education process, seeing his role in the church, and the church itself, as vehicles of support for the government and its social reforms. He attended the Beijing Socialism School and organized many conferences. Some lasted as long as three months. Participants, often clergy, immersed themselves in self-reflective issues: religion in a socialist country, the relationship between Christianity and imperialism, and personal spiritual and political transformation. Since social programs dealing with education, medical care, and community support were provided by the government, the church could concentrate on its spiritual and moral mission. Some participants were changed by these programs; others became more entrenched in opposition to ideological remolding. Robin had little tolerance for those who failed to exert themselves to resolve internal contradictions, calling them "sluggards" and "lazy thinkers."

He was enamored with the progress China had made from the days of beggars in the streets, urchins stealing watches, and soldiers running rampant over people. Babies were no longer routinely dying from typhoid, scarlet fever, and smallpox. The elderly were not left in the streets to die for lack of food or financial support. Women were contributing equally to society, and foot-binding was finally a historic relic. Japanese soldiers had long ago been ousted as unwanted occupiers, raping Chinese women and beheading Chinese men. The better China became, the more impatient he was.

"My idea of patriotism is not just talk," he wrote Grace.

His legs began to swell. The pain from a gastric ulcer returned. He tired more easily, and his breathing became heavy at times. He sensed time was limited.

"I want action ... not empty words!"

Grace replied: *Which of what you wrote is true? What is propaganda? What can I believe?*

"That you are planning to return after Hsun-Piao finishes his training is most happy news," Robin responded after receiving one of Grace's placating letters. "You should not miss the opportunity to serve your father-land, to participate in building the country. To answer your question, I have not been brainwashed. That does not mean I have not changed my way of thinking. The purpose of reconstructing one's thought is to recognize one's incorrect thinking, to strengthen patriotism and pursue socialism, to dif-ferentiate truth from untruth."

He was approaching retirement and still seeking his truth.

GRACE AND ROBERT BOUGHT A SMALL, BUT COMFORTABLE, house in Quincy, a working- and middle-class suburb of Boston. She heard from the FBI again in 1954. She swore to the field agent that she was not, and never was, a member of the Communist Party, nor had she ever received any pro-communist publications. A month later, McCarthy was censured by Congress and the Red Scare cooled down.

The young couple settled quickly into American family life. Within four and a half years of their wedding, they had three children and a growing circle of similarly stranded Chinese intellectuals, most of whom were also Christian. Returning to China seemed more and more remote, even unde-sirable. Grace made the important decision to apply for permanent residency the year before their last child was born.

One evening, Grace broached the unthinkable as she carried her young-est, Annette, in her arms. Mei Mei was watching a new black-and-white television in the living room and Dei Dei played with a red toy truck on the floor. Looking at her three children, she had to get it off her mind.

Robert retorted quickly. "Go back? It would be suicide!" News out of China was not good. A drought had hit the country and there were stories of a "crackdown" against thinkers and intellectuals. *Intellectuals* meant people like them. He was too practical to get caught up in all that oppressive culture. America was the land of the free and of opportunity. America's greatness was its future, China's was its past.

"It is not possible," he scoffed dismissively.

What did he have to gain? He had no parents, and his grandfather, Bishop Sing, had died long ago. His half-brother, John, also married, was living in the States. He would have to forfeit his appointment to the neu-rosurgical staff at the New England Medical Center. And what about the children? Give up living in America to live in China? There was no compar-ison. It *was* unthinkable.

That was it. His decision was as definitive as his scalpel was sharp. They would not speak of going home.

ANOTHER LETTER ARRIVED FROM CHINA. IT WAS THE THIRD this month. Grace opened each with trepidation, looking forward to words from her parents, yet dreading what news those words would bring.

For the past few years, it had been good news: a wedding, a new nephew, another wedding, a second nephew, then a third and a niece. But informa-tion of the Anti-Rightist campaign and the criticism of the Hundred Flowers Bloom movement brought an underlying sense of dread. The envelopes were emotional surprises. She anticipated upsetting contents and was relieved when they bore pleasantries. She welcomed news from her mother of some-one's successful operation and of a relative's baby. She learned that Helen was sent to teach in a very poor area of Northeast China and Hui was given a job in remote Harbin. From her father, it was mostly about China.

She carefully unfolded the letter, reflecting for a moment at the familiar writing. The characters were well-proportioned and graceful, like pieces of art. She traced her mother's words with her fingertips; the lines were thin and soft. The ideograms seemed to float on the paper, imparting calm mes-sages of family life.

Her father's was the opposite—bold, tight, efficient—half the size of her mother's, characters frenetically and densely etched into the paper. The paper was covered edge to edge, with four times as many characters, crammed together like an army of dutiful tiny soldiers, standing shoulder-to-shoulder, impatient with marching orders.

She stared at the characters and tried to imagine each voice: her moth-er's quiet, songlike voice cascading softly as a morning's sprinkle, and her father's forceful and direct tone, crashing, at times pounding, like the con-stant, irrepressible cadence of a summer storm. She strained to hear their voices in the distinctive handwriting, afraid of forgetting what her parents sounded like.

"The last time I wrote to persuade you to return to China as early as you can," her father spoke to her. "This is entirely because of our love for you. I will never force you to make a decision you do not want to make. Do not feel we misunderstand you if you choose not to return immediately."

She wanted to cry, not only because she missed her father, or could hardly remember his singular voice, but because she knew she was a disappointment. His words washed over her. She had not lived up to his dreams. She had not accomplished anything. She felt as if she were drowning in his delusions.

Her father spoke of China's great achievements. He related hardships he and her mother willingly endured because it aided the country's progress. He revealed the sacrifices every individual and family was making for the good of all Chinese people. He stressed how the church was growing stronger, more unified, and how the number of Protestants had climbed back to the level of just before the takeover. It was too much.

She went to her second-floor bedroom and entered the walk-in closet. She stooped to open a small storage chest. At the bottom was a shoebox. She took off the cardboard cover. The shoebox was crammed with a collection of letters, organized into each year's precious trove. She folded the letter and filed it neatly with the others. She fit the cover snugly back onto the shoebox and pushed down firmly, sealing away her parent's voices. The memory of her baby brother's coffin rushed over her—the inexplicable emptiness, the aloneness, the finality she felt when his body disappeared.

Bu ku, she heard father say to her.

Grace closed the chest, exited the closet, and shut the door. She did not cry. She walked out the bedroom and left the voices behind.

Chapter 61

GODLESS AGENTS

H ollington Tong waited for his turn in the pulpit at the Washington National Cathedral, a Neo-Gothic church where voices from the sanctuary resonated through a massive nave three hundred feet high. Tong was born in Chekiang Province in 1887, as was Generalissimo Chiang, one week before him. He was a journalism graduate of the University of Missouri and Columbia University. Tong first met the future Generalissimo when Chiang was one of his young English students in a Ningpo school. Tong was raised in a Christian household and eventually served as vice-minister of information in the fledgling propaganda office of Chiang's Republic of China. His task was to represent China's side of the story in the war with Japan, particularly to those within the United States.

After the Kuomintang lost their battle with the Communists and Chiang moved his army and government to Taiwan, Tong became its ambassador to Japan. After a couple of years in that post, he was appointed by Chiang to be ambassador to the United States. It was natural that he would look unfavorably upon the new Communist government overseeing China. He had been loyal to Chiang and the Republic for all of his adult life, and he wasn't about to mitigate his criticism of their foe. As a fellow Christian, that included fervent opposition to the transformation of Christianity and its church on the mainland.

What was happening in his homeland was disgraceful. A totalitarian dictatorship controlling all aspects of their poor citizens' lives. The church, a casualty of the ideological war. Its leaders, complicit co-conspirators.

The sound of his name descended from the vaulted ceiling, breaking his thoughts.

"—the Honorable Hollington Tong, Republic of China ambassador to the United States," announced the minister.

Tong, over seventy but still filled with the fiery vigor of his Ningpo youth, rose and shook the minister's hand. He ascended the pulpit, carved from stones that originated from Canterbury Cathedral. He wore his Western suit and tie in a very natural way and touched his tall forehead to smooth his silver hair. He cleared his thoughts and began in fluent English.

"Fellow Christians, I highly appreciate your invitation to speak at your evening service on the subject, 'What Can Christians in America Do for China?' It is true there are still organizations in China which call themselves Christian churches, but they are not. They are police agencies of the Communist state."

His American allies needed to hear the truth.

ROBIN AND HIS FAMILY GATHERED IN THE COURTYARD OF HIS home, awaiting cars to drive them to a park for a family outing. He had been busy with Three-Self affairs and felt guilty about not having written Grace for a while. As two government cars arrived, Robin thanked Constance and the rest of the family for allowing him to remain behind.

After they departed, he went inside. He settled into a chair at his desk. It was a decade ago that he had left his daughter in Philadelphia. Now, she was a wife with her own family. Had she forgotten them? He tried to swallow the bitterness he felt deep inside. He wanted her in New China. She needed to be here. Was she afraid? Did she not understand?

I want to take this opportunity to write you, so I asked the family's permission to stay home. Hsun-Piao mentioned: 'There are about two to three thousand Chinese students in the States who do not know much of the real situation back in China.' This is because of the anti-New China propaganda by the American imperialism.

Some people think there isn't any democratic freedom in China.

The fact is our democratic freedom is not only for the few powerful, rich, capitalistic, or anti-revolutionary criminals but for the majority of people .... The great masses of working people, farmers, laborers, working intellectuals, as well as those who love democracy, are enjoying the privileges of real freedom.

THE AUDIENCE RESPONDED TO TONG'S OPENING REMARKS WITH polite applause.

"A few months ago, nineteen prominent Chinese church leaders, including Y.T. Wu, Wu Yi-fang, Bishop Robin Chen, and Y.C. Tu exhibited their anti-Americanism by writing to Mr. and Mrs. John Powell and Julius Schuman, former editors of the *China Monthly Review*, who await trial for anti-American statements. These Chinese strongly expressed their sympathy over such "unjust indictment" .... The nineteen say, 'We feel it our duty as Christians to register our strong protest against such a flagrant infringement of human rights and civil liberties.'"

That he would name the Christian traitors showed how personal he felt the betrayal was. The enemy was not some faceless entity; they were individuals to be flushed from their protected positions, called out, and attacked for their show of support for this trio of American traitors!

IN THE QUIET OF HIS HOUSE, ROBIN TRIED A MORE DIRECT APPEAL to Grace.

"Another change is that working women have gained economic independence," he wrote.

As an American-trained medical doctor, Grace could be among the women leaders of the country. She could fulfill the promise she held as an outstanding college student.

"Women have entered all areas of reconstructive work and have become one of the great forces in building our socialism," he continued.

Perhaps Grace would see the kind of future she could enjoy back home.

TONG NEEDED TO MAKE PEOPLE UNDERSTAND THE TRAPS BEING set by this openness and invitations of friendship and the depths of the Chinese Christian connivance. There was too much at stake.

"The Powells and Schuman had published lying articles, under the supervision of the Communist masters of Shanghai, charging the American government with the use of germ warfare in the Korean War," he persisted.

He was determined to make the case against the Christian propagandists.

HUI STOOPED BY THE POND BURSTING WITH WATER LILIES TO feed a family of ducks. The ducks were free to fly to the countryside, but they remained in the city park. They had water to drink and swim in. Food was plentiful as long as visitors came. There was no reason to fly away.

Hui and her family laughed as the adult ducks dunked their heads into the water and upended their bottoms. With their heads immersed in the water, the duck tails looked like lotus flowers floating on the surface. They popped back up, shook their bills, then dove back in. Again and again. It was a simple pleasure.

"WE SOLVE RACIAL PROBLEMS WITH DEMOCRACY AND THE PRINciple of racial equality," wrote Robin. "We do not have racial oppression. We are trying to set policies for the autonomies to assist minorities to improve their economy, living standard, cultures. Since the working people have become the Master and the head of a big family, determining to rid itself of capitalists and building a prosperous socialist society, the nation is no longer a pan of sand, but a united family."

TONG RAILED AGAINST THE CHINESE CHRISTIANS IN MUCH THE same way that nationalistic Chinese railed against foreign missionaries. The accused inherited sins by their association with a political system. Christians were suspected of nefarious betrayal of their religious beliefs; church and state were intertwined. Friends of enemies are enemies.

"A minority of Protestant clergymen in this country … are urging that American Christians should hold out the right hand of friendship to the godless agents of Communism who are posing as spokesmen for the Christian body in Communist China today. It is tragic, but it is true."

THE PARK WAS FILLED WITH THE CASUAL CHATTER BETWEEN friends and family. The recitation of revolutionary slogans from loudspeakers scattered throughout the park cut harshly through the clear winter air. An old man wearing a thick cotton coat was playing a familiar, if not grating, erhu tune. In the distance, someone was singing a distinctly revolutionary folk song. Hui and Constance walked arm in arm, taking in all the sounds clashing and blending and weaving with each other. It was at once mellifluous and disruptive. Melodious and dissonant. Yin and yang.

"WE SINCERELY BELIEVE THE SOCIALIST ROAD IS THE RIGHT ONE," Robin wrote.

It was not propaganda. It was from his heart.

"COMMUNIST CHINA, IN ITS DIABOLICAL ENDEAVOR TO UPROOT true Christianity, has wiped out, in less than a decade, the missionary work done by Western Christians during the last hundred years," Tong continued. "It has hounded and driven from China the dedicated American men and women who have devoted their lives to foreign missions. It has imprisoned, tortured, and killed some of the finest foreign missionaries in China. It has confiscated and turned to political use the churches and institutions of the foreign missions in China, most of them paid for by the contributions of the American churches, including nickels and dimes given by American children. It has corrupted and broken the spirit of thousands of weakened native Christians and has turned them into evil servitors of the godless Communist state. And now it is proposed that American churchmen recognize these persecutors of God's church as fellow Christians! Could folly be more complete?

"God will lead us to victory in the worldwide crusade against the Communist anti-Christ, but we cannot achieve it by dishonorable gestures of friendship to those whose work is not to build the church but to destroy it!"

If we really love our country, we must be willing to sacrifice and to contribute. What a grand, glorious democratic freedom and privilege that would be.

In order to have the right thinking, one has to do it voluntarily and willingly. In order to conform into the thinking of the whole mass, effects on individual thoughts cannot be avoided. That is also true. That everything is being under control, including essential needs, to be deprived of freedom of thoughts, is not true."

Robin was spent. He didn't know what Grace or Hsun-Piao were really thinking. He didn't know if she ever intended to return, even though she had promised she would. He would have to let one thing or another go at some point: his dreams, or his daughter. But why should he? He had faith that both would come true. Perhaps not now—not during his lifetime—but sometime.

"I do not wish to force you in making decisions, but I do hope you will seriously consider it," he finished gently. "The socialist road will definitely take over that of capitalism."

Once again, as he had done on dozens and dozens of other occasions, he folded and sealed the letter. He prayed his words would reach his daughter's heart. He could only hope that she would read it carefully with her family and country in mind, believe his words, and keep them close to her heart. And then, he hoped and prayed that she would soon return home to her family and her homeland.

AMBASSADOR TONG STEPPED BACK FROM THE PULPIT. HE WAS pleased. The cathedral resounded with thunderous applause as the audience stood to salute the Ambassador's address. They had heard the message and the truth. The Chinese Church leaders were traitors to Christianity; the Church, a puppet of the government.

Onward, true Christian soldiers!

Chapter 62

RED BISHOP

"Is there religious freedom in China?"

Robin heard this question from every foreigner who visited China. He, too, had presumed that Marxist Communism could not coexist with Christianity, that Christianity had to reach the people before Communism did—or else be destroyed. But he had witnessed support from the government and the church was producing honey for the country.

"We enjoy full freedom of religious belief," he replied confidently to the Japanese reporter who was covering the Beijing meeting of the National Committee of Protestant Churches in China for Self-Administration.

Robin was the new committee's vice-chairman. Since this was a government-sponsored bureaucracy, he represented both the church and the government. He did not see it as a contradiction; everyone in China should support the government.

"Then why did China ban the activities of Jehovah's Witnesses? Why arrest two British missionaries?" asked the reporter, referring to recent international incidents.

"The government cannot tolerate destructive actions carried out by Western imperialists and their counterrevolutionary agents under the cloak of religion."

It was now the British reporter's turn.

"What actions are they guilty of?"

"Slandering and attacking the Party. Undermining social reconstruction," Robin answered.

The words slid easily off his tongue.

"That is not very specific," said the Brit.

"The sect advocated a third world war by fostering and spreading reactionary rumors."

"Are you a mouthpiece for the party, repeating common revolutionary slogans?" asked another reporter from the West. "How do you justify your role?"

"Our people believe in Chairman Mao. We believe in the socialist path for our country. Our lives are stable and we have prosperity. China is free of war for the first time this century ... the first time in my life," he answered patiently. "My role is to help people in their lives and with their spirit."

"Many in America, particularly your fellow clergy, believe the Three-Self church is a servant of Chairman Mao. Can there be true religious freedom without separation of church and state?" came another query.

Robin thought carefully, as he had debated this question many times. He remembered how difficult it was to sign the Christian Manifesto. He had believed the Communist Party was the right party for China. But for the church? That was still to be seen. He *was* skeptical then.

"Religion is what you believe in your heart," he answered. "Faith is a private matter."

"A private matter," challenged the reporter, "dictated by the state?"

It was a familiar line of attack for which, remembering Bishop Mowll's answer, he replied, "St. Paul said, 'Let every person be subject to the governing authorities, for there is no authority except from God. Those that exist have been instituted by God.' Perhaps direct your question regarding the separation of church and state to our good friend, the Archbishop of Canterbury," he concluded.

Earlier this year, Robin had faced a difficult decision. The Chinese were invited and encouraged to participate in the Lambeth Conference. But disappointment over the defeat of their resolutions in 1948 lingered. The Anti-Rightist Campaign also weighed heavily on the religious community and, with such preoccupation on domestic issues, the bishops engaged in serious debate about whether or not to send a delegation. Robin sent Bishop Ting to address the conference's preparatory sessions.

Many Christian leaders from the West accepted the hydrogen bomb as a deterrent to war. Archbishop Fisher inserted his church into the politics of the nuclear warfare by stating, "For all I know it is within the providence of God that the human race should destroy itself in this manner." With that, Robin made up his mind—China would not attend the conference.

"Would the monarch relinquish her role as head of the church?" he deflected back.

The British reporter chuckled and nodded in agreement. But he had one more burning question.

"Some in the West, especially among your Episcopalians, call you—" he hesitated, tightening his lips. "They call you the Red Bishop."

Robin had heard that rumor. It was a serious allegation—a sharp rebuke that put party over God—but it had little true meaning. The West did not understand China. They looked at China, and Christianity in China, through their own, self-interested myopia. Their enemy was Communism and everything that Communism touched. That was their biggest mistake and largest blind spot.

"Bishop Chen, are you a red bishop?"

The room became deathly silent. All movement stopped.

"Red bishop?" Robin repeated with a curious smile.

He let the words sink in.

Red. Bishop.

It sounded contradictory and accusatory. Anti-theological. A villainous traitor of faith.

Red.

He felt people in the room begin to stir uncomfortably. The reporter didn't flinch but looked straight at him, waiting.

Robin's smile slowly faded and he took a deep breath.

"Before Chairman Mao, before Communism, before the Kuomintang and the Manchus, red was good. Red, in China, has *always* been good. China has *always* been red. Red bishop?" He paused for full effect, the kind when the long wait is rewarded with truth.

"We are *all* red bishops."

He chuckled lightly, gave a slight wave of his hand, and quickly took leave of the reporters. It was one the last times truth would hold some humor for him.

JOHN POWELL AND HIS WIFE WENT TO HELL AND BACK. FIRST was the failure of their publication. Then there were the contentious hearings before Jenner and the Senate Subcommittee. There followed the solo vendetta by Senator Herman Welker, with more interrogations leading to charges of sedition: thirteen counts for Powell, and one each for his wife and Schuman. They were accused of knowingly publishing false reports of biological warfare by the United States.

"Something happened in Korea. Something sure as heck must have happened there," Powell publicly asserted. "I found it almost impossible to believe. It's too big of a hoax to perpetrate."

The government claims against the trio's actions were serious: that their articles about germ warfare were false; that the articles had been used to promote insubordination and disloyalty among U.S. prisoners of war; that they had obstructed recruitment and interfered with the success of the armed forces. Their defense hinged on the testimony of hundreds of witnesses. But these witnesses lived in China. None could expect to obtain visas to America. Neither side could access corroborative witnesses or evidence.

The trio's initial trial in San Francisco opened and closed within days. The Powells did not even show up in court. The call came that the judge had ruled a mistrial. The prosecution could not submit any witnesses in China to support their case. Powell's defense was that he, as a journalist, was merely reporting the news as told to him. He could not possibly be found guilty of sedition. His defense counsel's request for classified documents from federal departments and congressional committees was objected to on grounds that the evidentiary information would threaten military security.

The federal district judge stated to the press that the evidence so far was prima facie supportive of treason. Press coverage of his inappropriate comments justifying the charges generated prejudicial publicity. A fair trial was impossible. It was a non-trial from the beginning.

But the trio's troubles were far from over; freedom was not so easily won. Just as quickly, the government sought to file new complaints—this time for treason. Stakes were even higher. Conviction could mean the death penalty.

MAO'S HUNDRED FLOWERS MOVEMENT PROVED DISASTROUS FOR those emboldened enough to criticize the government leadership. The goal was to allow constructive criticism to strengthen the country. But as criticism grew more damaging to Mao, it was most effective in exposing opponents who dared raise their heads, hands, and voices. The resulting purge of critics, government officials, and intellectuals cast a countrywide freeze on further protests. Prior to the end of his Anti-Rightist campaign, Mao conceived of the Great Leap Forward to propel China past the United Kingdom in industrial steel production within fifteen years.

Peasants who used to farm their own private plots were organized into collective farms to increase production. People lived, worked, ate, and schooled together, to boost agricultural and industrial efficiency. The country pulsated with the forced unity expected of a homogeneous people who dressed, thought, and believed similarly.

All across the countryside, workers in communes melted down scraps of metal in homemade smelters. Peasants paraded incessantly from forest to commune, hoisting firewood like an army of ants transporting precious debris. All day and night, row after row of fires burned brightly in the countryside, spewing smoke high into the air from clay kilns that appeared like large cocoons planted on the open plains, incubating the country's fortunes.

Officials in charge of the new campaign ignored expert scientific advice. Patriotic fervor and mindless devotion to Chairman Mao trumped scientific facts and educated advice. The technology used was so crude and of such poor quality that the resulting pig iron was useless.

The single-minded race to increase steel production sucked the energy, efforts, and resources of the country. Crops were neglected, left rotting in the fields. Farmers, too busy tending to their backyard smelters, failed to plant new crops. Professionals abandoned their intellectual work in the patriotic call to produce steel. Everything metal, including farming tools, machinery parts, cooking pots, and household items, was sacrificed for a national goal. The project was devouring the country. Steel had become the new opium of the people.

To put on a good face for the world, ubiquitous propaganda propped up the people's spirit, glorifying their productivity. Banners promoting the socialist road and colorful posters with smiling, flag-waving peasants, workers, and soldiers decorated the streets, factories, and farms. Promotional films showing Chairman Mao with joyous farm and factory workers with their successful harvest or products painted a utopian façade that perpetuated the activities themselves. But enthusiastic competition among patriotic communes, fearful of being swept up as rightists, caused over-reporting of farm production, leading to over-taxation. Along with over-taxation, redistribution of rice to the cities, gifting of produce to Communist allies in North Vietnam, North Korea, and Albania, and remittance of grain to repay Soviet loans led to a countrywide famine, which worsened from year to year. Peasants in the countryside suffered the worst, but the cities were progressively rationed with vouchers for food and clothing. Coupled with a severe drought in the north and flooding in the east, the great famine spread throughout the country. Typhoons, hurricanes, hailstorms, insect pests, and crop diseases heaped additional death on the populace. The Great Leap Forward became a national disaster of gigantic proportions. Hunger gripped the nation. Economic output plummeted. Mao bore the brunt of the failure and resigned as head of state under heavy criticism.

The country's misery reached all corners. Old men, shameless in hunger, crawled on hands and knees, scooping up precious grains of rice scattered as waste on the floor. Young women complained ineffectively about the insufficient allotment of coal for their families during winter, then froze overnight in their huts. People weak from starvation fell in the street, to die neglected and alone. Children whose mothers could not nurse them developed painful swollen bellies and succumbed to malnutrition in large numbers; an insufficient supply of trained pediatricians could not service the multitude of sick children.

Hui was sent to the harsh northern plains in Harbin to work on a vegetable farm. Coal was necessary for warmth through the winter—the difference between life and death, when temperatures often reached -30° F. Robin used his extra coal supplement from the government to make it through the Shanghai winter. But occasionally one of their bricks would secretly find its way into a stranger's basket. It was only one brick, but for some it meant life itself.

Besides rationing of coal, food was carefully regulated. Robin hoarded his allotted vouchers—forgoing his noon meal—to treat family members to precious bowls of bean soup, *hsi fan*, and dumplings. Family members gathered on the weekends to share in these "feasts." The children were first to bolt into the room and devour the stockpiled food. Food was often the only thing the children thought of.

The rationing lasted for three years. Despite the efforts of the central government to stem the famine by purchasing wheat from Canada and Australia, by the end of the Great Leap Forward, tens of millions of Chinese citizens had starved to death.

"NO SET DATE FOR RETURNING HOME? REALLY CONCERNED."

Grace relinquished her residency in pediatrics, but had no definitive plan to appease her mother. Robert was secure as the youngest staff neurosurgeon at the New England Medical Center. They had a large and growing circle of like-minded, highly educated, professional, and mainly Christian, Chinese friends. There were three young children to raise. The post-war boom years had rewarded them well. Life in America looked bright. Even John Powell had all charges dropped by the US attorney general in 1961 and, by year's end, Robert had become a naturalized U.S. citizen.

While Grace and Robert loved America and assimilated easily, they were Chinese in their core. They organized a Chinese family summer camp, started a Chinese language school, and founded the Greater Boston Chinese Cultural Association with their friends. Robert was initiated into an international fraternity of successful Chinese pledged to "labor for the welfare of Chinese people." Both were active in their respective alumni associations. Their lives were happy, healthy, and full. Good fortune and long lives were possible in America.

Her children could sit before a warm fireplace during a New England blizzard drinking Nestle's hot chocolate. They might build snowmen or snow forts with their neighborhood friends the morning after. But Grace did not know that thousands back home did not wake, after a freezing night sleeping in rags on bamboo mats, because they lacked enough coal for their *kangs*.

During one of these storms, Grace sat in front of a glowing fire. The house was warm and the logs smelled of Christmas. Her children sprawled out on the hardwood floor watching television. Robert was out on an emergency, a common occurrence as low man on the neurosurgical totem pole.

She opened a letter from Shanghai. They came every one or two months, routed through Hong Kong. She had noticed a gradual change of tone in those voices. Initially, it was concern for her studies and settling in America. Work hard. Eat healthy. Be pleasant. Make friends. Then, especially from her father, she heard of the great things that were happening and explanations of changes the church, the country, and the people were experiencing. It was always so positive, in spite of the weeding out of "bad elements." The country was moving forward to a brighter future. Come home. It was always, when was she coming home to serve the people?

Now, she noticed a bitterness creeping in.

Why wasn't she home? Did she forget about them?

"Wonder if we will see each other in this life," her mother wrote. "Think of you when lying in bed."

Was mother sick?

"Hope you decide to return early. Outside is good; home is better. Covet the present good day. But this is too selfish. Forget oneself and love others. Be a brave patriot."

Patriot. Why was it always about being a good patriot? Must people sacrifice everything for the country? Am I really being selfish?

"Why have you changed entirely? The early years, you think of home, with a soft heart. We are getting less and less in our days here. Why are you not thinking of us? I guarantee that the whole country will welcome you!" her mother wrote.

Grace wished she had never read the letters, never received any news from home. What good was it to hear of these things—these dreams, these hopes. She could do nothing to change them. Why the need to choose between two worlds?

Grace looked at her three children on the floor. Robert was right. It was not possible to go back.

She went to the closet and pulled out her Hoover vacuum cleaner. Did they have vacuum cleaners in China? Her mother would be sweeping with a bamboo broom as thin, light, and sturdy as herself—methodically, without complaint.

She turned on the Hoover and began to vacuum the living room; pushing back and forth, over and over, like the meticulous sketching of flowers on a remote mountain path. Her children cast annoyed looks at her, but the monotonous hum of the motor was calming to her. Finished, she went to the kitchen and began to wash the counters. She removed every crumb and wiped every corner. Once the counters were clean, she polished the sink. The water stains bothered her. And once the sink was shiny, she scrubbed the oven—the sides, the bottom, inside the door. Then the refrigerator. She had never had a refrigerator back home. Only the rich had refrigerators. An hour later, she was done and sat down in a chair. She liked things clean. Clean as Mr. Clean.

But she could not sit still. She got up and went to her bedroom. She approached her desk and opened the drawer where she kept the family's checkbook. Robert was too busy and cared little about money. If he worked, took good care of his patients, the family would be fine. He trusted Grace to make the family run well. She defended her small turf and would chastise him when she found an error in the ledger.

Grace opened the checkbook and tore out a check. She wrote her mother's name, an amount, signed it, and put it in an envelope. After carefully recording the check, doing the math, and accurately adjusting the balance, she replaced the checkbook in the drawer. Then she addressed the envelope and left it on the desk so she would not forget to mail it. Tomorrow she would go to the post office and send it to Shanghai. It was not that much, but enough in China. It would not make up for lost time. It would not balance the pain on either side. But it was really all that she could do—for now.

Chapter 63

ALWAYS STAYS HOME

Robin went to his desk and pulled out an old box from the recesses of the bottom drawer. Its edges were frayed and tattered. The top was worn and stained with the oil and grime of fingertips from a lifetime ago. The box had traveled with him every time his family moved from Wuhu to Nanling and Maolin, and from Anking through the countryside back to Wuhu and onto Shanghai. Everywhere the family went, it was there—tucked away, but not wholly forgotten, like a trusted childhood friend.

He lifted the lid and looked at the neatly stacked, round playing pieces. He slowly rolled the wooden discs in his fingertips, remembering the day he first heard about bishops and knights. It had been years since he last played the game, but the pieces felt familiar.

Paul, Helene, their three children, and Helen with her three children had gathered for a Sunday afternoon visit. Together, they had endured the last three years, when life seemed to hang in the balance. They all had sacrificed, living on less and less. He called over Helen's number one son.

"Xiao Ding! *Lai le!*"

Before liberation, he had written to Grace in English. But now, he only wrote in Chinese. No one spoke English. No one learned English. Children learned Russian.

The little boy was only five and dutifully ran to his grandfather. Robin gathered him in his arms and pointed to the Chinese chess piece.

"I am going to teach you. It is a good game for smart boys," he said with a smile as he tapped his finger gently on the boy's head.

He set up the board, showing the little boy each piece and its position on the board. He had never had a chance to teach his own son: too occupied with learning about Christianity; too busy studying how to become a good minister and how to help his people and country; running from the Japanese and their bombs; and traveling from here to there to America and back and forth from mission to mission, city to city, small village to small village.

He had so many children in the church. Had he neglected his own? And Grace? Surely, she had her own life to live, too. He had been angry with her. He tried to squelch that feeling that was still there. He had not wanted to burden her with guilt, but he knew that he did.

Humans are all selfish, he thought.

Robin picked up a round piece. The black elephant. He pointed at the ideogram written on the top of the piece.

"This is *hsiang*," he explained. He picked up the red bishop. "This also is *hsiang*."

The boy repeated the words with accurate tones, took the two pieces and studied them. Robin watched him turn the pieces over in his small, fat fingers. They were hard and smooth, but not perfect. Small chips were present and sharp cracks had been polished by time. The pieces looked worn and the black and red paint dulled by use. Familiar, but tired, old friends.

"What does *hsiang* do, Ye Ye?" the little boy asked of his grandfather.

Robin's mind went to that day with Sister Louise—the day he learned about a bishop. He hadn't really understood it at the time, not as he did now. The pieces might have aged with use, but their use did not change with age.

"*Hsiang* moves like this," he explained, showing the boy how the piece moved. "Two spaces. Never cross the river. *Hsiang* protects the general. Always protects." The words came back clearly. He wanted to teach the little boy everything. He recalled when all he saw was the poverty, the confusion in the world around the mission. He did not understand anything then. He only knew it was not right and he wanted to make it better. God did not even exist then. He just wanted to give hopeless people hope—something beyond survival.

"*Hsiang* never crosses the river," said Robin, pointing at the middle of the playing field. "*Hsiang* always protects the general. Always stays home."

He smiled and patted the boy's head. The boy looked up and smiled at his grandfather. Each piece was in its place. The set was complete, and they started to play.

Chapter 64

HSIAO WANG

I t was not more than a month later when Robin suddenly curled over with intense pain, his body heaving with paroxysms of retching. A gush of red blood mixed with fresh clots exploded out of his throat, splattering with a thick, moist sound onto the kitchen floor. It left a crimson puddle.

"Mother!" he cried out to Constance. His face was pale, eyes wide open. His hands trembled as he reached to steady himself against a stool.

Constance and Helene rushed to his side, propped him up, and within an hour had him sitting in the noisy, crowded waiting area at the hospital. He had passed some dark stools and nearly lost consciousness before the ambulance came. A nurse brought him into a large ward with twenty other patients lying in beds separated by white curtains. There was a gentle chorus of moans in the background and the smell of musty sweat, pus, and acrid body fluids saturating the stale air.

A young doctor took his blood pressure, looking curiously at him.

"What happened, *lao shi*?" Old teacher.

A nurse recognized Robin and explained, "He is Bishop Chen. He has cirrhosis, from hepatitis."

The liver disease caused vessels in Robin's esophagus to dilate and occasionally bleed. A stomach ulcer brought on the sharp pain. The nurse reported to the young doctor that Robin had needed blood transfusions in the past.

"How much blood did he lose?" asked the doctor, listening to Robin's heart with a stethoscope.

"About two rice bowls," answered Constance.

The doctor took some samples from his arm, put a few drops into a tiny glass tube, and placed it in a centrifuge. After a couple of minutes, he took the tube out and looked at the red fraction that separated from the amber plasma. He frowned and instructed the nurse to insert an intravenous needle and bring a tube to put into Robin's stomach. He would need another transfusion.

The nurse returned with a rubber tube and the doctor placed the tip into Robin's nostril. The doctor threaded it slowly into the stomach. Robin shut his eyes to keep from choking. The doctor drew out syringeful after syringeful of red blood. By the time he was done, there was almost a quarter pan of blood lying by his feet on the floor.

"He needs blood," the doctor told Constance.

Robin was admitted to a hospital ward. He felt better, having vomited and gotten the blood pumped out of his stomach, but there was still a dull ache in his abdomen. The ward he was in was filled to capacity. Nurses bustled around. It was different than in the days of the KMT, when elites such as he were separated from the common people. He would have been in a private room with a Western-trained doctor. He actually felt at ease knowing everyone was being treated with the same care. The standard of training and medical care had improved since liberation. And the activity of all the white coats brought thoughts of Grace.

The curtain swung open. A friendly face appeared, unmistakably familiar, startling him. The surgeon spoke to the nurse as he placed his hand on Robin's torso, avoiding eye contact.

"*Ta hai zai liuxue ma?*" Is he still bleeding, the surgeon asked.

"*Bu!*"

The surgeon's hand felt the firmness in Robin's protruding abdomen, tense like a ripe winter melon. Robin suddenly grabbed the hand and pulled it close to his chest.

"Hsiao Wang!"

His old friend managed a weak smile. His quiet eyes still reflected the shyness of his youth, but his face was marked with deep furrows from years of untold worry. He hardly acknowledged Robin. They had gone their own ways after St. James and lost half a century together. Such was China.

"Jian Chen," replied the gentle voice—deeper, a bit rougher, but recognizable.

It was the Chinese name from his boyhood. His old friend hesitantly extended his hand. Robin quickly grasped it with both of his. He noted that the handshake was soft, like an empty mitten, almost without substance. Soft enough to have not recently planted any rice.

"Too much blood," Hsiao Wang stated.

The verdict was delivered clinically, without alarm. Robin nodded resignedly to Hsiao Wang. Perhaps they would catch up later.

Other doctors came in to explain that the problem was due to his cirrhosis, a common problem in China because of the hepatitis virus that had infected more than ten percent of the population. The scarring in the liver affected the veins around his esophagus and the size of his spleen. He would eventually need an operation. The doctors warned that they could not guarantee his survival. But without the operation, any bleeding in the future could be fatal.

That night, Robin received 1200 cc's of blood, almost a quarter of his entire body's volume. He stayed in the hospital for twenty-two more days. Constance cared for him during the day; Helene during the evening after work; and Helen and Paul on the weekends. He had only the briefest of conversations with Hsiao Wang, who told him he had gone to medical school and then worked for the government. When the Communists took over, he switched sides and worked for the PLA. He only cared about the patients, not the uniform. He took orders and did his job.

Hsiao Wang confessed he was too busy to go to church. It was a subject he was reluctant to take on with Robin, since his life could not compare favorably in that respect. Robin never asked if he was still Christian. That was one's own business and not always good for others to know. Robin did invite him to visit Trinity Church. It was evident that Hsiao Wang did not want him to know much about his past. Perhaps he already knew too much about Robin's.

WHEN ROBIN RETURNED HOME, HE WELCOMED COLLEAGUES, both Chinese and foreign. While the church's activities were not as vigorous

since the Anti-Rightist Campaign and the struggles following the Great
Leap Forward debacle, the Three-Self Patriotic Movement leadership,
headed by Y.T. Wu, still sought his advice on church matters. Their prayers
and friendship helped him regain strength.

He resumed work in the church and was beginning to feel normal. His
abdominal pain subsided. But his illness made him think more of Grace.

"Pen!" he demanded gruffly and with uncharacteristic impatience one
evening at home.

"Rest," Constance implored him. "You must rest."

She had seen how agitated he could get, thinking about Grace. What was
the use, she would scold him. Grace was no longer a child and had her own life.

"*Bi zi!*" Pen!

Constance relented and brought him his writing materials. He took the
pen and bent his head. His hand was steady, momentarily poised in midair
as he stared at the blank paper. Then he began to write.

*My dear Grace, Mother is here with me. We are well. I discovered that
you more than once sent money to Mother. I asked her not to write to
you. What I need is not money, not food to eat! But rather, understanding and concern for our country. Your photos are displayed on my desk
under the glass cover, constantly reminding me of all the promises, but
no idea to return.*

He glanced at the pictures, then gazed out the window at the bare
autumn trees in the courtyard. The weather was beginning to chill, and each
morning breeze stirred the fallen leaves more forcefully—unmistakable
signs that winter was just ahead.

Yesterday was a national holiday. The sixteenth year of liberation.

Shanghai was indeed alive with celebration as people danced in the
streets, singing patriotic songs that blared over ubiquitous loudspeakers
throughout the city. They waved red flags and twirled red ribbons. Colorful
balloons drifted over the buildings, and white doves were released into the
sky. A large parade of students, soldiers, farmers, and workers marched in

strict synchrony down the main boulevard. Robin noted the troops of medical and science students and imagined Grace in stride with them.

They showed off the socialist revolution's accomplishments, which far surpassed the world standard, encouraging our national peoples' rebirth. Our hard work overcame hardship, establishing a spirit of revolution. We hope you return ... and serve your people.

It was just another futile letter. Sixteen years of waiting and wishing did not bring her any closer to home. He did not intend to sound desperate. But passage of time brought more medical problems—of that he was aware.

Constance was right. The writing made him weary. He needed to rest. He set his pen down and signaled her to help him to the couch. He lay down and fell asleep.

Two months later, a little after midnight on November 29, he again was rushed to the hospital and transfused with 900 cc's of blood. This was about the tenth visit to the hospital in the last three years since he was found to have ascites. Doctors recommended that he undergo surgery to control the bleeding. Officials from the church and the Three-Self office, along with Paul, were consulted. Everyone promptly agreed.

At 9:30 the next morning, Robin went into the operating theater, scheduled to have ligation of esophageal varices, a splenectomy, and biopsy of his liver. He had faith that God would see him through the operation. He trusted Him to guide Hsiao Wang's hands.

HSIAO WANG ENTERED THE OPERATING THEATER AFTER IMMERSing his hands in a bucket of alcohol. With Robin peacefully asleep under the effects of anesthesia, he donned a gown and a pair of latex gloves that was among dozens hanging on a drying rack, waiting to be reused. He painted Robin's abdomen with iodine and made a deliberate incision down the center of the old scar. Pale amber fluid gushed out, like *huangcha,* yellow tea, boiling over its pot, spilling onto the table and running down the drapes to pool on the floor. Robin's abdomen deflated to a loose sack.

Before he even inspected the internal organs, Hsiao Wang was shaking his head. He paused to close his eyes. He did not admit to himself that what he wished was actually a prayer. But it was. It had been years since he had prayed. He moved swiftly to ligate the varices and remove Robin's gallbladder, which was exacerbating the liver disease. He did a sweep of the organs, inspecting each as if dissecting the clues in the life he had missed.

As he placed large silk sutures to close the gaping incision, he felt ashamed. He knew little of his friend—the joys and suffering and challenges his body and soul had experienced over the past fifty years to bring him to this table. He only saw the story of what was to come. The signs were clear, and no amount of praying to any god would help. The copious fluid and the pebbled, sickly grey liver told him everything he needed to know.

WHEN HSIAO WANG SAW ROBIN AFTER THE OPERATION, HE DID not have good news. The liver was badly damaged, he explained. The ascites fluid was drained but would come back, even more abundantly. Worse, there was not much he could do about the dilated blood vessels lining his stomach and esophagus. They would continue to sprout, enlarge, and leak.

What would that mean, Robin asked of Hsiao Wang.

"You will bleed again," Hsiao Wang said without emotion. He couldn't look at Robin, and fiddled with the dressings instead.

Robin thought for a moment, then asked, "How long?"

Hsiao Wang glanced painfully at Robin as he contemplated an answer, but then dropped his gaze to the floor. He shook his head, answering in a whisper, "Hard to say."

"Hsiao Wang!" Robin shouted harshly as he grabbed Hsiao Wang's arm. His voice startled his friend. *"Ni xiang shenma? Shuo!"* What do you think? Speak!

Hsiao Wang took a deep breath.

"Shuo chen!" Speak the truth! Robin demanded.

"If you are lucky, two, maybe three, years," Hsiao Wang answered, looking at his friend now.

Robin nodded. He pondered a moment.

"And if I am not?" he finally asked.

Hsiao Wang volunteered quickly, "Perhaps tomorrow. Next week. Next month."

They looked each other straight in the eye. Fifty years melted away.

"My good friend," Robin said, shaking Hsiao Wang's hand. "Pray for me to be lucky."

Chapter 65

RED GUARDS

On a warm Shanghai evening late in the summer of 1966, Right Rev. Robin Chen, the last Presiding Bishop of the extinct Holy Catholic Church of China, was suddenly eliminated. Without forewarning, Red Guards wearing red armbands burst into his house and began to ransack the rooms. They opened every drawer and checked every closet. They clucked orders to each other in excited tones, like fowls fluttering about in a chicken coop.

"*Zuo!*" Sit, the leader commanded, pushing Constance and Robin towards the couch in the sitting area.

"*Ni yao shenma?*" What do you want? Constance demanded, as Robin stood calmly between her and the intruders.

"Old woman, *bu shuo hua!*" Do not talk! crowed one of the Red Guards as he strode by her.

By the time the guards reached the bedrooms, they were in a frenzy, hunting for something. Anything. They tore through the rooms, peering under beds and overturning mattresses. They rummaged through clothes and upended a storage chest. Just as they talked about leaving, the closet in one of the bedrooms gave them their excuse.

On the top shelf, in a plain pine box tucked in the back corner, was the unmistakable red, white, and blue flag. It meant nothing. Robin had never ever flown it himself. He had forgotten it. It was neatly folded, as it was the day he received it; a token of an old friendship, hardly symbolic of anything but the distant past. But it was everything to the Red Guards—proof of Robin's secret anti-revolutionary loyalty to China's reactionary, imperialist enemy. The bishop was obviously a traitor.

The leader squawked to his comrades, who immediately took the American flag and arrested Robin. They rushed him outside in a noisy commotion and placed him in a car, still clucking at each other. Constance began screaming.

"What is happening? What are you doing? Where are you taking him?"

Hers was such a tiny voice amid the clamor. None of the Red Guards paid her any mind, and they drove away, leaving her solitary voice echoing off the courtyard walls.

THE WEEKS BEFORE THIS ABRUPT END TO BISHOP ROBIN CHEN were ordinary. People shopped, strolled through the city parks, and rode bicycles. They ate at local dumpling houses and went to work as usual. Farmers tilled their fields and fed their livestock. Robin was recovering from his last operation and retired from daily church work. For the last five years, church membership had declined and, after regaining much of its popularity since liberation, was now halved.

In Beijing, beneath this mundane calm, Mao became discontent with members of his party who he felt were reactionary, too bourgeois-like and corrupt. His stature within the party had waned since the Great Leap Forward disaster. He needed to recapture his old greatness and the spirit of the country's revolutionary past. Early in the spring of 1966, he set about purging the party of obstructionists: first, the mayor of Beijing, then, the PLA's chief of staff and head of the propaganda department. Later, in the fall, it reached higher up: the president of China, Liu Shaoqi, and the Party's General Secretary, Deng Xiao-ping. With swift and unfettered control of the press, Mao called for the rooting-out of reactionary and bourgeois leaders who were obstructing the revolutionary path he envisioned for China.

"Sweep out all the oxen, ghosts, snakes, and spirits!" he demanded.

Mao closed schools and universities and called forth the zealous youth to revolt against the Four Olds: old ideas, old habits, old cultures, old customs. The young listened to their paramount leader and rebelled against their teachers, their employers, even their parents—anyone in authority. The Red Guards were quickly formed by university students, imbued with Mao's Thoughts and armed with the authority of the Supreme Leader. Mao, wearing the red arm band as a public endorsement, unleashed the Red Guards, exhorting them with the rhetoric of violent revolution.

Rebellion is justified! Bombard the headquarters! Smash the Four Olds!

Mao reiterated his chilling statement at the beginning of the revolution forty years ago.

Revolution is not a dinner party. Revolution is messy and bloody.

Havoc and chaos swept through the cities, like the rabid slaughter of farm animals for market. Everything in the path of the brutal Red Guards was destroyed: schools, churches, homes, temples, factories, families. Nothing could oppose the terrorization as citizens of China became their own police, prosecutor, jury, judge, and executioner.

Robin was swept up, as were all the religious leaders. It happened as quickly as a spring flood. He was brought before government officials and harshly criticized for his ties to the United States and his worship of false gods opposed to the revolutionary cause. The government quickly closed the Three-Self Church and its offices. Other churches throughout the country followed.

The insults tossed at him were not rational. Nor truthful.

American imperialist, traitor, American spy, anti-revolutionary revisionist, capitalist.

None of this sounded correct, just as it had not forty years ago in Nanling. But he offered no rebuttal or defense. He did not fully understand the country's sudden descent into destruction and hate. The full force of Mao and the Communist Party was behind the movement to cleanse society. He was a mere stone tossed about in a stormy sea. Resistance would only bring more harm to his family, causing it to crack into tiny pieces. Better to hold firm to his core but tractable to the waves.

Shui luo, shi chu. When the water recedes, the stone will emerge ... smooth and shiny.

Faith is a private matter, he recited to himself.

Faith is a private matter.

~⚬~ 🏵 ~⚬~

THE PERSECUTIONS DID NO FAVORS TO ROBIN'S HEALTH. DURING another visit to the hospital, he was left in a waiting area for twelve hours. There were few doctors present; none would speak to him. Some had been sent to the countryside to serve the workers, peasants, and soldiers, where barefoot doctors, *chijiao yisheng*, were being trained.

Hospital personnel with red arm bands marched in and took away his medications. They smashed his glass syringes and forbade the nurses from administering his injections for anemia. A change had swept over the hospital like the red loess dust storms of the northern plains, blocking out light and suffocating life. As a mission-educated religious leader with associates from the West, he was branded a counterrevolutionary who did not deserve medical treatment. He lashed out and criticized their attitude.

"We are all Chinese!" he admonished. "Why do you not care?"

They continued to ignore him. After the twelfth hour, he left.

Constance brought him to the local alley clinic run by cadres. They would surely help. But, ever loyal to the Party's directives, they also refused him medicine. Counterrevolutionaries were enemies of the people.

An enemy of the people? Constance could not understand how that could be.

"Go away, old revisionist!" ordered the cadre.

"*Bu xing, bu xing!*" No, no! Not permitted, echoed the cadre's assistant, waving them away.

"Please. We need medicine," explained Constance.

"Go away. We cannot help you."

"You must help!" she pleaded. "Please!"

The cadre turned in retreat and began to close the door.

"Please!" she repeated, leaning into the doorway.

"No!"

The sharp rebuke came from behind her, out of the duskiness of day.

It was Robin. He placed a firm hand on her shoulder and pulled her back. "Do not beg!"

As everyone in the clinic stared at them, the cadre shooed him away. Constance led Robin home empty-handed. She did not know what else she could do.

THAT NIGHT, WHILE THEY WERE SLEEPING FITFULLY, THERE WAS light tapping on the door. Constance arose first and went to the door as quietly as she could.

Who could be there?

People were nosy, paying too much attention to other people's business. She slowly opened the door. The woman was a neighbor. A friend.

Was she a true friend? Constance asked herself. *What did she want?*

The neighbor looked nervously over her shoulder—first right, then left. The street was dark and deserted. Wandering around at night was seen as suspicious, and neighborhood watchdogs were everywhere.

When Constance saw the lone man standing in the empty shadows behind her neighbor, her body shook with a chill. The PLA uniform was unmistakable. The faint streetlight backlit the man's head so the face was obscured, like a solar eclipse.

Was she being betrayed? Arrested?

Before she could cry out, her neighbor hushed her and the soldier stepped forward. He looked at least sixty years old, with weighty eyebrows and grey hairs around the ears. His flaccid skin dripped off his facial skeleton. His teeth were crooked—a few were missing—and his eyes lacked sparkle, as if tired of living. Instead of arresting her, he bowed.

"*Chen Tai Tai. Wo xing Tang.*" Mrs. Chen. I am Tang, he said.

The voice was unexpectedly soft and respectful.

"*Cong* Wuhu." From Wuhu. Then in English, he added, "St. James."

Constance gasped. She hardly recognized him. Tang, the Communist teacher. His hollow face bore testament to China's turmoil, yet his gentle demeanor offered a glimmer of hope.

He presented a package wrapped in cloth, extending it deferentially toward her with both hands. He was wearing a uniform but seemed unsure of himself—almost out of place—certainly different than the Red Guards who tore apart their home.

"For Reverend Chen," he continued in English and bowed again.

Constance took the package and scrutinized it cautiously. She placed it on a small table in the unlit entryway and began to untie the twine encircling the cloth. She unwrapped the cloth, exposing the contents. She stared, almost crying at the sight of the gift.

There were vials of medicine, a bottle of alcohol, a couple of glass syringes, and some needles. Tang must have stolen the supplies from the hospital, she thought. But how? Her neighbor, the watchdog from Robin's congregation? Constance's eyes misted up. She rewrapped the package and looked up to thank Tang. But Tang and the watchdog had already slipped back into the night, absorbed by the pervasive gloom, merely a fleeting notion of a spontaneous act of kindness.

IN THE SHADOWS, BY THE HALF-OPENED DOOR, WHICH LET IN just a sliver of dull light from the electric streetlamps, Constance steadily drew out a small dose of the medication, as she had seen the nurses do in the hospital. She held Robin's left arm tightly and readied the syringe.

She had killed geese, beheaded chickens, and gutted fish. She had seen mangled bodies and torn limbs and was not afraid of blood. War and life had made her fearless. But she had never given injections before this day. Her hands trembled. If she wavered, penetrating too shallow or plunging too deep, she might cause more pain and harm.

Medication was a precious blessing many did not have. She was grateful for Tang's courage and glad the young teacher had survived years of tumult. It could not have been easy. So many like him had died during the KMT campaigns. Perhaps faith did him some good.

She continued to stare at the syringe in her hand.

Robin saw her hesitation. He gently held his wife's hand, smiled, and nodded reassuringly.

Constance pressed her lips together, held her breath, and, following Robin's guiding hand, firmly stabbed the needle into his arm. She depressed the plunger and smoothly withdrew the needle. The medicine was in and she released her breath.

Robin never flinched. He did not say a word. And he never stopped smiling at Constance.

DEMONSTRATIONS AND MARCHES BECAME A DAILY EVENT. Demonstrators moved in unison, flowing in the streets and infiltrating back alleys. They grew as they marched. Their tide swept through the streets of Shanghai, swelled in mass, and gathered in strength, threatening to crash onto Robin's house.

"American imperialist spy! Revisionist capitalist! Anti-revolutionary dog! Idol worshiper! Smash the Four Olds!" chanted the demonstrators, waving their banners and newly accompanied by the jarring clang of cymbals and gongs, as if to exorcise demons at a wedding celebration.

Constance and Robin heard them coming. They hoped the demonstrators would only make their voices heard in the streets and not bother them. Constance prepared the syringe and expertly gave Robin his shot, as she had done every day the last few weeks. By now, her hands did not shake. The commotion continued to grow and became louder and nearer until the demonstrators were right outside their door. Constance knew their house would not be spared; it was the tide's destination and it would not be turned.

Constance went to the front and flung the door open. Her tiny body blocked the entrance.

"Go away! This is our home. Go away!" she said firmly.

"Friends of imperialists. Enemy of the people," they shouted, shaking their fists in her face.

"Why are you here? What do you want?" she asked.

"This is Chairman Mao's home! The people's house! Preacher of false doctrine! Long live Chairman Mao! Long live the revolution!"

"You, go away!" she responded in a shrill voice.

Red Guards easily swept her aside as if she were no more than an ancient silk screen. Storming through the house, they stripped it of all books and manuscripts deemed reactionary. Gone were magazines and texts written in English, notebooks and publications from his college and graduate days in mission schools, English and American novels and journals, letters from America, England, Australia, and Canada and, of course, his English Bibles, hymnals, and prayer books. They pulled crosses and pictures of Jesus from the shelves and off the wall. They took all vestiges of corrupt Western culture: photographs with his foreign friends and colleagues, religious artifacts, his priestly garments and Western suits and top hat. They piled them high in the middle of the courtyard, then threw in a few pieces of furniture for greater incendiary effect. The last item they took from over his desk was his honorary diploma.

The revolutionaries built a pyre and began to incinerate his life. Neither he nor his family could bear to watch.

Constance was incensed, not about their belongings, but about the young Red Guards' disrespectful treatment of her husband. They were younger than her own children, and she wanted to scold them. He did not deserve this treatment. But he was one of the elements that had to be exterminated to revive and purify the revolution.

"Why are you doing this?" she yelled at the Red Guards with her own fieriness.

"Let them be. All this will pass," Robin cautioned her. "Society will rebuild itself."

As the flames danced high in the courtyard, the Red Guard leader brought them to the hallway adjacent to the kitchen. It was as small as a pantry, no larger than one and a half beds, end to end. There were no windows, no heating unit. No escape.

"Stay!" she commanded curtly. "Do not leave unless you request it from authorities."

With that, the leader closed the door and left Constance and Robin standing side by side, listening to the noise of the demonstrators recede from the courtyard. Constance was shaking, not from fear, but anger. Robin held her trembling body in his steady arms and leaned toward her, speaking in a quiet voice as if imparting a closely held secret.

"They do not know what they do," he said.

The intruders were gone. The house became still and empty. Their heartbeats pounding against each other's chests and their quickened breaths striking each other's cheeks were the sole signs of life.

Robin was formally under house arrest.

Over two days, the Red Guards cremated the bishop's literary and Western life. The neighbors bore witness to the incineration; the lingering smoke served to them as a cautionary warning. At the end, there was nothing left but a worthless mound of ash, as if those charred words and foreign trappings would forever snuff the ideas, memories, and lessons of a Christian schoolboy's life journey.

Chapter 66

HOUSE ARREST

Within a week of his detention, Robin was removed from his house by Red Guards. Whether the directive came from the neighborhood watchdog committee or the central government, he did not know.

As he was led into the street, he passed by big-character posters hanging limply from walls and tree branches throughout the courtyard, like banners on funeral wreaths.

"*Ni kan!*" You look! ordered the leader.

Imperialist dog! Guilty of worshiping false gods! Blind believer of false doctrine! Traitor to Chairman Mao! Down with Christianity! Down with religious ideas of the old society!

When a poster whipped at him with a strong breeze, it was as if a scourge was flogging his soul. A gaggle of Red Guards quickly surrounded him as a crowd gathered. They pushed him through the neighborhood; a large sign with his name weighing down his neck hung to his knees. *Chen Tseng-su,* his birth name, tagged him as a traitor, preacher of false doctrines. Epithets were again flung at him with blind, bilious intent.

"American imperialist spy!"

"Revisionist capitalist!"

"Anti-revolutionary dog!"

Someone placed a hand on his head and forced him into supplication. Another tied something on the crown of his head. A tall, conical paper hat. A dunce's cap.

The group stood him on a short platform. He faced his accusers, their faces unsmiling. They were not the faces of strangers nor enemies. They were neighbors, local cadres, their children, and students. Some of the curious, silent bystanders were his congregation. All he could do was to bow his head as he was commanded and swallow the criticism. Not a single voice rose up in his defense.

The public "trial" lasted an hour. But the Red Guards were not done. They took Robin off the platform and ushered him through the crowded streets to another area of Shanghai. Again, the leader and her comrades berated and criticized Robin. The crowd grew larger as the leader used a bullhorn to broadcast her accusations. Her comrades piled on.

"You betray Chairman Mao! You poison the minds of our people!"

"Down with revisionist religions! Out with old beliefs!"

"Confess your collaboration with American imperialists and Western conspirators!"

"State your crimes against the Chinese people!"

For the entire morning, in the suffocating humidity of the Shanghai summer, the Red Guards paraded Robin from one neighborhood to another, making a mockery of him as a believer in foreign gods and preacher of superstitious and capitalistic ideas. They beat down the bishop, tore down the man, and obliterated his past; they stomped on his church and his Christian beliefs. For them, there was nothing but the thoughts and words of Chairman Mao. Everyone carried "Quotations from Chairman Mao Tse-Tung," Mao's Little Red Book, and waved it proudly like the national flag at a victory parade. The madness was earnest. The masses had a new bible, and the Red Bishop was no more.

When the Red Guards were done, they escorted him home. The leader took him into the house and shoved him into the kitchen hallway with Constance. Before she closed the door, the leader broke the solitary bare light bulb with her bullhorn. It was an unnecessary gesture, blindness born of blindness.

After she left, Robin and Constance huddled together in the stifling room. Their hands groped in the dark, searching for the other's. Robin's fingertips found Constance's and their fingers curled together. Robin could not see Constance's face, nor Constance Robin's, but they clung to each other in their prison; a home without light, without hope—just shards of glass littered on the cold concrete floor.

For great is your reward in heaven …

WHILE ROBIN SLEPT, CONSTANCE CREPT QUIETLY OUT OF THE pantry and went to the front door. Very carefully she cracked open the door, taking care not to make any noise.

Seeing no one in the courtyard, Constance went to the faucet at the side of the house. She slowly turned the valve and filled the bucket hanging on the spigot. It was so heavy she needed both hands to lift it. She struggled toward the nearest big-character poster. Water sloshed out as she waddled her way across the courtyard. The weight of the bucket nearly bent her in two.

Cupping her delicate hands like a ladle, she began to splash one of the posters. Very quickly, the ink began to run, effacing the vile words. Gone was *traitor*.

She splashed another poster. Down ran the ink onto the ground. Gone was *imperialist devil*.

Again and again, she tossed the water, filled the empty bucket, then splashed some more. The sound of the water hitting the stone pavement echoed through the courtyard; one after another, rhythmically, like muted chime bells marking time. The sound made the courtyard seem even more empty. She was such a diminutive person: thin as a twig and weak as a city squirrel. But nothing could hold back her fury this midnight hour.

Over and over, with more and more anger, she flung the water as hard as she could so that the beads ricocheted off the paper like tiny missiles. She continued until her arms were fatigued and hung listlessly by her side. All the posters had been bled of their insults. The ground ran dark with the blatant lies, like blood pooling on the floor of a slaughterhouse.

But erasing words was not enough. She strode up to the posters and began to tear at them. She flailed at the hanging paper, as if trying to scratch the eyes out of a monster. A shadow approached her from the side. She froze when she spied the other woman.

She did not recognize her, but the woman began to tear at the posters. She did not say a word. Then a second woman joined them. In the muted darkness of their upended world, the three continued in silence, shredding the posters until nothing was left of the accusations except fibers hanging like torn flesh dangling from a mutilated corpse.

When she was done, she replaced the bucket. The two women disappeared, apparitions in the night. She quietly went back into the house, breathing hard from the effort.

As she entered the pantry prison, sweat dripped off her forehead in thin rivulets like toxic humors coaxed from the flesh. Her clothes were drenched, her short hair matted, and her sandals soiled with ink. She had rarely felt such anger and was surprised at herself, as if her mind were not her own. But she had never felt as clean in her heart as she had felt with the two angels by her side.

"WHAT DO YOU ACCOMPLISH?" ROBIN REPROACHED HER.

He was not afraid of what they would do to him but of what they might do to her and his family.

"I am not afraid!" she raised her voice sharply.

"Foolishness! Red Guards will bring trouble!" Robin retorted sternly. He had never seen her so angry.

"Let them come!" she said defiantly. "Jian Chen! Seek truth!"

It was too late to do anything. Robin sat with her. They would have to suffer the punishment. It was early morning, and all they could do was wait.

Constance changed her clothes from the night before, then washed and combed her hair. She took a wooden stool from the kitchen and went outside, ignoring Robin's warnings. The courtyard was a mess of melted pulp, black puddles, and remnant strands of shredded rice paper. Some people glanced into the courtyard and walked on. Those on bicycles hardly noticed as they rushed by. She put her stool down and sat. She stared straight ahead and waited for the Red Guards. The tin-like clinking of the passing bicycle bells comforted her as if they were a secret salute.

Constance patiently sat the whole morning. Robin told her to come back into the house. Why bait the Red Guards? She refused and continued to wait—arms folded and eyes fixed ahead at the street.

The day passed. People came through the courtyard but said nothing as they glanced vacantly at her. Children stared curiously until their parents pulled them away. Pigeons strolled at her feet, bobbing and bowing their heads while scavenging for treasured scraps of food. At the end of the day, the Red Guards never came. Constance went back into the house as the sun began to set.

Robin was eating *hsi fan*. He had not moved all day. They sat across from each other at the small table. The fight and fury were gone from their eyes. They could hardly make out each other's face in the fading light of dusk.

Constance reached for a syringe and went about filling it with Robin's medicine. He dutifully rolled up his sleeve and Constance administered the shot. As he unrolled his sleeve and swallowed, some porridge dribbled from the corner of his thin lips. She took a cloth and gently wiped the rice from his mouth.

"Mother—" Robin said quietly as his dull, once-active eyes gazed gently upon her wrinkled face.

She waited for another admonition for her reckless rebellion. Perhaps she deserved it, she thought. Red Guard punishment could be harsh.

"*Xie ni,*" Robin spoke.

Thank you.

Constance simply nodded. She understood he was not talking about the dribble of porridge she had wiped from his mouth.

Chapter 67

THE BEAST

Constance and Robin survived their confinement. As the feverish pitch of the Great Proletarian Cultural Revolution showed tenuous signs of subsiding, they were gradually allowed more freedom. But to seal their demotion, officials allotted half their home to a family of strangers—a stark reminder that everything belonged to the government and those out of favor were subservient to the people.

They lived with Paul, Helene, and their three children in two remaining rooms while the new family took up the rest of the house. Their beds occupied most of the living space. There was no room for anything but a small table and a couple of sitting chairs; they possessed very little after the raid. They shared their kitchen and its small pot stove with the strangers. Nobody complained.

With the end of the Three-Self Church, Robin's supplemental benefits were gone. He was still luckier than many fellow Christians. Some were sent to labor camps to be re-educated or to work in the fields or on livestock farms. Others were imprisoned. A few clergymen took matters into their own hands and dropped a well-tested noose around their necks or threw their weary bodies off of a conveniently tall building. The Red Guards had their own bloodied hands in the suffering, forcing Christians to renounce their beliefs. Those who refused were whipped, beaten, burned, or, for one Catholic priest, buried alive.

Even Y.T. Wu ended up in a labor camp. His close association with Premier Chou could not save him. Not much could.

Robin's body was in its eighth decade. If not for his age and poor health, he, too, would be planting rice, feeding pigs, or mining coal for the government. Seeing Hui sent off to the countryside, he was thankful Grace was in America. Everything he had lived for and believed in was smothered by the dark cloud that had descended on the country. Only Grace was safe.

Mao unleashed his supporters on the Five Black Categories of society, encouraging them to oppose the Four Olds and turn the hierarchy of society upside down. Wealthy landlords and bourgeois elites were attacked, their land repossessed and property confiscated. Intellectuals were denounced and sent into the countryside. Higher education in colleges and universities was abandoned and science and medicine rejected. Counterrevolutionaries were criminalized or executed. Ethnic minorities were oppressed and killed by the Han majority, erasing the gains they made the previous decade. The press was propagandized and the most important book that people read was Mao's Little Red Book. Only the peasants, workers, soldiers, Communist Party members, and revolutionary martyrs mattered in the revolution. They were Mao's favored Five Reds, who used colorful slogans attacking the Five Blacks, boastfully elevating Mao with Lin Biao's Four Greats epithets: greatest teacher, greatest leader, greatest commander, and greatest helmsman. Robin saw that people who were dismissive of his God now worshiped Mao as their one and only deity.

Robin's health continued to deteriorate. He wrestled with the bile that affected his body and his mind; all that he envisioned for China, the church, and his family had rapidly disintegrated in violent chaos. Everything in his life disappeared. His daughters were sent to the countryside. Paul and his family remained at home to help care for him and Constance. Education, so important to him, was nonexistent. The future was only as far away as the next day, and during the winter he had doubts about waking to the following dawn.

His time was spent pondering questions. What had brought this upon all the good people he knew? Was his persecution justifiable retribution for his betrayal of Bishop Tsu? Had he been completely wrong about the Three-Self Church? Would he pass through this life without anything to show, arriving empty-handed at the narrow gates of heaven?

Even as he doubted God, he still believed. He just did not understand.

He was a mortal vessel: unvarnished, imperfect, amorphous. He thought back to all the times he sought to put the world into perspective for his congregation. He had believed himself and those words.

Wait patiently for the Lord; be brave and courageous; love of God conquers evil.

They are not empty words, he kept telling himself. *This will all pass.*

Constance continued to give him his injections until the medicine ran out. Comrade Tang did all he could through the back door. But it was dangerous and not consistent. If caught, he could be imprisoned or purged from the Party, even executed. He, too, was just a twig twisting in turbulent times.

As the turmoil persisted, Robin could see that order would not be restored for a long time. The heads of the beasts were removed, but the bodies writhed sporadically, without direction. Military officers, party heads, educational leaders, scientists, and research investigators were decimated and their underlings entrusted with authority to run amok. Soon, Red Guard factions in various cities were fighting each other for dominance, competing for Mao's favor. They turned their lethal madness against each other.

Robin spent most of his time sitting in a chair or lying in bed with periodic fatigue. He had nothing to read except the *People's Daily* newspaper, the official publication of the Party, and Mao's Little Red Book. His legs were constantly swollen, and his abdomen protruded, pregnant with proteinaceous fluid, draining fullness from his face and producing a ghostly gauntness. He dozed off under his family's watchful eye. His slow, heavy breathing would become rhythmic, indicating deep sleep.

At night, Constance placed pillows under his legs to try to reduce the swelling; he slept nearly upright as his breathing labored with the extra circulating fluid. Propped up at his head and feet, he remained deathly still while asleep. Constance was ever vigilant, her ears attuned to changes in his breathing. A sudden break or gasp in his breath would startle her from her sleep.

"Chen I! Chen I!" he screamed as his body jerked upright one night—his eyes opened wide, staring into the darkness as if seeing an apparition in the room.

Paul and Helene rushed in from the adjacent room. With Constance by his side, they calmed Robin until he fell unconscious. They never told him Grace was not in the room; that it was just the fog of his failing liver clouding his mind. They allowed him that one pleasurable dream among his nightmares. It was his way to keep his daughter alive.

～ ✦ ～

GRACE RECEIVED THE LAST LETTER FROM HER FATHER ON JUNE 29, 1966, in Newton Centre, Massachusetts. The previous year, her family had moved from Quincy after Robert left the full-time staff at the New England Medical Center to enter private practice. He was in high demand, with a stellar reputation as a surgeon's neurosurgeon, surpassing the two more senior staff members in referrals. The Tudor house was three times the size of their Quincy house, and the Newton public school system was ranked in the country's top ten, with the highest number of local students entering Harvard. To Robert, Harvard was the St. John's of America. That was where his son would go.

Robin wrote of the hopes he had for China, touting its advances and social equities. As usual, he made a plea for Grace to return to help serve the people. Come home.

Then, communication suddenly stopped.

Every day, Grace looked in the mail, expecting a letter like the ones she had received each month for the last nineteen years. Even though she knew returning to China was impossible, and even though each letter put another tiny dagger in her homesick heart, she needed to stay connected to her family. It was the bitter pill she had to swallow. She took her medicine every time it came, and it kept her going. But something was happening in China.

The more the days and weeks a letter did not come turned into months and years, the more Grace immersed herself in American life. She became a naturalized citizen. She worked as a researcher in labs at MIT and Harvard. There were violin and piano lessons for the children, skating and ballet lessons for her daughters, Boy Scouts meetings and Little League practice for her son, Saturday Chinese school, Sunday church school, Chinese cultural association activities, Robert's fraternity gatherings, Ginling College and St. John's University Alumni events, winter ski trips, and vacations out west, up north, and down south. Dei Dei's music activities took them to

Switzerland, Israel, and the World's Fair in Montreal. She began to play tennis—first an hour, then two, and, finally, up to three hours a day. She would hit balls spat out one after the other from the machine, marking time with each swing of her racquet. She would play until she was exhausted. Life was busy and life was good. That was her saving grace.

∾ 🌟 ∿

"THE LIGHT SHINES IN THE DARKNESS, AND THE DARKNESS HAS not overcome it."

Proteins continued to accumulate in Robin's abdomen, distending it like a balloon and dulling his senses. The room was always dark even when it was light outside, and he sat most days with his eyes closed, thinking of those words he had said in sermons. He focused his energy on drawing air into his chest. When he opened his eyes, it was only to eat and to stare at the small photograph he carried of Grace at her college graduation. He wanted to be angry at her. But could he really be angry at someone he hardly knew? How many years had it been? He had lost count. He wished he could have met her children and her husband. He wanted to relate all the magnificent events that occurred since he last saw her in Philadelphia.

He regretted some of the harsh words he had written to her. Could he truly blame her for her lack of loyalty, lack of patriotism? There were times he thought her selfish and uncaring. He didn't understand how she could forsake her family and her home, and he wanted to shout sense into her: *You are Chinese! Come home!*

As much as he tried to explain to her husband how he felt, how China had evolved, he couldn't help think that Hsun-Piao was to blame for Grace's absence. No, that was wrong. He could not blame her. He should not be mad at Hsun-Piao. Life was what God intended. He challenged us. China was turning the soil, upending the dirt, stirring the ground. A new crop will be planted. It was not the time for Grace to come. It was winter. Her time will come. It was time for him to go.

Lord, call me home.

In his drifting in and out, he sought out Constance, ever present by his side, always within arm's reach. He held firm and pulled her close. He felt no anger when with her. He felt no bitterness. He only imagined light. The light was hope.

I am the Light.

He saw the truth.

"Believe the Party! Trust Chairman Mao!" he implored his family with momentary lucidity. Then he settled back into a peaceful stupor.

Chapter 68

THE WORD

Robin saw no finality to the country's descent into its disorderly morass. The Red Guard movement, aided by the local police and army, became an uncontrollable revolution within a revolution, shredding the fabric of society. The country had lost all direction and leadership.

In the summer of 1967, Chairman Mao called an end to the violence of the Great Proletarian Cultural Revolution, now that it had served its purpose of purging bad elements and recharging the socialist revolution. But his struggle with different factions within the Communist Party continued, leaving the country unsettled.

Lin Biao maneuvered to be Mao's right-hand man, occasionally overstepping his role and drawing Mao's ire. Mao's wife, Jiang Qing, his left hand, grew more radical and outspoken, and clashed with Lin Biao. Former president Liu Shaoqi was removed from office, placed under house arrest in 1967, and expelled from the Party the following year. Like Robin, he was refused medical treatment. The head of the dragon was devouring its own shoulders—its tail striking at its own writhing body and blood spilling out of its flailing limbs. The beast was twisting and tumbling on the cold, soulless ground. Mao finally set his army against the fanatical Red Guards, quashing the movement in brutal fashion. The beast had tamed itself.

On his last trip to the hospital, late in 1968, Robin thought life was surely over. Helene pedaled her bicycle desperately, pulling her human cargo as he lay in Constance's lap at the bottom of the wooden cart. Shanghai was torn apart. He saw remnants of the Red Guards haul down the cross at the top of a church's steeple. He heard youths parading in the streets, shouting the revolutionary slogans that were as common to the people as verses of the Psalms were to him. He lifted his head to peer out of the cart. The streets were empty and quiet; the dust from the fallen cross was nowhere to be seen. Was it only his imagination?

The nurses at the hospital refused to open the door for him. His insults and caustic attitude from the last time had not faded from their memory. Constance called out for the doctors. None came. She demanded Hsiao Wang. But things had changed. Reactionaries and counterrevolutionaries were the enemy of the people. *He* was an enemy of the people. Even doctors themselves were enemies of the people. The directive was given from the dragon's head.

Constance pleaded with the nurse and called out.

"Hsiao Wang!"

Robin said it was useless. The Red Guards were gone, but society was still upside down. No one could oppose the Party.

"Hsiao Wang!" she called again.

"Do not beg!" he ordered.

The door remained closed.

SITTING IN HIS SPARTAN OFFICE, HSIAO WANG BOWED HIS HEAD and folded his shoulders into his chest. He muffled his ears with his surgeon's hands so he would not hear the futile banging on the hospital doors. The pounding echoed through the empty corridors like a hammer to his head. But it was his own heart beating, as if trying to escape.

He had tried to warn Jian Chen long ago how difficult and dangerous it was going to be to be a man of God. He *told* him he would need big courage. He *was not* naïve. But it was not to warn Jian Chen, not for his sake. It was his own weakness. The time had come when there was no choice; there was only one side, one uniform, one authority. He refused to hear Constance's desperate voice. He pushed his hands more forcefully into the side of his skull until it hurt and turned his head away from the sound at the end of the hall. He wished the knifelike pain in his ears could exorcise his friend's suffering. But it only made him squeeze harder. The harder he squeezed, the more pain he felt.

LYING AT THE BOTTOM OF THE WOODEN HUMAN CART, ROBIN was done.

"No more," he whispered.

He silently thanked a parade of people in his life: his parents, Mr. Lund, Sister Louise, Miss Gregg, Lloyd, Bishop Huntington, Lindel, Miss Sherman. Even Hsiao Wang. One after another, they passed before his closed eyes. There were too many; his mind couldn't remember them all. He had so much for which to be grateful—even as much about which to be bitter. He did not want to leave like that. The cross was the place where death occurred, but also the place from which hope sprung. The cross was not only a symbol of sacrifice and suffering, but a symbol of God's infinite love, a beacon of salvation. He now understood. The cross was not about the sins of the past. It was about hope for the future.

On that last trip to the hospital, he had pulled Constance close to him, her ear nearly touching his mouth. Her face was speckled with his blood, which continued to trickle from between his purple lips. He had drawn in a breath and whispered the only word to her that mattered, the only word that made sense.

"Forgive."

It was a wholly Christian word.

"Forgive."

SO IT WAS THAT THE NEXT TIME—THE LAST TIME—IN THE MIDdle of winter on one of the coldest days, when Robin again vomited bright red blood, there was no excitement. No frantic rush to any hospital or clinic. He heard the call and, willingly and happily, accepted it. All his children were summoned from the countryside. Everyone gathered in his home on

Wan Han Du Road. There were no trumpets or angels. Church bells did not ring. White doves did not fly. No congregation or fellow clergymen or bishops were notified; they were all spirits from the old society.

ON FEB. 18, 1969, ROBIN JIAN CHEN CHEN, THE LAST PRESIDING Bishop from the long, tortuous history of the Anglican Church in China, passed peacefully at home. Condemned by some in the West as the Red Bishop, he grew sympathetic to the Chinese socialist revolution. Living under house arrest by his own government, to which he remained loyal, his only "sins" were love of God, his church and family, and an unwavering patriotism to China and its people.

In the end, it was only family members surrounding him. They were what mattered most. All had come home—except beloved Grace.

Chapter 69

VISA

I n the early months of 1971, a phone call in the middle of the night woke the colonel, a pilot in the United States Naval Air Force. His father, William Sung, a track and field athlete who led the Chinese delegation in the 1932 and 1936 Olympics, was the first Chinese president of St. John's University in Shanghai during the Japanese occupation in 1937. The elder Sung was credited with preserving the university during that hostile period. But after the Kuomintang regained control of Shanghai, some thought he was traitorous and accused him of colluding with the Japanese, for which he spent a brief time in prison and then under house arrest. After Japan's surrender, President Sung was acquitted in a public trial and his Japanese guard committed suicide. Sung's own father, the colonel's grandfather, was Bishop Sing of Chekiang.

The voice on the other end explained the top-secret nature of the call and requested advice from the seasoned airman. He was ordered to report for briefings: What was the best route to Beijing? How do they navigate entry into China airspace? Whom do they contact in China to ensure safe transit? There would be a high-level contingent of diplomats flying to China in February, the first official flight in decades: a carefully-guarded mission with a high-value cargo. The main passenger on the long leg to China would be the President of the United States. Following months of clandestine negotiations between Secretary of State Henry Kissinger and Premier Chou En-lai, Richard M. Nixon was on his way to a historic meeting in Beijing with Mao Tse-tung.

Nixon made the trip for several reasons. He had been thinking of making overtures to the People's Republic of China ever since he was elected president in 1968. He believed the free world, and especially the United States, could not afford to ignore nearly three-quarters of a billion people and he foresaw the leverage that could be exerted over the Soviet Union if the United States had a closer relationship with its Asian rival. Also, the destructive morass of the United States' military and political involvement in Communist Vietnam might be effectively balanced for history's sake by a constructive friendship with the Communist nation of China. For these reasons, President Nixon made the politically risky gamble of courting a Communist government with which his country had not had communications for over two decades. He did it by traveling thousands of miles away from Washington, D.C., meeting its leaders on their own home turf—a fully intentional sign of respect.

For Grace and all her Chinese friends living in the United States, none of these geopolitical reasons amounted to anything important. For them, Nixon's gesture unlocked the floodgates of suppressed emotions that washed over them with the purely personal possibility that they could go home to see their relatives and loved ones—if they could get a visa. Grace immediately applied for permission to visit her family. Because the United States had no formal relations with China, she had to apply through China's embassy in Ottawa.

After a few months, while many of her friends had already obtained their visas, Grace still heard nothing. She and Robert were law-abiding citizens. They were both honest doctors, English-speaking, financially upper middle class, with three children in top-notch universities.

What was the problem?

Frustrated by the lack of progress, she wrote a letter to Massachusetts Senator Ted Kennedy pleading for assistance. He would certainly hear her case and expedite a visa. But the letter bore no fruit—just a form reply with curt apologies.

Sorry, we cannot help you.

Why was she unable to get a visa, she asked. She wrote more letters. This time, Grace went to the senator's Beacon Hill office, petition in hand. She didn't have time or patience for small talk. She had learned that in America you needed to be bold and outspoken. Go straight to the top.

"My name is Grace Yuan," she declared to the senator's assistant. "I am a doctor. I applied for a visa to visit my family in China six months ago. I received a letter saying my application is pending. Another three months. No answer."

"I'm sorry, but we do not handle visas," replied the assistant.

"I am a U.S. citizen!" asserted Grace. "You can help me."

"I'm sorry, but you should contact their consulate," the assistant responded dismissively.

"Twenty-five years," Grace protested. "I haven't seen my family for twenty-five years."

"I'm sorry," came the pat response again.

"Sorry! Why are people always sorry? Is there a problem here?"

"We have good relations with Taiwan," the assistant said, shrugging off the implication.

"Not Taiwan. China!"

The assistant grimaced. Grace noticed the second hand of the clock on the wall behind her move staccato-like with inexorable deliberateness, like the drip-drip of a slowly leaking faucet.

"People's Republic? They are not very efficient."

Grace handed her the letter.

"Please, give this to the Senator. He can help."

"I think you must wait," the assistant answered as she took the letter and placed it in a pile of other correspondence on her desk. "But I will see the Senator gets it."

"Twenty-five years. You know I am a United States citizen," she stated.

The words fell on the assistant's ears like the undistinguished ticking of the clock. With that, Grace left.

It was early 1973, and Grace would go on to write more letters. She continued to wait. Time was passing. It was running out. Nixon had freed China for Americans, but for Grace, it was like she was in prison.

CONSTANCE WROTE GRACE THAT YEAR, SAYING SHE HAD SENT a letter to the central government to support her visa application, but she refrained from telling Grace about her father's death. It would only worry Grace unnecessarily. There was nothing anyone could do. What was the use? No one in China liked talking about death. How could one explain death ten thousand miles away and four years old?

Because of her hard work, Hui earned a promotion to supervisor of vegetable production at her farm collective in Harbin. She took time off and went to Shanghai to ask government officials about Grace's request to return home.

Grace traveled to Ottawa to visit the Chinese Embassy, since Canada, not the United States, was first to establish formal relations with China in 1970. No one could do anything for her. She paid another visit to Senator Kennedy's office.

"Six more months. No visa!" Grace complained. "Nothing! Nothing!"

The secretary had nothing reassuring to tell her. Grace placed another letter on her desk and walked out. She really did not want to cry.

Be brave, her father would say. *Do not cry.*

Crying never helped, she thought. Instead, she wanted to scream.

There was nothing anyone could do except wait.

Chapter 70

BEYOND CONTROL

The phone rang, harsh and metallic, in the alcove adjacent to the spacious living room. The interior of the English Tudor boasted red cedar beams and casement windows with glass set in lead cames. There was a decorative replica Stradivarius violin Robert had brought from China hanging on the wall. Dei Dei had played violin since age five, and his sisters learned piano on the ebony Baldwin baby grand. Music was a third language in the home.

The closed piano top was populated with framed photographs: school yearbook and graduation portraits, family holiday sittings, ski outings. Two decades of civil American life. The rest of the room was adorned with ceramic Chinese vases, floral porcelain lamps, and hanging scrolls of misty mountain scenes and grassroots calligraphy. It was comfortable—tasteful, not ostentatious—evolving over the years into a pleasant, balanced mix of East and West. The family often gathered in the room around the piano, singing hymns, Easter songs, and Christmas carols.

The phone rang again, and Robert rose from his easy chair. Grace barely acknowledged her husband as he left the room. She was happiest with her children.

Annette helped her mother with the laundry, organizing and stacking the sheets and towels that Grace meticulously folded into neatly creased, perfectly proportioned rectangles. Folding laundry was an art form.

Robert's rough Shanghainese leaked into the room. He had the simultaneously amusing and annoying habit of shouting as if he could not hear, understandably the case in China where phones were of poor quality. But it was not necessary in America. The children often thought he was trying to holler his conversation all the way to China.

"Talk so loud!" Grace complained subconsciously to no one in particular. Her face quickly registered a faint scowl and she waved her right hand in the air dismissively. It was a common reaction toward Robert lately.

The three children said nothing. Mei Mei stared at the television while Annette moved on to socks and tee-shirts, each avoiding their mother's momentary glare. It happened like a tic, involuntarily and spontaneously, then just as quickly ended with a discomforting snicker.

Dei Dei tried to pick up pieces of the phone call. His father's voice sounded serious, then went silent.

Robert came back into the living room.

"Grace," he said plainly, indicating the telephone room.

Grace put down her spoon and got up. Without a word to Robert, she went into the adjoining room and closed the glass-paned door.

Dei Dei watched his mother disappear. He could tell something was amiss by the look on his father's face. Dei Dei's gaze went back to the television screen, his ears straining to hear his mother's voice. It was like the times in his upstairs bedroom listening to the Red Sox, Bruins, or Celtics games on the transistor radio tucked under his pillow. One ear was tuned to the game's action and the other to his parents' heated conversation, coming from their bedroom or leaking up from the kitchen.

Were they arguing about him or his sisters? Was his father working too much? Was it about money? Did they no longer love each other? The conflicts occurred with increased frequency.

He had grown more curious ever since his mother seemed to change a year or two ago. He tried to imagine what their previous life had been like in China and how they adjusted to America. They never said much about that time of their lives. And because he was afraid to ask, much of it was a mystery. Topics like school, music, and baseball were easier. He sensed something had changed since there was talk of visiting China, but his parents, like most Chinese people, were reticent about their past and even more reserved about their feelings.

Recently, he and his mother did discuss the topic of divorce; rather, he listened to her. She seemed troubled at the time, not herself.

"I would never get divorced," she confessed to him during this singular moment of openness. "We are Christian. We do not divorce. We learn to suffer."

Suffering seemed acceptable, even expected. But to him, it was quite un-American. *Why be unhappy?*

"Family stays together," she told him. "Once you make a promise, you keep it."

He knew his mother was not happy, as if she wanted to be somewhere else. He wanted his parents to be happy, but he also wanted them together. It was something he could not fix.

The laugh track grew louder with each punch line. Her voice pitched higher as well, sounding agitated. Dei Dei heard a soft cry.

"Aiyaaaah—"

The sound froze him. It was more animal-like than human, as if someone had stepped on a dog's tail. It was two and a half decades of anguish released into the Tudor house, causing a chill to shoot up the back of his neck.

His mother's voice went silent. A sickening thud immediately followed, then a clatter of falling objects and the clang of the telephone striking the hardwood floor.

The whole family rushed to the alcove, leaving the television show to play to an empty room. Robert was first to reach the glass door, with the children close behind. A monotonous hum emanated from the upended telephone as he opened the door. Within seconds, they all had reached her limp body.

GRACE PICKED UP THE RECEIVER. SHE EXPECTED A FAMILIAR voice, one from her large circle of Chinese friends.

"Chen I?" asked the voice.

The connection was scratchy, passing through the imperfect filter of time and space. She didn't recognize the man. Who was this? Other than those she grew up with in China, few people called her by the Chinese name. In America, she was known as Grace.

"Hello," she answered.

There was an annoying delay. It seemed forever.

"*Wo shi Gu … yisheng,*" I am Dr. Gu, announced the fragmented voice, breaking through the static. "From Anhwei."

Anhwei. China. She froze. Home. She hadn't heard anything from China since Mao began the great upheaval seven years ago. It was as if her family had disappeared into the earth. One day, she was reading letters from her father about how wonderfully the church was doing and how prosperous the people were. *Come home and serve the people*, he pleaded again and again, like morning birds in her backyard—ever chirping, singing, pleading. *Come home.* But the next day, next month, next seven years—nothing. China swallowed itself and her family into its soil. Only vague, uncomfortable stories of turmoil and revolution seeped out to America.

Until recently. Last year. Finally, a letter from her mother:

Family and I are good. Children are good. The country has become more and more prosperous. Try to return to our country to serve the people.
—*Mother*

That was it. It was not much. But it said a lot without saying anything. It spoke of family. It spoke of country. It spoke of expectations.

Dr. Gu was a family friend. She immediately thought about her family. Dr. Gu and her father went back many years, to their days in Wuhu. Did he have news from her parents?

"*Ni shi Chen I?*" You are Chen I, he assumed. "*Dui bu chi.*"

Sorry.

Sorry, she thought.

"Chen Jian Chen, your father … " the voice continued, now in briefly accented English.

She didn't know if she had heard correctly. *Jian Chen.* She hadn't heard that name for decades. She knew her father as Robin. The last time she saw him, twenty-six years ago, people called him Robin. Bishop *Robin* Chen. She had named her only son after him.

What about her father?

"*Ta si le*," said Dr Gu.

Si le.

Died. Dead.

It sounded like air rushing out of a hole in a rapidly deflating balloon.

Ssss....

She was stunned. *Did he really say ...? Father ...?*

She felt nothing. She heard nothing. She couldn't breathe. China had suddenly disgorged her family in the most unthinkable and heartless way. Her longing was over. The bitterness bottled inside exploded, and she expelled twenty-six years of suffering in one chilling scream.

Aiyaaaah!

Then the room began to blur.

GRACE CAME TO ON THE ROYAL BLUE SOFA. ANNETTE HELD HER hand while Mei Mei dabbed her forehead with a cold cloth. Grace's eyes were misted, but her face was a strange void, as if drained of vital energy. Her eyes drifted, wandering, as if searching for a resting place. Her eyes went slowly from the photos on the Baldwin, to the frames on the fireplace mantel, finally resting on a portrait perched on a short cabinet in a far corner of the room.

The frame was plain black. The photo was glossy black and white. It was a photograph of a man with dark hair dressed in a black cassock, the white clerical collar illuminating the center of the dark photo. The face was typically rectangular, with a strong jawline, from the Southern coastal provinces. His expression was serene, but reassuring, with a hint of a Mona Lisa-like smile. Grace rested her gaze on the soft eyes staring back, remembering him as he drove away for the last time. Her tears came easily now. The long wait was over. Her father, the bishop, was gone.

Dei Dei leaned towards his mother from his seat on the other side of the coffee table. Her color had returned to a healthy tan, and her breathing was regular. Her body and head sustained no visible injury. She was in no physical pain. All appeared normal—except he realized now that he had never before seen his mother cry.

His view of her changed in that moment, as she looked at the photo of her father. She was no longer only his mother, the assertive matriarch. She was someone's daughter, someone's child. She seemed so small, so vulnerable. She seemed lost.

He looked away and let his mother have her time with her father.

WHILE FRIEND AFTER FRIEND RECEIVED PERMISSION TO RETURN, Grace's visa application continued to languish. There was no explanation. Grace saw her friends prepare for their trips with excitement, loading their luggage with gifts from America. She heard them, upon their return, talk emotionally of their visits with relatives and long-lost friends. She sat quietly when they spoke glowingly of China's progress: the miraculous use of acupuncture anesthesia, their cheerful, singing children, their productive communes, and industrious factories. She remained skeptical, knowing how protective and selective the government would be of their image, showing off only their best.

IT WAS AN INTERMINABLE NEARLY THREE YEARS. NIXON HAD instilled an excitement among overseas Chinese families. Home was within their grasp. But when the mail failed to bring a visa, Grace began to lose hope. Loss of hope brought frustration, and, after learning of her father's death, frustration brought anger. In turn, anger induced more arguments with Robert. Why didn't they go back when her father asked them to? Why didn't he let her return to China when she had the chance? Should she have left medical school and not married? Was his career as a neurosurgeon in America more important than her family in China?

At times, she worried, was *she* the selfish one?

Robert always told her he was an orphan, having lost his mother at one and his father at five. But she still had parents she wanted to see. He was the reason she never saw her father again before he died. He was the one that said no, it would be suicide. She feared she would never see her mother again; she was already eighty. How could he say he was an orphan? To her, being an orphan meant being alone, having no one. He had seven sisters, a half-brother, and a boatload of cousins who lived in America. That is not *no one*. She was the one without family. She was the one who was the orphan. As much as she tried, she could not shake the resentment.

DEI DEI SAW THE CHANGE IN HIS MOTHER'S DEMEANOR. THERE were times, more and more frequent, when he saw her being mean and unfair to his father: angry when he came home late at night; angry when they were at a restaurant with friends and he did not grab the check fast enough. That was a cardinal sin among Chinese friends.

"How could you let them pay?" she yelled at him.

She was angry when he received too much attention and compliments from their friends. *He is the big-shot neurosurgeon*, he heard her tell their friends. But she had given up her medical career for him and the children. She was irritated when he missed a shot and they lost to friends at tennis. She complained of not receiving credit for her contributions in the research lab. Women are discriminated against, she complained to him. It seemed all of these complaints were about things she could not do anything to change. He felt sorry for her. Her whole life seemed beyond her control.

THE INABILITY TO GET A VISA HAD NOTHING TO DO WITH Robert. Grace knew that. But she felt powerless, like when the FBI interrogated her in Philadelphia. Her life was caught up in other people's dreams and aspirations: their rules, their obligations, their expectations.

It was obviously something else that had prevented her from getting a visa. But what? Was it that incident in her apartment over twenty years ago? Did a fellow student, faculty member, or friend misrepresent her to government authorities? Had she revealed something in the second FBI interview? Did someone in her family cause a problem with the Chinese government? Was her family blacklisted because her father was a member of one of the five reactionary classes? Question after unanswered question bombarded her mind. At times, she thought she was going crazy.

Her father earned the good graces of the Communist Party, she argued to friends. He was loyal to the people. He knew Premier Chou. He loved Chairman Mao. His letters were proof of his patriotism. Was believing in the right to believe in God really a crime in China?

Then, just when she thought she would never see China again, her visa was approved. It came for no apparent reason and with no explanation. She was too happy to ask why. Perhaps someone in China had listened.

Chapter 71

LOVE SO GREAT

G race sat in a window seat, watching the scattered lights twinkle dimly below in the otherwise black-as-Chinese-ink landscape. The sleeping city came into view as the Swissair plane started its descent into the Shanghai airport. Staring down, it seemed like she was looking at stars floating upside-down. The trip from Boston in the summer of 1975 had taken thirty-six hours, nine flights, and thirteen meals, with stops in New York, Dublin, Zurich, Athens, Bombay, Beijing, and who knows where else while she was asleep. It was one of the first trips to Shanghai by Swissair after the normalization of Western relations with the People's Republic of China. It wasn't efficient, but it would get her home.

She looked at her family as the plane continued its descent. They were all awake, peering out the small port windows. The children had never been so far away from home, in such a foreign place, going to meet relatives they did not know. After twenty-seven years, Robert had classmates from St. John's, medical colleagues, and cousins to meet, and he would see her family for the very first time.

The plane glided through the patchy layer of clouds. It felt like they were traversing a time warp and entering an alternate reality as they broke through to the other side and taxied onto the tarmac. Unlike airports in the United States, the Shanghai Airport was nearly dark, with a few pale floodlights giving off a rust-colored hue. The plane came to a stop and the group deplaned down the mobile stairway. The acrid smell of burning coal and firewood hit their noses. It was as if they had just walked into a campfire site. To Grace, it immediately smelled like home.

The family passed through customs, handing their passports to officers in khaki green uniforms with red and yellow trim. The PLA soldiers were everywhere, in conspicuous clusters of two or three. They looked like costumed characters in a stage play, watching their every movement. Their skin was uniformly tanned, their cheeks ruddy as if highlighted with rouge, and their hair as deeply black as the night. Robert and the three children retrieved their luggage and walked down the barely lit corridor towards the terminal's exit. It was late at night, and the airport was nearly empty. The unrelenting gaze of the soldiers scrutinized their every movement. Grace walked ahead of her family. This was *her* time.

They could see a throng of plainly dressed Chinese; the only bright color among the white, olive green, and pale grey was the red bandana dangling around the neck of the youngest. Their bodies pressed collectively forward against a metal barrier at the end of the walkway, as if a single organism. Their heads bobbed and weaved around each other, trying to catch a glimpse of their relatives. They strained against airport guards, who firmly pushed back, preventing them from breaking through.

Grace walked more briskly. She tried to see who these people were. There were probably thirty in all. Was that her number two sister, Helen? Could that be her older brother, Paul, and his wife, Helene? He was only twenty-eight the last time they argued in Philadelphia. Where was her little sister, Hui? And the baby, Little Constance? She began to feel stirrings of her youth in her stomach. Where was her mother? Her eyes searched, jumping from one smiling face to another.

Then she saw her.

The family dwarfed her mother's tiny frame as they pushed her toward the front. Her mother's face, in stunned disbelief, emerged from the crowd. Her deep wrinkles had multiplied with the years, etching a map of her life. Their eyes met and locked together. Grace's tears found their way up from their last time together, twenty-nine years ago. Her mother's face suddenly came to life, her eyes glistening with the overflow. It felt familiar to Grace— the bright morning sun rising after an eternity of the deepest darkness. They reached their arms over the barrier, beckoning to each other.

The two groups of families surged towards each other, and Grace pushed through the guards and burst through the barrier. Her mother clutched her with thin arms and pulled her close, and her relatives engulfed her. With that familiar embrace of her past came forth an ocean of tears, flowing together on their closely pressed cheeks. And echoing against the concrete walls, waves of joyful wailing.

Grace, at long last, was home.

THE ALL-TOO-BRIEF REUNION LASTED JUST A FEW DAYS. GRACE had brought Hershey's chocolate and Maxwell House Instant Coffee—such novelties. Her children showed off a Polaroid camera that instantly spat out color pictures like magic, amazing crowds of curious strangers. Robert bought a small electric refrigerator at the Foreign Friendship Store that he snuck into their cramped quarters in the middle of the night so as not to cause embarrassment for the family; jealousy and gossip traveled quickly in such a communal neighborhood.

They chatted in the living room in front of open windows as neighbors, faces perched on top of faces, peered in unabashedly. There was no privacy in Red China; everyone's business was everyone else's business. Mutual surveillance was a behavioral tool the government relied on to great effect.

When they spoke, it was mainly of the present and of the very distant past of childhood. The immediate past was too painful and complex to address. Her father's passing was only related to Grace to reassure her that he did not suffer—that he was happy for his family and hopeful for his country. Her family told her he missed her and forgave her for not returning—and hoped she would forgive him. She didn't know if all that was true. But they didn't dwell on it.

Grace and her brother and sisters talked mainly of life in America and of their children's activities. Paul, the head of the clan now, welcomed his sister with open arms even as he praised the government's achievements. Grace and her mother could only look at each other and hold hands. Memories they shared were of Grace's childhood. Her adulthood did not exist to her mother. Her family's hardship did not exist for her. Both were imagined tales told scantily through their cryptic letters passed across the ocean. Words were left unsaid. Their eyes spoke enough, of longing and loving.

Like the child she used to be a lifetime ago, Grace slept with her mother in her bed while her family stayed at the Friendship Hotel. Every hour together rehabilitated a lost year. There were few questions and no explanations of the decades of separation. After hundreds of letters, all that could be said had been said. Talk could not bring back the last three decades or reunite Grace and her father. It could only bring assurances of future visits, even when the next time was yet unknown.

Yes, we will return, Grace promised.

FROM THE TIME OF HER FATHER'S DEATH, HUI WROTE TO THE heads of the Central Committee, the nidus of power: Chairman Mao Tse-Tung, Premier Chou En-lai, and First Vice-Premier Deng Xiao-ping—each time entreating for Bishop Chen's exoneration. Hui had suffered a double tragedy; her husband died the same day as her father. They were both wrongly accused of being traitors, of being reactionary and anti-revolutionary, of communicating with foreign enemies, of betraying the Chinese people and its government. It was fictitious nonsense. Her father loved his country and its citizens, she wrote. He tried to do good and help people in their lives. He believed in Chairman Mao and supported the Communist Party.

Hui traveled to Beijing to hand-deliver letters asking the leadership to reconsider the criticism against her father and husband. She was willing to forgive their wrongdoings, but things must be put right. She wrote again and again, acting on her own, not knowing if her appeal and complaints would produce rectification, or bring the police to her home—or if they were even read. She sought neither retribution nor revenge, but recognition and restoration. It did not matter that party officials might be offended; they could not hurt her. She was beyond being hurt.

A year after their reunion and a month following Mao's death in September 1976, the era of the Great Proletarian Cultural Revolution came to an abrupt and bloodless end. Chou En-lai had died earlier, in January. The members of the Gang of Four were arrested and endured a public trial that

Grace and Robert and all Americans watched with surreal interest on television half a world away. Order was restored to Chinese society and Mao's wife, Jiang Qing, the gang leader, defiantly committed suicide at age 77 while in prison. It was a global event.

In 1979, the country returned to some normalcy with Deng Xiao-ping's resurrection as China's paramount leader, after he had been demoted and sent to the countryside three times. Hui's prayers were answered. The Shanghai Religious Council took up her request to rectify her father and husband's record. An official government-sponsored memorial was held for Bishop Robin Jian Chen Chen in Shanghai. Government officials, religious leaders, family members, and remaining friends attended to hear of his devotion to his church and his country.

The official pronouncement, roughly translated, in part, read:

During the Cultural Revolution, Bishop Robin Jian Chen Chen was persecuted by Lin Biao, the Gang of Four, and all the leftist party line. He suffered bodily and spiritual harm and died on February 18th (8 p.m.) in 1969. We have a heavy heart holding the memorial service for Bishop Chen to express our deep sympathy and remembrance.

Bishop Robin Chen saw love of the country's socialist doctrine and encouraged his children to support the path of socialism. We are saddened by his passing. The Shanghai Religious Council declares today we want to overthrow the damage done to the Bishop, obtain his rehabilitation, recover his reputation, and clean up the residual poison.

Bishop Chen, may you rest in peace.

Hui had accomplished her task. She had requested and accepted their concession. Perhaps it was not possible to fully forgive, but it made her wounded heart heal more quickly. She understood the lesson her father taught her when she was just a little girl playing with paper planes.

Bishop Chen's "crime" against China was erased and his loyalty to his country officially recognized. His ashes were moved to the Revolutionary Headquarters and later interned in the Longhua Cemetery of Revolutionary Heroes outside of Shanghai. That same year, the Three-Self Church, which had been shuttered during the Cultural Revolution, was officially re-established. One of the former bishops consecrated by Robin, Bishop K.H. Ting, became its head. Freedom of religious belief was reaffirmed and the church, in its different form, was resurrected from the ashes of revolution. A year later, the China Christian Council was formed as the religious umbrella organization for all Protestant Churches, with Bishop Ting as its president. The goal of the Three-Self principles was finally realized.

Grace and Robert also kept their promises. Grace went back nearly every other year after the United States normalized relations with China in 1979. She supported her family financially, and their lives improved.

Her mother chose to stay in China despite Grace's invitation to live in the United States. She and Robin had always rejected the opportunity to leave China, especially in its time of turmoil. She thought it unnecessary to leave when standards improved.

"Your father visited America many times. He loved America, its ways and its people. But our home is here. Your father never left China," she explained to Grace.

Robert returned multiple times to revisit family but also to re-establish contact with schoolmates from St. John's University and its medical school. Although he never fulfilled his childhood aspiration of practicing neurosurgery in his homeland, he shared his experience, knowledge, and advice with his Chinese counterparts. His classmates were now leaders in their field and eager to learn from American-trained doctors. He helped establish, and was president of, the Chinese American Neurosurgical Society, formed to improve communication and relations between neurosurgeons of the two countries.

Grace and Robert hosted, sponsored, and entertained Chinese students, doctors, trade groups, government officials, religious representatives, and Three-Self Church clergy and bishops during their excursions to Boston. Robin's old colleagues, Alice Gregg and Blanche Myers, visited their bishop's family in Newton Centre to recount their adventures. As cooperation and exchanges increased between the People's Republic of China and the United States, Grace and Robert opened their home to relatives and doctors, including neurologists, neurosurgeons, cardiothoracic surgeons, and internists coming to the United States for education. Many of these visitors shared one of the two guest bedrooms in their house.

Dei Dei, now a plastic surgeon, traveled to different Chinese provinces every other year to perform reconstructive surgery and exchange ideas with Chinese plastic surgeons. During one trip to Shanghai, he and his mother attended a church service at the same Trinity Cathedral that his grandfather had preached in. The Neo-Gothic cathedral was known as the Red Church, not for any Communist affiliation, but simply because it was built with distinctive red bricks. Over a thousand people packed into the cathedral. Another five hundred of the overflow congregation sat in an adjoining room, listening to the service on loudspeakers. The early service they attended was just the first of five services that Sunday. He had never seen anything like this in America.

Dei Dei understood his mother's frustration, sadness, and anger as she stood as small as a child, lost among strangers, singing hymns from a lifetime ago, with tears pooling in her eyes. He saw the pain of her family's absence for so many years. He understood the sense of shortcomings of her aspirations. He knew the impotence she experienced as a woman emerging too soon in a man's world, unable to effect the changes in her country her father believed she could help realize. Her family, career, and country had passed her by, dwarfed by the history surrounding her.

But *he* was here—her only son. Everything had been for him, and his sisters, and his father. They were her love. *Love so great.*

The capacity crowd, with its enthusiastic singing, was testament to his grandfather's courage, perseverance, and vision. When they began to sing "God Be With You Till We Meet Again," he knew the tears streaming down his mother's cheeks were real. She finally was able to say goodbye and to sing for her father. It was her last song to him.

Epilogue

On June 20, 2010, at age eighty-six, Grace died peacefully at her home in Newton Centre. She was surrounded only by her immediate family, just like her father and her mother, who had passed at eighty-eight.

Robert cared for her in her final eight years, as she slipped into the deep, debilitating unknown of Alzheimer's disease. The illness crept through her mind stealthily. It was during the earliest manifestation that she attended her 50th medical school reunion in Philadelphia, the only woman in the remaining group of fifty alumni. Losing her bearings on the drive home, she tried to exit the car on the freeway at sixty miles per hour. Life was no longer the same.

Since that incident, her mind went on momentary vacations, then returned to normalcy, only to forget where she was or what she was doing. She wore her emotions openly on her face, expressing them freely, like an innocent child without constraints, untrained yet in social norms. Soon she could no longer be trusted to drive or be on her own. Robert devoted every minute to her care and companionship. He himself was over eighty and long retired, but he bathed her, clothed her, and fed her—attending to her every need. He would not allow anyone except family to touch her. Every bath he gave cleansed away the anger of the past. Every spoon-fed meal nourished her with his love.

Near the end, as a stone mask replaced Grace's expressive face, she would sit quietly for hours, staring vacuously as life played itself out before her. Her children might wake her for a moment, when she would issue a grunt or mumble something incoherent. Her grandchildren could elicit a smile, even a hearty laugh or two if they joked around or danced in front of her. She could catch a beach ball and throw it back to her grandchildren while staring at nothing, and, miraculously, she could stand at one end of the ping pong table, paddle in hand, and dispassionately return a batted ball with robotic regularity as if programmed by years of practice.

But what brought her back to life, back into the brief communion with friends and family, was music. Singing familiar melodies as Mei Mei or Annette played the Baldwin brought her out of her trance. Her soprano voice rang crystal clear, without hesitation, climbing to the purest pitch with the precise vigor of youth. Whether it was "Joy to the World," "Happy Birthday," or a Christian hymn, her vibrato gave each note, each melody, life and meaning. When the actual words could not escape the trap of her mind, she sang *la la la*. It was not her faith, or hope, or even love that rose from the void. It was her irrepressible spirit, implanted in her young soul long, long ago.

She seemed to know when it was time to go. Her family did not object when she refused to eat or drink, stubbornly shaking her head with clenched lips at the proffered nourishment. They realized and accepted that she was done with her suffering. She had made up her mind. She wanted to see her parents, and they would let her go.

Mei Mei called Dei Dei at his home in California.

"I think you should come home. Mom is not eating. It is time."

Dei Dei immediately flew across the country. He saw his mother lying on a bed the family had placed in the living room, since she was unable to safely negotiate the stairs to her second-floor bedroom. Her hair was pure white, her eyes closed without tension, and her face serene and calm.

He kept vigil by her side, and on the third day of his return, Dei Dei watched as his mother heaved her final breath at the end of the three-day coma. When she came to perfect stillness on her bed, he stroked her face, touched her hands, and spoke his last words to her.

"I love you, Mom. Go see Grandma and Grandpa," his shaking voice whispered.

Robert came into the room and listened to her heart. He confirmed the obvious with a slow nod. Then, he closed his eyes and sat in his chair, unable to utter a single word.

∽ ✦ ∽

IN SIXTY YEARS SINCE MAO'S COMMUNIST PARTY ASSUMED control of China, despite severe persecution during the Cultural Revolution, when all open practice of religion was banned, hundreds of thousands of Chinese killed, and churches closed or destroyed, the population of professing Christians rose from under one million Protestants and three million Catholics to nearly a hundred million worshipers. Almost forty million are officially registered with the Three-Self Church, and at least that many are estimated to belong to unregistered churches. By 2025, the number of Christians in China could reach one hundred and fifty million. Despite a delicate, sometimes violent, balance between freedom and regulation, tolerance and persecution, projected growth over the next two decades will make China the largest Christian country in the world.

Grace was buried three blocks from her home in Newton Centre, Massachusetts, in the front lawn of Trinity Church, serendipitously the namesake of her father's home church. As the church had no cemetery, she is the only person laid to rest there, in a private garden surrounded by her precious flowers, beside a solitary tree providing shade to her remains. It was Robert, her husband of fifty-eight years almost to the day, who single-handedly designed and orchestrated her unique final resting place.

A stone plaque with her name is set in the ground. A simple granite bench, overlying an urn carrying her ashes, also bears her name: In loving memory, Grace I Chen Yuan, M.D. 1923-2010. The "M.D." was very important to her in life and in death.

Two years after his mother's passing, Dei Dei brought his children—her grandson, Ryan Christian, 17, and her granddaughter, Robyn Nicole, 14—to pay respects at her grave. He had just returned from China with his father. They visited his father's grandfather's small church, located next to his father's primary school in Ningpo. They attended a Sunday service at the Centennial Church in Ningpo with thousands of worshipers of all ages, some carrying their cellular phones and dressed in brightly colored clothes. All were passionate in their worship. None appeared to need rice.

"Mom never saw her father again after she came to America," Dei Dei explained to his children.

Ryan and Robyn Nicole stood respectfully, listening to their lineage as they stared at their grandmother's stone memorial for the first time.

"It was four years before she even knew he had died."

It was too much for children to think about parents dying.

"It took her three years to get a visa to go home," Dei Dei continued, trying to give them a sense of his mother before her illness. "She never gave up."

"Twenty-eight years. A long time ... without family." Dei Dei felt the lump in his throat and stumbled on the words. "But your grandparents never forgot China. Over the years, they helped a lot of people."

Dei Dei held one of his children's hands in each of his. They took a final look at the grave.

"In some small way, they did serve their people and help rebuild China."

Dei Dei had felt sad when he brought his children to his mother's grave. He felt her pain, her frustration, certainly her anger at times. But now, he felt proud. Perhaps his grandfather also felt proud of his mother. Perhaps they each forgave the other for their suffering. Perhaps that was the only thing anyone could do.

Forgive.

With that, the Red Bishop's grandson and great-grandchildren turned around, took a final glance over their shoulders, and left the gravesite. They walked with each other, hand in hand, and without a word, returned home.

Together.

Afterword

My mother hardly mentioned her father when I was growing up. She simply told me he was a bishop and kept a photograph of him in clerical garb hanging on our living room wall. Neither of my parents related much to me of their early lives.

As I learned more about 20th century China, I became curious about what life might have been like. Periodicals propagated idyllic pictures of a communal utopia with caring barefoot doctors, smiling farmers, and singing factory workers. I wondered how my parents' lives fit into China's past and how they managed to end up so incongruously removed from their homeland. In particular, the contradictory role of my maternal grandfather as a Christian leader within an avowedly atheistic Communist revolution intrigued me.

By the time my mother passed in 2010, I saw her life quite differently than before. I had learned about her struggles in America and my grandfather's death under house arrest. I understood her life as tragic, centered predominantly on her long separation from family. Her dramatic turn with Alzheimer's disease rendered her dependent and childlike, and I realized that she had once been a young woman facing an uncertain future in a foreign country. With a great sense of admiration for my grandfather and mother, mixed with sorrow for them both, I began writing their story.

I started with my grandfather's conversion to Christianity as a schoolboy at an Anglican mission school. This seminal event was the necessary first step to his story. As I discovered his life and his words in newspapers, books, and magazines, especially publications of the Episcopal Church, such as the *Living Church, Forth,* and the *Spirit of Missions,* his story, and my mother's, became clearer. Research was difficult because of the various romanizations of his name: Robin Chien-tsen Chen, Ch'en Chien-chen, C.T. Chen, Ch'en Chien-Tsen, Chen Jianzhen, Chen Tseng-su, T.S. Chen, Robin T.S. Chen, and Chen Jian-chen—often preceded by Rev., Reverend, Right Reverend, Rt. Rev., Bishop, or, simply, Mr. As I delved deeper, it was evident that comprehending the sociopolitical landscape of China and its relationship with the West was fundamental to understanding their journeys.

This story contains actual dialogue and statements memorialized in magazines, newspapers, letters, and academic and personal journals. At times, I took the liberty of altering the context to serve the storyline. Thoughts and events expressed in letters and newspaper articles were sometimes reimagined within sermons or conversations. Many people in the book are real—either personal friends and relatives or well known in history, as with Dr. Harry Taylor, Bishop Huntington, Dean Hewlett Johnson, Y.T. Wu, or Chou En-lai. The events, while factual, have been dramatized, and the characterizations of, and interactions between, these people imagined. I have never met any of these figures, now all deceased, and much of the dialogue between them, both public and private, has not been recorded nor perhaps even witnessed. Some additional liberties have been taken with the temporal order of events when not precisely known. Otherwise, I have tried to present the events as they have, or might have, occurred. The value of heartfelt, authentic recollections by relatives, especially my mother and my aunt, Hui, cannot be overstated. Letters my mother saved from her parents were invaluable and often quoted verbatim. But this is a work of fiction, even as it is inspired completely by real events and people.

I try to explain some of the crucial happenings and sentiments of the times as they affected the lives of the characters, yet there is so much written in other excellent academic or historical references that this book should not be read as anything more than a shorthand narrative of a complex history. If readers are motivated to learn more about China and how its history affects current events and politics, I will have succeeded. I hope the narrative will tell the epic story of my grandfather's courageous, extraordinary, and complicated life, and reveal the complex and intricate relationships among Christianity, China, and the Western world. In the end, it is a story of inspiration rising from within tragedy and of the desire to do good, pitted against persistent adversity.

As for the Chinese names in the book, most of the romanization is derived either from the traditional forms of translation, the postal romanization system of Herbert Giles, or the Wade-Giles system prevalent at the time of the story. Some romanizations were preserved exactly as written in the original texts. Changes to the more contemporary pinyin system (for example, *Peking* to *Beijing*) are made to reflect historical changes within the storyline.

Finally, my appreciation goes to those professionals who helped me realize the final form of my manuscript: editors Cindy Marsch and Doreen Martens, cover designer Liz Demeter, cartographer Nat Case, and interior designer Domini Dragoone.

PEOPLE

Bishop Robin Jian Chen Chen

Constance Nieh and Robin Chen wedding party

ABOVE: *Grace Chen I Yuan (with the author)*
BELOW: *Drs. Grace and Robert Hsun-Piao Yuan*

ABOVE: *Chen family (early 1930s when Robin was studying in the U.S.)*
BELOW: *Chen family (1946 when Robin was in the U.S.)*

LEFT: *Grace with her mother (1975)*
RIGHT: *Hui (Mary) Chen and Grace in Massachusetts*

Bishop Chen's ashes at Longhua Cemetery for Revolutionary Heroes

ABOVE: *Bishop Chen's family (1979 at Bishop Chen's official memorial)*
BELOW: *Constance Chen (1979 at Bishop Chen's official memorial)*

List of Sources

MEMOIRS:

Remembering my parents, unpublished memoir by Chen Hui

Biographical notes, Grace I Chen Yuan

The Craighills of China, Marian G. Craighill, Trinity Press, 1972

Collection of personal letters to Grace I Chen Yuan from Robin Chen and Constance Nieh Chen

Project Canterbury: The Diocese of Anking, Right Reverend Daniel Trumbull Huntington, D.D., Bishop of Anking, Hartford: Church Missions Publishing, 1943.

The Last Missionary in China, Marion Naifeh, Woodward/White, Inc., 2003

My Cup Runneth Over, Harry B. Taylor, M.D., Trinity Press, Ambler, PA, 1968

Friend of Fishermen, Andrew Y.Y. Tsu, Trinity Press, 1951

NEWSPAPERS AND PERIODICALS:

Spirit of Missions

Forth magazine

The Living Church and the Layman's Magazine of the Living Church

The Churchman

The Dayton Herald

The Wilkes-Barre Record

The Tampa Times

The Cincinnati Enquirer

The Philadelphia Enquirer

The Bristol Daily Courier

The Hawaiian Church Chronicle

The Courier Journal (Louisville, Kentucky)

The Denton Record-Chronicle

The Bee (Danville, Virginia)

Detroit Free Press

Daily Independent Journal (San Rafael, California)

Hawaiian Church Chronicle, Vol. 28, No. 3, 1938

Wikipedia

FBI Files

ARTICLES IN PERIODICALS:

Hansard July 15, 1952, Transcripts of British Parliament Debates

"The First Chinese Bishop" Reverend S. Harrington Littell, Spirit of Missions 1918

Interlocking subversion in Government Department: hearings before the Subcommittee to Investigate the Administration of the Internal Security Act and Other Internal Security Laws of the Committee on the Judiciary, United States Senate, 83rd Congress, second session, 1953-1956

"What Can Christians in America do for China?" Hollington K Tong, Taiwan Today, 1958

"China and the Anglican Communion: The Chung Hua Sheng Kung Hui" Charles H. Long, Anglican and Episcopal History Vol. 67, No. 2, Essays on the Anglican Church in China: 1844-1997 (June 1998), pp. 161-190

"The Ideological Persuasion of Chiang Kai-shek" Pichon P.Y. Loh, Modern Asian Studies, Vol. 4, No. 3 (1970), pp. 211-238, Cambridge University Press

"Shanghai during the Takeover, 1949" Randall Gould, The Annals of the American Academy of Political and Social Sciences, Vol. 277, Report on China (Sept. 1951), pp. 182-192, Sage Publications, Inc.

"History of Three Mobilizations: A Reexamination of the Chinese Biological Warfare Allegations against the United States in the Korean War" Shiwen Chen, The Journal of American–East Asian Relations, Vol. 16, No. 3, pp. 213-247, 2009

"The Christian Church in Communist China" Frank P. Jones, Far Eastern Survey, V 24, N 12, December 1955, p184-188

"China's Use of the Boycott as a Political Weapon" Dorothy J. Orchard, The Annals of the American Academy of Political and Social Science, Vol. 152, China, Nov. 1930, pp. 252-261

"History of Three Mobilizations: A Reexamination of the Chinese Biological Warfare Allegations against the United States in the Korean War" Shiwei Chen, The Journal of American-East Asian Relations, Vol. 16, No. 3 (Fall 2009), pp. 213-247 (35 pages)

"Urban Mass Movement: The May Thirtieth Movement in Shanghai" Hung-Ting Ku, Modern Asian Studies, Cambridge University Press, Vol. 13, No. 2 (1979), pp. 197-216 (20 pages)

Wilson Center Digital Archives, Dec. 23, 1954

BOOKS AND MANUSCRIPTS:

Anglicans in China, A History of the Zhonghua Shenggong Hui (Chung Hua Sheng Kung Huei) G.F.S. Gray with editorial revision by Martha Lund Smalley, The Episcopal China Mission History Project 1996

Documents of the Three-Self Movement, Source Materials for the Study of the Protestant Church in Communist China, Wallace C. Merwin and Francis P. Jones, National Council of the Churches of Christ in the USA, New York, 1963

St. John's University, Shanghai 1979-1951, Mary Lamberton, United Board for Christian Colleges in China, 1955

Christian Voices in China, Chester Miao and Jim Lee, Friendship Press, New York, 1948

While China Faced West: American Reformers in Nationalist China, 1928-1937, James Clause Thomson, Jr., Harvard University Press, 1969

Protestants, The Faith That Made the Modern World, Alec Ryrie, Viking, 2017

Reconstructing Christianity in China: K. H. Ting and the Chinese Church (American Society of Missiology), Philip L Wickeri, Orbis Books 2007

Seeking the Common Ground: Protestant Christianity, the Three-Self Movement, and China's United Front 2011, Philip L. Wickeri, Wipf and Stock Pub., 2011

Biographical Dictionary of Republican China, Howard Boorman and Richard C. Howard, Columbia University Press, New York, 1967

The United States and Biological Warfare: Secrets from the Early Cold War and Korea, Stephen Endicott and Edward Hagerman, Indiana University Press, 1998

*American Editor in Early Revolutionary Chi*na: John William Powell and the China Weekly/Monthly Review, Neil Obrien, Routledge, 2015

The Great Migration and the Church in West China: Reports of a Survey of the Nanking Theological Seminary and the National Christian Council of China, Robin Chen and Carlton Lacy, Thomas Chu, 1941

DISSERTATIONS:

Origins of the Three-Self Patriotic Movement: John Livingston Nevius, Caleb Seibel, Kent State University, 2011

John William Powell and "The China Weekly Review": An analysis of his reporting and his McCarthy era ordeal, Fuyuan Shen, The University of Montana 1993

Protesting Protestants: Missionaries During the Anti-imperialist Movement in China, 1920s, Kimberly Cionca Sebesanu, Department of History, Barnard College, 2017

Chiang Kai-Shek and Christianity, John Douglas Powell, Texas Tech University, 1980

Anglicanism, Anti-communism, and Cold War Australia, Doris LeRoy, School of Social Sciences and Psychology, Victoria University 2010

About the Author

Robin T.W. Yuan is a plastic surgeon practicing in Beverly Hills, CA. A graduate of Harvard College and Harvard Medical School, he enjoys tennis, golf, charity work, his violins, and the company of his two children. He is the author of three previous books: *Cheer Up! You're Only Half-Dead: Reflections at Midlife; Behind the Mask, Beneath the Glitter: The Deeper Truths About Safe, Smart Cosmetic Surgery;* and *The Skinny on Marriage: A Plastic Surgeon's Practical Guide.*